YOU WILL SUFFER

"Did they tell you anything that could help?" she demanded.

Nate grimaced. "Just that Daniel assured them that he was going to make some money that night so he could pay them."

"Doing what?"

"He was supposedly hired to cause chaos."

"What does that mean?"

"That was all Daniel said, but if I had to make a guess, I'd say he was responsible for your slashed tires and Mandy's broken window."

"Someone paid him to harass me?"

He shrugged. "It's one theory."

It was bad enough to believe that anyone would want to deliberately vandalize her property. Now he was implying there was some mystery person paying the citizens of Curry to pester her, along with Mandy and maybe even Tia.

"But why? What would be the point?" she asked.

"I don't know . . ."

Alexandra Ivy is a *New York Times* bestselling author of romantic suspense, paranormal and erotic romance. She has also written Regency historicals under the name Deborah Raleigh. A five-time *Romantic Times* Book Award Finalist, Ivy has received much acclaim for her Guardians of Eternity, ARES Security, Immortal Rogues and Sentinels series. She lives with her family in Missouri.

Find Alexandra online at **www.AlexandraIvy.com**, and connect with her on Facebook at **www.facebook.com/alexandraivyfanpage** and on Twitter **@AlexandraIvy**.

By Alexandra Ivy

Pretend You're Safe
What Are You Afraid Of?
You Will Suffer

YOU WILL SUFFER

ALEXANDRA IVY

Published by arrangement with Zebra Books,
an imprint of Kensington Publishing Corp.

First published in Great Britain in 2019
by HEADLINE ETERNAL
An imprint of HEADLINE PUBLISHING GROUP

2

Cataloguing in Publication Data is available from the British Library

ISBN 978 1 4722 5296 8

Offset in 11.23/13.32 pt Times New Roman by Jouve (UK), Milton Keynes

Printed and bound in Great Britain by CPI Group (UK) Ltd, Croydon, CR0 4YY

Headline's policy is to use papers that are natural, renewable and recyclable
products and made from wood grown in well-managed forests and other
controlled sources. The logging and manufacturing processes are expected
to conform to the environmental regulations of the country of origin.

HEADLINE PUBLISHING GROUP
An Hachette UK Company
Carmelite House
50 Victoria Embankment
London EC4Y 0DZ

www.headlineeternal.com
www.headline.co.uk
www.hachette.co.uk

Prologue

Once there was a time when the solid brick building on the corner of Main Street and First Street had been the proud headquarters of the local Masonic Lodge. The men of means and stature in the community would gather behind locked doors and discuss their secret business. In other words, they shared the latest gossip while they ate dinner and enjoyed the barrels of moonshine they kept hidden in the cellar.

As the years had passed, however, the small town of Curry, Oklahoma, dwindled in population. The younger folks moved fifty miles west to Oklahoma City in the hopes of better jobs, and there was nothing in the area to attract new blood. As they'd aged, the Masons died off, while the younger men had no interest in the traditions of the past. The Lodge had threatened to become yet another empty shell.

Thankfully, the building had been purchased by Harry Massie, a local rancher who'd had the brilliant idea to turn it into a tavern. Gutting the main floor, he'd spent the bare minimum on ensuring the ceiling didn't cave in on his customers, and that it was relatively clean. He was also smart enough not to bother to name his new establishment. It would always be "the Lodge" in the minds of the locals.

Now it was a dark, dingy place that had worn brick walls with the obligatory neon beer signs. Along one side of the cavernous room was a line of booths and in the middle was a handful of tables. At the very back was a dance floor with a small stage.

Harry insisted that the warped wooden floors and bare light bulbs that hung from electrical wires gave the place atmosphere, but the truth was that the building should have been condemned years ago. The locals didn't care. They just wanted someplace they could occasionally get together and have a drink.

Of course, there were some locals who did more than come in occasionally for a drink. There were a dozen or so customers who could be found in the dark interior on a nightly basis.

One of those customers was Daniel Perry.

Seated in the corner booth, he was nursing his beer and ruefully glancing toward the woman that Harry had hired to manage the place. Paula Raye was a hard-ass who claimed to have come from Oklahoma City, but Daniel suspected she was fresh out of jail. He knew enough men who rotated in and out of the penitentiary system to recognize an ex-con.

She was a squat woman with brown hair that was chopped short and ugly tats that covered her arms and crawled up her thick neck. She'd arrived in town a year ago and had promptly taken firm control of the Lodge. Including putting an end to Daniel's habit of charging his drinks to his tab.

Bitch.

Daniel returned his gaze to his beer, wishing he was anyplace but here.

Although he was still in his mid-twenties, he looked at least a decade older. His narrow face was sallow and already lined with wrinkles. And his once broad frame was now to the point of being gaunt.

Years of substance abuse had taken their toll.

Taking another sip, he ran his fingers through the long, tangled strands of his dark hair. His father had bitched for an hour this morning that it needed to be cut, but Daniel had ignored the old man. Walter Perry had once been the sheriff of this godforsaken county. The illusion of power had gone to his head, making him think he could bully everyone into obeying his commands.

Including his own son.

Lost in daydreams of the moment he could afford to walk away from Curry and never look back, Daniel didn't notice the two men who strolled into the tavern and headed directly toward his booth. It wasn't until the floorboards squeaked that he belatedly glanced up to watch as the men slid into the bench seat across the table from him.

Bert and Larry Harper.

The brothers were originally from Curry, but had moved to Tulsa after they'd flunked out of high school. They were both thin and wiry, with dirt-blond hair and sharply defined faces. They looked and dressed like hillbillies, but they tried to act like they were some sort of bad-ass gangsters. Bert had even tattooed a couple teardrops beneath his eye to add to the illusion.

It would have been funny if they weren't so willing to shoot anyone who pissed them off.

"Shit," Daniel muttered, scooting toward the edge of the booth.

Bert reached out with his leg and planted his cowboy boot at the end of the seat, effectively blocking Daniel's escape.

"Going someplace, Danny boy?" the man drawled.

Daniel grimaced. He'd been avoiding this meeting for two weeks. Ever since he'd sobered up long enough to realize that he'd managed to smoke his way through the entire stash of meth that he was supposed to be dealing. The Harper brothers were expecting him to hand over a thousand dollars. Or else.

The knowledge had gnawed at him for days. But then an unexpected stroke of luck had happened. He'd been offered an employment opportunity that might just save his ass. As long as he could survive this unwelcome meeting.

"It's getting late." He pointedly glanced toward the clock. Ten minutes until eleven p.m.

Bert flashed an ugly smile. "You run off and you're going to make me think you don't want to spend time with me."

"Yeah," Larry chimed in. "You'll hurt our feelings."

"We're real sensitive that way," Bert added.

Daniel resisted the urge to roll his eyes. The two were idiots. But that didn't make them any less dangerous. Just the opposite.

They didn't have any ability to think through their actions to the inevitable conclusions. Meaning they shot first and asked questions later.

"Maybe next time."

Daniel placed his palms flat on the table, trying to shove himself upright. He had a brief hope that the two would want to avoid a scene.

A hope that was squashed when Bert moved his foot to sharply kick Daniel in the knee.

"Sit," he ordered.

Daniel sucked in a pained breath as he flopped back down. "No need to get violent."

Larry leaned forward, his blue eyes cold and empty. Like he was dead inside. And maybe he was. It was rumored that the Harper brothers' dad had been a mean drunk who liked to knock around his family whenever he bothered to go home.

"If you think that's violent, Danny boy, just wait to see what we have planned for you if I don't get the money you owe us," Larry warned.

Daniel licked his dry lips. At his very core, he was a

coward. Long ago it'd bothered him, but now he simply accepted he'd do anything to save his own skin.

"You'll get it," he told them.

"Good boy," Bert commended, sending his brother a mocking smile. "See, I told you we could depend on him."

Larry scowled. "I ain't seen the money."

Bert kept his gaze locked on Daniel. "He's about to hand it over, isn't that right, Danny boy? You're not going to prove me a liar, are you?"

Daniel's teeth clenched. Christ. He hated the Harpers. They were crude, disgusting pigs. Sadly, they'd been his drug dealers since he'd started experimenting in the ninth grade. What choice did he have but to kiss their asses?

"My name is Daniel, not Danny boy," he snapped.

Bert held out his hand. "I don't care if your name is fucking Santa Claus. Give me the money."

Daniel hunched his shoulders. "I don't have it on me."

There was a tense pause, emphasizing the silence in the tavern. The sparse crowd had thinned out while Paula was sweeping the floor, clearly preparing to close for the night.

"Then we'll all go together to get it," Bert at last said. "My car's outside."

Daniel swallowed a resigned sigh. He couldn't tell the brothers that he'd used the product he was supposed to be selling for them. Or what he'd agreed to do to earn the money to pay them back.

"Look, it's been a little tough to unload what you gave me, but I have a buyer who promised to take the whole stash. We're meeting tomorrow night," he smoothly lied.

Bert narrowed his gaze. "Do I look stupid?"

Daniel lifted his hand. There was an edge in Bert's voice that warned he was starting to consider the pleasure of putting a bullet through Daniel's heart.

"It's true," Daniel insisted.

"I asked you a question." Bert slammed his hand flat on the table. "Do I look stupid?"

Daniel gave a cautious shake of his head. "No."

"Then I shouldn't have to tell you that I can smell bullshit a mile away."

"It isn't bullshit." Daniel pressed a hand over his heart. He didn't have many talents, but he was a master at lying. He'd managed to cover his drug addiction for years. "Not this time. I swear."

Bert paused. Then, no doubt realizing that killing Daniel wasn't going to get his money, he settled back in his seat.

"Tell me about this score," he commanded.

Daniel released a slow breath and weaved a story that he silently prayed would convince the brothers not to kill him.

Chapter One

Ellie Guthrie was savoring her second cup of coffee when her cell phone rang.

Grabbing it off the linoleum countertop, she glanced at the screen out of habit rather than necessity. She already knew who was calling. Less than a handful of people had her private number, and of those, only her secretary, Doris Harvey, would be phoning before breakfast.

"What's the disaster?" she demanded, not bothering with pleasantries.

After a year of working together, Doris had learned that Ellie was single-minded when it came to work.

"No disaster," the older woman assured her. Doris was a tiny wisp of a woman with steel-gray hair she kept cut short and dark eyes that sparkled with good humor. Beneath her sweet-old-lady façade, however, was the tenacity of a bulldog. Over the past year she'd proven to be more than just an employee. She was a loyal friend who protected Ellie with a ferocious diligence. "I was sorting through your emails and there was one from the district attorney's office that your meeting has been delayed."

Ellie frowned. She'd recently taken over the defense of a man who'd been accused of a series of thefts in the area.

Today she was supposed to pick up the discovery packet so she could prepare for the pretrial hearing.

"Delayed? Did they give a reason why?" she demanded.

"A scheduling conflict is the official reason, but I would guess that the prosecutor discovered you had taken over the defense and realized that he'd better have his ducks in a row," Doris said.

Ellie's lips twitched. She couldn't see her secretary's face, but she could hear the hint of smug satisfaction in her voice.

"Ducks in a row?"

"Greg Stone is used to being the smartest man in the room," Doris said, referring to the local prosecutor. "The fact that there is a woman who can challenge him in the courtroom has him scrambling to bring his A game."

Ellie felt a stab of pride. It was one thing to graduate from a fancy law school with a 4.0; it was another to put everything she'd learned to the test by opening her own law firm.

The knowledge that she'd succeeded despite her father's stern disapproval at her walking away from a prestigious position he'd arranged for her in Oklahoma City added an extra dash of satisfaction.

She'd accomplished her success on her own.

That was important.

"Then I'd better make sure I bring my A game as well," Ellie said.

"Your game is A-plus, baby."

Ellie chuckled. "You're very colorful this morning," she told her secretary. "Did you spend the weekend binge watching *The Sopranos* again?"

"Nope. It was *Dragnet* this time."

"Ah." Ellie's smile widened. She'd watched reruns of the show when she was just a child. "Just the facts, ma'am."

"Exactly."

She wrinkled her nose. She hated having her tightly

controlled schedule disrupted. Still, she understood the game. Greg Stone had a legal obligation to hand over the files he had on her client, but if she became a pain, then he'd drag his feet as long as possible.

It was better just to allow him to enjoy his power play. It was one skirmish in a war she was fully confident she would win.

"I'll head straight to the office."

"No hurry," Doris told her. "It's pretty quiet here this morning."

"Then I'll catch up on my paperwork."

Doris heaved a deep sigh. "It's supposed to be a beautiful spring morning. Don't you have something better to do than sit in your office?"

Ellie glanced around her kitchen and grimaced. She had lots and lots of better things to do.

Thousands of things.

Since buying the old ranch house five miles south of Curry, she'd done nothing more than unpack the necessities. At the beginning, she'd had grand plans of remodeling. She intended to gut the place and create an open floor plan as well as enclosing the wraparound porch for a place to sit and enjoy the peace on warm nights.

Instead, she'd piled her boxes in a spare bedroom and concentrated on the office she'd purchased in downtown Curry. It was far more important that she make the perfect first impression to her potential clientele. The only real updating she'd done at her house was buying a state-of-the-art coffee machine that looked like some sort of alien technology on the chipped countertop.

With a shrug, she shoved aside thoughts of the enormous number of repairs that were waiting for her. She'd muddled along for the past year. She could muddle along a couple more months. Once summer arrived she might have more enthusiasm to tackle at least a few projects.

"I have work to do," she told her secretary.

"You always have work to do," the older woman chastised. "And don't try to pretend you didn't spend last night at the office."

Ellie was caught off guard by the accusation. "How do you know?"

"It was bingo night at my church. Whose car do you suppose I spotted in front of the office when I drove home at ten o'clock?"

Ellie rolled her eyes. "I sometimes forget I live in a fishbowl now."

"It's not a fishbowl. Our interest in each other's lives comes from a place of love, Ellie."

"Hmm." Ellie had spent the majority of her life in Oklahoma City. She hadn't realized the cultural shock of moving to a small town. Some days she loved feeling a part of a community. Other days she hated the sensation she was constantly being watched and judged by her neighbors. "I'm going to change into something more comfortable and I'll be in."

"Suit yourself," Doris said.

"I always do."

"Amen."

Ellie ended the conversation and headed toward her bedroom. She quickly stripped off the black skirt and crisp white shirt that matched the other black skirts and white shirts hanging in her closet. She reserved them for her appearances in court or meeting with the DA, preferring slacks and soft sweaters for her day-to-day office uniform.

Stepping into the bathroom that had an old claw-foot tub and a sink that was chipped and yellowed from age, she grabbed a brush and stood in front of the mirror.

With a quick efficiency, she pulled her honey-brown hair into a ponytail. She usually kept it shoulder length, but she was well overdue for a trim. Now it fell almost to the middle of her back and it always seemed to be in the way.

She grimaced as she caught sight of her reflection. She looked like she was twelve, not a woman approaching her twenty-ninth birthday. And it wasn't just the ponytail. Her features were delicate, with large brown eyes that were heavily lashed. Even worse, she barely topped five-foot-four, with a slender body that still looked like she was in her tomboy years.

Her elegant mother had rued Ellie's lack of sophistication, incapable of understanding why Ellie wanted to play softball and run in marathons rather than prance around in a pretty dress.

Ellie scowled, tossing aside the brush.

She'd moved to Curry to get away from the heavy sense of duty she always felt when she was in the presence of her parents. She wasn't going to let bad memories haunt her.

Pausing long enough to grab her purse and a light jacket, she stepped out of her house and locked the door. She headed to the driveway, where she'd left her car. She had an attached garage, but the door was jammed. Just another project on her to-do list.

At least it promised to be a lovely spring day. The sun was peeking over the horizon, spreading a golden warmth that battled against the crisp air. Ellie paused, glancing around the rolling fields that spread as far as the eye could see.

Not many women her age would choose to live alone in such an isolated area. She had friends from law school who had all leaped at the opportunity to join firms in large cities where they could quickly climb the corporate ladder. When she told them she was happy in her shabby ranch house in the middle of nowhere, they shook their heads and heaved resigned sighs. With Ellie's powerful family connections, she could have her choice of plum jobs.

Sucking in a deep breath, she caught the scent of rich earth and winter wheat. Much better than the smell that wafted from the dumpster when she stepped out of the door at her old apartment in Oklahoma City.

A smile touched her lips as she neared the silver BMW her parents had given her when she'd graduated from law school. Okay, she hadn't totally turned her back on the finer things in life. The sports car wasn't the most sensible vehicle, but she loved it too much to give it up.

Eventually she'd have to buy an old truck for those days when the roads were too muddy or too icy to get her car into town. But she hadn't had time to look around.

Reaching the vehicle, her smile abruptly vanished.

She squatted down, staring at her tire. It was flat. Completely and totally flat.

Annoyance soured her mood. This was a trade-off to avoiding the problems that plagued big cities: gravel roads were hell on tires.

On the point of rising to her feet so she could pop the trunk and pull out her spare, she caught sight of the back tire. Crap. It was as flat as the front one.

What had she run over?

Impossible to know for sure, she acknowledged with a rueful sigh. And it didn't really matter now. She was going to have to call the local auto shop to come out with two new tires.

She was pulling her cell from her purse when she heard the sound of a loud engine. Her stomach tensed. She didn't need to turn her head to see who was headed up the gravel road. She'd recognize the racket of Nate Marcel's old pickup a mile away.

Keeping her gaze focused on her phone, she scrolled

through her contacts. She was sure that she'd put in the name of the garage. What was it called? Something that started with a G?

Fiercely trying to concentrate, Ellie found herself distracted as she heard the truck begin to slow.

Drive on, drive on, drive on, she softly whispered.

Of course, he didn't.

Her nearest neighbor would never, ever be the sort of guy who would drive past a woman who looked like she might need his help.

She didn't know if it was his training as a former FBI agent. Or if he'd been born with a hero complex. Either way, he'd been the first to arrive on her doorstep after she'd moved to Curry, offering to help her with the numerous repairs on her property.

The sight of him had frankly taken her breath away.

He was gorgeous in a rugged sort of way. He had a strong, square jaw that constantly looked like it was a few hours past a five o'clock shadow. His nose was bold and his mouth bracketed by a pair of unexpected dimples. He kept his dark hair cut short, but it lay like glossy satin and her fingers had itched to touch it. And his pale eyes seemed to hover somewhere between blue and gray.

He had been wearing the traditional uniform of all men in the area: flannel shirt, faded jeans, and cowboy boots. But no one could mistake him as just one of the guys. His body was rock hard with muscles, while he managed to move with a smooth grace that came from years of some sort of martial arts training.

Her first impulse had been to look for a wedding band. When she didn't see one, she'd made the firm decision to get him into her bed as quickly as possible. He was just so damned sexy.

Then, he'd started offering to help with her unpacking

and showing up with tools to fix her clogged sink, and she'd panicked. She was eager to enjoy a brief sexual relationship with the man. Just being close to him was enough to make her body sizzle with awareness. But it hadn't taken long to realize that Nate wasn't a man who indulged in meaningless hookups. At least not with his neighbors.

He was looking for a relationship with a woman who could give him more than her body.

Instinctively she retreated from his bold flirtations, going so far as to try and avoid him whenever they happened to be in town at the same time. It was a habit she'd developed when she was younger and her mother would invite over boys in the hope she could influence Ellie to settle down with a socially suitable husband.

Her only defense was to crawl into a shell like a turtle, taking cover until the danger passed.

Within a few weeks Nate had accepted her rebuffs, his smile mocking as he watched her scurry away when he walked into a room. The knowledge that she was acting like an awkward teenager instead of an intelligent, successful lawyer only intensified her discomfort.

Now she felt heat crawling beneath her cheeks as the noisy truck pulled into her driveway and the sound of a door opening and closing forced her to glance toward the approaching man. It was that or scampering back into her house and closing the door.

Not even she was that childish.

"Trouble?" he asked, his voice low and slightly gravelly.

A strange sensation fluttered in the pit of her stomach and her mouth went dry. He was wearing a Henley shirt that hugged the width of his chest and a pair of faded jeans that hung low on his hips. The wind ruffled his dark hair, and he had a shadow of whiskers on his jaw.

A tall, dark invitation to sin.

Inside she melted. Outside she forced her lips into her "courtroom" smile. Professional, meaningless.

"Nothing I can't handle."

"So you've told me before," he said in dry tones.

"Because it's true."

The pale eyes that were more blue than gray in the morning sunlight narrowed, his jaw tightening at her cool dismissal.

"Yeah, yeah. I got it. You're Wonder Woman and I'm an annoying male who is too stupid to take the hint." He flicked a glance toward her flat tires. "Have a great day."

Ellie grimaced. Christ, what was wrong with her? She was acting like a bitch.

"Wait," she called out. "I'm sorry."

He slowly turned back to face her, his expression unreadable. "Are you?"

She blinked in confusion. "What?"

"Are you sorry?"

Ellie's lips twitched at the blunt question. Nate came across as a down-to-earth guy who said exactly what was on his mind, but Ellie had never been fooled. He'd been an FBI agent for years. Which meant he was a master of deception. He could be the naïve boy next door. The sophisticated charmer. Or the reckless playboy. Whatever was needed to get what he wanted.

This morning, however, she sensed his reaction was genuine. Here was a man who'd reached his limit with an aggravating female.

"I'm trying to be sorry, does that count?"

His tension eased, his own smile rueful. "Do you have a spare tire?"

"Yes, but I'll need to call the garage to get one for the back."

His brows arched as he realized the back tire was as flat as the front.

“Did you run over something?” he demanded.

“I didn’t notice anything, but I must have. I had these tires put on less than three months ago.”

He frowned, a strange expression settling on his face as he circled the hood of the car to study the tires on the other side. Then, without warning, he was disappearing from view as he bent down.

Curious, Ellie followed to see what had captured his interest. Instantly her heart dropped to her toes. She didn’t have two flat tires. She had four.

“Crap,” she muttered.

Nate reached out to touch the tire. “Slashed,” he said.

Ellie swallowed a resigned sigh. She could see they were slashed. And trashed. And beyond any hope of repair.

“There must have been something metal in the road,” she said. “Probably a strand of barbed wire.”

With a shake of his head, Nate straightened. His expression was grim as he met her gaze.

“These weren’t caused by a stray piece of metal,” he told her. “They were deliberately slashed with a knife.”

Ellie stiffened. “How can you know?”

“I was an FBI agent.”

She resisted the urge to roll her eyes. “And your training included identifying weird holes in tires?”

“Only knife holes.”

She flinched, her gaze zeroing back on the car. Was he right? Had someone crept onto her property and used a knife to slash her tires?

The mere thought made her stomach clench with an icy sense of revulsion.

“That’s ridiculous,” she finally said, more in an effort to ease her fear than to convince Nate he was wrong. “No one would do that to my tires.”

“Are you claiming you don’t have any enemies?”

Her gaze snapped back to his face. "Why would you assume I do?"

"You're a lawyer."

He said the words without apology. As if he hadn't just insulted her.

"Not everyone has your prejudiced opinion of my profession."

He shrugged. "Maybe not everyone, but your work involves keeping bad guys from being punished for their crimes. That pisses people off."

She felt a burst of irritation. Of course an FBI agent would assume that everyone who needed a lawyer was guilty.

"I represent clients who are presumed innocent until they're proven guilty."

He ignored her chastisement.

"And a few bad guys that hire you actually go to jail," he continued, seeming to enjoy pointing out the number of people who held grudges against lawyers. "Which pisses off even more people."

"Fine. I piss people off." She glared at him, trying to pretend her heart didn't skip a beat at the sight of his fiercely male features. "Including FBI agents. How do I know you didn't slash my tires?"

"I wouldn't have bothered with a knife. I would have shot them."

His smile remained, but there was an edge to his voice that assured her that he really would have shot her tires if he decided it was necessary.

Ellie gave a sharp shake of her head. "I'm not going to leap to some wild conclusion."

"It's not a wild conclusion. You should report this to the sheriff."

Her lips parted to tell him that she could decide whether she wanted to make a police report or not. But, with an effort, she bit back the words. He wasn't being bossy. He was simply concerned for her safety.

Just as she should be concerned, she reluctantly acknowledged.

It was possible that she'd run over a piece of barbed wire. And it was equally possible that someone had deliberately slashed the tires. Until she knew for sure, it was only sensible to take a few precautions.

"Okay," she finally agreed. "I'll call when I get to the office."

"Do you need a ride?"

This time she didn't hesitate to agree. She didn't want to drag Doris away from the office, and it could take an hour if she had to wait for the one taxi in town to come pick her up.

"Yes, thanks."

A hint of surprise flashed through his eyes and she hid a smile. He hadn't expected her to accept his offer. At least not without a fight.

Quickly recovering, he turned to lead her toward his vehicle. She doubted that he was ever completely caught off guard.

He opened the door and she climbed into the passenger seat, glad that she'd changed into her slacks. She was short enough that it was always an awkward scramble to get in and out of a truck.

At least it was clean, she realized as she took a quick inventory of the interior. The outside might be battered, but the leather seats had been recently refurbished and the dashboard was polished until it glowed.

She'd just finished buckling herself in when Nate slid into his seat and turned the key. The engine grumbled to life, and he backed out of the driveway and headed down the gravel road.

Ellie searched her mind for some sort of meaningless

chatter to fill the silence, but she kept getting distracted by the warm scent of male skin that filled the cab. It'd been over a year since she'd last spent time with a man.

Clearly, she was overdue for a bit of romance.

Unfortunately, Curry wasn't overflowing with eligible men. And those who might be interested in the sort of relationship she wanted couldn't possibly compare to the man at her side.

"Do you want me to stop by Green's and have him run out to your place to change your tires?" Nate thankfully interrupted her dangerous musings, slowing the truck as they reached the paved county road that led into town.

She cleared her throat, trying to suppress the blush that she could feel staining her cheeks.

"I can call him when I get to the office," she assured him, making a mental note of the garage name. Green's. She'd been right. It did start with a G.

His lips tightened. "Do you have to do everything yourself?" he demanded, pressing his foot hard on the gas.

The truck shuddered, as if it was on the point of simply collapsing, then with a loud backfire it was zooming forward at an impressive pace.

"Actually, I was going to offer to call the garage to have a look at this pile of scrap metal," she said in dry tones.

There was a startled silence, as if Nate was shocked that she actually had a sense of humor. Then he released a sudden laugh.

"Are you insulting June?"

"June?"

He reached a hand to lightly pat the dashboard. "My truck."

She snorted. "You call your truck June?"

"It's my mother's name," he said. "When I turned sixteen and wanted to buy this beauty, my mother loaned me the down payment." He gave the dashboard another loving pat. "It only seemed fair to honor her in some way."

Ellie studied his profile, noting the fond expression that softened his chiseled features. That expression wasn't for his truck, or at least not entirely. It was for his mother.

She swallowed a sigh. There were few things more charming than a man who openly adored his mother.

"I apologize. I didn't realize your truck was an antique," she murmured.

He gave another chuckle. "It's not an antique, it's a classic."

"Hmm." She paused, the rattle of the engine filling the air. "Didn't the FBI pay well enough to buy a new truck?"

"I drove a Bureau car when I was working," he said with a lift of one shoulder. "But it wouldn't have mattered. Nothing could ever replace June."

Ellie resisted the urge to continue bantering with her companion. She was already sexually obsessed with Nate Marcel. She didn't need his potent charm swaying her into making a decision they would both regret in the end.

Turning her head to glance out the side window, she remained silent as they entered the outskirts of Curry. Nate accepted her tactical withdrawal without comment. Instead, he concentrated on navigating the narrow streets that were lined with trees.

They passed by the strip mall that had a dollar store, a laundromat, and a pizza joint that served amazingly delicious calzones. Then they turned the corner that led to the center of town.

In the middle of the square was a large stone building that housed the courthouse and city hall, as well as the sheriff's office. The jail had recently been moved from the basement to a new building north of town.

Ellie's own office was across the street. Not only because it was a convenient location, but it'd belonged to the previous lawyer, which meant the locals would know where to find her.

The downside had been that she'd had to completely gut the place. For two weeks, the construction crew had pulled out the dark paneling and shag carpeting that had been installed during the sixties. Then she'd had the walls painted a pale gray and installed tile floors and sleek furniture that offered a sense of sophistication.

She'd never compete with the old lawyer's reputation for solid dependability. Not until she'd been there for twenty years or so. Oh, and changed her sex to male. Instead, she gave them the appearance of a glossy professional while she proved her ability to be a shark in the courtroom.

"You can let me off at the corner." She abruptly broke the silence.

The traffic was one-way in front of her building. She didn't want him to drive all the way around the square to park. His jaw tightened, but he swerved to pull to a halt in front of the post office.

She hastily unbuckled her seat belt and opened the door. "Thanks for the lift," she said, ignoring the small pang of regret that she'd once again managed to make things awkward between them.

Without warning, he reached out to lightly grab her arm. "Ellie."

She glanced over her shoulder, meeting his somber gaze. "Yes?"

"Be careful."

She gave a slow nod. This time she didn't try to dismiss his concern. Not when a tingle of unease fluttered through the pit of her stomach.

"I will."

Chapter Two

It's a perfect day. Crisp air, golden sunlight, and the sound of birds singing in the nearby trees.

I hum beneath my breath as I work. It's hard. Daniel Perry might look like a scarecrow after his years of abusing drugs and alcohol, but he is heavy enough to make me breathe hard as I drag him across the hard ground.

Once he's in the middle of the field, I carefully create the scene I desire. He's still unconscious from the drugs I injected when he'd so foolishly agreed to meet me last night. It makes it easy to curl him into a fetal ball. I step back, surveying my handiwork. He's surrounded by prairie grass and a sprinkling of early spring wildflowers.

Beautiful.

I move back to ensure everything is perfect.

Daniel's curled up like a small child and I smooth the dark hair from his face. He looks peaceful when he's sleeping. Not at all like the tense, angry man who stalked around town with a chip on his shoulder.

He is going to look even more peaceful.

I tug at the sleeve of his leather jacket until his forearm is exposed. Then, reaching into the pocket of my coat, I pull out the syringe that I prepared in advance.

Stabbing the needle into his arm, I press the plunger and fill his veins with enough pure heroin to kill an elephant. I watch in fascination, waiting for some sign that the drug is flowing through his body, destroying what few cells he hasn't already fried. I don't know what I expect. Pain. Ecstasy. Fear.

There's nothing.

I wait. And wait.

Overhead the sun continues to shine and the birds are singing. I hum my soft tune. Then Daniel makes a sound. Like a low grunt. I lean forward, watching his lips part as he releases his last breath.

Death creeps into the meadow, brushing past me as it collects Daniel's miserable soul, leaving as silently as it arrived.

The complete opposite of life, I realize with a small jolt of surprise. Birth was a noisy, messy business. Blood and screams and pain. The death I offer is a quiet, peaceful event.

Fascinating.

I slowly straighten, pulling the needle from his arm. I look down.

I've done good work, but I feel no pleasure.

Daniel isn't my victim.

No. He's a message.

You. Will. Pay.

Nate watched as Ellie traveled down the sidewalk, her chin tilted and her pace brisk.

She looked like a woman headed into war.

He snorted, pulling away from the curb as she entered her office without glancing back. Ellie Guthrie was a woman who constantly acted like she was ready to battle. At least with him.

At first, he'd assumed her prickly attitude was a result of a woman forging a path through a man's world. He'd known female FBI agents with the same brittle façade. They'd endured too many insults, harassment, and downright bullying over the years not to become defensive.

But then he'd seen her with other men around town. She hadn't been flirtatious. That wasn't her style. But she'd certainly appeared a lot friendlier.

Another man might have been offended. Who wanted to have the most beautiful woman in town treat him like he carried the plague? Nate, however, was a man with a healthy ego. He told himself that Ellie's cold-shoulder treatment wasn't because she didn't like him.

It was because she was afraid she might like him too much.

His lips twitched as he turned the corner and pulled his truck into the parking lot of the local diner. Okay, he could be way off base. She might genuinely believe he was an ass. She wouldn't be the first or the last. But he'd convinced himself over the past year that her elaborate effort to avoid him was wariness at the fiery awareness that had sparked between them.

He chose a spot where he could easily exit the lot and switched off the noisy engine. Old habits died hard. Even after two years of being retired from the Bureau. Then, leaning back in his seat, he sucked in a deep breath. Ellie's light floral scent lingered in the air. It teased at him, like a promise.

Abruptly he recalled the first time he'd seen her.

He'd heard that the new owner of the property next to his had arrived. At the time, the only thing he'd known was that she was the daughter of Colin Guthrie, who'd once worked in the local prosecutor's office before moving to Oklahoma City and eventually becoming a judge. Oh, and that she was a defense attorney who was opening her own law firm in Curry.

A part of him wanted to ignore her arrival. He'd worked in the FBI long enough to have watched perps who were guilty as hell walk away from justice because of some technicality used by their devious lawyer. But his mother had deeply ingrained a sense of proper manners into all four of her sons. The older woman would travel to Curry and whack him on the head with a wooden spoon if she discovered he hadn't done his duty.

So, he'd arrived on Ellie's doorstep with a forced smile and an offer to help with any repairs.

His first impression hadn't been great.

It wasn't because she'd been dressed in jeans and an old sweatshirt, with smudges on her face. Any fool could detect the ethereal beauty that was hidden beneath the dirt and cobwebs that clung to her glossy hair. But she'd had an aloof, frosty expression that made him think of an ice princess.

It hadn't taken long, however, to stir his fascination. It started with the sensual awareness that smoldered in her dark eyes whenever she thought he wasn't looking. She might pretend that she wasn't interested, but she wanted him.

Bad.

Then, she'd opened her mouth and her sharp, slightly snarky banter had sealed the deal.

Smart and sexy.

His ultimate weakness.

And the fact that she'd spent the past year attempting to elude him had only intensified his determination to charm his way past her defenses. Like how he'd been when he'd set his mind on buying this truck. It didn't matter how many extra chores his mother had demanded he do, or how many nights out with his friends he had to miss to earn enough money for gas; he'd set his heart on the rusty old pickup and nothing was going to stop him.

Hell, the fact he'd had to struggle to finally achieve his goal only made his final victory all the sweeter.

Nate gave a short laugh. Ellie would cut off his balls if she knew he was comparing her to his truck.

Giving a rueful shake of his head, Nate jumped out of

the vehicle and headed toward the diner. He had a meeting this morning with the bank manager. But first he needed coffee. Strong and black. Not only for the jolt of caffeine, but he needed to clear his brain before he made his pitch for a loan.

He'd mulled over his decision for six months before making the appointment. He wasn't going to ruin everything because he was still worried about Ellie Guthrie.

Crossing the small lot, he'd nearly reached the glass door when it was pushed open and Walter Perry stepped out of the diner.

Nate moved back, waiting for Walter to clear the doorway. The retired sheriff was a short, wiry man with features that always reminded Nate of a rat. Small and beady. He had a rapidly balding head that he kept hidden beneath his stained cowboy hat and a gray stubble on his jaw. This morning he was wearing a western-style shirt with pearl snaps for buttons and dark jeans.

Nate forced a smile to his lips. The older man was a blowhard who'd latched onto Nate as soon as he moved to the area. Walter seemed to believe that the fact they'd both worked in law enforcement meant they were destined to be best buddies.

Nate didn't agree, but he was too polite to blatantly snub the retired sheriff.

"Hey, Walter," he said, glancing through the glass door to the table at the back of the dining room.

Every morning, rain or shine, the local men gathered to play four-point pitch and drink coffee.

"Finished with your card game already?"

"Yep." Walter's lips twisted into a humorless smile. "We drank a pot of coffee, now we all have to go home and take a piss." He shook his head. "Getting old stinks."

Nate could sympathize. Although he'd just celebrated his

thirty-fourth birthday, he already had a few aches and pains when he woke in the morning.

"I suppose it could be worse," he murmured.

Walter turned his head to spit out the juice from his chewing tobacco.

"You know, I used to have a calendar on my desk where every morning I would mark off the days to my retirement," he said.

Nate kept his smile in place. He didn't talk about his own early retirement. Even after two years it still gave him nightmares.

"A lot of lawmen have those calendars," he instead said.

Walter gave a faint shake of his head, his eyes growing distant as he became lost in his inner thoughts.

"I had some crazy fantasy that my days were going to be filled with fishing and playing cards with my pals and teaching my grandkids how to throw a curveball."

"Sounds like a perfect retirement."

Walter snorted. "Turns out that I hate fishing, and my son . . ." The older man's words trailed away. He didn't have to say that his only child was a burnout who was headed for jail. Or just as likely, the morgue. "Well, he isn't going to be giving me grandkids anytime soon," he finally muttered. "And years of playing cards with the same five guys is enough to make a man wish he was still at his desk and retirement was just a distant dream."

Nate frowned. The onetime sheriff was always gruff. Most people in town called him cantankerous. But there was a bitter edge in his voice that Nate hadn't noticed before.

"Is everything okay, Walter?"

A shadow darkened the rat features before Walter was waving away Nate's concern.

"Fine."

"Are you sure?"

The man forced out a laugh. "You know how it is. When it rains it pours."

Nate had heard rumors that Walter's wife had left town years ago with the math teacher, so he couldn't be talking about marital problems. And the older man seemed to have plenty of money in his retirement. At least, he drove a brand-new truck and he had a beautiful brick home just a few blocks away.

Which left his son, Daniel.

A constant pain in Walter's ass.

"Is there anything I can do to help?" he offered, even as he knew there was nothing he could do.

Daniel was an addict. No one could save him. Not until he was ready.

"Maybe we'll go fishing together next week," Walter said, his smile strained.

"Sounds good," Nate agreed.

"See ya around."

Nate watched the older man walk toward the end of the squat building, his steps slow and precise, as if he was concentrating to make sure he didn't stumble.

Giving a shake of his head, Nate entered the diner.

Walter might not be his favorite person in Curry, but it pained him to see the old man looking so troubled. A damned shame he couldn't beat some sense into Daniel.

Chapter Three

Ellie leaned back in her office chair and heaved a sigh. She'd spent the past two hours trying to concentrate on the appeal she hoped to file before the end of the week. Instead, she found herself unable to focus on the computer screen in front of her.

It was annoying. Nothing ever interfered with her dedication to her clients. But even after she'd called Green's Auto and arranged for them to replace her tires, she couldn't completely quash the vague unease that someone had actually snuck onto her property and stabbed her tires.

It was creepy.

Who could possibly hate her that much?

Oh, she had people who she'd angered since moving to Curry. As Nate had pointed out, her job as a defense attorney meant that the victim's family blamed her if she managed to prove her client's innocence. Or occasionally to get him off on a technicality. And, of course, her client's family was angry if their loved one ended up in jail. No matter how guilty they might be.

But she couldn't imagine any of them creeping through the dark to vandalize her car, which was parked miles outside of town. Why not throw a rock through her office window?

She released a breath through clenched teeth.

She blamed Nate.

If he hadn't been so certain that someone had slashed her tires, she would have assumed it was nothing more than an aggravating accident.

She should change into her jogging clothes she kept stashed in her file cabinet, she abruptly decided. A run always cleared her mind, and Curry had a paved bike path along the nearby river. It was a perfect place to burn off her excess energy.

Not as fun as getting Nate in her bed . . . *No, no, no.*

Nate Marcel had caused enough disruption in her day. She wasn't going to waste another second thinking about him. Or his hard, naked body.

With a sharp motion, she was on her feet and turning away from her desk. Yep. Definitely time for a run.

She was preoccupied with her inner thoughts, but a sudden movement outside her window instantly distracted her.

With a frown, she crossed the silver rug to peer out the clear glass. She didn't have a great view. The real estate agent had called it a private garden. Ellie called it a cement slab surrounded by low hedges.

She assumed at one time it'd been a parking spot for the office, but the previous owner had transformed it into a place to enjoy a cigarette in private. She'd found ashtrays hidden beneath the hedges and a lighter on the wrought-iron table in the center of the slab.

Now she turned her head from side to side, trying to catch sight of who'd been lurking near her window.

A shadow darted across the edge of the patio, but even as she pushed the window open, whoever was there had disappeared behind the bakery next to her building.

A chill snaked down her spine. With a shiver, she slammed down the window and backed away. At the same time the door behind her was shoved open and her secretary stepped into the office.

Doris was dressed in her usual uniform of knee-length skirt and wool sweater. Her short gray hair was held in place by a coat of lacquer, or maybe it was hairspray—either way, it wasn't going anywhere. Her thin, lined face held a hint of worry as she cast a glance around the office before studying Ellie with confusion.

"God Almighty," she breathed, pressing a hand to the pearl necklace hung around her birdlike neck. "I thought you'd fallen."

Ellie released a shaky breath. "Sorry."

The older woman frowned, her head tilting to the side as she noticed Ellie's pallor.

"What's wrong?"

Ellie forced a smile. "Nothing."

"Nothing, eh?" Doris took a step toward her. The secretary might be in her sixties, but her gaze was still razor sharp. "You look like you've seen a ghost."

Ellie shivered, unable to halt her instinctive glance toward the window.

"I'm jumping at shadows."

Doris wasn't fooled. "What kind of shadow?"

Ellie hesitated. She'd told Doris about her tires. It wasn't like she had a choice when she'd shown up at the office without her car. But she didn't want to frighten her secretary with the thought there might be some pervert out there peeking through windows.

Then she gave a roll of her eyes. What was she thinking? It would take more than a pervert to scare Doris.

The older woman had spent a few youthful years on the rodeo circuit. She'd shared enough colorful stories with Ellie to prove she had nerves of steel.

"There was someone on the patio," she confessed. "When

I stepped toward the window to see who was there, they ran behind the bakery."

On cue, the secretary pivoted to head out of the office. "I'll go see if I can find out who it was."

Ellie quickly moved to block her path. The older woman wouldn't think twice about marching around the bakery in search of the intruder.

"No, Doris."

"Why not?" The secretary came to a reluctant halt. "It's probably the same person who ruined your tires."

Ellie swallowed a sigh. Doris had been as quick as Nate to assume that her flat tires had been caused by deliberate vandalism.

"I'm still not convinced they were slashed, but I'm not going to let you take any chances," Ellie said.

Doris clicked her tongue. "You need to go see the sheriff."

"You sound like Nate," she complained.

"He's always struck me as a sensible man."

"I suppose."

"And hot as hell."

Ellie made a choked sound. "Doris."

"Hey, I'm old, not dead."

With a rueful shake of her head, Ellie moved to the desk to grab her purse. The older woman would continue to nag until Ellie finally gave in. It was easier just to concede defeat and get it over with.

"Fine. I'll go talk to the sheriff." She pointed a finger toward the smugly smiling secretary. "You stay here and behave yourself."

Doris's smile faded. "You be careful."

With a nod Ellie left the office and crossed the reception room to step out of the building. The sun was shining, but there was a chilled breeze that whipped around the corner, slicing through her sweater. She paused. Maybe she should go back in and grab her jacket.

Then she gave a shake of her head. The courthouse was across the street. She was just trying to procrastinate.

Squaring her shoulders, she marched toward the large stone structure that had been built over a hundred years ago. It had massive windows and hand-carved shutters. The copper roof had turned green with a patina long ago.

Ellie crossed the neatly manicured lawn and climbed the wide steps to enter the arched double doorway. She was forced to halt and allow her eyes to adjust to the darkness of the foyer. At the same time, she breathed in the musty scent.

There was a sensation of ponderous age that had settled into the very air of the courthouse. She liked the feeling. It offered a silent promise of tradition that Ellie appreciated.

The law was the law. It was something she could depend on.

Maybe it was because she'd spent most of her life being uprooted from one house to another. When she was three they'd moved from Curry to Oklahoma City. From there they'd stayed in the same city, but they'd traded in one house for another, increasing in size as her father had climbed the judicial ladder of success.

All Ellie had wanted was a home. Instead she'd gotten a mansion as cold and empty as a museum.

She abruptly rolled her eyes and crossed the tiled floor to enter the nearest corridor. *Poor little rich girl*, she mocked at her bout of self-pity. She had everything, including two parents who loved her.

Minutes later she was sitting in a small waiting room. She'd hoped to make her report to the receptionist. Regrettably, she hadn't realized it was nearly noon, which meant most of the staff was out for lunch. She'd been met by a young deputy who was clearly nervous at her entrance. No doubt the sheriff and prosecuting attorney spent hours describing her as a bitch who did everything in her power to thwart the brave men in law enforcement.

So now she was stuck twiddling her thumbs.

Pulling out her phone, she did her best to ignore the large clock on the wall, and the *tick*, *tick*, *tick* of the second hand that was an audible reminder that she was wasting time. She'd managed to check her email and order a new bra before the sheriff, Gary Clark, at last strolled into the room.

He was a square, stocky man with a large hook of a nose and rapidly thinning blond hair. His eyes were pale and watery, as if he suffered from allergies. Currently he was wearing a dark uniform with a shiny badge on the shirt pocket and a patch sewn onto one sleeve. He also had a heavy utility belt strapped around his thick waist that held a plethora of objects, including his gun.

She rose to her feet, as always caught off guard by the fact that the man barely topped her by a few inches. She was used to having people towering over her. It was nice when she didn't have to crane her neck to meet someone's gaze.

"Morning, Ms. Guthrie," the sheriff said with a faint nod.

He insisted on formality. Which was fine with Ellie. Even if they didn't find themselves on opposite sides of the law, she would never have encouraged a friendlier relationship.

The man was quite frankly an incompetent jerk.

He was lazy, and always willing to take shortcuts. Since Ellie had moved to Curry, his sloppiness had led to dismissal of charges for one of her clients, and two overturned verdicts. She suspected he held on to his job because no one else wanted it.

"Thanks for seeing me," she said, thankful that her time in the courtroom had taught her the trick of sounding sincere no matter what the situation.

"Clay said you needed to report a crime?"

His tone was less than encouraging. Ellie didn't know if

it was because he didn't like her, or because he didn't want to be bothered with doing his job.

Probably a combination of both.

"Actually, I'm not sure if it's a crime or not," she conceded.

He heaved a resigned sigh. "Come into my office."

She followed him through a door that had a frosted glass window with SHERIFF CLARK painted on it in big gold letters. She arched her brows as she caught sight of the cavernous office. It was filled with heavy antique furniture that was polished until it reflected the light filtering through the high, arched window. The rug looked like it was handwoven in some oriental pattern and the walls were covered with framed pictures of the current sheriff at various functions. A groundbreaking ceremony. Singing in the church choir. A fundraising event with the governor.

Heading straight toward his desk, the lawman waved a vague hand toward the visitor chairs.

"Make yourself comfortable," he said, settling in his own leather seat.

"I'm fine," she said, standing in the center of the room. The office made her uncomfortable. It was unabashed shrine to an egotist. "I know you must be busy."

He nodded, impervious to her subtle taunt. "Tell me what happened," he said.

She quickly told him about waking up to find her tires ruined, not surprised when he looked far from impressed by her concern.

"You had flat tires?"

"Yes."

There was a pause before he pointed out the obvious. "You could have run over something."

"That was my first thought, but Nate insisted that they were slashed with a knife."

"Nate Marcel?" For the first time the sheriff managed to look genuinely interested. "He was at your house?"

Ellie swallowed a curse. Of course, the idiot would leap to the conclusion that Nate had spent the night with her.

"He was driving past and stopped to see if he could help."

"Right." A skeptical smile twisted his lips. "Just driving past."

She pasted on her lawyer face. She'd discovered in the courtroom that demanding a direct answer was the only answer to ugly insinuations.

"Is there a problem, Sheriff?" she asked in cool tones.

"It just seems convenient that he happened to be there just when you needed him."

"I can assure you that there was nothing convenient about having my property destroyed."

Gary shifted in his seat, a ruddy color crawling beneath his skin before he cleared his throat and tried to act professional.

"Did you notice anyone near your vehicle last night?"

"No."

"What time did you get home?"

She had to stop and consider. "Around ten thirty," she at last said.

"Alone?"

"Yes. Alone." She tried not to take offense. It was a reasonable question. "And before you ask, I didn't have any guests stopping by."

He tapped his finger on the top of his desk, which was oddly bare. Or maybe it just seemed bare to her, she wryly acknowledged. Her own desk was always littered with files and law books and empty coffee cups.

"What time did you notice the tires were flat?"

She absently noted that he didn't mention the word *slashed*. "Around seven thirty this morning."

Tap, tap, tap with his finger. She wondered why he wasn't taking notes, or filling out some sort of form. No doubt because he had no intention of doing a damned thing after she left his office.

"Have you recently broken up with your lover?" he demanded.

She scowled. "No."

"Have you had any threats?"

"Nothing out of the ordinary."

The pale eyes hardened. "Is that a yes or a no?"

She shrugged. "There are always people unhappy with lawyers."

"No shit," he muttered softly. Not soft enough, however, for her to miss it. "Make out a list of anyone who has recently threatened you."

Ellie resisted the urge to turn and walk out. She didn't doubt this was a complete waste of time, but she was already there. She might as well finish what she'd come to do.

"Fine. I'll send it over later."

The sheriff rose to his feet, a visible indication he was done with the conversation.

"Anything else?"

"I think there was someone peeking in my office window."

His brows arched. "When?"

"Right before I came here."

"I assume you didn't recognize them?"

She shook her head. "I only caught a glimpse of their shadow."

"A shadow?"

"Yeah."

"So, no description?"

Ellie clenched her purse tight enough that her knuckles turned white. She wanted to reach across the desk and smack the impatient expression off the man's face.

Probably not a good idea, she ruefully told herself. No matter how much pleasure it might give her.

"No, no description."

"Anything else?"

"That's it."

He didn't even pretend that he was concerned she was being harassed by some unknown enemy. Instead he sent her a condescending smile.

"I'll have a deputy drive by your house and your office."

"Great."

Turning on her heel, she strolled out of the office with her head held high and her spine stiff.

Lazy, conceited ass. Someday there would be a brave soul to run against him in the election for sheriff and Ellie intended to donate as much money as necessary to see that Gary Clark was kicked out of office.

Still fuming, Ellie was leaving the outer office when she bumped into someone trying to enter. There was a painful impact and Ellie was knocked backward.

Shaken out of her dark thoughts, Ellie reached out a hand in an apologetic gesture to the woman who had come to a halt and was staring at her in surprise.

"Oh, Tia. I'm so sorry," she breathed. "I wasn't paying attention to where I was going."

Tia Chambers was several inches taller than Ellie, with a stocky frame and shoulder-length brown hair and a sprinkling of freckles across her broad face. The daughter of the mayor, she had the money to wear expensive designer clothes, but she always looked awkward. Like her mother picked out her wardrobe and she was forced to wear it.

Ellie could sympathize.

"It's fine." Tia stepped back. "It was probably my fault. I was in a hurry."

Ellie paused. Tia's face was flushed, and she was breathing hard. As if she'd been running down the hallway before Ellie crashed into her.

"Is everything okay?" she asked.

"Of course." The woman's smile was just a tad too bright.

"Are you sure?" Ellie pressed. She didn't know Tia as more than a distant acquaintance, but it was easy to sense the woman's tension.

Tia's smile faltered. "It's silly, but I think someone was following me while I was walking to town this morning."

Ellie's heart missed a beat. There was no reason to believe that Tia's suspicion she was being followed had anything to do with her own weird incidents. But on the other hand, Curry was a small town. What was the likelihood that two women would feel threatened on the same day?

"I don't think it's silly," she told Tia. "Did you see anyone?"

"No." Tia wrapped her arms around her waist. The motion stretched the fabric of her red wool sweater over her large breasts. "It probably was just a figment of my imagination."

"There had to be something that freaked you out."

Tia hesitated. Almost as if she was afraid Ellie would laugh at her.

"I'm certain I heard footsteps behind me, but whenever I turned to look, I couldn't see anyone," she at last admitted.

"Has it happened before?"

"I've occasionally felt like someone was watching me whenever I was out in our garden," Tia admitted, "but my father told me I was imagining it."

Ellie bit her bottom lip. Was it possible that there was some local nutcase who was stalking single women in town?

"I believe you," she assured her companion.

"Thank you." Tia glanced nervously into the sheriff's office. "I'm not sure anyone else will."

Ellie made a heroic effort not to share her opinion of Sheriff Gary Clark or his lack of concern for his citizens.

She reached out to lightly touch Tia's arm. "It doesn't matter. If your instincts are telling you that something is wrong, then you should pay attention to them."

Tia sucked in a deep breath, visibly gathering her courage. "You're right. I'm going to report it."

"Good." Ellie moved out of the way of the door. "Take care, Tia."

"You too." Tia headed into the office and Ellie hurried down the hallway.

She had a sudden urge to pick up a sandwich and her favorite red velvet cupcake from the bakery.

It was going to be a long afternoon.

Chapter Four

Nate waited until nearly six o'clock before he drove back into Curry. He didn't know Ellie Guthrie as well as he wanted, but he'd driven by her house often enough to notice that she was rarely home before seven.

He circled the block, parking directly in front of her office. Then, jumping out of his truck, he paused to glance around.

He'd rarely had a reason to be in the town center at night. Now he frowned as he realized how isolated it felt with the stores shut down and the streets empty of traffic. A frown tugged at his brows as he reached for the door.

Locked. Thank God for that. He half expected Ellie to leave it wide open, even when she was there alone.

Clenching his hand, he rapped on the glass, waiting for the light to be flipped on and Ellie to peer out of her office. With a frown, she crossed the reception area to unlock the door and pull it open.

"Nate." She looked confused. "What are you doing here?"

"I was about to head back to the ranch," he said, mentally crossing his fingers at the harmless lie. "I thought I'd see if you needed a ride."

She glanced over his shoulder at his truck parked next to

the curb. Did she suspect that he'd gone home hours ago and had driven back to town to pick her up?

There was a long pause, then without warning, she was tilting back her head to meet his steady gaze.

"Actually, that would be great. If you don't mind waiting while I lock up."

His heart squeezed with pleasure and Nate swallowed a sigh. He was an idiot. There were a dozen lovely women in town who were eager to attract his attention, but not one of them had managed to give him the same thrill as Ellie agreeing to a simple lift back to her house.

Pathetic.

"Take your time. I'll wait in the truck," he said, turning to head back to his vehicle before she could change her mind.

Sliding behind the steering wheel, he started the engine and flicked on the heat. The night air had grown chilly and his truck wasn't exactly dependable. Sometimes the air came out as hot as blazes and with the force of a hurricane. Other times, it was barely a lukewarm trickle.

Tonight, it was the trickle.

He settled back in his seat, prepared to be patient. He'd come from a family of four boys, plus a cop for a father. That meant his mother ran a constant chauffeuring service from school to football practice to the thousand other places young boys wanted to go. As the youngest, Nate had learned to wait his turn.

Surprisingly, however, Ellie was climbing into the passenger seat in less than ten minutes.

He waited for her to place her purse and a stack of files on the floorboard and buckle her seat belt before he put the truck in gear and pulled away from the curb.

"Do you need anything before we leave town?" he asked.

She shook her head. "No. The shop called to say that they put new tires on my car, so I'm all set."

He'd already driven by her house to make sure that the repairs were done. He couldn't help himself.

It was like a compulsion.

They made the short journey through town without saying anything more, then, turning onto the county road, he pressed his foot on the gas.

"Did you talk to the sheriff?" He at last broke the silence.

She snorted. "Yeah, for all the good it did. He made it clear that he wasn't going to waste his time worrying about my flat tires."

Nate flashed a startled glance toward her tense profile before returning his attention to the road. She'd actually done as he asked?

He didn't know if it was a miracle or if the sky was about to fall.

Of course, the fact that the sheriff had dismissed her concern made his fingers tighten on the steering wheel. Someday he was going to have a very long conversation with Gary Clark about the responsibility of wearing a badge.

"Do you have a security system installed at your house?" he demanded.

She shifted on the seat. "My father arranged to have new locks on the doors and windows when I moved in."

There was an edge in her voice when she mentioned her father that Nate had noticed before. He wondered what sort of relationship Ellie had with Judge Guthrie. Families could be complicated.

"You need a dog," he told her.

She released a startled laugh. "Are you kidding? I can't keep a house plant alive, let alone an animal."

Nate was distracted by the unexpected sound of sirens wailing in the distance. Slowing the truck, he pulled onto the shoulder and watched as the ambulance zoomed past him, followed by a dark vehicle with a flashing light, going at top speed.

The coroner?

Ellie leaned forward as the emergency vehicles turned onto a narrow dirt road.

"There must have been a wreck."

Nate pressed on the gas and hurried after them. "Let's find out."

She sent him a startled glance. "What are you doing?"

"Following them."

"No," she protested.

He sent her a startled glance. "Don't you want to know what happened?"

"I'm a lawyer," she said in dry tones. "I try to avoid the appearance of chasing ambulances."

His lips twitched. He loved her humor. Probably because she so rarely shared it with him.

"I might be able to help."

"You have medical training?"

"I have many talents."

She rolled her eyes. "You're nosy."

He was. The reason he'd been such a good investigator was because he was fascinated by people and why they did the things they did.

"Neighborly," he corrected.

They bumped down the narrow road, seemingly headed into the middle of nowhere. It was nearly a quarter of an hour later when they rounded a sharp curve and suddenly the darkness was lit by a dozen flashing emergency lights.

There were cop cars, fire trucks, the ambulance that had passed them, along with the coroner.

Nate pulled off the road, studying the line of vehicles to the empty field, where he could see a large group of people gathered in the center.

"I don't think it was a wreck," Ellie muttered.

Neither did Nate. By the glow of the lights he could see a shadowed man draping police tape across an opening in the barbed-wire fence.

"Stay here," he muttered, shoving open his door.

"Excuse me?"

He flinched at her sharp words. He was so used to giving orders to civilians when he'd been with the Bureau that he'd spoken before he could think.

"Habit," he told her.

She sniffed, climbing out of the truck. Together they walked toward the deputy, who was now standing near the side of the road. Presumably he was there to protect the crime scene.

Nate's gaze moved toward the group that was gathered in a semicircle a hundred feet away. He had a bad feeling in the pit of his stomach.

The men looked grim, but there was no urgency in the movements of the EMTs who were carrying the stretcher across the field. They moved with the slow formality of pallbearers.

Halting in front of the deputy, he nodded his head toward the knot of officials.

"What's going on?" he asked.

The young man hesitated, clearly aware that he shouldn't be speaking with the local gawkers. Then, Nate's time as an FBI agent paid off. The deputy glanced around to make sure no one was looking in their direction, and then leaned toward Nate.

He spoke in a low voice, lawman to lawman.

"A 911 call came in an hour ago, saying that there was a dead body found in the middle of this field," he said.

He heard Ellie give a faint gasp, but he kept his gaze

focused on the deputy. He'd already suspected what the deputy would say. He was just glad there was only one body.

Murder/suicides had become far too common in areas that had been hit hard by the opioid epidemic.

"Do you have an ID?" he asked.

The man gave another hesitant glance over his shoulder before answering.

"Daniel Perry."

"Jesus." Nate's breath hissed through his teeth.

He'd known that Walter was troubled when he'd talked to him this morning. Had the older man realized that Daniel was spiraling out of control? Or had it been the sixth sense of a father who loved his son regardless of the choices he made?

"Yeah." The deputy offered a somber nod of his head. Daniel had been a pain in the ass, but it was still a tragedy for such a young man to die.

"Was there an accident?" Nate asked.

The deputy grimaced. "I didn't see any injuries. My guess is that he died of an overdose."

Nate would have made the same guess. His gaze swept the area, absently noting the emergency vehicles that blocked the road. Where was Daniel's car? It couldn't have been towed yet.

"Was someone with him?"

The deputy shrugged. "Nope."

Nate's gaze shifted back to the field. They were miles from the nearest house.

"Then who called it in?"

"Don't know. They didn't leave a name."

"Can't you trace the call?"

Another shrug. "Probably."

Nate hid his grimace. He was used to thinking like an FBI agent, not a local deputy who was convinced the death was a tragic accident.

"Any idea how long he's been here?" he asked.

"The coroner can't say. We'll ship the body off to the medical examiner's office." The deputy glanced over his shoulder as someone called out. "I have to go."

Nate hesitated before turning to head back to his truck.

This was none of his business. Whether Daniel had been out here alone, or partying with a bunch of friends who'd abandoned him after he'd OD'd, it was the sheriff's problem to clean up.

"So sad," Ellie breathed as they climbed into the truck.

Nate nodded, cranking the engine. Her words summed up the situation perfectly.

So fucking sad.

He turned his vehicle around and they drove to Ellie's house in subdued silence. As hard as he tried, he couldn't shake a strange sense of unease.

Not just the disquiet that came from learning that someone he knew was now dead. But a heaviness that filled his heart with anxiety.

It was an anxiety that only intensified as he pulled into Ellie's driveway and glanced around the empty darkness that surrounded her house. Statistically speaking, she was much safer in this remote area than in a large town. The violent crime rate in Curry was almost nonexistent. But it was hard not to react to the knowledge that she was completely alone in such an isolated spot.

She pushed open her door and was jumping out of the truck before he could get out to help.

"Thanks for the lift."

He leaned across the seat, angling his head to catch a glimpse of her profile visible in the glow from his headlights.

"Ellie." He waited for her to turn her head and meet his gaze. "Make sure you lock up tight once you're inside."

She gave a sharp nod before she was closing the door and hurrying toward the house.

Nate waited until she was inside and she'd flicked on the lights. Even then, he found himself reluctant to pull away. If there were someone lurking in the dark . . .

Muttering a curse, he shoved the truck into reverse and pulled back onto the gravel road. Ellie was safely tucked in her house. If she needed anything from him she would call.

He snorted. He was fairly sure that hell would freeze over before Ellie dialed his number.

Nate was up before dawn. Not an unusual occurrence.

After six or seven hours in bed his old wound felt like someone was shoving a hot poker through his hip. The only cure was to get up and spend a half hour in a hot shower, relaxing his knotted muscles. Then he would pour himself a cup of coffee and head out the door to stand on his back porch.

He enjoyed watching the sun crest the horizon, the colors of dawn brushing over the flat prairie as his livestock stirred in preparation of a new day.

Leaning against the railing, he sipped his coffee and glanced toward the north. He couldn't see Ellie's house, but she often enjoyed an early morning jog along the road. He took great pleasure in watching her progress.

Hey, he was a man.

He liked to look, even if he couldn't touch.

He'd just switched on his old-fashioned coffeemaker when he heard a vehicle pull into his driveway. He felt a stab of surprise as he headed toward the living room. It was early for a visitor, even in an area where most people were up at the crack of dawn.

Pulling open his door, he initially assumed that whoever was there must be lost. At first he didn't recognize the shiny new truck that was parked in front of his garage. Then a slender man climbed out of the vehicle and Nate's heart squeezed with pity.

It'd been less than twenty-four hours since he'd last seen Walter, but in the early dawn light he looked like he'd aged fifty years.

The man's shoulders were slumped and his head hung low, as if it was too heavy for his neck. He was wearing the same clothes as yesterday, and his cheeks were bristled with his unshaved whiskers. Even worse, there was a shell-shocked expression on his narrow face that made him look like he'd just wandered off a battlefield.

Nate walked to the edge of the porch as his unexpected guest climbed the stairs.

"Walter," he murmured.

"Nate." Reaching the top step, Walter cleared his throat. "I know it's early."

Nate couldn't imagine what had brought the grieving father to his house, but right now it didn't matter. First, he wanted to get the man off his feet before he collapsed.

Grasping his arm, Nate steered him across the porch and into the house. Walter shuffled at his side like a zombie, allowing himself to be pulled through the living room and into the small kitchen.

"Have a seat."

Nate pressed him into one of the wooden chairs that matched his table. He'd carved it with his own hands. Just as he'd carved all the furniture in the old ranch house. He'd discovered an unexpected peace when shaping and polishing wood after his early retirement.

Moving to the counter, he poured a large mug of coffee and added several teaspoons of sugar before placing it in Walter's shaky hand. Wasn't sugar supposed to help with shock?

"Thanks." Walter absently sipped the steaming liquid.

"Have you eaten?" Nate asked. "I have some fresh muffins or I can scramble some eggs."

"No." Walter shook his head. "I couldn't eat. Not today."

Nate grimaced. "I really don't know what to say except that I'm sorry as hell."

"It's crazy." Walter shook his head. "I've spent years waiting for something bad to happen to Daniel. I thought he'd end up in jail. Or dead in a drunk driving accident." There was a painful pause. "Not this."

"No one can ever be prepared to lose a child," Nate murmured, then he flinched. Jesus, the words sounded so trite.

Walter seemed to agree. He released a sharp, humorless laugh.

"That's what I told folks for thirty years. But now the shoe is on the other foot and it doesn't fit so well."

"How can I help?"

Walter set the coffee mug on the table, the cresting sun slanting through the window over the sink to expose the man's unnatural pallor.

"I want the truth."

"The truth?"

"I want to know who murdered my boy."

Nate studied his companion, not sure he'd heard correctly. "You think someone deliberately killed him?"

Walter jutted his lower jaw. "That's exactly what I think."

Nate tried to ignore the questions that had nagged at him when he'd been observing the field where Daniel's body had been found. He was a rancher, not an FBI agent. And Walter was a father who was in the first brutal hours of his grief. Encouraging any wild fantasies could only cause Walter more pain in the long run.

Nate, however, couldn't restrain his fierce curiosity. He had to know why Walter thought his son had been murdered.

"What about the sheriff?" he asked. "Does he suspect murder?"

Walter curled his lips in disgust. "That man has the investigative instincts of a turnip."

Hard to argue with that. "Have they determined a cause of death?"

A muscle ticked at the base of Walter's jaw. As if he was clenching and unclenching his teeth.

"Nothing official, but everyone assumes Daniel died of an overdose."

"But not you?"

Walter instantly looked defensive. "I'm not a fool. I know Daniel did more than just drink. From what I heard he was willing to experiment with anything that could get him high. Hell, he was caught trying to steal painkillers from the local nursing home."

Nate studied the older man. "So why don't you believe he died of an overdose?"

"If he had enough drugs in his system to kill him, then how did he get thirteen miles outside town?"

Nate stilled. The question proved that Walter wasn't blindly grasping at someone to blame for his son's death. He was thinking as a lawman on some level.

"Where is Daniel's vehicle?"

"They found it parked behind the tavern."

"Which one?" Nate asked. There was a grand total of three taverns in town.

"The Lodge."

Nate leaned against the counter. The Lodge was the largest bar and it attracted a younger, rougher crowd than the others.

"He could have hooked up with friends and then headed out to the field to party with them in private. If something happened to Daniel, they might have bailed on him," Nate said, unable to think of a kind way to describe the life of an addict. Lost in the grip of their habit, they had no morals or principles.

Without warning, Walter slammed his open hand on the table. The mug bounced to the side from the force of the blow, slopping coffee onto the glossy wood.

"But why there?" he snarled.

Nate frowned. Was that fear in the man's pale eyes?

"What do you mean?"

"Why that field?"

It was a question that Nate hadn't really considered. Not until this moment.

"It's isolated," he at last said.

"There are a lot of fields closer to town that are just as isolated," Walter snapped. "Besides, Daniel has his own trailer that I bought for him. Why not party there?"

Nate paused. He wasn't sure why Walter was obsessing over where Daniel had gone to party. Maybe it was because he'd grown up in a city, but one field was like another as far as he was concerned.

"What do you think happened?" he demanded.

Walter abruptly looked away, his chest expanding as he sucked in a deep breath. It was like he was swallowing some huge emotion.

Then, with an effort, he forced himself to answer Nate's question.

"Two months ago, I caught Daniel dealing drugs out of my basement. That's why I kicked him out," he said. "I wasn't going to tolerate having a line of losers going in and out of my own damned house."

Nate had a vague suspicion that Walter wasn't being completely honest with him. Or rather, that he was leaving out information.

A typical response.

Even people who were desperate to learn what had happened to their loved ones would often be less than truthful. Sometimes it was to protect the reputation of the recently dead. Or to hide a family secret. Or sometimes, it was a reflexive action when talking to law enforcement.

Nate didn't try to press the older man. Right now, he was more interested in Walter's gut instincts about his son and the people who might have been with him when he died.

"You think it might have been a drug deal gone bad?"

"It's possible. Or . . ." His words trailed away.

"Or what?"

Walter hunched a shoulder. "I just want to know if someone deliberately lured my boy to that field and killed him. Will you do that for me?"

Ah. So, Walter wanted more than just to vent his frustrated grief. He actually expected Nate to investigate his son's death.

Nate parted his lips to say no. The last thing he needed was to aggravate the local officials by sticking his nose in where it didn't belong.

Then he remembered Ellie's flat tires, and his belief that someone had deliberately slashed them. It was far-fetched to think the two events could be related, but until he could be 100 percent certain he was going to be worried.

"I'll check around, but if the sheriff decides there was a crime committed, he's not going to want me butting into his investigation," he warned the older man.

Walter snorted. "That lazy jackass won't give a crap. He's already decided to call it an accidental death and nothing short of someone coming into his office and confessing they killed Daniel is going to change his mind."

Nate held up a hand. He agreed with Walter; the odds of Gary Clark actually doing his duty were slim to none. Still, he didn't want to get Walter's hopes up.

There was a good chance there was nothing to investigate beyond a tragic accident.

"I'll do what I can," he said.

Walter rose to his feet and reached to grab Nate's hand in a tight grip.

"Thank you."

Chapter Five

Barb Adams cursed as she tossed her cell phone on the sofa and paced across her living room, which was cramped and dark. Dammit. Where was Eloise? No, wait . . . she liked to be called Ellie, right?

When Ellie had first returned to Curry, it'd been hard for Barb to think of her as a grown woman with her own law practice. In her mind, she was still a precocious toddler who'd zipped around the office whenever Colin Guthrie would bring his daughter to work. But after Barb had gotten caught driving with a suspended license, she'd had no choice but to ask Ellie to represent her. She'd long ago burned her bridges with her old acquaintances, and there wasn't anyone who would lift a finger to help her.

Now she paced back and forth, grimacing at the thought that she'd managed to drive Ellie away too.

Maybe she should call back and tell that stupid secretary that she didn't need Ellie's legal help. Or even more money, although she wouldn't say no if the younger woman wanted to slip her a couple of twenties.

Barb abruptly froze. Was that a creak? Had someone opened a window? No. She was being paranoid. She tried to soothe her rattled nerves. It wouldn't be the first time, right? Since she'd gone from a glass of wine after dinner to relax, to drinking an entire bottle of vodka just to get through the night, she'd started imagining all sorts of crazy things. She'd once been convinced she could hear people whispering when she tried to sleep. And that a car was following her whenever she was driving around town. And that she'd seen the face of her dead mother peering through the living room window.

Of course, this time she actually had reason to be on edge, she reminded herself. Last night she might have been hammered, but she'd seen more clearly than she had in years.

She had to warn the others.

There was another creak and Barb whirled around, her eyes widening in horror. She lifted her hands, as if she could ward off the fate that had been stalking her for years.

Oh God. She was too late.

Too. Damn. Late.

Ellie woke early. Nothing unusual in that. But she didn't usually creep out the door with a flashlight in one hand and a softball bat in the other. Once reassured that no one had been skulking around during the night, she headed out for her morning run.

Jogging down the road, she kept her pace steady and her gaze locked on the distant windmills. She was never going to win a marathon, but there was something deeply satisfying in the feel of her feet hitting the red-dirt road. It was her version of meditation.

Out of habit, she circled past Nate's home, experiencing the familiar sensation that she was being watched. But it wasn't a creepy, stalker sort of sensation. Actually, she'd always savored the warmth that flowed through her as she passed by the old ranch house. As if someone who cared about her safety was always close by, keeping away the monsters.

Concentrating on her breathing, Ellie managed to pretend she didn't have a ball of unease lodged in the pit of her stomach. It actually worked, even when she returned home.

Taking a quick shower, she dried off and gathered her damp hair into a ponytail. Then, sipping her second cup of coffee, she pulled on black slacks and a light sweater before she jumped in her car and headed into town.

It wasn't until she stepped into her office and Doris surged to her feet with an eager expression that her pretense cracked and crumbled. She just wanted to go to her desk and bury herself in the stack of files awaiting her attention. Instead, it was obvious that Doris was impatient to discuss the shocking news that was already buzzing through town.

Swallowing a resigned sigh, she forced a smile. "Morning, Doris."

"Did you hear?" the older woman demanded.

"About Daniel?"

Doris was briefly disappointed at the realization that she couldn't amaze Ellie with the latest gossip, but she quickly rallied to offer an expression of sympathy that was laced with a large dose of judgmental satisfaction.

The good citizens of Curry believed in loving thy neighbor, but they also believed in karma. Or as they would say, *Let justice roll on like a river, righteousness like a never-failing stream.*

You got what was coming to you . . . eventually.

"A tragedy," Doris said, "but I suppose we all knew it was just a matter of time."

Ellie grimaced. The older woman had a point. Daniel had chased death with a vengeance. Still, it was hard to accept that such a young, seemingly healthy man was dead. "Have you heard what happened to him?"

Doris looked surprised by the question. "Everyone assumes it was an overdose. What else could it be?" There was a short pause as the older woman pressed a hand to the center of her chest. "Oh. You don't think he committed suicide, do you?"

"No, I don't think anything," Ellie hastily denied. Christ, the last thing she wanted was to start the rumor that Daniel had killed himself. Once she'd told her secretary that her lunch at the local café caused her heartburn, and the next thing she knew the owner was calling to say that he'd heard she was telling people that he'd given her food poisoning. Lesson learned. "I was asking if you'd been told how he died."

Doris gave a shake of her head. "All I know is that Daniel was found in the middle of Neville Morse's field."

Ellie hadn't known who owned the land. Although she'd been born in Curry, she'd spent the majority of her life in Oklahoma City. She was still acquainting herself with the locals.

"Neville Morse," she murmured. "I don't recognize the name."

"He doesn't come to town much. To be honest, he's almost a hermit," Doris told her. "But you know his daughter, Mandy."

Ellie only knew one Mandy. The woman who worked next door at the bakery.

"Mandy Gibson?"

Doris nodded. "She married Neil Gibson straight out of high school. It was a rushed ceremony, if you know what I mean. They were divorced a year later. She's been working at the bakery ever since to take care of herself and her son."

"Was she friends with Daniel?"

Doris snorted. "I doubt it. She's a hardworking mother who doesn't have time for the sort of nonsense that killed Daniel."

The ring of the office phone interrupted their conversation and Doris reached for the receiver to answer in a professional voice.

"Guthrie Law Firm, how may I help you?" She listened, her lips thinning with displeasure at whoever was at the other end of the line. "I'm sorry, she's not in yet. I'll pass along your messages when she gets here."

Ellie arched a brow. Doris was bossy, and inclined to gossip, but she was always gracious to Ellie's clients. Even those who were more than a little sketchy.

"Who was that?" Ellie demanded as Doris replaced the receiver with a loud bang.

"Barb Adams," the older woman said.

Ah. Ellie suddenly understood the woman's prickly response.

Barb Adams had been her father's secretary when he'd worked in the prosecutor's office in town. Ellie had seen pictures of the vivacious, redheaded woman when Barb was younger, but she hadn't recognized her when she'd stumbled through the front door. The woman's hair had faded, her face was sallow and deeply wrinkled, and her body was gaunt after years of abusing alcohol.

Ellie had often heard the term "death warmed over," but she hadn't truly understood it until she'd seen Barb. Which might have explained why she'd allowed herself to be talked into agreeing to represent her, pro bono, despite the fact that she didn't usually take DUI cases. And even giving her money to pay her electric bill. Frankly, she felt sorry for the woman.

Doris hadn't been nearly so sympathetic. She claimed she was angered that the older woman had used her connection to Ellie's father to take advantage of her, but Ellie suspected there was more to her disapproval than that.

From everything that Ellie had heard from her father, Barb Adams had once been a top-notch secretary, who'd been offered several lucrative positions while she was working at the prosecutor's office. No doubt Doris was worried her own performance was being judged against the other woman's before Barb had taken to drinking. Or perhaps she thought Barb was hoping to replace her as Ellie's secretary.

Whatever the case, Doris always looked like she'd swallowed a lemon when Barb was around.

"Was she arrested?"

"Either that or she wants to play on your sympathy for more money," Doris said. "She left a dozen messages last night on the answering machine asking you to come and see her. I assumed she was drunk out of her mind and erased them."

"Maybe I should go see what she needs," Ellie said, swallowing a sigh. She hated to admit the fact that she found Barb Adams a pain in the ass.

At one time, she'd no doubt been a highly efficient woman with a bright future. Now she was just a sad drunk drowning in self-pity and alcohol.

Still, her house was only a couple of blocks away. Ellie could walk there in less than ten minutes. And if she didn't go see the woman, there was a good chance she would stumble into the office drunk as a skunk, demanding to see Ellie.

Doris flattened her lips in disapproval. "What she needs is to stop trying to take advantage of you just because she worked for your father."

"She's lonely."

"Perhaps she'd have a few friends if she wasn't always three sheets to the wind."

Ellie turned back to the door. The sooner she found out

what Barb wanted, the sooner she could concentrate on her work.

"I'll be back."

"Don't give her any money," Doris called out as Ellie left the office and headed down the sidewalk.

Ellie rolled her eyes, glad that she'd pulled on a sweater before she'd left the house. The sun had crested the horizon, but it hadn't managed to take the chill out of the morning air.

Not that Ellie minded. She liked when the breeze was crisp and the sun a mere promise of warmth. In a couple of months, it would be unbearably hot.

Hurrying past the businesses that were beginning to open for the day, she turned north to enter a residential section of town. At one time, it had been an elegant neighborhood with a nice mix of Victorian and Craftsman homes. Now the wealthy citizens lived in the new subdivision south of town, and the Victorian homes had been converted to cheap apartments. A sad but inevitable decline.

She reached the small corner house with white siding and black shutters and headed up the sidewalk to climb the steps that led to the covered porch. Knocking on the door, she frowned as it swung open.

"Barb?" she called out. She stuck her head into the house, her nose wrinkling at the overpowering stench of stale cigarette smoke. "Hello? Barb." Nothing.

Ellie hesitated before she stepped inside. The older woman might be unstable, but she wouldn't have left without locking her door, would she?

It took a few seconds for her eyes to adjust to the darkness of the front room. The heavy drapes were pulled across the windows, as if Barb was allergic to daylight. Or maybe it was a preventive measure, knowing she was going to wake with a hangover.

Taking a cautious step forward, Ellie peered through the

shadows. She could make out a couch and two armchairs as well as a low coffee table. Nothing looked out of place. Then, as she was about to turn and leave, she caught sight of the lump lying on the floor near the window.

"Barb."

Ellie hurried forward and crouched down next to Barb. Carefully she reached out to roll the woman onto her back, feeling for a pulse.

It was faint. Unsteady.

Ellie dug in her purse, finding her phone to dial 911. As soon as she heard the call answered, she gave Barb's address and tossed the phone back in her purse. Thankfully there was a rural hospital on the edge of town. It shouldn't take them more than a couple of minutes to reach the house.

Barb suddenly coughed, her lashes lifting to reveal eyes that looked dull and unfocused.

"Eloise?"

Ellie reached up to yank open the nearest curtain. The darkness was unnerving. Sunlight slanted into the room, revealing the stark pallor of Barb's face.

"I'm here," she assured the woman, grabbing one thin hand to give it a squeeze. "Don't try to move. The ambulance is on its way."

The woman grimaced, her face twisting with regret. "Too late."

"It's not. You need to hang on," Ellie urged.

Barb coughed again, her already pale skin turning a nasty shade of gray.

"You have to warn them," she rasped.

Ellie's stomach twisted into a tight knot. Was the woman delusional?

"I don't understand."

"It isn't safe. None of us."

"What isn't safe?" Ellie leaned closer as the woman's eyes fluttered shut. "Barb?"

A long, shaky breath escaped the woman's lips and then she went limp. Ellie bit her bottom lip, silently urging the ambulance to hurry.

She wasn't a doctor, but she was fairly certain that the older woman was dying. Once again, she pressed her fingers to the woman's wrist, desperately searching for a pulse.

This time there was nothing.

Ellie was trying to remember her rusty CPR classes when she heard the sound of an approaching siren. Thank God. She rose to her feet only to freeze at the unmistakable sound of footsteps.

Someone was in the house.

"Hello?" Ellie cautiously crossed the living room and peered down the hallway.

Dark. Dusty. And empty.

Had she been hearing things? God knew her nerves felt raw enough to imagine ghostly sounds. Still . . .

There was another patter of footsteps. These, however, were firm and loud as they entered the house.

Turning, Ellie watched as the EMTs rushed to Barb, one man hooking her up to various monitors while another started CPR. Their grim expressions didn't inspire a lot of confidence in Barb's prognosis.

Pressed against the wall in an effort to stay out of the way, Ellie's gaze remained locked on Barb as she was transferred to a gurney. Which meant that she didn't notice the man who was crossing the floor until he was standing directly in front of her.

"Nate." She blinked, caught off guard by the sheer relief that raced through her. It was like Nate Marcel had become her personal shot of Prozac. "What are you doing here?"

He gave a lift of his shoulder, his gaze studying her with a strange intensity.

"You know my habit of chasing ambulances."

"Hmm." She didn't believe him for a minute. "Doris told you I was coming to see Barb, didn't she?"

He nodded, his gaze darting toward the emergency crew who were heading out the door with Barb on the gurney.

"Do you know what happened to her?"

"No. I knocked on the door and it swung open, so I came in to check on her." Ellie wrapped her arms around her waist. Suddenly she wasn't such a fan of the crisp morning air. She felt chilled to the bone. "I found her on the floor."

"Was she injured?"

"Not that I could see. She's—" Ellie bit off her words. It was no secret in town that Barb Adams was an alcoholic, but since she'd been a client, even a non-paying client, Ellie had a policy of not discussing personal matters over and beyond what was demanded by the law. Better safe than sorry. "She's not in very good health."

Outside there was a crunch of tires as the ambulance pulled out of the driveway. Ellie grimaced. No siren. That couldn't be a good sign.

"Maybe I should go to the hospital," she abruptly decided.

Nate regarded her in confusion. "Wouldn't it be better to call her family to be with her?"

"I don't know if she has anyone. She worked for my father until we moved to Oklahoma City, but I don't think she ever married or had kids."

"It's still not your responsibility."

"Maybe not, but it seems wrong to let her wake up alone in a hospital room," she said, not voicing her fear that Barb wasn't going to be waking up anywhere. "Besides, she was trying to tell me something," she added as she suddenly recalled why she was at the house.

"Was it important?"

Ellie furrowed her brow. "I'm not sure. She called several times during the night, asking me to come see her. Then, when I found her this morning, she said I needed to warn them, but she didn't tell me who or why."

"That's all?"

"She said something about no one being safe and then she passed out." Recalling her short conversation with Barb, she abruptly pushed away from the wall and moved toward the nearby hallway.

Nate was quickly following behind her. "Ellie?"

"I thought I heard footsteps, but I was distracted when the ambulance arrived."

He hurriedly stepped past her, taking the lead as they moved down the hallway. Together they glanced into a bedroom that was messy, but clearly empty. They checked out a small bathroom and then a closet before Nate pushed open the door at the end of the corridor.

This one looked like a guest room with a narrow bed and peeling wallpaper. On the far wall a window was wide open and a stack of old magazines had been knocked over to clutter the shag carpet.

Nate quickly moved across the room, bending down to study the window frame. He made a small sound, pushing his head through the open space to survey the backyard before he was straightening.

"It's possible that someone jimmied the window," he said, waiting for her to join him so he could point at the deep gouges visible in the wood around the lock. "Plus, the dirt outside is disturbed, like someone was recently standing there."

"Maybe that's why she collapsed," Ellie said slowly. "If someone broke in and frightened her, it could have put too much stress on her heart."

Nate's jaw hardened. "Or she had information that she wanted to share with you and someone broke in to stop her."

Ellie bit her bottom lip. If Nate was right, then the person who'd attacked Barb had still been there when she'd entered the house. Perhaps they'd even been watching her as she'd called 911, debating whether to make sure Barb was dead and maybe her as well.

"She warned me that no one was safe," she murmured, her dark thoughts interrupted as Nate abruptly turned to head out of the room. "What are you doing?" she demanded, following him down the hallway and into the kitchen.

"Searching to see if anything is disturbed," he murmured, coming to a sharp halt as they turned into the kitchen.

Ellie made a small sound of disgust. She couldn't help herself. Her own house might need repairs, not to mention several boxes that needed to be unpacked, but it was clean. This place . . . yikes. The sink overflowed with dishes that had been sitting there for days, if not weeks. The countertops were loaded with empty takeout boxes, and trash overflowed from the bag to spill across the floor.

With a mutual shudder, both Nate and Ellie backed into the living room.

"I can't imagine anyone breaking in with the hope of stealing something," Nate muttered.

Before Ellie could speak, the sound of someone climbing the porch stairs had her turning to watch an older man in a deputy uniform step into the house.

The lawman arched a brow, his gaze taking in Ellie before moving to the man who stood at her side. Instantly his expression eased. As if everything was fine as long as Nate Marcel was with her.

She swallowed a sigh. Male chauvinism was alive and well in Curry.

"Hey, Nate. I didn't know you were here."

"We were just about to head to the hospital to check on Barb." Nate wrapped an arm around her shoulders. Her heart warmed. He was making a silent statement that she was an equal. His partner.

The deputy grimaced. "I wouldn't bother, if I was you."

Nate frowned. "Why not?"

"Just between us, I got a call that said she was pronounced dead in the emergency room."

"Oh no," Ellie breathed. She'd already suspected that Barb was gone, but the confirmation still hit her like a blow.

The deputy sent her a curious glance. "I'm sorry. Were you friends?"

"She worked for my father."

The older man snapped his fingers. He'd no doubt been around long enough to remember Colin Guthrie when he was a local prosecutor.

"That's right."

"Do you know what happened to her?" Nate asked before the man could reminisce about old times.

"Nope. I was just told that she was gone and that the sheriff wanted me to come by and make sure the place was locked up." He nodded toward the door. "So, if you folks don't mind."

"Certainly," Nate murmured, steering Ellie forward. They paused long enough for Ellie to grab her purse off the floor, before they were heading out of the house and off the porch.

She didn't protest, not even when he urged her into the passenger seat of his truck. She was busy trying to process the knowledge that Barb was dead.

Why had the older woman called her? Was it to pass along the vague warning? Or had she needed something else and the intruder caused her to alert Ellie to the danger lurking just out of sight?

Impossible to know now.

They drove back to her office in silence. Nate was either lost in his own thoughts, or he sensed that she wasn't in the mood to discuss what had just occurred. She'd been trained as a lawyer to think on her feet in a courtroom, but she preferred to internalize and process stuff before she formed a conclusion.

It wasn't until Nate had pulled the truck to a halt that he finally spoke.

"Looks like Doris has been waiting for you."

With a blink, Ellie glanced toward the glass door of her office, which was pushed open. Doris was standing there with a worried expression.

With a grimace, Ellie climbed out of the truck and hurried forward. She should have realized that her secretary would have heard the ambulance heading down the street and be concerned.

"I didn't realize I'd been gone so long," she said with genuine regret. "I'm sorry, I should have called."

Doris waved aside her words. "I heard they were taking Barb to the hospital," the older woman said, proving once again her astonishing ability to be the first to know what was happening in town. Then Doris glanced toward Nate. "I'm glad you're here."

Belatedly Ellie realized that the secretary's tension had nothing to do with Barb.

"What's going on?" Nate demanded.

Doris waved a hand. "I'll show you."

Ellie stepped into the office and followed her secretary as she crossed the reception room and headed down the short hallway.

Doris was unflappable. When one of Ellie's clients had stripped off his clothes and run around the office naked to prove he qualified for an insanity defense, the older woman had picked up the phone and threatened to call his mother. And when another client refused to put out his cigarette, she'd blasted him with the fire extinguisher.

What could have her so rattled?

Nate hurried to ensure that he was slightly ahead of her. His protective instincts were clearly on full alert today.

Doris guided them to the back exit that led to the patio,

but she didn't go outside. Instead she stepped to the side and wrapped her arms around her waist.

"Out there."

Nate shoved open the door, and with a twinge of trepidation, Ellie peeked around his broad shoulder.

She frowned. There was nothing there. Had whoever spooked Doris run off? Or were they still lurking in the hedges? Then Nate stepped forward, allowing her the full view of the patio. That's when her gaze landed on the dead rats that were piled in the center of the cement pad.

"Oh my God." She pressed a hand to her mouth, nausea rolling through her stomach.

Nate pivoted, blocking her view of the gruesome sight. "Go to your office," he commanded. "I'll deal with this."

Her lips parted. She was going to remind him that she was a strong, independent woman who could deal with her own troubles, thank you very much. But the words refused to come out.

She hated rats. On an epic scale.

With a shudder, she turned to head through the nearby door to her office. She walked straight to her desk and sat down, grimly refusing to look out her window. Instead, she stared at one of the open files, fiercely trying to scrub the sight of the bloody rodents from her mind.

Ten minutes passed before she heard the back door close and the sound of approaching footsteps. Glancing up, she watched as Nate strolled into the office, his expression unreadable.

"Did you get rid of them?" she asked, even knowing that he wouldn't have returned until he'd disposed of the mess along with searching the area to make sure there were no other nasty surprises.

Nate was a man who wouldn't stop until he accomplished his mission.

He gave a short nod. "Yes."

She shivered. "Someone must have dumped them there."

"Have there been any other incidents?"

"I thought there was someone on the patio yesterday, but they disappeared before I could see more than a shadow."

A muscle ticked in his jaw at her confession, his gaze flicking toward the corner of the ceiling where a small camera was visible.

"Did you check your surveillance footage?"

"I only have cameras in here and in the reception room. There never seemed any point in having them outside."

Doris appeared in the doorway before he could express his opinion of her safety precautions.

"I don't like this," the older woman announced.

Ellie grimaced. "Neither do I, but I'm not sure what to do to stop it."

"We catch whoever the hell is responsible," Nate growled.

"And how do you suggest I do that?" Ellie demanded.

His expression hardened with determination. "I'm going to talk to your neighbors. They might have noticed something that will help."

Chapter Six

An hour later, Nate entered the bakery next to Ellie's office. The front eating area was empty, but a woman hurried out of the kitchen as the bell attached to the door tinkled.

Mandy Gibson was a few years younger than Nate, with curly brown hair that framed her face like a halo, brown eyes, and pale skin. Her features were plain and she had a slight overbite. She was average height and pleasantly plump. She was the type of woman who was easily overlooked in a crowd, but Nate had made an effort to always take a few minutes to speak with her whenever they were at the same event.

At least until it'd become obvious that she was harboring hopes for more than just friendship between them.

For the past few months he'd done his best to discourage her flirtations. Now he swallowed a sigh as she hurried toward him with a wide smile.

"Nate, I haven't seen you forever."

He waved a hand toward one of the small tables that were placed in front of the long, glass display counter.

"I know you're busy," he said. "But can I ask you a few questions?"

"Never too busy for you," she assured him, wiping her

hands on her apron as she took a seat. She waited for him to slide into a chair across the table before sending him another encouraging smile. "How can I help?"

"I was wondering if you'd noticed anyone in the alley who shouldn't be there."

She frowned at his question. Obviously, he'd caught her off guard.

"The alley?"

"Yes, the one that runs behind your building."

"Why?"

"Ellie has had some trouble," he told her.

Mandy wrinkled her brow. "You mean Ms. Guthrie next door?"

He nodded. Although Ellie had been born in Curry before moving to Oklahoma City, she was still considered an outsider by many locals. It probably didn't help that she was a highly educated, career-focused woman who rarely spent time outside her office.

She was an intimidating force of nature to those people who enjoyed a slower pace of life.

Mandy's frown deepened, her female intuition clearly on full alert.

"Are the two of you together?"

His lips twisted. "It's complicated," he told her.

And it was. Complicated and exciting and exasperating. Just like Ellie.

Disappointment rippled over Mandy's round face. "Ah."

Nate ignored his small pang of guilt. He'd never encouraged Mandy to consider him more than a friend.

"Have you seen anyone?" he pressed.

Mandy shrugged. "I haven't seen them, but I know there's been some kids causing trouble. They tipped over my trash cans three nights ago, and this morning I found the back window had been smashed." She made a sound of disgust. "It took me an hour to clean up the mess."

"How do you know it was kids?"

She looked confused. "Who else would it be?"

Small towns. You had to love their innocence.

"You haven't had any trouble with customers?"

"I don't think so, but I'm usually in the kitchen. Peter takes care of the customers, as well as dealing with all money issues."

Peter Jordan had inherited the bakery from his mother, who'd inherited it from her father. It was a family dynasty that used to be common in rural America, but was now being eroded as more and more young people flocked to cities in search of well-paying jobs.

"Does he own the building?" he asked.

Mandy nodded. "Yeah. I rent the apartment upstairs from him."

Nate tapped the tip of his finger on the table. He was used to interviewing potential witnesses, but right now he was at a loss.

He didn't know if the sleepy town of Curry was suddenly a hotbed of crime with two dead bodies and a stalker who was targeting Ellie. Or if it was two tragic deaths and a couple bored teenagers who were causing trouble.

All he could do was flounder around until he could get a better feel for what the hell was going on.

"If you do catch sight of the kids that have been pestering you, could you give me a call?" he asked.

Mandy reached into the pocket of her apron and pulled out her cell phone, pushing it across the table to Nate. He quickly programed his number into her contacts and returned the phone to her.

Mandy's lips curved into a self-derisive smile as she studied the screen. "This isn't how I wanted to get your number."

Nate lifted himself to his feet. There was nothing he could say. Since Ellie had moved to Curry, there just wasn't any other woman who could interest him.

"Take care," he murmured.

Leaving the bakery, he walked the short distance to Ellie's office. He entered the reception area, not surprised to find the two women pacing the floor. The rats had spooked them. It would take a while before they could concentrate on work.

Ellie hurried toward him as soon as he pushed open the door, her face pale.

"Well?"

He held up a hand. He'd driven into town early that morning to meet with the real estate agent and then stopped by this office to see if he could lure Ellie into sharing breakfast with him.

From there his morning had been a blur of activity.

He was in dire need of caffeine.

"Do you have any coffee?"

"Of course." Ellie grimaced in apology. "I should have offered you a cup."

Doris clicked her tongue, bustling toward the hallway. "I'll make you a fresh pot. Ellie likes hers strong enough to strip the paint off the walls."

They waited until the older woman disappeared from view, then Ellie turned back to Nate.

"Did you find out anything?"

Nate resisted the urge to say that he'd learned that Will Pruitt, who owned the hardware store, had no use for Feds, even ex-Feds, poking their noses into his business. And that the dentist's office was closed for the week so Dr. Cox could take his wife on an anniversary cruise. Oh, or that Violet Pickering, who owned the hair salon, hadn't seen anyone in the alley, but she was sure that someone had stolen her hummingbird feeder.

Ellie wasn't in the mood.

And neither was he.

"I found out that you're not the only one in town being harassed," he told her.

She pressed her fingers to her mouth. "Rats?"

"No." He reached out to lightly touch her cheek. It was as cold as ice. "The bakery next door had their trash turned over and a back window busted. Not quite the same as dead rats or slashed tires, but certainly it's vandalism."

"They don't know who's responsible?"

He shrugged, dropping his hand. "Mandy assumed it was kids."

"She was the only one who had something happen?"

He studied her tense expression. "She's the only one who admitted that there was trouble. Why?"

Her gaze moved to the front window that offered a view of the courthouse across the street.

"When I went to the sheriff's office yesterday I ran into Tia Chambers."

"The mayor's daughter?"

"Yes."

Nate arched a brow. He didn't rub elbows with the families who lived in the big houses near the local golf course, but he could recognize most of their names.

They made sure of that by giving money to plaster their names all over town. A gold plaque at the church. And on a fountain in the park. And a whole wing on the local library.

"Why was she there?" he demanded.

"Tia said that she thought someone had been following her, but she hadn't managed to see who it was," Ellie said. "She was spooked, but she was trying to convince herself that it was just a figment of her imagination."

Nate didn't need his FBI training to see his first possible connection.

"Is she married?" he asked.

"No."

He lifted his hand, counting on his fingers. "You. Mandy. Tia. Three single women in Curry who are being harassed."

She sucked in a sharp breath, then her eyes widened. "Maybe four."

"Who?"

"Barb." Ellie pressed her hands together, probably trying to hide the fact that they were trembling. "She was single."

"She doesn't fit the age group, but it's possible she was a victim," Nate said. Most stalkers were like serial killers. They had a preferred type. But until he knew the exact connection between the women, he had to consider the possibility. "Or perhaps she suspected who was responsible and tried to warn you."

"She did say that *they* were in danger, meaning more than one person."

Frustration blasted through Nate. If Barb had a warning for Ellie, why didn't she come to her earlier? Was it a threat that she'd just discovered? Or had she just been too frightened to say anything?

"Did she have anyone she might have confided in?" he asked.

Ellie gave a helpless lift of her hands. "I'm not sure. I really didn't know her very well. I think she spent most of her time at the tavern."

"Which one?"

She hesitated, no doubt doing her lawyer thing. She wouldn't want to give away private information that her client had given to her. Then, deciding that she wasn't breaking confidence, she answered.

"The Lodge."

He nodded. "I think I might be in need of a beer."

"At this hour?"

Nate shrugged. "It's five o'clock somewhere."

She stepped toward him, her head tilted back to reveal her worried expression.

"You'll let me know what you find out?"

"Of course." He swept his gaze over her face, lingering on the delicate perfection of each feature. The wide, velvet brown eyes. The slender nose and lush curve of her lips. Heat raced through him. He'd behaved himself for an entire year. He couldn't resist temptation any longer. "In the meantime . . ."

"What?"

"This."

He framed her face in his hands and leaned down, claiming her lips in a slow, searching kiss. He groaned. It was just as magical as he'd expected.

Her lips were soft. Like satin. And she tasted of warm coffee and cream. His favorite.

Nate wrapped his arms around her waist as the sparks exploded and his breath was wrenched from his lungs. He wanted to devour her. Hell, he wanted to toss her onto the low sofa and ease his pent-up passion right this second.

But for today, he put a firm leash on his hunger.

This was a promise. A pledge that he was done being held at arm's length.

The world faded away as he explored her lips, his tongue dipping into the warm wetness of her mouth. She shivered in pleasure, then her hands were lifting to press against his chest.

"Nate," she rasped.

Grudgingly he lifted his head, his body hard as a rock. "I've waited an entire year to do that," he confessed.

Her cheeks were flushed, her breath coming fast between her parted lips.

"Are you happy now?" she asked.

He snorted at the ridiculous question. "Not even close. But I'm a patient man," he warned, his voice thick with shameless need. "Eventually I intend to be very, very happy."

Her blush darkened. "What about me?"

"Oh, you'll be happy. That's a promise."

She released a reluctant laugh. "I'll admit that you're persistent."

"That's what made me such a good investigator," he said without modesty.

He had been a good investigator. And when there was something he wanted, he didn't let anything stop him.

Not even a bullet.

She gave him a light push. "Then go and investigate."

He allowed his fingers to brush over her cheeks and down the slender curve of her neck.

"I'll bring back lunch," he promised before turning to head out the door. "Tell Doris I'll take a raincheck on that coffee."

Chapter Seven

It wasn't noon yet, but the door to the Lodge was unlocked. Nate pulled it open and stepped into the long, narrow bar that was wrapped in shadows.

"We're not open yet," a voice called from the back.

Nate paused to allow his eyes to adjust to the darkness. He could catch the pungent scent of bleach—probably the manager cleaning the bathrooms—as well as the deeper smell of old leather and musty wood. He'd seen pictures of the Lodge when it belonged to the Masons.

It was a shame that the once stately building was now nothing more than a dank, ratty tavern.

By the time he could at last see through the gloom, he heard the sound of approaching footsteps.

"I said we're not open."

Paula Raye, the current manager of the Lodge, had short brown hair and a square body that was attired in a black sweatshirt with the logo of some band Nate had never heard of, and baggy jeans.

Nate flashed what he hoped was a charming smile. "Sorry, but if you don't mind, I have a few questions."

The woman studied him with a frank gaze. "Are you working with the cops?" she abruptly demanded.

Nate swallowed a sigh. He hadn't told anyone he was retired from the Bureau when he'd moved to Curry, but it hadn't taken long for the gossips to somehow discover his past and spread it around town.

"Why do you ask?" he hedged. It wasn't a yes, or a no.

Hey, if she wanted to think he was there in an official capacity, he wasn't going to protest. He needed information and he no longer had a badge to ensure he could get it.

Paula moved toward the bar that ran along the wall. "I've been expecting them to stop by ever since I heard they found Daniel dead in that field."

Nate followed her, taking a seat on one of the high stools as the woman began polishing the wood. He felt like he was a character in an old film noir. All he needed was a fedora and a cigarette.

Squashing his ridiculous thoughts, he studied the woman. Clearly, she assumed he was there because of Daniel.

"Because he was here the night he died?" He hazarded a guess.

"Yep." She waved the rag toward a booth in the corner. "Sitting at that table."

Nate paused. He was here to find out if Barb Adams had recently been at the tavern. And if she ever met with friends when she came there.

But he suddenly realized that he might have found another connection to the strange events swirling through Curry. Both Barb and Daniel spent their evenings drinking at the Lodge.

It might be meaningless, but he couldn't ignore the possibility.

"Was he alone?" he asked Paula, leaning his elbows on the brass railing that ran the length of the bar.

Paula resumed her polishing. "Most of the night, but around closing time a couple of guys came in and joined him."

"You didn't recognize them?"

She gave a decisive shake of her head. "They weren't local."

Hmm. There weren't many reasons for strangers to come to Curry. Not unless they were visiting family.

"Were they friends of Daniel's?"

Paula paused, considering her answer. "They knew each other, but I don't think they were friends."

"Why not?"

Paula tossed aside her rag and reached beneath the bar to pull out a laptop.

"See for yourself," she said, firing up the computer and tapping on the keyboard. There was an unexpected jiggle of charms from the silver bracelet around her wrist. Was it to distract attention from those ugly tats? She didn't seem like the jewelry type of woman. "I saved the surveillance video. You wouldn't believe how many people come back and try to claim they gave me a fifty instead of a ten, or that they left their wallet on the bar and accuse me of stealing it."

It took a few minutes for her to find the file she wanted and then fast-forward to the end of the night. At last she turned the computer so Nate could see the screen.

There was no sound, but he could make out the grainy image of Daniel hunched over his beer as he sat in the corner booth. He appeared impervious to his surroundings. At least until two men strolled through the front door and headed directly to where he was seated.

Nate leaned closer, watching as Daniel tried to leave, only to have the men stop him. It was clear that Daniel wasn't happy with the appearance of the two. And equally obvious that he couldn't tell them to go away.

"Tense," he muttered. He didn't have to see Daniel's expression to read the stiff set of his shoulders and the nervous twitching of his fingers.

"Yeah," Paula agreed. "I had my phone in hand, ready to dial 911."

"I don't suppose you managed to overhear what they were discussing?"

Paula shrugged. Nate guessed that she didn't get too excited about anything. Probably a good trait for a woman running a tavern. Curry might not be a big town, but alcohol made people act stupid no matter where they were.

"No, but I've been a bartender long enough to recognize when someone is collecting a debt," she said.

Nate was impressed. That was exactly what he was thinking.

He focused on the screen as he watched the two men have an intense conversation with Daniel. One leaned forward, revealing the teardrop tattoos on his face. Then, with jerky motions, the two strangers slid out of the booth and headed toward the door.

"They didn't leave together?" he demanded.

"I didn't really notice," Paula admitted. "I was tired and ready to go home. I was trying to get as much done as I could so I could lock up when the clock hit midnight."

"I guess they came to some sort of agreement," Nate murmured. Or more likely the threat had been delivered, he silently acknowledged.

Daniel slumped back in his seat, wiping his forehead. Relief? Or just a druggie needing his next fix?

Five minutes passed before Daniel abruptly grabbed his phone off the table and glanced at the screen. Then he slid out of his seat and headed for the door.

If Nate had to guess, he'd say that Daniel had been waiting to hook up with his dealer. Of course, if the sheriff would get his lazy ass in gear, no one would have to guess. They could get Daniel's phone records and find out exactly who sent him the text.

Nate sat back as the video continued to run, showing Paula as she finished her late-night cleaning.

"His car was found out back, wasn't it?" he finally demanded.

"Yeah."

Daniel had left through the front door.

"So, either he walked to meet a friend, or someone picked him up," he surmised. "Do you have a camera outside?"

Paula snorted. "No, most of the trouble happens in here."

Nate sighed. A perp couldn't walk ten feet in a large city without being on camera. Around here a person could dance naked around the town square without fearing they were being recorded.

Making a mental note to ask Walter if he had access to Daniel's phone records, Nate turned his attention back to the reason he'd come to the tavern in the first place.

"Can I see the video from last night?"

Paula stilled, her expression suddenly wary. "Why?"

"I want to see if Barb Adams was here," Nate admitted with blunt honesty. He didn't want the woman afraid he was searching for any illegal activity in her dubious establishment.

He didn't care if someone was sneaking a joint in the corner or having sex in the bathrooms.

"Oh." A portion of the woman's tension eased, although she was still wary. As if she didn't completely trust Nate. Or maybe she just didn't trust anyone connected to law enforcement. Nate sensed she was a woman who'd been on the wrong side of an interrogation table. "I'm sure she was. Barb's here almost every night," she admitted.

Nate nodded his head toward the computer. "Do you mind?"

"Knock yourself out," Paula said, clicking on a new file. Once the video was running, she shoved the laptop close enough for Nate to fast-forward the video until he reached the point that Barb entered the tavern and made a beeline for the bar. "Are you looking for something specific?"

Nate grimaced. He was sitting on the same stool that Barb had chosen. It was weirdly disturbing.

"I want to see if Barb talked to anyone."

Paula folded her arms on the bar, eyeing Nate with blatant curiosity.

"What's your interest in her? Do you think she's connected to Daniel's death?"

Nate paused. If he thought that the sheriff might treat the older woman's death as a murder, he might hesitate to discuss his interest. Unfortunately, he was willing to bet good money that Gary Clark was going to try and pass off her death as natural causes. Or even a tragic accident. Which was why he hadn't bothered sharing his suspicion that someone had broken into Barb's house before her death.

"She passed away today."

"Passed away?" Paula looked confused, then she went rigid with shock. "Are you saying she's dead?" Nate nodded. "Oh God, she wasn't driving, was she?" Paula demanded.

"No. She was at home."

"Jesus." Paula grimaced. "I assumed she'd drink herself into an early grave, but not this early."

Nate didn't bother to argue with the woman's assumption that Barb's death was related to her alcohol abuse. For all he knew, that was exactly what had killed her.

"How well did you know her?" he instead asked, watching the video as Barb leaned on the bar and abruptly motioned toward Paula, who was pouring a beer a few feet away.

"She was here most nights, and if it was slow I would spend a few minutes chatting with her, but she was just another customer," Paula told him.

Nate pointed at the screen that revealed Paula strolling toward Barb, then abruptly the older woman lunged across the bar to grab Paula's arm.

"What's going on here?"

Paula frowned. "I don't remember." The bartender abruptly snapped her fingers. "Wait. She was asking to run a tab."

"And?"

"And I told her no. I have a strict policy of not extending credit. Not to anyone." Paula's square face reddened. As if she thought Nate was judging her business decision. "It saves any misunderstandings."

Nate gave an absent nod, his gaze returning to the video. Paula had pulled away from Barb and the older woman was giving a vague shake of her head.

"She looks confused," he murmured.

"She was more drunk than usual. To be honest, I was glad when she left. Now she's dead." Paula grimaced. "Damn."

Nate continued to watch the video until Barb slid off the stool and headed toward the door. She stumbled more than once and walked with a lean to the right, as if the floor was slanted. Paula hadn't been wrong. The woman was toasted.

"No one spoke to her?" he asked.

Paula shook her head. "Not that I noticed. Why?"

"Just trying to piece together her last hours."

"Do you think someone slipped her something that killed her?"

He gave a vague shrug, closing the laptop and shoving it across the bar. "It's possible."

Paula studied him, clearly sensing there was more to his questions than he was willing to admit.

"Barb liked to drink, but I don't think she took drugs," she told him.

Nate slid off his stool. "You never know."

"That's the God's truth."

There was a sincerity in the woman's voice that told Nate she'd seen and endured more than most people.

He reached into his pocket and pulled out his wallet. Finding a twenty, he dropped the bill on the bar. He might have more questions later. He liked to keep witnesses eager to talk.

"Thanks for your help."

"No problem."

He walked out of the tavern, feeling Paula's gaze until he was out the door and headed down the sidewalk.

He hadn't really found out anything that could help discover who was bothering Ellie, but he knew how both Barb and Daniel had spent their nights before they died.

Whether or not that was information that would actually lead to anything remained a question.

For now, however, he wanted to concentrate on something besides death and mutilated rodents and potential stalkers.

Ellie needed a distraction.

He intended to give her one.

Chapter Eight

After Nate left, Ellie refused to dwell on the kiss. The explosive sensations were too confusing to be sorted through. Not without a large bottle of wine. Instead, Ellie forced herself to return to her office. She didn't get any work done. She was still too freaked out by the rats to concentrate. But she at least had stopped pacing the floor.

Progress.

In an effort to keep busy, she sorted through her files, searching for anyone who might have an axe to grind. Not literally. Or at least she hoped not.

A shiver raced through her as she finished her list and sat back in her chair.

She had some names scribbled down. A couple of them were relatives of clients who blamed her for their family member going to jail. One was a victim of a hit-and-run who was furious when she managed to get her client, the driver, off on a technicality. And a couple of local men who'd taken it personally when she'd brushed off their attempts to get her into bed.

She truly didn't believe that any of them would slash her tires or leave dead rats on her patio, but she needed to feel as if she was doing something productive.

It was well past noon when she at last heard the sound of footsteps headed down the hallway, and Nate stepped into the office. Ellie lifted herself to her feet. It was an instinctive reaction to the sheer force of his personality.

It would be easy to be intimidated by Nate Marcel. His potent masculinity was like a punch to the gut.

He halted in the middle of the room, his expression impossible to read.

"Ready for lunch?"

She glanced toward his empty hands. "I thought you were going to bring something with you."

He flashed a crooked grin. "I have a better idea."

Her heart skipped a beat. The treacherous sensation put her in full retreat-mode.

"I really don't have time to leave the office."

"It's nearby." He held out his hand. "I promise."

Ellie paused, then blew out a deep sigh. She really did want to get out of the office. It was starting to feel like the walls were closing in.

She grabbed her keys and cell phone off the desk, and headed toward the door. Nate stepped aside, allowing her to take the lead as they left her office and headed into the reception room.

Ellie halted next to Doris's desk. The older woman was busy shuffling files, but Ellie wasn't fooled. Her secretary was still rattled. Even if she would rather have her tongue cut out than admit it.

"Why don't you go home for lunch today, Doris," Ellie urged. Both women usually shared lunch on the patio. "I'll lock the door."

Doris nodded, rising to her feet. "A good idea. Those rodents were a nasty shock."

"Take the afternoon off," Nate abruptly announced. As if he had every right to tell her employee what to do.

Doris paused, her probing gaze studying Nate. Then her lips twitched.

"You know, I think I will."

Without even a glance toward Ellie—the woman who signed her paychecks—Doris turned and walked toward the small closet so she could grab her coat and purse.

Five minutes later, the secretary was gone and Nate was escorting her out of the office. Ellie glared at her companion as she locked the office door and they headed down the sidewalk.

"Did I miss the memo that says you're now in charge of my office?"

He reached out to tuck her hair behind her ear. "We all need a few hours to clear our heads."

A shiver of pleasure raced through her at his tender touch. Once again, she was reminded just how long it'd been since she'd shared her bed with a man.

With an effort, Ellie relaxed her tense muscles and sent her companion a rueful smile. Nate was going above and beyond the call of duty to help her. The least she could do was appreciate his efforts.

"And that's what you have planned? Clearing our heads?"

His fingers trailed down her cheek. "What else?"

"Hmm."

He chuckled, lowering his hand to grasp her elbow as they reached the corner.

"First, lunch," he said, steering her to the north side of the square.

Ellie sent him a puzzled glance. "You do know the diner is in the other direction?"

"I have something better."

She frowned. She was willing to be nice, but she wasn't prepared to offer more. At least not this afternoon.

"Nate."

"Really," he promised.

"There'd better be food wherever you're taking me or you'll discover that there are few things more dangerous than a woman denied her lunch," she warned.

He laughed. "I grew up in Chicago, crammed into a house with four boys and a dozen of our friends. Mealtime is a sacred event to the Marcel clan."

They strolled past the storefronts at a leisurely pace, the afternoon sunlight adding a welcome warmth to combat the chilled breeze.

"Do your parents still live there?"

"Yep. My dad's a cop and my mom takes care of every kid in the neighborhood." He shrugged. "I don't think they'll ever change."

"Did all your brothers follow your father into law enforcement?" she asked.

"In one way or another. I have one brother who is a detective in Chicago. One brother who works in the CSI division. And another who is a professor who teaches criminal justice."

She tilted her head, studying his perfectly chiseled profile. There was no way to miss his affection for his brothers. His love was etched on his face.

She felt a tiny pang of envy. She'd always longed for a sister or brother. Perhaps then she wouldn't have felt so achingly alone.

"Impressive," she said. "Your parents must be very proud."

He shrugged. "My mother would be proud of us no matter what we wanted to do. I carved a rocking chair for her for Christmas and everyone who comes into her house has to sit in it before they leave."

"And your father?"

The lean features tightened. "I think he was pleased. In his own way."

Ellie was caught off guard. What father wouldn't be doing backflips to raise four sons who'd followed in his footsteps?

"What way was that?" she asked.

His lips twisted, but there was more resignation than humor in his smile.

"My mother used to say that my father loved us, but he was married to his job. That was her way of excusing his habit of blowing us off after promising to help with a school project or coming to watch us play football."

Ellie was fascinated by Nate's unconcealed bitterness. Not because he was angry. A young boy would naturally long to have his father's attention. But she'd been raised to believe that you never revealed your true feelings when it came to your parents. Image was everything and she was expected to pretend that the Guthries were a perfect family.

"I'm sure being a cop means a constant choice between duty to his family and duty to his job," she said, not quite sure why she would defend Nate's father.

Perhaps because she was a workaholic and she understood the compulsion to lose herself in a case?

"There are some things in life more important than others." His tone was flat, uncompromising.

Before she could respond, he halted in front of a three-story brick building. There was an ornate medallion over the double wooden doors that was hand-carved with curlicues and the word *Mercer* in the center.

She sent him a startled glance.

"Didn't this used to be the old mercantile store?"

He nodded. "Yep. At one time it had household goods, groceries, women's clothing, a full-time tailor, and even a small restaurant on the third floor."

She smiled, studying the old structure. The red brick had faded, but the massive display windows remained intact along with the decorative stone garland that framed the entryway. The building maintained an air of worn elegance that Ellie had always admired.

"I love to imagine what Curry must have been like a

hundred years ago. This store was probably bustling with customers who spent hours browsing through the merchandise." She sighed. "It makes me sad to see it abandoned."

"Not to ruin the glamorous fantasies of the past, but from what I could discover, this building was first constructed by a shyster from Missouri who used to cheat his customers with weighted scales in the grocery store, and shoddy clothing that he swore came in from France. Eventually he was run out of town by a group of ranchers who threatened to hang him in front of the courthouse."

She sent him a chiding frown. "Spoilsport."

He laughed, stepping forward. "I'm hoping the future for the building will be much brighter, not to mention, less felonious," he assured her.

"What are you doing?" she demanded as he took a key from his pocket and pushed open one of the doors.

"Taking you to lunch," he said, gesturing for her to enter.

Confused, she stepped through the door, glancing around the large, empty room. Her gaze swept over the floorboards, which were dusty but in remarkably good shape, and plaster walls that had once been painted a soft ivory with crown molding and gold sconces. Toward the back of the open space was a heavy oak staircase that led to the upper floors.

"Here?"

He closed the door. "This building is officially mine. I recently signed the paperwork with the real estate agent. As well as taking out a hefty loan to get my business off the ground."

His answer only added to her confusion. "You bought this building?"

"Yep."

"Why?"

"I intend to convert it into a showroom."

Ellie arched a brow. "I don't know much about being a rancher, but I've never heard of one needing a showroom."

"My ranch is too small to make much of a living. I've been scraping by, but I hope to sell some of the furniture I have been building for the past two years, to add in some extra income."

"Seriously?"

"Yeah." He glanced around, his features softening. Could he already visualize the room filled with his treasures? She found herself mentally crossing her fingers that the store was a success. "It started as a necessity. After buying the ranch I didn't have any spare money. I got tired of eating and sleeping on the floor, so I taught myself woodcraft."

"A man of many talents," she murmured.

"You have no idea." He grabbed her hand, lifting her fingers to his lips. "Not yet."

She burst out in laughter. "Good Lord."

He grinned. "Okay. That was pretty cheesy," he admitted, lowering her hand. "Wait here."

Ellie watched as Nate hurried toward the staircase at the rear of the building, resisting the urge to touch her hand where her skin still tingled. She told herself it was the predictable reaction of a woman who was in lust with a gorgeous, sexy guy. But that didn't explain why her heart felt so ridiculously full as he moved back toward her with a picnic basket in one hand and a blanket in the other.

She was thankful that Nate was unaware of her dangerous thoughts as he spread the blanket on the floor and knelt at one edge. Then, with efficient movement, he unloaded the picnic basket.

"Lunch is served." He grinned. "Sorry about the lack of furniture. Kind of ironic considering what sort of store I want to open."

Ellie moved to sit on the opposite end of the blanket, her gaze on the meat and cheese tray that had obviously come from the nearby butcher shop, along with a bowl of grapes and a bottle of wine.

"It looks delicious."

Nate filled two plates and handed her one. Then he held up the bottle.

"Wine?" Ellie hesitated. She had work piling up on her desk. She was going to spend the next six hours just trying to catch up. Then Nate sent her a rueful smile. "I think we've earned a glass."

She nodded. He was right. Over the past couple of days, they'd more than earned a glass. Maybe two.

Accepting the wine he poured for her, Ellie nibbled at the food, enjoying the hushed peace that surrounded them. Even without furnishings, it felt as if they'd stepped back into a slower, more gracious time.

Far away from the horrid sight of Barb lying on her filthy carpet, and the nasty pranks that were rubbing her nerves raw.

At last she broke the companionable silence. "Are you going to tell me what you discovered at the Lodge?"

Nate poured them both another glass of wine. "Later. First I want to know more about you."

She glanced away. She never talked about her personal life. Which might explain why she was so reluctant to have a real relationship with a man.

She sipped her wine, her gaze locked on her nearly empty plate. "There isn't much to know. I live alone. I don't have any cool talents. And I spend every day working." She shrugged. "Boring."

He braced his hands on the floor and leaned back, his expression warning her that he wasn't going to be easily diverted. She heaved a sigh of resignation.

"What made you come to Curry?" he asked.

"I was born here."

"You consider this place your home?"

She hesitated, thinking about the boxes that were packed in her garage a year after she'd moved in. Was this home? Her actions indicated she hadn't made her final decision.

"Maybe not yet," she conceded. "But I hope it will be one day."

He nodded, as if he understood exactly what she meant. "What about Oklahoma City?"

"It's a beautiful city, but I prefer to work for myself. It was easier to open my own practice here."

"Certainly, there's less competition."

"Exactly."

His gaze swept over her face, clearly aware that there was more than a lack of competition that had driven her to Curry.

"How do your parents feel about you fleeing the nest?"

She grimly refused to let the memory of their heated arguments rise to her mind. She had enough crap clogging up her brain.

"My father was disappointed," she carefully admitted. "He'd arranged a position for me in a prestigious law firm in Oklahoma City. He didn't understand my need to prove I could achieve success without his help."

"And your mother?"

Ellie wrinkled her nose. Her relationship with her father had been fiery on occasion. They were both strong-willed and both enjoyed a good argument. No doubt that's why they'd both chosen to become trial lawyers. But she'd told herself that beneath all his bluster he cared about her.

Her mother . . .

Well, Allison Guthrie was a beautiful, sophisticated woman who'd met Ellie's father when she'd traveled from England to visit a friend who was attending Oklahoma State University. They'd enjoyed a long-distance relationship until Colin had graduated from law school. They'd wed and settled down in Curry, where Colin had landed a job in the local prosecutor's office.

Ellie couldn't imagine her mother living in the small town, but within seven years her father had moved up the ladder of success, leading eventually to his impressive career as a judge in Oklahoma City. A place where Allison could truly shine as a leader of society.

It also gave her plenty of opportunity to be disappointed in her only child.

"She accepted I was never going to be the daughter she wanted," Ellie finally admitted.

Nate's brows snapped together, as if he was personally offended by her words.

"She didn't want a daughter who is intelligent, articulate, and beautiful? Not to mention a kick-ass lawyer who champions the underdog?"

Hot color stained her cheeks. She'd spent her life trying to live up to her parents' grinding expectations. She was used to criticism. She didn't know how to handle compliments.

"My mother was raised to believe a woman's worth comes from her husband," she muttered, hoping the shadows hid her blush.

"Yikes."

Ellie relaxed at Nate's expression of horror. Nothing seemed as bad, even the oppressive displeasure from her mother, when he was near.

"Yeah, we started butting heads when I was five."

"Families are always difficult."

She gave a slow nod. She wasn't one of those people who was constantly trying to make herself into a victim. She'd been raised in a safe, comfortable home with plenty of money and the opportunity to follow her dreams. But then again, she no longer tried to pretend that her childhood was perfect.

"My parents were older when I was born. They had a strictly defined idea of what their daughter should be." She grimaced. "There were times when I—"

His brows lifted as she abruptly swallowed her words. "When you what?"

"I felt like they must have taken home the wrong baby from the hospital. I never really fit into the Guthrie household." She polished off the last of her wine, feeling like an idiot for confessing her deepest secret.

Already braced for an unwanted display of pity, Ellie was relieved when Nate flashed his charming grin.

"My oldest brother told me my parents found me in a dumpster and brought me home. I believed that stupid story for years."

She lifted her empty glass in a mocking toast. "To families."

"And moving far, far away," he added in wry tones.

Chapter Nine

Ellie set aside her glass and plate, her brief smile fading. She really did have to get back to her office and get some work done. But first she needed to know what Nate had learned.

"Are you going to tell me what you found out?" she demanded.

His gaze roamed over her face. "I'd rather kiss you."

Something that felt like liquid fire flowed through her blood. She had a sudden vision of Nate pressing her onto the blanket and exploring her with his mouth. From head to toe and back again. Then her gaze shifted to the large windows that offered a view for everyone walking past the building.

"The entire town can see us," she pointed out.

"And?"

Ellie rolled her eyes. "I can't believe your mother had four boys and still managed to spoil you rotten."

"I was the youngest," he explained without apology. "And the cutest."

Ellie wondered if Nate's brothers were like him. And how his poor mother had survived.

She returned the conversation to more important matters. "Tell me what happened when you went to the Lodge."

Nate collected the plates and placed them in the picnic basket.

"I talked to the bartender."

"And?"

"Barb was there last night."

A flicker of sadness touched Ellie's heart. She'd be a liar if she said that she'd found Barb anything more than a pain in the neck, but it was difficult to accept that someone might have deliberately ended her life.

"Was she there alone?"

"Yes." He held up his hand. "And before you ask, I watched the surveillance tape and she didn't talk to anyone except Paula."

It took a minute for Ellie to remember that Paula was the name of the woman who was now in charge of the Lodge.

"Did you ask if she had any friends?"

Nate nodded. "If she does, she never meets them at the tavern."

Ellie tried to recall if Barb had mentioned an acquaintance during their conversations. She couldn't remember anyone. Most of the time, Barb had seemed lost in the past, talking about her years as Colin Guthrie's secretary and her important connections to men in power.

So, who else could she ask?

She hit on the most obvious solution.

"Maybe I could talk to her neighbors. They might know if she ever had any visitors."

Nate scowled, not nearly impressed by her stroke of genius as he should be.

"Ellie, we don't know if someone attacked Barb or why she was trying to warn you."

"Which is only more reason to find out if she shared her secrets with anyone."

Grasping the middle of the blanket, he tugged. Ellie found herself being scooted along with the blanket until she was just inches away from Nate.

"No, it's more reason to be careful," he said, his expression suddenly grim. "You start stirring a hornet's nest and you're going to get stung."

She refused to back down. Her job as a defense lawyer meant that she dealt with criminals every day. Granted, Curry didn't have an overwhelming number of killers, but she was used to dealing with violent offenders.

"But you can stir the nest?" she demanded.

"It's what I'm trained to do."

Okay. She couldn't argue with that. He was certainly better trained than she was, but that didn't mean that she couldn't be a part of the investigation.

"We need to know what Barb wanted to tell me."

Nate reached out, tucking her hair behind her ear. "We will. I promise."

He was careful not to sound patronizing, but Ellie pushed away his hand as she glared into his handsome face.

"And I'm supposed to be a good girl and let the tough FBI agent take care of my business?"

"If I say yes, something bad is going to happen, isn't it?"

"Yes."

He heaved a sigh, his features tight with frustration. Was he debating whether or not she was worth the effort? Probably. She had that effect on people.

"Right now your stalker is content to try and torment you with nasty pranks," he said, his tone sharp. "If he senses you're a danger to his game, he might decide he's tired of playing."

"We don't know that whoever left the rats is connected to Barb," she reminded him. She was a lawyer. She never jumped to conclusions.

"And we don't know it isn't."

Nate's clenched jaw warned he wasn't going to debate the issue. He wasn't a lawyer, he was an FBI agent. No doubt he assumed the worst, and prepared for the even worser. Was that a word? She gave a mental shrug. She knew what she meant.

Nate was hyperalert. But that wasn't necessarily a bad thing, she abruptly acknowledged. As long as he understood she wasn't going to be some passive bystander in her own life, she was willing to accept he had skills that she didn't.

"So, what do we do?"

He thought for a minute. No doubt he was trying to consider ways she could feel useful without putting her in danger.

"I think you should start with a list of any recent clients who might be violent or have a history of stalking."

Ellie's lips curved into a smile. Had she prepared the listing knowing that Nate would demand one? Probably. And in the back of her mind, she'd already devised how she intended to use it as a leverage.

Hey . . . she was a lawyer.

"I already did."

He studied her, like he was expecting a trap. Wise man.

"Will you share it with me?" he asked.

"Only if you agree to go on my payroll as an investigator and sign a confidentiality agreement."

He blinked, as if caught off guard by her demands. "Seriously?"

"Yes." And she was. Most of the people who came to her had been accused of committing petty crimes. Shoplifting. Misdemeanor theft. Squabbling neighbors who assumed that throwing a few punches would somehow solve their dispute. And in this area, most people knew as much about her cases as she did. Gossip spread through this small town like the plague. But she had a legal and moral obligation to protect their secrets. "I have a duty to my clients."

There was a long pause before Nate once again reached out; this time he stroked his fingers along the line of her jaw.

"Are you sure that's the only reason?" he asked.

"What do you mean?"

"I think you want me to be on the payroll so you can have me at your beck and call."

Her brain started to sputter as his fingers cupped her chin in a warm grip.

"Why would I want you at my beck and call?"

"So I can do this."

His head dipped down, his gaze holding hers as he waited for her to protest. When she simply shivered in anticipation, he claimed her lips. Instantly, Ellie jerked in shock. It felt as if she'd been struck by lightning. His mouth was hot. Demanding. Possessive.

A voice whispered in the back of her mind that she needed to pull away. She wasn't stupid. She understood the difference between a casual kiss and a brand of ownership.

But even as she tried to force her melting muscles to stiffen, his lips were brushing over her cheek and down the curve of her throat. Pleasure cascaded through her.

"Or this," he murmured against the pulse that was pounding at the base of her neck. His arms wrapped around her, hauling her into his lap. "And maybe a little of this."

The woman steps out of the back of the bakery. She glances from side to side, making sure she is alone in the alley. Then, unaware she is being watched, she pulls out a cigarette and a lighter.

I silently laugh. She is a grown woman, but she is sneaking a smoke like she is a teenager.

Weak. Needy. Pathetic.

Just like Daniel.

The sins of the father truly were visited upon the children.

And now payment is due.

I wait for the woman to finish her cigarette and grind the butt beneath her heel. Then, she squares her shoulders and heads for the entrance of the alley.

I knew she would.

It is her routine.

She finished her work day at three. She stepped outside to indulge in her daily cigarette. Then she walked the six blocks to meet her son at the local school.

I hurry to my car and wait.

The woman appears around the corner as I pull open my door. I smile and wave my hand, indicating I'd be happy to drive her to the school.

She hesitates. Not out of caution. It's a small town. We all trust each other. But she's probably eaten a few cookies or cupcakes during the day with the mental promise she would walk off the calories later.

At last she smiles and moves toward my car. After a day on her feet she is clearly willing to trade off the positives of walking for the comfort of riding.

I smile.

It is all so remarkably easy.

Chapter Ten

Nate had never understood the term "a spring in my step." He assumed he wasn't the springy type.

But this afternoon he had an unmistakable bounce as he crossed the street and walked past the courthouse that sat in the center of the square.

It was Ellie's fault, of course.

First she'd stolen a chunk of his heart when she'd revealed her past. He'd already suspected that there was a reason she'd left Oklahoma City. Now he understood that she needed to forge her own path, without the constant disapproval from her parents.

He respected that she'd stood for her principles. And that she'd managed to start her own law firm with nothing more than skill and grim determination. She had an inner strength that had attracted him from the beginning.

He grinned. That wasn't the only thing that had attracted him.

Just thinking about the feel of her snuggled in his lap, the taste of her satin skin on his tongue, was enough to make him hard and aching. Unfortunately, Ellie had been right. The entire town could walk by and peer in at them. Which meant he'd had to content himself with a few heated kisses.

And even those had been all too brief after the sound of a car horn had Ellie scrambling out of his arms. Five seconds later she was insisting she had a pile of work waiting for her and dashed out the door.

And still he had a stupid spring in his step.

Ellie Guthrie had clearly rattled his brains. He was acting like a hormonal teenager who couldn't think about anything but the woman who'd captured his interest.

Nate shrugged, crossing to the south side of the square. He couldn't control his reaction to Ellie, so he was just going to accept the inevitable. If she ripped out his heart and stomped on it, then that's what was going to happen. On the other hand, something wonderful might be in their future.

He stopped in front of a narrow building with a glass door painted with MAGIC MIRROR BARBERSHOP in gold letters.

Nate glanced through the large window. The mirror didn't look magical to Nate. It was actually silvered with age, just like the barber, Leland Reed, who was lazily sweeping the floor. The older man was tall and thin with a thick mane of gray hair. His face was lean, but without the weathered wrinkles of most men who worked outdoors. Nate didn't know how long the man had owned the shop, but he was guessing it was at least forty years.

Nate's gaze shifted to take in the two red leather and chrome barber chairs that were arranged in front of the long mirror. Empty. As were the four wooden chairs that lined the opposite wall.

Leland usually closed up around three. His customers were early risers who filled the shop to exchange the morning gossip and drink the coffee he doled out as he trimmed hair and the occasional beard.

Pulling open the door, Nate stepped inside. Leland turned, a wide smile tugging his lips as he realized who had entered.

"Hey, Nate. Need a trim?"

"If you aren't in a hurry to close up," Nate said.

Leland propped his broom against a shelf that was filled with cheap jewelry that Leland's wife sold in the back of the shop and waved a hand toward the nearest barber chair.

"You know I always have time for you. Have a seat."

Nate moved to settle into the aged leather. Not long after he'd moved to Curry, Leland had arrived on Nate's doorstep with a request to help locate his grandson. Leland's ex-son-in-law had taken off without warning, and the barber had been deeply worried that he might harm the boy.

Calling in a few favors, Nate had located the man in Texas, where he'd been unconscious after a three-day bender in a seedy hotel. The authorities had returned the boy to Leland's daughter and thrown the son-in-law in jail for endangerment of a child.

With a flick of his wrist, Leland had a cape tucked around Nate and grabbed his comb and clippers from the nearby counter.

"Quite a week in Curry, eh?" Leland said, efficiently trimming the edges of Nate's hair. The old barber didn't know the first thing about new styles, but he was quick and efficient, the only thing that mattered to the locals. Plus, he always knew the best gossip. Which was exactly why Nate was there. "First Daniel and now Barb."

"Yep. Quite a week," Nate agreed.

"Don't suppose you know anything about what happened?"

Nate glanced into the mirror, meeting the older man's gaze. Clearly the word had already spread through town that he was at Barb's when she'd been carted off in the ambulance. And probably that he was asking questions at the Lodge. It was almost impossible to keep a secret in Curry.

So why didn't anyone know about Ellie's stalker?

"I did speak with Paula," he conceded.

"That new lady at the Lodge?"

Nate nodded. "She said that Daniel was in the bar drinking the night before he died."

"No surprise there. I think that boy spent his entire life high or drunk," Leland said.

"True. Paula said that he was joined by two men she didn't recognize."

Leland lifted his brows. It wasn't often there were strangers in town.

"Some of his druggie friends?"

"That's my guess. I happened to see them on the security tape," Nate said. "They were both skinny with dirty blond hair that hung to their shoulders. One of them had teardrops tattooed on his face."

"Tattoos right here?" Leland demanded, touching a place below his left eye.

"Do you recognize them?" Nate demanded.

"Sounds like the Harper brothers."

Harper. Nate shuffled the name through his brain. "I'm not familiar with them."

Leland continued to trim Nate's hair, but his expression hardened. "Their dad passed away when they were young, and their mother let them run wild. They were trouble from start to finish. They left town several years ago, but they come back to peddle their wares."

"Drugs?"

Leland nodded. "They're bad news. Really bad news," he repeated. Nate silently wondered if the brothers had been friends with Leland's ex-son-in-law. "Do you think they had something to do with Daniel's death?"

"I really don't know any more than you, Leland." Nate grimaced. He didn't want any rumors spreading through town. If the Harper boys were involved, they might go into hiding. He didn't want to have to check every gutter to find them. "Right now it looks like a tragic accident."

Leland nodded, but he didn't look convinced. "Accident?"

It was Nate's turn to probe for answers. "What have you heard?"

"Overdose. Suicide." He shrugged. "A drug deal gone bad."

"Did Daniel have any enemies?" Nate pressed. "Did he mess around with other men's wives? Did he owe anyone money? Did he have an angry girlfriend?"

Leland finished the trim and reached for a brush to swipe over his nape.

"A few years ago I would have said yes to all those, but the past year he was . . . what does my daughter call him?" Leland struggled for the word. Finally he snapped his fingers. "A burnout. He spent most of his time alone, either sleeping or trying to get high. I don't think anyone cared enough to want him dead."

There was a brutal truth in Leland's words. By the end, Daniel had destroyed any connection to the world around him. He'd been completely and utterly alone.

"Did you ever see him with Barb?" Nate abruptly asked.

A speculative expression settled on Leland's face. "Not that I can remember."

"Does she have any friends I can talk to?"

The barber considered the question as he removed the plastic cape.

"Sorry. I really can't think of anyone. She spent a lot of time at the bars around town. Maybe someone there might know about her."

Nate nodded and pushed himself out of the chair. If Leland hadn't heard any whispers about Barb or Daniel's death, then there weren't any going around.

Still, he'd gotten the name of the men who'd been with Daniel at the Lodge. He intended to have a word with them ASAP.

"Thanks," he said, pulling out his wallet.

Leland held up a hand. "On the house. And if you have

any questions, just stop by. There's not much that happens in this town that I don't hear about."

Nate nodded. "I'll be back."

Mandy woke with a shudder of pain.

It was dark.

Not the darkness that had surrounded her earlier. That had been the result of being stuffed in a cellar or a closet. Someplace where the sun couldn't reach. This was the darkness of night.

Mandy groaned.

It felt like someone was whacking a rolling pin against the back of her head. The star-bursts of pain made it difficult to think.

Where was she?

She knew she was lying on her side on the ground. There was the smell of rich dirt and grass beneath her head. Distantly she heard the sound of water as it splashed over a shallow creek-bed.

She was in a field, she at last decided. Far enough from town that she couldn't hear the usual sounds of people. Even at night there was the buzz of streetlights and the muffled echo of televisions.

Okay. She was in a field.

Now the big question.

How had she gotten there?

She had a vague memory of waking in the darkness with her brain aching, but before then . . .

Something teased at the edge of her mind.

A car. Yes. She'd gotten into a car. But why? Had she been going somewhere? Or had they forced her to get in? Straining, Mandy tried to piece together her fragmented memories.

Maybe if she started from the beginning.

She'd gone to work. Just as she had six days a week for

the past ten years. Working at the bakery wasn't a bad job, but it wasn't what she'd dreamed about when she was young. She'd intended to become a world-famous chef in a restaurant far away from Curry.

Mandy grunted, continuing to focus on the events of the day.

It'd been a normal morning. She was certain of that. She'd baked muffins and donuts and bagels for the early morning crowd. Then she'd focused on bread and pastries. She'd just finished putting the last batch of cupcakes in the oven when Nate Marcel had strolled into the bakery. Instantly her heart had started pounding in her chest.

Nate was everything she ever wanted in a man. Strong. Honorable. A man a woman could depend on.

The exact opposite of her jackass of an ex-husband.

Plus, he was sexy as hell.

It was no wonder he'd played the starring role in her fantasies since she'd first set eyes on him.

But despite her best efforts he'd never returned her interest. Oh, he'd always been nice. More than nice. He'd gone out of his way to make her feel special when their paths had crossed. But she'd known he would never consider her more than a friend.

And today he'd put the final nail in the coffin when he'd revealed his interest in Ellie Guthrie.

Mandy had been forced to swallow her rueful laughter. She liked Ellie, she really did. But Mandy had harbored a deep sense of jealousy of the woman since she'd moved back to Curry. Who could blame her? Ellie was smart. Ambitious. And beautiful. Everything that Mandy wasn't . . .

Realizing that she was once again allowing her fuzzy thoughts to wander, Mandy struggled to open her eyes. Maybe if she could figure out where she was, her memories would return.

She was still in the process of lifting her heavy lids when she sensed someone standing over her.

Oh God.

This was bad. Really, really bad.

She could hear the rustle of grass as the person knelt beside her. Then strong fingers grabbed her arm and she felt the stab of a needle being shoved into her flesh.

Mandy helplessly tried to pull away as a last vivid image seared through her brain.

She had been getting into a car because she was accepting a ride to pick up Charlie.

Poor Charlie.

She was all he had.

And now she was gone.

Her heart raced as heat seared through her veins, then with one last painful spasm it went still.

Death claimed her.

Chapter Eleven

Ellie managed to finish her work, but it was dark by the time she was stepping out of her office and locking the door.

She had actually been relieved to have her caseload to concentrate on. It was better than dwelling on Nate's earth-shaking kisses. Or the unnerving events of the past couple of days.

Clutching her keys in one hand and her briefcase in the other, Ellie turned toward her car, which was parked next to the curb. It was only then that she noticed the small figure standing in the doorway of the bakery.

She stiffened, briefly worried it might be one of the vandals who'd been harassing her. Then, as she took a step forward, she caught sight of the childish profile and ruffled hair in the glow of the streetlight.

Concerned, she hurried toward the child she recognized as Charlie Gibson.

It wasn't that late, but Mandy was hyper-protective of her only child. She would never have let him roam around the streets by himself at nine o'clock at night.

"Charlie? What's going on?" she demanded.

The boy turned to watch her approach, his hands stuffed

in his jeans as he tried to look casual. Ellie, however, didn't miss the pinched expression on his narrow face.

"Oh, hey, Ms. Guthrie."

"Is something wrong?" Ellie demanded, glancing through the door at the dark bakery.

She could only assume that Charlie had snuck out of the upstairs apartment. Or that some emergency had called Mandy away and the boy had become spooked being alone.

"Naw." He tried to smile, but it was more a grimace. "It's all good."

"Where's your mom?"

"She . . ." The boy hunched his shoulders. "She musta had something to do. I haven't seen her since breakfast."

Ellie's mild concern shifted into major concern. Mandy would never, ever have left Charlie alone for an entire evening. Not for any reason.

"She didn't walk you home from school?" Ellie asked, keeping her voice light. She could already sense the boy was on edge. She didn't want to add to his fear.

Charlie tilted his chin. "I can walk by myself, I'm not a baby."

"Of course you're not," Ellie hurriedly soothed. Did the other boys tease Charlie because his mother insisted on meeting him after school? She pushed away the inane thought. "Did you look to see if she left a note?" she instead asked.

Charlie's hands clenched and unclenched, revealing his effort to pretend he wasn't worried.

"The door's locked. And she's not answering her phone." He licked his lips. "She always answers when I call."

Ellie's heart clenched. The poor boy had been standing out there for hours. Something was definitely wrong.

With an effort, she maintained a calm composure and pulled her cell phone from her purse.

"You know what, maybe we should make a few calls to

see where she is," she said in matter-of-fact tones. "Just in case she needs us to come pick her up or something."

Charlie swallowed hard, giving a slow nod of his head. "I guess that would be okay."

She smiled before she turned away and hit the number of the one person she knew could help.

"Hi, Nate," she said as soon as she heard his voice. "This is my first beck and call."

Chapter Twelve

It was six in the morning when Nate pulled his car into the driveway in front of Ellie's house.

When she'd called him to say that she needed him to find Mandy Gibson, there'd been enough concern in her voice that he hadn't asked questions. Instead, he'd hopped in his truck and headed for town.

Along the way he'd contacted the owner of the bakery, learning that the man had last seen Mandy at three o'clock that afternoon when she'd left to pick up her son. Next he'd called Mandy's best friend, Kelly Vaughn, and asked her to start calling everyone who might know where the young mother could be.

He didn't have the authority to contact the hospitals in the area, but he did get ahold of Charlie's father. He hadn't heard anything about his ex-wife being in an accident, but he did promise to head over and pick up his son.

By the time he reached Curry, Ellie was alone and pacing outside her office. Even in the dim light from the street lamp he could see her face was pale and her eyes shadowed with weariness. He'd wanted to pull her into his arms and promise her that everything was going to be okay. Unfortunately, it wasn't a promise he could make.

He could, however, insist that she go home and wait for any news.

She'd agreed, but only after his firm promise that he would stop by and tell her whatever he might discover.

Now he switched off the motor and climbed out of the truck. By the time he reached the front porch, Ellie had the door pulled open.

Nate scooted past her slender frame to enter the house. He cast a quick glance around the living room, his lips twitching. Very little had changed from the day that she'd moved in. There were no pictures on the walls. The couch and mismatched chair were in the exact same position. And there were no curtains on the windows.

The only real difference was the desk in the corner that was loaded with files.

He turned his attention to the woman watching him with blatant impatience. During the night, she'd exchanged her work clothes for a pair of yoga pants and a sweatshirt. She'd also scrubbed her face of the light makeup and pulled her hair into a ponytail. She looked closer to sixteen than thirty.

"Well?" she demanded when he simply stood there, absorbing her quiet beauty.

He sucked in a deep breath, reluctantly turning his thoughts to the terrible news he had to share.

"They found her," he said in low tones.

"Oh God." She lifted a hand to her parted lips. "Is she . . ."

"Yes." He'd been searching the bike path that ran along the river when he'd heard the sirens. Jumping in his truck, he'd followed the ambulance out of town and along the gravel road. "Her body was left in the same field as Daniel's," he admitted.

Ellie made a sound of distress, turning to pace the worn floorboards. She was clearly shaken by the realization the young woman was dead. Nate didn't blame her. He'd felt sick to his stomach when he'd parked behind the emergency vehicles and a nearby deputy had shared the information that they'd found Mandy's body.

At last regaining her composure, she turned back to meet his worried gaze.

"Do they know what happened to her?"

Nate's lips twisted. He hadn't had an opportunity to speak directly with the sheriff, but he'd managed to overhear the man's loud pronouncement as the body was loaded into the back of the coroner's vehicle.

"Gary Clark is trying to pass it off as another overdose. He's saying there must be a bad batch of heroin in town."

Ellie made a sound of disbelief. "Mandy would never take drugs."

"I agree."

Over the years Nate had learned that you could never assume that you knew what happened behind closed doors. He'd arrested cops, politicians, and preachers for everything from drugs to murder. Still, he'd known Mandy for two years. She never missed a day of work. She was at every one of Charlie's school events and baseball games. Plus, she volunteered at the food bank. Never once had he suspected that she was high.

"So why is the sheriff claiming it was an overdose?" Ellie demanded.

"They found a hypodermic needle stuck in her arm."

Ellie faltered at his explanation. Then she gave a shake of her head.

"None of this makes any sense."

He agreed. It didn't make sense.

Just a few hours ago he was seated across the table from Mandy, discussing the vandals who'd broken her window and turned over her trash. Now she was dead, and not from any damned drug overdose.

Which meant whoever was responsible was out there. Perhaps plotting to strike again.

He had to stop them.

Raising his hand, he ticked off the names on his fingers. "Daniel. Barb. Now Mandy," he said, needing to spark some connection in his brain. "What did they have in common?"

Ellie squared her shoulders. She easily understood what he wanted from her.

"They all lived in Curry. Daniel and Mandy are . . ." She grimaced as she corrected herself. "They were about the same age. Daniel and Barb hung out at the Lodge. Both Daniel and Mandy ended up in the same field."

"Yes," Nate breathed. Having Ellie speak the words out loud allowed him to focus on the nagging sense there was something he should remember.

Ellie stepped toward him. "What is it?"

"Walter came to my house yesterday," he told her. "He asked me to look into his son's death."

She appeared more curious than surprised by his confession. "Why?"

"He was convinced there was something suspicious about his son's sudden overdose."

Ellie's expression softened with pity. "I'm sure it's hard for him to accept that Daniel is truly gone."

"He's struggling," Nate agreed. "But he seemed weirdly disturbed by the fact that Daniel was found in that particular spot. And now Mandy was discovered in the same place."

Ellie frowned. Then her eyes widened. "Oh."

"What is it?"

"I just remembered that Doris told me that the field belongs to Neville Morse, Mandy's father."

"The land belongs to her father?"

"Yeah."

"Christ." Nate grimaced. Not only had the poor man lost his daughter, but she'd either died in his field, or her body had been dumped there. It seemed like salt in the wound. "Do you know anything about him?"

Ellie shook her head. "Doris said he was some sort of hermit."

Which would explain why Nate wasn't familiar with the name.

His jaw tightened. He was tired of constantly reacting to events. It was time he took the initiative.

"I think I should have a word with Mr. Morse," he said. "But first I want to track down the Harper brothers."

"Who?"

"The last people to speak with Daniel the night he died," he explained.

"Okay." She offered a weary nod. "I need to get ready for work."

He moved forward, framing her face in his hands. Her skin was pale and there were purple shadows beneath her eyes. He wondered how long it'd been since she'd had a decent night's sleep.

"You should go to bed and get some rest," he said.

"I can't sleep. I might as well go to the office." She held his gaze. "You'll stop by if you discover anything?"

He nodded, his hands tightening as he was struck by an unexplainable fear that there was something—someone—out there waiting to strike again. Like a spider sitting at the edge of its web, patiently anticipating its next prey.

"Just be careful."

He pressed a lingering kiss on her mouth before he forced himself to turn and walk out of her house. As much as he wanted to stay, he logically understood that Ellie needed an FBI agent right now. Once she was safe he could concentrate on his role as her lover.

After all, he intended to have her in his bed for a very long time.

Swinging by his house, Nate took a quick shower and ate some breakfast while he called in a favor from his oldest brother, Jax. He needed to find the Harper brothers, and he didn't have time to waste.

There was an astonished silence before Jax was demanding to know exactly what the hell was going on. Like the rest of his family, Jax had been relieved when Nate had turned in his badge and moved to his ranch in the middle of nowhere. Not that his older brother disapproved of the Bureau, but Nate had been a reckless, thrill-seeking agent who'd taken far too many risks. When he'd been shot, the Marcel clan had gathered at his hospital bed for an intervention. Well, all of the clan except his father, of course. They'd demanded he quit the FBI and find an occupation that didn't include him getting killed.

Giving an abbreviated explanation of what he knew about the deaths in Curry, he endured Jax's stern lecture on staying out of trouble; after all, his brother was putting his ass on the line by giving Nate the information.

An hour later he was back in his truck and headed for Tulsa.

The drive took less time than he'd expected. One of the benefits of living in Oklahoma. He never had to worry about traffic. At least not until he hit the suburbs of the city.

Following the GPS on his phone, he skirted along the west side of the city, at last parking his truck a block away from his destination. He liked an opportunity to scope out an area before he made contact with his target.

It was late morning, but the shabby neighborhood was shrouded in near silence. A few residents were no doubt at work, or school. The rest were more than likely sleeping off a hard night of partying.

Nate strolled down the street, his gaze constantly moving from side to side. This looked like the sort of area where a man could find himself on the wrong end of a gun.

He reached the long, narrow apartment complex that ran the length of the block. It was two stories, with brick on the bottom of the structure and cheap white siding on the top floor. The parking lot was framed by a towering chain-link fence. Nate assumed it was to keep out intruders, although he couldn't imagine anyone was actually trying to get in.

Circling the block, Nate at last made his way to the lower apartment at the end of the complex.

His gaze skimmed the yellow Camaro parked in front of the door. It was spotted with rust and the back window was covered with duct tape. Nothing like a classic, he acknowledged wryly. Next, he took in the bags of trash that had been tossed onto the walkway. Seemingly it was too much of an effort to walk the ten feet to the dumpster.

Moving forward, he pressed his back against the brick wall and leaned toward the window. Peering through the slit in the curtains, he could make out a cramped living room that was littered with empty fast food containers and beer cans. There was a sectional couch where he could make out two forms sprawled on the cushions.

The Harper brothers.

Nate touched the gun holstered beneath his sweatshirt. He had a permit to carry, both open and concealed, although he was hoping there wouldn't be any need to pull his weapon.

Once bullets started flying, there was never a good end.

Turning around, he raised his hand and thumped it loudly against the door. Once. Twice. Three times.

He was about to go for number four when the door was jerked open to reveal a man with greasy blond hair and a gaunt face that was beginning to show the ravages of heavy drug use.

There were no tattoos beneath his eyes, which meant this must be the younger brother, Larry.

"What?" the man growled.

"Morning, sunshine," Nate drawled.

"Who the hell are you?"

Nate shrugged. "I would say your worst nightmare, but it's just so cliché."

The man blinked, his eyes painfully bloodshot and his hands unsteady as he clenched them into tight fists. "A funny guy?"

"Some people think so."

"Oh yeah?" Larry lifted his arm, telecasting his intention so even a child could have dodged the clumsy punch. "Laugh at this."

Nate easily dipped beneath the wild swing, grabbing the man by the throat. Digging his fingers into the man's flesh, he shoved him back into the apartment and slammed him against the wall.

Larry grunted in pain, futilely trying to break free of Nate's ruthless grip.

"I'm calling the cops. You have no right—"

"FBI," Nate interrupted.

He didn't actually claim he was an active agent, but Larry jumped to the obvious conclusion.

His pasty face paled to white. "You're a Fed?"

"I have a few questions for you," Nate said without answering the question.

The man licked his lips, sending a desperate glance toward his brother, who was snoring loudly on the nearby couch. Realizing there wasn't going to be any help from the passed-out Bert, Larry returned his gaze to Nate.

"I don't know nothing." His expression was as petulant as his tone.

Nate rolled his eyes. "Truer words have never been spoken."

"What?"

Nate shook his head. The apartment was filthy and

smelled like old socks. He didn't even want to think about what might be crawling beneath the piles of trash.

The sooner he had his answers, the sooner he could go home and jump back in the shower.

"Daniel Perry."

Larry looked blank. "What about him?"

"Was it an accident or did you deliberately kill him?"

Nate had discovered over the years of interrogating junkies it was always best to go for a direct assault. Their fried brains couldn't handle subtle.

"Kill him?" The man looked genuinely perplexed. "Is this a joke?"

"There's nothing funny about death row."

Larry scowled. "Daniel's fine. We just saw him the other night. If he said we tried to hurt him, then he's a liar. I wanted to pound in his face, but my brother wouldn't let me."

"So instead you watched him overdose and just walked away?"

Larry resumed his struggle to get free. "Why do you keep blabbering about Daniel? I told you, he's fine."

Nate tightened his grip. The man was about the same size, but he'd been using for so long he didn't have the strength or balance to gain any leverage.

"I doubt he would agree with you," Nate drawled. "They found his dead body where you dumped him."

The man's struggles abruptly halted. "Dead." His mouth hung open. "Daniel's dead?"

His shock was palpable. And unless he was the best actor in the entire world, he truly hadn't known about Daniel.

Not that Nate was about to let up on the pressure. Even if the Harper brothers hadn't killed Daniel, they might have information that would lead Nate to the person responsible.

"Don't act like you didn't know," he growled.

Larry's gaze flicked wildly toward the door, as if hoping

one of his stoner friends would make a sudden appearance and rescue him.

Unfortunately for him, there was nothing but a stray dog sniffing around the nearby trash.

"Look, I barely knew him. In fact, it's been years since—"

"You already admitted that you were just with him, you idiot," Nate interrupted. Larry's brain was even more fried than he'd first suspected. "Plus, your ugly mug was caught on camera with Daniel when you met him at the Lodge. It all looked very cozy."

Larry flushed, hatred twisting his features. "I told you. We did a little business," he hissed. "Nothing else. And if we were on camera then you know when we left town he was alive and well."

"As a matter of fact, I don't know that. All the video shows is you and your brother leaving the Lodge and then Daniel following you a couple minutes later. You could have easily been waiting for him outside."

The man glared at him in frustration. "Why the hell would I want to off Daniel?"

"It could have been an accidental overdose. And if that's the case, you need to confess. That's the only way to avoid a lethal injection," Nate warned.

There truly was no honor among thieves. If Larry knew who was responsible, it would only take a little pressure to make him name the culprit.

"This is bullshit." The man's anger was replaced by fear. "You're not pinning this on me or my brother."

"Then tell me what happened."

Larry hesitated, licking his lips as Bert's snores filled the air.

"Nothing happened," he at last muttered.

Nate leaned forward, ignoring the stench of the man's

breath. Meth not only rotted the brain, but it decayed the user's teeth as well.

"Lethal. Injection."

"Fine. We met him at the Lodge. That's it," Larry insisted. "Nothing illegal about that."

Nate swallowed a curse. Did the idiot think he cared about any drug deals they had going?

"He owed you money?" he directly demanded.

There was a long pause before Larry blew out a resigned sigh. "Yeah. Okay. He owed us money."

"And you decided to teach him a lesson?"

"I wanted to, but Bert wouldn't let me."

"Why not?"

"Because Daniel promised us he would pay us in full after he completed a job he had later that night," Larry groused. "Bert said it was better to get the money than pound the shit out of him."

Nate felt a stab of satisfaction. At last they were getting somewhere. "What job?"

Larry reached up to grab Nate's wrist, his pale eyes darkening with pain. Was he suffering a hangover? Or was he already going into withdrawal?

"He didn't get into details," he rasped.

Nate tightened his grip and banged Larry against the wall, rattling his already sore head.

"You're going to have to come up with a better lie before your trial."

The man cursed, spittle forming at the corners of his mouth. "He said someone had hired him to cause some chaos."

Chaos? Nate frowned. What sort of job involved chaos in the middle of the night?

"What's that mean?" he demanded.

"I don't know. Daniel pulled a switchblade from his

pocket and waved it around like he was stabbing someone, but he refused to say anything else."

It was the switchblade that stirred Nate's suspicion.

What did you do with a knife? He could have been implying he was going to kill someone, and instead ended up dead himself. Nate, however, thought it was far more likely that he'd been hired to slash Ellie's tires and break Mandy's window and perhaps even spook Tia Chambers.

Of course, that wouldn't explain how the harassment had continued after Daniel's death. Unless whoever had hired Daniel had also hired others to torment the women.

It was a leap, but it was a place to start.

"Did he say who was paying him for his chaos?" Nate demanded.

"Bert asked him."

Ah, Bert. Clearly the brains of the operation. At least when he wasn't lying face-first on a filthy couch, drool dripping from his open mouth.

"And?" Nate prompted.

"Daniel laughed and said we wouldn't believe him if he told us."

Nate absorbed the words. What did Daniel mean? That his employer was an upright citizen of Curry? Or a complete stranger? Nate grimaced. It was impossible to know.

"I need a name."

"I don't have one," Larry snapped, then his screams ripped through the air as Nate grasped his arm and wrenched it behind his back. Nate pressed until the elbow was in danger of snapping.

"A name."

"I don't know." Sweat ran down Larry's white face. "I swear."

Chapter Thirteen

Ellie parked in front of her office. After a sleepless night followed by three hours with the local prosecutor, she was exhausted. Greg Stone could be an arrogant ass, but when he decided to concentrate on his job, he was a fierce opponent.

Now she considered the pleasure of crawling beneath her desk and taking a short power nap. She needed sleep more than she needed lunch. Or maybe she would go for a long run to clear the cobwebs from her brain.

Grabbing her briefcase, Ellie slid out of her car and slammed shut the door. At the same time, she caught sight of the tall woman barreling down the sidewalk with more purpose than grace.

Ellie hurried forward, giving a wave of her hand. "Tia."

The woman came to a halt, forcing a smile to her lips. "Hello, Ellie. How are you?"

Ellie glanced toward the bakery that was closed for the week. Perhaps for even longer if they didn't find someone to replace Mandy.

"In shock, like everyone else in town," she said, sadness tugging at her heart.

"I know." Tia heaved a sigh. Today she was wearing stretchy pants and a chunky black sweater that looked at least two sizes too small. "It's awful. I had no idea Mandy was into drugs. She always seemed so devoted to her son."

Ellie grimaced. Obviously, the sheriff had already spread around his theory about the cause of death.

"It's pretty unbelievable," she said dryly.

Tia sent her an odd glance, as if sensing Ellie's skepticism. Then, with a shake of her head, she stepped around Ellie.

"I should get going. I'm meeting a friend for lunch."

Ellie reached out to touch her arm. "Wait."

"Yes?"

"I was wondering if you'd had any more trouble?" Ellie asked.

Tia's eyes widened, a flush stealing beneath her skin. "How did you know?"

"Lucky guess," she said with complete honesty. "What happened?"

Tia blew out a shaky breath. "I'm not sure I want to tell you. My father insists I'm imagining things."

"I don't," Ellie said in fierce tones. "There're a lot of strange things happening in Curry."

"True."

"Tell me," Ellie urged. "Please."

Tia hesitated before she at last revealed what was troubling her. "I'm sure there was some man peeking in my bedroom window."

Ellie swallowed the sudden lump in her throat. Bloody rats and slashed tires for her. A strange stalker for Tia. Petty vandalism for Mandy.

All different, and yet, Ellie suspected they were all connected.

Just as the deaths of Daniel and Barb and now Mandy were connected.

But how?

"When did it happen?" she asked.

Tia shrugged. "Just this morning."

Ellie studied the woman. She seemed more annoyed than frightened. "You're sure it was a man?"

"Yes. But as soon as I caught sight of him in the mirror, he was running away."

"Do you remember anything that might help identify him?"

She furrowed her brow, giving a shake of her head. "Not really. It all happened so fast."

Ellie nodded in understanding. She'd cross-examined enough witnesses to know the mind was a strange thing. It could remember some things in perfect clarity. Others it could shut out completely. And still others remembered it in a garbled mess.

"Was he young or old?" she asked in gentle tones.

"I had the impression he was older."

"So not a teenager?"

Tia gave an emphatic shake of her head. "Definitely not."

"Was it a stranger?"

Tia hesitated. As if she didn't want to answer the question. "I'm not sure. I have a weird sense that I recognized something about him, but I can't put a name to him." She waved her hands, clearly embarrassed. "It sounds stupid, right?"

"No, it doesn't sound stupid," Ellie breathed, shivering despite the bright sunlight that spilled from the cloudless sky. "Will you let me know if you see him again?"

Tia studied her with a curious gaze. "Has he been bothering you too?"

"Possibly."

Tia heaved another sigh. "The entire town has gone insane."

"Amen."

Ellie watched Tia hurry away, wishing she had the evidence that would convince the woman she was in genuine danger. Until then Tia would no doubt listen to her father's insistence that her stalker was nothing more than a figment of her imagination.

"She seems to be in a hurry." The male voice whispered directly in her ear.

Ellie whirled around, her heart lodged in her throat. She half expected to find a serial killer with a hockey mask over his face standing behind her. Instead, her gaze landed on Nate, who was watching Tia scurry away with a curious expression.

Her jolt of fear transformed into anger as she glared into his handsome face.

"Crap. Don't sneak up on me."

His eyes—which were more gray than blue today—narrowed as he turned his gaze in her direction.

"I drove up in my truck that you once claimed sounds like a freight train on steroids and walked down the street like a normal person. I'm not sure how that qualifies as sneaking up on you."

She wrinkled her nose. Okay. She might have overreacted. "I'm a little jumpy."

"Yeah, me too," he admitted.

Ellie concentrated on slowing the pace of her racing heart. "Did you find the brothers you were looking for?"

His jaw tightened, as if he was clenching his teeth. "I did."

"Did they know anything about Daniel?"

"After some prompting, they admitted they were with him the night he died."

Ellie didn't ask what sort of prompting he used. Nate was a man who could intimidate others without resorting to violence, but then again, she suspected he could hold his own in a fight if necessary.

"Do you think they killed him?"

He gave a sharp shake of his head. "I think Daniel owed them money for drugs."

She heaved a resigned sigh. She'd dealt with enough drug

dealers to know what had happened between them and Daniel. Threats. Arm twisting. Maybe a few punches.

But that's it.

"No point in killing him," she muttered.

"Exactly," Nate agreed. "They might rough him up, but you can't get paid by a dead man."

Ellie frowned. She considered herself an intelligent woman who could take small fragments of information and piece them together to discover the truth. That's what she did as a trial lawyer. But now . . .

She felt like she was stumbling around in the dark.

"Did they tell you anything that could help?" she demanded.

Nate grimaced. "Just that Daniel assured them that he was going to make some money that night so he could pay them."

Ellie snorted. She'd lived in Curry for a year and had never seen Daniel lift a finger.

"Doing what?"

"He was supposedly hired to cause chaos."

Cause chaos? Was Nate joking? Or had Daniel been making up some crazy story to try and buy some time?

"What does that mean?"

"That was all Daniel said, but if I had to make a guess, I'd say he was responsible for your slashed tires."

"Someone paid him to harass me?"

He shrugged. "It's one theory."

She gave a sudden shake of her head. "But he was already dead when the rats were dumped on the patio."

"There could have been more than one person hired to cause the mysterious chaos."

Ellie studied him in horror.

It was bad enough to believe that anyone would want to deliberately vandalize her property. Now he was implying there was some mystery person paying the citizens of Curry to pester her, along with Mandy and maybe even Tia.

"But why? What would be the point?" she asked.

"I don't know."

She studied his lean face. She hadn't missed the grim edge in his voice.

"But you have a thought?"

He paused, as if considering whether or not he wanted to share his inner fears.

"If I wanted chaos, it would be to create a distraction," he at last told her.

She slowly nodded. Okay. That made sense. She once had a client who'd set fire to an empty warehouse so the cops would be across town when he robbed the local gas station.

"A distraction from what?"

"Daniel's death. Or Barb's. Or Mandy's. Maybe all three. Or . . ." He allowed his words to trail away.

"What?"

"Or more to come."

An icy ball of dread settled in the pit of Ellie's stomach. Drugs. Vandals. Stalkers. Three deaths. How were they connected? And why was she being targeted?

Those were questions she sensed she needed to answer. Sooner rather than later.

"How do we find out?"

Nate didn't hesitate. "Let's talk to Mandy's father."

Chapter Fourteen

Nate glanced toward his GPS as he turned down yet another dirt road. Since moving to Curry he'd become accustomed to remote locations. People liked to spread out across the prairie. But this was more remote than usual.

At his side, Ellie sat in silence.

He sensed her simmering concern. A part of him regretted sharing what he'd learned from the Harper brothers. And his own suspicion that Daniel had been hired to create a diversion. A larger part, however, understood that Ellie wasn't the sort of woman who would be satisfied sitting on the sidelines, waiting for him to protect her.

She needed to feel as if she was an active participant in discovering who was responsible for harassing her.

Plus, he wasn't too proud to admit that he needed help. So far he'd gone from one dead end to another. He hoped she could see some connection that he was missing.

Taking yet another turn, Nate drove until he reached the end of the road. He pulled the truck to a halt and switched off the engine.

Together, he and Ellie leaned forward, staring out the front windshield with mutual surprise.

The house was four times the size of Nate's home. Maybe

five times. It was a two-story structure built of pale stone with a wraparound porch and a second-floor terrace that ran the entire front of the home. The windows were large to allow in the blazing Oklahoma sunlight. Or perhaps for the owner to survey his domain from every angle.

It rose out of the flat, dusty landscape like a monolith, jarringly out of place.

"This must be it," Nate muttered.

Ellie released a low whistle, her brows pulled together in confusion.

"When Doris said he was a hermit I was expecting a shack with a tin roof. Not a mansion in the middle of nowhere."

No shit. Nate shook his head. "It's odd."

"What is?"

"That he lived in this huge house all alone while Mandy shared a cramped apartment above the bakery with her son."

"I suppose it was convenient for her to be so close to work," Ellie suggested. "Especially since she was probably in the kitchen at the crack of dawn."

"Or maybe her father didn't invite her to return after her divorce. Not all men want a young child underfoot."

Ellie's lips twisted. "It's just as likely she didn't want to return to her childhood home. Independence has its own rewards."

Nate felt a tug on his heart. Ellie took pride in having achieved her own success. It was what defined her, both as a woman and a lawyer. He wasn't so sure that Mandy had had her same ambition. He suspected she would have leapt at the chance to live in the big house so she could devote her days to raising her son.

Not that it mattered now.

With a small sigh of sadness, Nate turned his attention to the circle drive that ran along the side of the house. It was empty. Not one visitor, despite the fact the man had just lost his daughter.

"Doesn't look like Neville Morse has a lot of friends."

Ellie glanced toward the drive. "Do you think he's home?"

He pointed toward double glass doors. "I saw a shadow move inside when we pulled up."

"It could be a servant."

"There's one way to find out," Nate said.

They climbed out of the truck and crossed the gravel drive to the house. Before they could reach the porch, however, the door was pulled open to reveal a middle-aged man with the thick body of a bull and a face weathered by the sun.

He was wearing a pair of worn jeans and a flannel shirt that was only half buttoned. His thinning dark hair was mussed, as if he'd been running his fingers through it, and even from a distance, Nate could see the dark circles beneath his eyes.

Whatever this man's relationship to his daughter, it was obvious he was distressed by her death.

Moving across the porch, Neville folded his beefy arms over his chest and glared down at them.

"What ya want?"

Nate stopped at the foot of the steps, instinctively reaching to wrap his arm around Ellie's waist and tug her close to his side. It wasn't just the animosity in the man's dark eyes that sent a tiny tingle of warning down his spine. Or the empty silence that surrounded them.

It was the bulge on the side of the man's waist.

Neville had a handgun hidden beneath his shirt.

Nate offered a cautious nod of his head. "Mr. Morse."

"If you're a reporter—"

"I'm Nate Marcel," Nate interrupted, baffled why the man would assume a reporter would be showing up on his doorstep. He glanced toward the woman at his side. "And this is Ellie Guthrie."

The man's scowl deepened. "You're the Fed."

Nate swallowed a sigh. There were times his past profession was an asset, and other times it was a hindrance. He suspected right now it fell into the hindrance category.

"In another life. Now I'm just a local rancher," he told the man.

Neville didn't look particularly impressed. "Why are you here?"

Clearly sensing the prickles of aggression between the two men, Ellie attempted to soothe Neville's less-than-welcoming attitude.

"I know we haven't met, Mr. Morse, but my office is next to the bakery. I used to drop in and visit with Mandy in the mornings," she said in soft tones. "I wanted to offer my condolences."

The man jutted out his heavy jaw. "The funeral is on Monday. You can offer your sympathy then."

Without warning, Neville pivoted on his heel, clearly intending to head back into the house.

"Wait," Nate commanded.

The man grudgingly turned back. "Now what?"

Nate took a step forward. "I wonder if I could ask you a few questions."

"No."

"I promise it will only take a minute."

The man clenched his hands. "Are you deaf? I told you no," he growled.

Nate refused to accept defeat. He hated to be a jerk when the man was mourning the death of his daughter, but he couldn't continue to hope he would stumble across information that would expose the person, or persons, responsible for the sudden bout of crime in Curry. Not when people were dying.

Before he could continue, however, the sound of wheels crunching against the gravel had him glancing over his shoulder to watch a truck park next to his own.

Not that the two vehicles had much in common.

His poor old June looked like a relic when compared to the shiny black pickup with lots of chrome and wheels that cost as much as Nate's house.

He watched as the driver's door was shoved open and Walter Perry hopped out. He was dressed in an old-fashioned suit, complete with a western tie and a black Stetson hat.

Nate swallowed a rueful sigh at the realization that the man had probably just come from his son's funeral. There'd been so much going on he'd forgotten about the small, private service.

The wiry man glanced from Nate and Ellie to Neville before he spoke.

"Is there a problem here?" the retired sheriff demanded.

"These folks can't seem to understand when they're not wanted," Neville informed Walter, his voice sharp.

Walter held up his hand as he strolled to stand next to Nate. "Let me handle this, Neville," he soothed. "You go back inside."

The man quickly turned to scurry back into his house, slamming the door behind him. Nate swallowed a curse. He was fairly sure he'd just lost his opportunity to get the answers he needed from Neville Morse. The elusive man would no doubt make sure he found a way to avoid Nate in the future.

Walter tilted back his cowboy hat, his expression unreadable. "Nate. Miss Guthrie," he murmured. "I think it's best you go."

"We didn't mean to upset Mr. Morse," Ellie said.

Walter shrugged. "These are trying times. For a lot of us."

Ellie nodded in sympathy. "Do they know what happened to Mandy?"

Walter's features tightened. "The sheriff is saying there's a bad batch of heroin in town."

Nate snorted. "Sounds like a convenient explanation so he doesn't have to worry about doing any investigating."

"It's possible," Walter said, his expression hard and unreadable. "Curry wouldn't be the first small town to be plagued with a rash of overdoses. It's a national epidemic."

Nate jerked, feeling a burst of disbelief. He expected Gary Clark to dismiss Mandy's death. Just like he'd dismissed Daniel's and Barb's. The current sheriff didn't have the skills necessary to investigate a runaway dog, let alone three potential murders.

But Walter . . .

"You know very well that Mandy didn't do drugs," Nate said. What the hell was going on? Facts didn't change. The truth didn't change. But everything around him kept shifting and ebbing like he was standing on quicksand. "Certainly she didn't shoot heroin."

Walter's face flushed, his eyes flashing with anger. "My Daniel wasn't the only one with vices in this town."

Nate sliced his hand through the air, his patience level at zero. "Everyone has vices. Some more secret than others," he growled. "But we've had three deaths within the span of forty-eight hours. Something's going on in Curry, and I intend to find out what it is."

Walter glanced toward the house, visibly struggling to regain command of his composure. Eventually he returned his attention to Nate, his expression once more wiped of all emotion.

"Let it go," the man commanded.

Nate frowned. "The death of Mandy? Or your son?"

"All of it. Let it go."

Nate took a long moment to accept that Walter truly meant what he was saying. How could he have gone from furious certainty that someone had deliberately harmed his son to dismissing Daniel's death as if it meant nothing to him?

"Just twenty-four hours ago you were pleading with me to help discover who murdered Daniel," he reminded the man.

Walter hunched his shoulders. "I was mad with grief. Now I can see that it was a tragic accident. Just like Mandy."

Nate bit back his angry words. He didn't know what was going on, but he didn't believe for one second that Walter was now convinced there was nothing more sinister in town than a bad batch of heroin.

"And Barb?" he asked.

Walter looked confused. "What about her?"

"Was she an accidental overdose as well?"

Walter licked his lips, his hands clenching and unclenching. He hadn't been expecting the question.

"Perhaps. Or more likely she drank herself to death. I haven't seen her sober for the past twenty years."

"She was a friend of yours?"

Walter jerked, as if Nate had struck him. "Hell, no."

"But you recognized her name, and knew that she was a drunk."

"When I was sheriff I made an effort to know most people in town, but she certainly wasn't a friend," Walter growled. "I doubt I ever shared more than a dozen words with the woman."

He was lying. Nate could read it in the way the older man's gaze refused to meet his own. The question was why. Because he didn't want anyone to know he was friends with the town lush? Or because the woman was somehow connected to his son?

"What about Neville?" he abruptly demanded.

"What about him?"

"Was he friends with Barb?"

A strange emotion flickered over Walter's face before he was stepping back and nodding toward Nate's truck.

"It's time you were on your way."

Nate's lips parted to continue his questioning. He'd come there for answers and he wasn't going to leave without them. Thankfully, he hadn't forgotten all of his interrogation training.

If he pushed too hard, Walter would clam up completely. Plus, the one-time sheriff had enough influence in town to ensure that no one else would talk to them.

For now, he had to accept that he was going to have to find a new approach to getting the information he needed.

"Fine." He reached to grab Ellie's hand, sending her a warning glance as she made a sound of frustration. "If you and Neville are satisfied with the sheriff's cause of death, then there isn't anything more to discuss."

Clenching Ellie's fingers, he tugged her toward his truck. He had a few favors to cash in.

Chapter Fifteen

Ellie quashed her burst of frustrated anger as she climbed into the truck and slammed shut the door. As much as she wanted Nate to beat the truth out of the men, she understood that it was hardly a legitimate choice.

She had several clients who were currently sitting in jail for making the poor decision to use violence to solve their problems.

Besides, he was a former FBI agent, and she was a lawyer. They had better ways of discovering what the men were hiding. Or at least she hoped they did.

They drove in silence until the large house was out of sight. Then Ellie made a sound of soul-deep irritation.

"They're hiding something," she muttered.

Nate gave an absent nod. "And they're afraid."

Afraid? Ellie tried to recall the exact expressions on the men's faces. She'd noticed anger. And frustration. Two emotions that could be directly caused by fear.

But what were they afraid of?

"Do you think they know who's responsible for killing Daniel and Mandy?" she demanded.

"Either that, or they received some sort of warning not to cooperate with an investigation of the murders," Nate said.

Ellie heaved a sigh. "Every time we turn around we run into a brick wall."

Nate glanced at the GPS he'd set on his dashboard before turning onto a narrow dirt road. They were taking a different route back to town.

"We did learn one thing," he told her.

"We did?"

"Daniel and Mandy's deaths are definitely connected."

Ellie nodded. It'd been obvious that Walter had some sort of relationship with Neville Morse. And that they were putting on a united front to keep anyone from asking questions about the sudden deaths of their children.

"Not that I believe they were drug overdoses."

"So what else did they have in common?"

She paused, sorting through her limited knowledge of Mandy and Daniel. "We already went through the list. They were both from Curry. Both about the same age. I assume they both graduated from Curry High School and shared a few friends."

Nate made another turn. "And both were dumped in the same field."

Suddenly Ellie realized where they were going. "That makes sense now that we know it belongs to Mandy's father," she slowly conceded.

"Let's check it out."

He took several more turns before he stopped at the edge of the road, and switched off the engine. Together they climbed out of the truck and headed toward the gate that sagged at a drunken angle.

The ground had been trampled by recent footsteps and there were stray ribbons of police tape that had been left behind, but they didn't distract from the remote wildness of the field.

"Not much here," Ellie said, pointing out the obvious.

Nate moved forward. "I'm going to have a look around."

Ellie grimaced. She didn't know what Nate was looking for. All she could see was grass and weeds and dirt. But she wasn't going to just stand there.

Turning, she headed in the opposite direction, her gaze darting from side to side. Somewhere in the back of her mind she was acutely aware that Daniel and Mandy's dead bodies had been lying somewhere in the field, but she fiercely refused to consider the fact that she might be walking over where they had been dumped. She was already going to have nightmares.

They wandered in aimless circles for twenty minutes before Ellie's toe connected with something hard that was hidden in the tall prairie grass. She sucked in a pained breath, hopping on one foot. Had she kicked a rock? Leaning down, she parted the grass to discover that the hard object wasn't a rock, but a long piece of cement.

"There's something here," she called out.

Nate crossed to stand at her side. The late afternoon breeze tugged at his hair and molded his Henley to his broad chest. He absently allowed his fingers to brush down her back and Ellie felt her heart skip a beat.

He was just so damned gorgeous. And he smelled yummy. Warm male skin and soap with the faintest hint of sandalwood.

Then he bent down to push aside the grass and she pressed her lips together in annoyance. What was wrong with her? They were searching for clues to a potential murder and she was breathless and fluttering like they were on a date.

Thankfully unaware of her embarrassing reaction, Nate straightened and wiped his hands on his jeans.

"An old foundation," he said, his gaze focused on the ground as he began to walk along the crumbling line of cement.

Ellie walked a pace behind him, surprised to discover the foundation was far larger than she'd expected. This wasn't the ruins of some old storage shed. Or even a barn. This was five times the size of her house.

A warehouse that had gone bust? A storehouse for farm equipment?

Impossible to know.

Without warning, Nate halted. He used the tip of his boot to nudge a jagged plank of wood stuck into the ground.

"Charred," he said as the blackened edges flaked away at the touch of his boot. "Whatever was here must have burned down."

Ellie's attention was captured by the glint of something metal on the ground.

"What's this?" Bending down, she pulled a silver object out of a clump of weeds. "A charm bracelet."

As she straightened, Nate reached out to gently tug the jewelry from her hand. His brows drew together as he ran his fingers over the charms.

"I think I've seen this before," he slowly said.

Ellie studied him with raised brows. "Mandy?"

He frowned, his fingers rubbing over the cheap metal that was starting to turn green.

"I can't remember. But I will." With a sharp shake of his head, he shoved the bracelet into the front pocket of his jeans. "I don't think there's anything else to see here."

Ellie eagerly followed him back to the road. She wanted to be away from the field that was shrouded by a lingering darkness. As if the very air was tainted. And maybe it was.

Murder had to leave its mark. Didn't it?

Once they were back in the truck, Nate switched on the

engine and turned on the heat, as if he was capable of sensing the chill that was spreading through her body. Then he was pulling his phone from his pocket and tapping on the keyboard.

"What are you doing?" she asked.

"I want more information on Neville Morse," he said, continuing to concentrate on his phone. "I still have a few contacts in the Bureau. I'm hoping one of them can help."

She waited for him to tuck the phone back into his pocket before she revealed her own special method of obtaining information.

"If you want the history of anyone in Curry, I have a better way to get it."

He arched his brows. "Nothing's better than the FBI database."

Her lips twitched. "You don't know Doris."

"Your secretary?"

"There isn't anything that's happened in Curry that she doesn't know about," she assured him.

"Okay." He put his truck in gear. "Then let's go talk to Doris."

They bumped over the gravel roads in silence, both once again lost in their own dark thoughts. It was crazy. Just a week ago her greatest worry was making sure she could pay her monthly bills. Now she was mourning the loss of three acquaintances, and contemplating who might have murdered them.

Oh, and if the person responsible was also intending to kill her.

It wasn't until Nate reached the edge of town that Ellie shook herself out of her inner musings to direct him toward the quickie-mart where she grabbed a glazed donut and one of the gossip magazines off the rack. Five minutes later they were stopping in front of her office and Ellie jumped out of the truck. It was nearly five o'clock and she wanted to catch Doris before she left for the day.

As Ellie entered, the secretary lifted her head from the stack of folders she was sorting through.

"Greg Stone truly outdid himself this time," she said in dry tones. "I think he searched his trash can for crap to stuff into these discovery files. It'll be another day at least before I have them all sorted."

Ellie sent Doris a smile, setting the donut and magazine on top of the desk.

"No hurry. I brought you dessert."

"And my favorite gossip rag." The secretary glanced toward Nate, who'd just walked through the door, before returning her attention to Ellie. "What do you want?"

"To pick your brain," Ellie admitted without hesitation.

"That sounds ominous," Doris murmured, biting into her donut.

Ellie sensed Nate moving to lean against the wall. No doubt he realized that Doris loved to gossip. Once she got started it might be a while before she was done.

"What do you know about Neville Morse?" Ellie asked.

"He's Mandy's father, poor man."

"You told me that he was a hermit."

Doris nodded. "Ever since his wife died . . . oh, it must be ten or fifteen years ago."

"And before then?"

Doris's brow furrowed as she dug into the recesses of her memory. "Now that I think about it, he used to like rubbing elbows with the bigwigs."

Ellie snorted. "There are bigwigs in Curry?"

Doris gave a lift of her shoulder. "The mayor. Old Doc Booker. And your father when he lived here. Kind of like the Rat Pack. You know that group that hung around with Frank Sinatra?"

Ellie didn't have any trouble imagining her father being

at the center of a group of men who considered themselves the grand pooh-bahs of Curry. He craved power and attention. She was far more interested in the fact that the men used to be friends.

Almost as if able to read her mind, Nate asked the question hovering on the tip of her tongue.

"What about Walter Perry?"

Doris considered. "You know, I think the sheriff was a part of the same group." She took another sip of coffee. "Of course, that was all years ago. Curry isn't the same place it was then."

Hmm. Mandy's father. Daniel's father. Tia's father. And her own. Was that the connection they were searching for?

"Do you know how Neville Morse made his money?" Nate continued his questioning.

Doris looked confused. "He was a rancher like most folks in this area."

Nate shook his head. "Not like most folks. His home must be worth at least two million dollars."

"I'd heard he built some monstrosity. He brought in some fancy architect from San Francisco and everything." Doris grimaced. "I've never been out there."

"Did he inherit money?" Ellie asked.

Doris gave a slow shake of her head. "I don't think so . . . oh." She sat straighter, as if struck by a sudden thought. "Wait."

"What is it?" Ellie demanded.

Doris tapped her finger on the desk, her eyes growing distant as if she was traveling to the past.

"It's vague, but I seem to remember that Morse had a business with Doc several years ago."

Nate moved to stand directly behind Ellie, the heat of his body searing against her back.

"What sort of business?" he asked.

"A clinic for addicts," Doris answered, her tone vague.

"At first there was a big stink in town when Doc suggested he start the place, because it would mean bringing in a bunch of druggies who most folks thought should have been in jail, but then Neville stepped in and said he would be building the place well outside of Curry, and they promised the patients would be kept locked away."

"It was a residential facility?" Nate asked.

Doris nodded. "I'm not sure how many people stayed there. I was like most folks in town and tried to avoid the place."

"Was it in the same field where the bodies were found?" Nate pressed.

"It could be." Doris waved her hand in an absent gesture. "I was doing some traveling back in those days and I really didn't pay much attention."

Ellie assumed most citizens of Curry had tried to ignore the facility. It was the sort of place that might be necessary, but no one wanted in their particular neighborhood.

"What happened to the clinic?" she asked.

Doris continued to tap her fingers on the desk. "It burned down one night. I don't think it was arson, just a tragic accident." *Tap, tap, tap.* "And there was something else."

"What?" Nate demanded.

Doris gave a shake of her head. "I can't remember. It seemed like something happened around the same time, but I'm not sure if it was connected to the clinic or not."

Nate nodded, and Ellie suspected he was making a mental note to have his FBI contact investigate the clinic.

"Is there anything else you can tell us about Neville?" she asked Doris.

The older woman shook her head. "I don't think so."

"Thanks."

Ellie turned toward Nate, who looked like he was churning through the information Doris had shared.

"Can I use your computer?" he abruptly demanded.

Ellie shrugged. "Sure."

She was about to lead him to her office when her attention was captured by the sight of the front door being pushed open. Her brows lifted as she watched the sheriff step into her office. Gary Clark had never been there before, despite the fact the courthouse was just across the street. She suspected he liked the power of forcing her to come to him.

The sheriff watched as Nate moved to stand at her side before he spoke. "Ms. Guthrie."

Ellie frowned. She had a bad feeling. "Can I help you?"

Gary cleared his throat. "I'm afraid there's been some bad news."

Her heart squeezed with fear at his somber tone. "What is it?"

"The fire department got a call an hour ago about a blaze outside town."

She frowned in confusion. She didn't know what she'd been expecting, but it wasn't this.

"A blaze?"

The sheriff gave a dip of his head. "Yes, ma'am. Your house was on fire."

Nate wrapped his arm around her shoulders and tugged her close to his side. Instantly Ellie's fear eased. Without a word, he was telling her that no matter what had happened, she wasn't going to face it alone.

It was a powerful sensation.

"How bad?" she asked.

"The porch is gone, along with a portion of the roof," Gary told her, placing his hands on his hips. The gesture spread open his windbreaker to reveal his gun strapped at his side. Ellie often wondered why he bothered to carry a weapon when he spent 90 percent of his time sitting at his desk. "Not a total loss, but I don't think you'll be able to stay there until the repairs have been made."

Ellie released a shaky breath. Not as bad as it could have been. "How did it start?"

"Hard to say." The sheriff shrugged, looking predictably unconcerned. "Lots of the old ranch houses have faulty wiring."

Ellie's jaw clenched. "Not mine. My father insisted that it be thoroughly checked before I moved in."

"Then it could have been a frayed cord from a lamp," the lawman suggested.

"On my porch?"

The man sucked air between his front teeth. "Hard to say."

"It's not hard to say at all," Ellie snapped. "The most obvious explanation is arson."

"You'll have to check with the fire chief about that," Gary drawled. "Sorry for your loss."

Ellie made a sound of shock. "That's it? You're not going to make a report?"

"As I said, talk to the fire chief." With a sharp nod, the sheriff turned to head out of the office.

Ellie watched his exit with her mouth hanging open. Had he really just announced her house had been set on fire and strolled away as if it was nothing?

She'd known he was lazy, but this was outright negligence. Idiot.

Snapping her lips shut, she pulled away from Nate's arm. "I have to go."

Nate studied her with a grim expression. "I'll drive."

She hesitated before giving a grudging nod. She wasn't the sort of woman who fell apart in an emergency. In fact, she prided herself on being at her best when she was under pressure. But she knew her thoughts were too distracted to make it safe for her to be behind the wheel.

"Fine."

Doris rose from her chair to round the desk and pull Ellie into a tight hug.

"Let me know what I can do to help."

"I will," Ellie promised, gently pulling away. "Lock up when you leave. I don't know when I'll be back."

Doris waved her hand. "You just concentrate on getting your house sorted. I'll take care of things here."

"Thanks."

Offering her secretary a shaky smile, Ellie allowed Nate to lead her out of the office and back to his truck.

A couple minutes later she was buckled in and they were driving out of town at a speed that might have caused her alarm if she wasn't lost in the horrifying certainty that someone had tried to burn down her house.

Who would do such a thing?

And why?

Two questions she knew beyond a shadow of a doubt had to be answered before she became the next victim to be found dumped in the remote field.

Chapter Sixteen

Night had shrouded the charred house by the time the last of the emergency vehicles drove away. Unlike the worthless sheriff, the fire chief had listened to Ellie's concerns and promised that they would do a full investigation.

Nate had stayed in the background. He didn't need an investigation to know that the fire had been deliberate.

What he didn't know was what it meant.

Why would anyone set a small fire at a house where they had to know Ellie wasn't home? It was possible they assumed no one would notice the fire before it had a chance to destroy the house, and that it had just been bad luck for them that someone had spotted the smoke. But why start so small? Why not set a large enough blaze that it would burn in a matter of minutes, not hours?

Just another annoying case of vandalism? Or a warning?

Frustration and a large dose of fear churned through Nate as he walked toward Ellie, who was staring at her house with a sad expression. He didn't know how to protect this woman from an enemy who didn't make sense to him.

Reaching her side, he brushed his fingers down her cheek, finding them damp with tears.

"I'm sorry," he breathed. He hated like hell that he'd been unable to stop the person who was terrorizing her. Or persons.

She reached to touch his arm, as if sensing his sour feelings of guilt. "It's not as bad as it could have been."

His gaze moved toward the house, visible in the glow of the moonlight. The front porch had been turned into jagged bits of charred wood, and a corner of the roof had been burned. But overall, the majority of the damage had been caused by the water hoses used by the firefighters.

"True," he agreed. "It shouldn't take more than a week or so to make the repairs once the water dries."

Her hand dropped. "I was talking about my procrastination. I have most of my stuff stored in the garage."

He turned his head to study her tense profile. It'd been over a year and she still hadn't unpacked? That sounded like a woman who hadn't committed to staying in the area.

Now, however, wasn't the time to question whether she intended to simply walk away one day. Instead he gently wiped away her tears.

"A silver lining," he murmured.

Her lips twisted. "I suppose."

His thumbs brushed over her cheeks. "I have another silver lining."

"What's that?"

"You get to stay with me until your home has been repaired."

She stiffened, as if she was caught off guard by his offer. "I can stay in my office tonight. I have a full bathroom and a couch. Then I can look for other—"

He overrode her babbling words. "You're staying with me."

Her brows drew together. "Isn't it my decision?"

He bent his head to press his forehead against hers. In the distance, the droning song of frogs echoed through the night air, offering a sense of peace despite the acrid smell of smoke that hung over the nearby house.

"Let me take care of you, Ellie," he urged in low tones.

A hint of vulnerability touched her face. "I don't like having people take care of me."

His thumb traced her lower lip. "Why not?"

"They think they can control who I should be."

Nate swallowed a sigh. Her parents had done quite a number on her. Of course, he was dealing with his own daddy issues. Who was he to judge?

"Lucky for you, I like you just the way you are," he assured her. "Stay with me. I promise you'll have all the freedom you need."

There was a pause before she was giving a small nod. "Maybe for a night or two. Just until I can arrange to rent a place."

Nate straightened and grasped her hand, tugging her toward the back of the house. He wasn't going to allow her the opportunity for second thoughts.

"We'll grab clothes and whatever else you might need," he said.

They entered through the kitchen and Nate did a quick sweep of the rooms. He wasn't in the mood for any unpleasant surprises. Once assured that the house was empty, he inspected the ceilings, pleased to discover that none of the water had managed to leak into the house.

Tomorrow he would return and do a quick repair on the roof until she could have it replaced. Or maybe he would convince Ellie to sell the place and move in with him.

The thought hit him with the force of a freight train.

He wanted Ellie to stay with him . . . forever.

A realization that he intended to keep to himself for the moment. Ellie was wary enough. If she suspected that he was hearing wedding bells, she'd bolt so fast she'd leave skid marks on his floor.

And right now it was more important to keep her safe than to convince her they belonged together.

Smiling wryly, Nate helped Ellie carry her suitcases to his truck and drove them the short distance to his house. Then, carrying the cases to the spare bedroom, he headed into the kitchen to start their long overdue dinner.

He was on the back porch grilling the steaks and corn on the cob when Ellie at last wandered out to join him. Quickly he moved to pour her a glass of his favorite wine.

She lifted the glass to her lips, her face pale. "Someone deliberately tried to burn down my home."

Nate reached out to lay his finger across her lips. "We'll discuss it tomorrow. For tonight we'll enjoy a good dinner, and some well-earned peace."

She pushed away his hand, but even as her lips parted to argue, she heaved a weary sigh.

"You're right," she admitted in rueful tones. "I could use a little peace. And whatever you're cooking smells delicious."

"It'll be ready in just a few more minutes," he said.

Ellie moved to lean against the railing, sucking in a deep breath as she tilted back her head and studied the sky above them.

"I don't think I'll ever get tired of this view."

Nate followed her gaze, surveying the velvet black sky that was sprinkled with stars. It was big and vast and beautiful beyond words.

"It's stunning," he agreed, his attention returning to Ellie's face. He was far more interested in the beauty that was just a few feet away. "But is it lovely enough to encourage you to stay in Curry?"

She blinked, meeting his steady gaze. "Why do you ask?"

He shrugged, acting like his future happiness wasn't

hanging on her answer. "Because you haven't bothered to unpack."

"Oh." She sipped her wine. "I've been busy getting my law practice established."

"And that's the only reason?"

There was a long pause. "I'm not sure," she at last admitted.

His lips twisted. At least she was honest. "Fair enough."

She studied him over the rim of her glass. "What about you? Is Curry going to be your forever home?"

"Forever?" He forced himself to truly consider the question. He loved his ranch. And the prospect of opening his small furniture store. But did he want to grow old here, surrounded by wheat fields and cows? He shrugged. "That's impossible to know, but for now I'm satisfied."

"Do you miss Chicago?"

He chuckled, moving back to the grill to flip the steaks. "I miss my family, despite the fact they drive me nuts."

She tilted her head to the side. "You've never told me how you ended up in Curry."

He shrugged. "I took off one morning in my trusty old truck with all my things packed in the back and headed out on Route 66. I wanted to see something of the country before I decided where I was going to settle down." He allowed his gaze to skim over the countryside that was splashed in silver moonlight. "I stopped over in Oklahoma City and happened to pick up a paper, where I saw a classified ad for this ranch. Once I came out here and walked around, I knew this was the place I'd been wanting."

"And what about the FBI?" she pressed. "Do you regret retiring?"

He set down the tongs and grabbed his glass of wine, taking a deep drink as he slowly turned back to meet Ellie's curious gaze. He'd known the question was coming. It always did. A man didn't retire at the age of thirty-four without people wondering why.

But this time he didn't pull out his usual spiel about wanting to get away from city life and work with his hands. If Ellie was going to be a part of his life, she deserved the truth.

"Sometimes I have regrets," he told her. "From the time I was five I wanted to be an agent."

Her brow furrowed in confusion. "So why would you leave?"

The sizzle of the steaks had Nate grabbing the plates and filling them before he placed them on the small table in the middle of the porch.

"Sit down," he urged, refilling their glasses before taking a seat next to her.

He waited until she'd started to eat before he cleared his throat and forced himself to dredge up the memories he'd buried after he moved to Oklahoma.

"When I first started working for the FBI I believed I was impervious to danger," he said, wryly recalling the eager recruit who'd graduated from Quantico.

He'd been convinced that his reckless courage was an asset. And that rules were for other agents. He told himself that he was too ambitious to always follow the tedious guidelines that were no doubt established by stuffy bureaucrats who'd never spent a day in the field.

She polished off her corn before she spoke. "Recklessness is a failing for most of us when we're young."

He smiled. He could easily imagine her climbing the highest tree branch or sneaking out in her father's car and driving it at breakneck speed. But he hadn't been indulging teenage hormones.

He'd been working undercover for brutal gun dealers who would have put a bullet through his heart if they suspected he was a Fed. After that, he'd infiltrated a group of white-nationalists who were sending bomb threats to synagogues around the country.

With every success he'd grown more bold, and more convinced his instincts were never wrong.

"I took risks that would have turned my mother's hair gray if she'd known what I was doing," he said.

She snorted. "Somehow I'm not surprised."

"It was thrilling to think that I was putting my life on the line to help others."

"Like Superman?" she teased.

The tension he didn't even realize had clenched his muscles suddenly eased.

"I always preferred Batman," he corrected.

"Dark and mysterious?"

"He had all the cool gadgets."

"Ah." She sent him a fleeting smile. "What happened?"

He finished his dinner before continuing. He knew the rest of the story would put an end to his appetite.

Once done, he pushed away his empty plate and allowed his gaze to roam beyond his barn toward the rolling fields that were bathed in silver moonlight.

"We were working on a kidnapping case. The child of a high-profile drug lord who was taken by a rival family." His features hardened as he recalled the meetings where he'd heatedly pushed to do whatever necessary to save the child, while his boss calmly calculated the pros and cons. "My superiors didn't think the Bureau should get involved."

She sucked in a shocked breath. "They didn't care about the child?"

He held up his hand. That had been his first reaction as well. It was only with the wisdom of hindsight that he realized his boss had the responsibility to consider the case from every aspect, not just a kid in danger.

"Of course they did, but turf wars are messy," he told her.

"If I got the child back, there was a good chance the father would take justice into his own hands. He'd already killed at least thirty people that we knew about, including children."

She grimaced. "Why didn't you arrest him?"

Nate sat back in his chair, sipping his wine. He hadn't been on the case to bust the drug lord, but he'd known several agents who'd been working for years to bring him to justice.

"Every time the FBI had a solid case against him, the witnesses would be found floating in the river," he told her.

"Yikes."

"Getting in the middle wasn't going to solve anything. Not as far as the FBI was concerned," he continued. "Just more bloodshed."

She tilted her head to the side, studying him with an intensity that made his blood warm. She wasn't just being polite. She truly was interested in what had happened to him.

"But you didn't agree?" she asked.

Nate shook his head. "I was convinced I knew where they were hiding the child and that I could get her out. My boss told me to hand my intel to the local cops and walk away."

Her eyes widened, as if she couldn't believe anyone would suggest that he concede defeat.

"You're not a guy who walks away."

He smiled. Ah. She knew him so well.

"No. I went to the house and found the girl tied up in the basement just like my informant had told me."

"You saved her?"

He winced, the memory dragging him back to the cramped basement with the girl in his arms. It'd been hot. So hot that sweat had been dripping down his face as he'd cradled the child close to his chest. And without the ability to use a flashlight, he'd been stumbling through the dark. Even worse, the sound of the TV upstairs had been blasting so loud that he'd been unable to listen for any approaching footsteps.

In that moment he'd accepted that he was in over his head. It was one thing to risk his own life. It was another to endanger a five-year-old child.

Unfortunately, once the bullets had started flying, he hadn't had any choice but to go forward with his hasty plan.

"When I was carrying her out the back door, one of the guards opened fire on us," he said in grim tones.

"Were you hit?"

"Four times."

Her eyes darkened. "Oh, Nate."

He shrugged aside her sympathy. The last thing he deserved was sympathy. He'd made a poor choice and paid the consequences. Thank God it hadn't been worse.

"I've healed, although my hip hurts like a bitch when it rains," he said in deliberately light tones.

She wasn't fooled. Reaching across the table, she grabbed his hand and gave his fingers a comforting squeeze.

"And the child?"

"A bullet grazed her lower leg, but otherwise she was okay."

"You saved her," Ellie breathed.

He nodded, not sharing the fact that he still woke in the middle of the night with the sound of her screams in his ear.

"Yeah, but my arrogant assumption that I always know best nearly got us both killed," he said, his voice harsh.

She sat back, grabbing for her wineglass. She was wise enough not to try and convince him that he'd made the right choice to rescue the girl.

"Retiring still seems extreme," she instead said.

"While I was lying in my hospital bed I realized that I'd had my fill of danger." He waved his hand toward the dark emptiness that surrounded them. "It was time to slow down and appreciate each day."

"You don't ever get bored?"

He polished off his wine and set aside his glass. Enough of the past. He didn't want to talk about his FBI days. Or even the current danger that was stalking Ellie.

For the first time, he had this woman exactly where he wanted.

In his house.

He didn't want to waste one second of their time together.

"Not since a feisty lawyer moved next door," he murmured, his gaze skimming over her face and down to the scoop-neck sweater that showed a luscious glimpse of her breasts.

"Feisty?" she demanded.

He shrugged. "Stubborn? Ornery? Pain in the ass?"

She pushed away her empty plate and sent him a challenging smile. "Just because I don't let you order me around doesn't make me a pain in the ass."

He placed a hand over his chest, feigning innocence. "I don't order you around. I very politely share my opinion."

She rolled her eyes. "If anyone is the pain in the ass, it's you."

"Sometimes," he agreed. "Clearly we make a perfect pair."

Chapter Seventeen

Ellie's heart lurched and skipped as she met Nate's gaze. There was no mistaking the heat that smoldered in his pale eyes. He was making no effort to hide his passion.

A passion that was echoed deep inside her.

She wanted him. Not because she was scared. Or because she'd had a rotten day and she needed comfort. Or even because she'd been way too long without a man in her bed.

This was as pure as it got.

A deep, ruthless desire that wouldn't be satisfied by anyone but Nate Marcel.

Feeling ridiculously awkward, Ellie rose to her feet and offered what she hoped was a come-hither smile. She didn't know exactly how to do come-hither, but usually a man didn't need much encouragement.

"I think I'll take a shower," she murmured.

Nate lifted himself out of his chair, briskly reaching for the plates.

"A good idea. I'll take care of the dishes."

Ellie blinked. So much for her smile. Instead of tossing

her on the table and stripping off her clothes, he was thinking about dirty dishes. He hadn't even offered to join her in her shower.

She cleared her throat. "If you want . . ." Her words trailed away as he studied her with blatant curiosity.

"Yes?"

"Never mind. Thanks for dinner," she muttered. "It was delicious."

"It was my pleasure. Enjoy your shower."

Disgruntled by his polite indifference, she turned to scurry into the house. Maybe she'd misread the desire in his eyes. Maybe he had heartburn. Or maybe he was thinking of some other woman.

Pressing her lips together, she headed into the small spare bedroom. Fine. If he wasn't interested, then she would . . .

Well, there wasn't anything she could do but pretend that she didn't give a damn. And she was really good at that.

With jerky motions, she grabbed her nightgown. She was fortunate that the smell of smoke had largely been contained outside the house, so she didn't have to rewash her entire wardrobe. Next, she found the shower kit she always kept ready. She never knew when she might have to travel to interview witnesses or to obtain information for a case. Then she headed into the bathroom across the hall.

Unlike her own home, Nate had done extensive renovations. The white subway tiles and claw-foot tub were true to the original home, but they were obviously new, along with the glassed-in shower that was built in the corner.

She closed the door, not bothering to lock it. She'd already done a quick tour of the house before she'd joined Nate on the back porch. Including his bedroom. She knew he had an en suite bathroom, so there was no need for him to use this one.

Stripping off her clothes, she dropped them on the floor and turned on the shower. Once the water was warm, she stepped into the stall and allowed the spray to wash over her skin.

What was wrong with her? She'd never had any trouble letting a man know that she wanted to take their relationship to the next level. Of course, she'd never known a man who'd disturbed her on so many levels, she acknowledged.

And then there was Nate's rigid code of ethics. Maybe he was afraid he would be taking advantage of the situation since she was more or less homeless. It could be that he feared she would feel obligated to say yes if he tried to have sex with her.

She reached for her soap and worked up a thick lather. Okay. She clearly needed to stop acting like a teenage girl who was desperately waiting for some boy to call. She was a logical, well-educated lawyer. She would simply ask Nate what he wanted.

That's how adults handled relationships. Right?

She'd just finished covering herself in soap when she sensed Nate enter the bathroom.

It wasn't a sound that alerted her. She couldn't hear anything over the gush of water. Perhaps it was the swirl of mist that shrouded the bathroom. Or a faint vibration from his approaching footsteps. Or perhaps she was just so acutely aware of him that she could detect his presence on a soul-deep level.

The thought would have been unnerving if she actually allowed herself to consider the possibility. Instead she brushed it aside to concentrate on the shiver of anticipation that raced through her body.

He was here. Just as she'd so desperately wanted.

She bit her bottom lip, her nipples hardening as the

warm water slid over her. She could already imagine Nate's hands on her wet body. His calloused palms would rasp lightly over her skin, finding all those small, unexpectedly erotic spots.

Rinsing off the soap bubbles, Ellie could see the silhouette of Nate as he removed his clothing. Her mouth went dry, her heart pounding so hard it was difficult to breathe.

There was a *whoosh* as he opened the glass door behind her and stepped into the small stall. Ellie didn't turn. Instead, she held herself perfectly still as a pair of strong arms circled her waist and warm lips pressed to the side of her neck.

Pleasure swirled through her as he nuzzled a path of kisses to a spot just below her jaw.

"You startled me," she said in a husky voice.

"In a good way, or a bad way?"

Her heart thundered in her chest as she tilted her head to the side, silently offering him greater access. He groaned his approval, his fingers gliding up and down the curve of her back in a restless motion.

His touch was unbearably gentle, as if he feared she might bruise. The knowledge that his first concern was always her, even when he was in the throes of passion, made her heart give a funny little leap.

"Ellie?" he prompted when she didn't answer. "Do you want me to leave?"

She lifted her hands, bracing them against the slick tiles. There was a melting pleasure flowing through her veins.

"Stay." The word came out as a shaky whisper.

He chuckled, clearly enjoying the fact he could make her tremble. She swallowed a groan. He wasn't the only one enjoying the molten sensations sizzling through her. A part of her wanted to turn and press herself against his hard body. But a larger part feared breaking the dreamlike quality to his slow seduction.

On cue, Nate's broad hand swept a path along the curve of her waist. He paused, as if waiting for her to protest, then, when she arched her back to indicate her full approval, his hand continued upward to cup her breast.

"Thank God. I wasn't sure I could endure another cold shower."

Her breath hissed through her teeth. His calloused fingers were rough against her sensitive skin, but nothing had ever felt so good. She tilted back her head, allowing the warm water to rush over her face, moaning as he found the tip of her nipple and used his fingers to tease it to a hard nub.

"There's nothing cold about this one," she assured him.

"Mmm. And it's only getting hotter."

He nipped at her earlobe, pressing his arousal against her lower back. Unable to resist temptation, she reached behind her back to grab his erection. It was hard, and hot and slick as she brushed her fingers down the curved length.

"Yes, it is," she assured him.

A harsh sound was wrenched from his throat as she gave him a light squeeze, but even as she savored his reaction, she was being distracted as he allowed his free hand to skim down her body to slide between her thighs.

"Finally, we agree on something," he groaned. "A minor miracle."

She released a rueful laugh. He was right. It was a miracle. Since the day he'd appeared on her porch she'd done her best to drive him away. A wasted effort, of course. This moment had been inevitable.

Not that she was going to admit as much to Nate. His ego was big enough.

"I'm a lawyer. Arguing is in my DNA," she teased.

"Just as assuming I'm always right is in my DNA."

"Hmm. Obviously our time together is destined to be explosive."

"Fireworks," he whispered. "I love fireworks."

His finger reached its target and Ellie instinctively spread her legs, her head falling back to rest on his shoulder. He murmured his approval, stroking over her sweet spot.

Fireworks, indeed.

She bit her lip. It felt like she was wrapped in a sensual cocoon. The gentle spray of water. The scented cloud of steam. And the man who was creating magic with his touch.

She closed her eyes, allowing the world to fade away.

Later she would worry about her torched house and the mysterious deaths. In this moment, she didn't care about anything but the glorious heat spreading through her body like wildfire.

His lips stroked down the line of her jaw, his hands moving to grasp her arms. Slowly he turned her so they were face-to-face.

Her breath was slammed from her lungs as her gaze traveled down his naked body. Having this man in her fantasies was one thing. It was quite another to have him standing just a few inches away.

Barely capable of believing this was truly happening, Ellie reached out to run her hand over his hard, sculpted muscles. His skin was warm and slick from the water that continued to pour over them, and sprinkled with rough hair that sent tingles of excitement through her.

Male. He was deliciously, utterly male.

Her hands explored downward, tracing the six-pack that came from hard work, not the gym.

"Christ, Ellie," he rasped. "You take my breath away."

She tilted back her head, meeting his bemused gaze. "The feeling is mutual," she assured him.

He grasped her hips, tugging her tight against the hard

length of his erection. He bent his head, placing his lips directly against her ear.

"Shall we take this to the bedroom?"

Her hand slipped even lower, her fingers wrapping around his cock.

"Next time," she whispered.

He chuckled, giving the lobe of her ear a small nip. "I like the way you think, Ellie Guthrie."

Ellie smiled, even as she inwardly acknowledged she wasn't thinking. Not now. She was feeling. And it was glorious.

Holding her gaze, he opened the shower door and reached toward the nearby cabinet. She wasn't surprised as she watched him slip on the condom he'd obviously placed in a strategic spot. Nate was a man who liked to be prepared.

He also liked to be in control, she discovered as he grabbed her by the waist and lifted her off her feet. She sucked in a startled breath as she found herself pressed against the side of the shower stall. Then, refusing to let him have complete dominance, she used the strength she'd developed during her long morning runs to lift her legs and wrap them around his waist.

He chuckled. "A woman in charge."

"Always."

He gripped her butt as he leaned forward to allow his mouth to torment her nipple. He lapped and teased until her fingers dug into his shoulders.

She shuddered, her nails digging into his flesh. It felt like she was on fire.

"I like it," he murmured. "Too much. I wanted to take this slow and easy, but I don't think I can wait."

She didn't want him to wait. It'd been too long. And she wanted him too much.

Right now she had a pagan need to have him buried deep inside, pounding hard and fast.

As if sensing she wasn't looking for slow, Nate pulled back to study her with an expression that sent tremors racing up her spine. It was an expression that spoke of need and longing and a blatant ownership.

She shifted her hands to frame his face, leaning down to press their lips together. An aching sweetness flowed through her veins like molten honey. She groaned. She didn't know what the future might hold, but she intended to savor this night in Nate's arms.

His hands gripped her upper thighs, parting them so the tip of his erection was pushed against the entrance of her body. Ellie muttered her approval, trailing her lips over his face and down the strong column of his throat. Her stomach clenched in fierce need, her senses clouded with the clean scent of male skin.

"You're so tiny," he whispered. "I'm afraid I might accidentally crush you."

She gave a throaty chuckle, rubbing her body over the tip of his erection. Electric sparks danced through her at the friction she was creating.

Her every nerve was buzzing, perfectly attuned to this man.

"I'm tougher than I look," she assured him.

She pressed downward, the ache between her legs delighting at the sensation of his wide tip slipping just inside her body. But instead of shoving himself home, he clutched her hips and regarded her with smoldering eyes.

"Good. I intend to have my wicked way with you several times tonight."

"Ambitious," she murmured.

"Inspired," he corrected, branding her lips with a kiss of pure hunger.

Then, moving his mouth over her face, he stroked his

tongue down the length of her arched neck. Ellie once again grabbed onto his shoulders as he tugged a furled nipple between his teeth. Bliss, she decided with a raw sigh. Pure bliss.

He turned his attention to the other breast, deliberately urging her desire to a frenzy.

She needed to get him inside her.

Deep, deep inside.

Lifting her head, she gazed at his flushed face. Time passed as they simply stared at one another, silently sharing the connection she had struggled so hard to deny.

Then, slowly, he penetrated her damp channel.

Ellie hissed as he filled her. She felt stretched to the limit, in the best possible way. Yes. This was exactly what she needed tonight.

The heat. The steam. The spray of water.

It all combined to make her feel as if they were completely secluded from the world.

She wrapped her arms around his neck as he started to move. His pace was steady, creating an electric friction that made her entire body shudder.

Ellie made a sound of pleasure, rolling her hips to meet his upward thrust. She smiled with smug satisfaction as his fingers convulsively clutched her hips.

She liked the feeling that they were equals, working together toward one goal.

As if they were true partners . . .

Abruptly thrusting away the disturbing thought, she concentrated on the sensation of Nate's deepening thrusts. Her groans melded with the sound of water beating against the tiles, filling the air with a soft music as her muscles clenched in preparation for the impending orgasm.

Nate tightened his grip, pressing her back hard against the shower wall. Then, still pumping into her at a furious pace, he tilted his hips to a perfect angle, sending her into a shattering climax.

Ellie trembled in ecstasy, convulsing around him as he gave one more thrust and cried out with the violent pleasure of his own release.

I walk around the house. I'm not pleased. I had expected more. This was supposed to send a message. Instead there is nothing more than a missing porch and a few charred shingles. Not much of a message.

Sloppy. Inadequate.

I sigh. This is what happens when I allow others to take care of business.

Unfortunately, I can't be everywhere at once. And events are starting to move at an accelerated pace. I have a lot to accomplish before the pieces come into place and I can complete my revenge.

I can't afford any disruptions in my plans.

Slowly I turn to glance toward the lights burning in the distance.

Nate Marcel is a complication I didn't expect. The question is, how do I stop him?

A bullet through the head is the most obvious answer. But it would no doubt draw the sort of attention I don't need. The man might have retired from the FBI, but I'm quite certain his death would create an uproar. Curry would be crawling with Feds determined to solve his murder.

No. I can't kill Nate.

But there's more than one way to distract him long enough to complete my plans. I just need the proper diversion.

Pacing through the dark I consider my options. Five minutes pass. Then ten. At last I come to a sharp halt. Ah. I know exactly what I need to do. And how I need to do it.

Best of all, if it works, I will be killing two birds with one stone.

Quite literally.

A smile suddenly touches my face. There are times when my brilliance astonishes me.

Chapter Eighteen

Nate woke well before dawn.

Trying not to move, he lay with his eyes closed, simply savoring the sensation of having a naked female body wrapped in his arms.

Perfection. The word drifted through his fuzzy mind.

It'd been a long, long time since he'd had a woman in his bed. And never had it felt so right.

At last he allowed his eyes to open. The room was shadowed, but he'd left a light in the bathroom on, allowing him to appreciate Ellie's tousled beauty as she snuggled closer.

He brushed his lips over the top of her head, a small smile curving as her hands softly stroked up and down his back. Her fingers paused, tracing the scars that pockmarked his skin.

The long, thin scar where his oldest brother had split open his shoulder with a whip. The rough patch from a wound suffered while he was pulling a child from a burning car. And the more recent gunshots.

Her hand moved to his lower hip, lingering on the scar that was four inches wide and still tender to the touch.

"Is this the one that still hurts?" she asked in a husky voice.

Nate shivered. Sparks danced over his skin, igniting a heat that spread through his body. The woman had magic in her touch.

"Not right now," he assured her, his lips tracing a path of kisses over her wide brow.

She stroked her fingers over the side of his hip. "Did they operate to take out the bullet?"

Nate reached down to wrap her fingers in a gentle grip, tugging them to touch the deep indention that marred his lower stomach.

"No. It came out here," he told her, "but there were bone fragments they had to dig out. They've operated three times so far."

She tilted back her head, her eyes dark with emotion. "I'm glad you retired."

His fingers loosened their hold as he allowed his hand to skim up her arm. He explored the slope of her shoulder with a light, feathery touch that made her tremble. He was learning what made Ellie shiver and squirm in all the best ways.

"My mother agrees with you."

"Poor woman."

"Why do you say that?"

Her hand traced the tense muscles of his stomach, brushing the tip of his full-on erection. A groan was wrenched from his lips.

"She raised four boys," Ellie explained. "And if your brothers are anything like you, she must have the patience of a saint."

He chuckled. He wasn't sure he should admit that his

brothers were much worse than he could ever be. He sensed she would freak out the first time he took her home for the holidays.

A strange warmth filtered through his soul.

It was so damned easy to picture her in his parents' small home in the suburbs of Chicago, surrounded by his brothers and a small posse of children.

A wish. A dream. A fantasy.

Or maybe a prophecy.

For now he could only hope, and remain patient.

"I'm not sure if she qualifies for sainthood, but she should get a medal of honor for bravery," he said.

She studied his face, as if searching for some hidden truth. "You love her very much."

"She's something special," he instantly agreed. "And she's going to be anxious to meet you."

As expected, Ellie stiffened at his words. "Nate."

He leaned forward to press their mouths together. "You can pretend if you want, but I'm not going to."

"I'm not pretending."

He nipped her lower lip. "Of course you are. We both know that what's happening between us is destiny." His fingers threaded through her hair. "There's no point in fighting it. It's too powerful."

He heard her breath catch in her throat.

"I don't believe in destiny," she whispered.

"I didn't either." He kissed her. Slow and deep. "Until you. Now I understand exactly why Fate brought me to Curry."

She sighed, wrapping her arms around his neck. "I'm not ready to think about the future," she said. "Not yet."

He disguised his pang of disappointment behind a teasing smile. "Then let's concentrate on this moment."

She hooked her leg over his hip, pressing her lower body tight against his aching arousal.

"I'm good with that."

Excitement blasted through him. "You're more than good. You're great."

She wrinkled her nose, giving a small shake of her head. "We really need to work on your cheesy lines."

"Don't worry. We have all the time in the world to practice. Years and years and years."

Her rueful chuckle filled the room. "You're wrong."

Nate found it increasingly difficult to think about anything beyond the feel of her soft body perfectly fitted against his own.

"About what?"

"Your mother had to be a saint to survive you," she said.

He rolled her flat on her back, reaching toward the nightstand where he kept his decreasing stash of condoms.

"Probably," he absently agreed.

Right now, all he wanted to think about was hearing Ellie's soft moans as he thrust deep inside her.

It was nearly seven a.m. and Ellie was showered and dressed, ready for work. Unfortunately, there was a six-foot male blocking the doorway with a stubborn expression etched on his face.

"I'm going to my office and that's final," she said, trying to ignore the warm scent of his skin.

She'd spent the past twelve hours distracting herself with glorious sex. Now it was time to return to the real world. First a few hours at the office. And then figuring out what she needed to do to start the repairs on her house.

Nate, however, had other ideas.

He'd been arguing with her since she'd pulled on her ivory slacks and a soft cashmere sweater.

"Just give me one good reason why you can't work from here," he growled.

She planted her hands on her hips, glaring at his handsome face. Even with his hair mussed and his jaw dark with unshaven whiskers, he was sinfully gorgeous.

Her heart jumped and skittered even as she did her best to scowl at him.

"I need my files."

"I'll go pick them up."

"I also have two clients coming in today."

He shrugged. "Reschedule."

"No, Nate." She gave a sharp shake of her head. "I'm not going to be bullied into changing my life."

He made a sound deep in his throat. "It's not forever."

"No?" She held his fierce gaze. "Can you be sure of that?"

"Stubborn—"

"Look, my office is just across the street from the sheriff's office," she interrupted. "There's no safer place in Curry."

"My bed," he shot back.

Ellie rolled her eyes, hoping he didn't notice her shiver of yearning. It was bad enough to know that a secret part of her wanted to stay in this house and pretend everything was perfect. She didn't want Nate realizing just how weak she was beneath her pretense of bravado.

"Now I know why you're so determined to keep me here," she accused.

He released a rough sigh, framing her face in his hands. "Ellie, there's some lunatic out there. A lunatic who has potentially killed three people."

"I know that."

"Do you?"

She grimaced. She wasn't sure she'd fully accepted all

the ugly things happening in Curry, but she wasn't oblivious to them.

Or the fact that she was somehow involved in the madness.

"Yes, but I won't run and I won't hide," she said in defiant tones.

His thumbs brushed her cheeks. "I've learned that there's nothing wrong with choosing to avoid danger. It doesn't make you a coward."

Her breath caught in her throat as regret twisted her heart. Did he think she thought he was somehow a coward because he'd left the FBI? Nothing could be further from the truth.

She had infinite admiration for his ability to accept that his temperament wasn't suited to be an FBI agent. Too many people clung to old dreams, refusing to see that happiness might be waiting in another direction.

Or sold their souls to make them come true.

The vision of her mother and father seated in their formal salon that felt more like a hotel lobby than a home seared through her mind. Then she gave a small shake of her head.

"I have no intention of deliberately putting myself at risk," she promised, reaching to place her hand on his forearm. She could feel the tension in his muscles and she experienced another pang of regret. He was truly concerned for her safety. Still, she couldn't hide away. It wasn't who she was. "All I want is to spend a few hours at my office concentrating on something besides how scared I am."

"Christ." He closed his eyes before he forced them back open. "You promise not to leave the office?"

She flicked a brow upward. A silent warning that she wasn't a woman who took commands. From anyone.

"The only promise I'm willing to make is that I'll let you know if I need to go anywhere," she said.

A smile ghosted over his lips. "You negotiate a hard bargain, Ellie Guthrie."

"It's good to know my expensive education didn't go to waste."

"Hmm." Another sigh. This one resigned. "I'll drive you to town."

Larry Harper tried to peer through the gloom that shrouded the back of the room. It was midmorning, but the windows were boarded over, leaving the space in total darkness.

When his brother had shared his crazy idea to try and earn a few extra dollars, Larry had expected to meet his contact in a secluded field. Or even a house in a quiet neighborhood. Somewhere private, not a building on the town square.

For a second he wondered if he'd made a mistake. He turned in a full circle. The place was empty. And it smelled like sawdust and polish. As if someone was in the middle of a renovation project.

Weird.

Then again, everything about the past couple of days had been weird.

Daniel getting snuffed. The FBI dude who'd acted like he was going to pin the death on him. Then Bert's sudden announcement that he'd seen something the night they'd met with Daniel.

Larry hadn't wanted to come. This was all Bert's idea and Larry feared it was a setup that was going to land him in jail. Then his brother had pointed out that there might be Feds watching their apartment. Bert promised he would stroll around the neighborhood to lead them away so Larry could head to Curry without being followed.

Larry wasn't fully convinced that was the reason. Bert would always protect his ass, while expecting his younger brother to take all the risks.

Not bothering to hide his annoyance at the entire situation, Larry glared through the thick shadows. He was waiting another five minutes, then he was going to bail. He'd already wasted half his night coming here. He wanted to get back to the apartment to sample the new stash of meth his brother had promised to bring home after he sent the Feds on a wild-goose chase.

"Where's your brother?" A voice suddenly sliced through the darkness.

Larry jumped. He hadn't heard anyone approaching. Then he allowed a smug smile to touch his lips. Bert had been right. He'd actually seen Daniel's killer.

Why else would they actually show up to this meeting?

Damn. This was going to give them the payday they'd been dreaming of for years. Maybe enough to get out of the squalid apartment and into a real house.

That's all he'd truly wanted since leaving Curry all those years ago.

"Bert is standing outside the Tulsa police station," he lied, shoving his hands in his pockets in an attempt to appear casual. In truth, his heart was banging in his chest so hard it made it difficult to breathe. "He's waiting to make sure I get the money. Otherwise, he's headed inside to tell the cops everything he saw that night."

"You're a terrible liar, Larry Harper."

There was a faint rustle as his companion moved forward. Larry narrowed his gaze. His eyes were beginning to adjust to the darkness. Just enough for him to see the silhouette of his companion.

He frowned, belatedly realizing that the shadowed form was holding something. What? A phone? No, it was bigger than that. It had to be a . . .

Fear exploded through him.

A gun.

The realization burned through his brain at the same time the person lifted their arm.

Stumbling backward, he stared at the weapon in horror.

"Wait!" he cried out. "We can negotiate the price."

"Two birds, one stone," came the whispered reply.

Then a bullet drilled through Larry's forehead and blasted out the back of his skull.

Chapter Nineteen

Nate tried to leash his frustration. Ellie was a big girl. He knew that with intimate certainty. But that didn't keep him from wanting to insist she remain locked in his house.

In his bed.

Now he held on to his steering wheel with a white-knuckle grip as she pushed open the passenger door of his truck and jumped down to the sidewalk.

"You'll call me if you leave the office, right?" he demanded.

"I promise."

"I'll be back to take you to lunch."

She didn't bother to argue. "Fine."

Nate idled next to the curb until Ellie was inside her office. He could see that Doris was already at her desk. Still, he lingered for another few minutes, reluctant to leave.

At last he muttered a curse and shoved his truck into gear. If he wanted to protect Ellie, he needed to discover who was responsible for harassing her. And if they were connected to the spate of deaths.

Something that wasn't going to happen if he spent his day keeping watch on her office.

He circled the square, then headed out of town. He

wanted to stop by Ellie's house and see if he could find any clues as to how the fire was started, and who might have been responsible. Then he intended to have a conversation with Walter.

There was some reason Walter had gone from believing there was something sketchy about Daniel's death to asserting that he, along with Mandy, had died of a bad batch of heroin. A woman who had never been known to drink more than a half glass of wine.

He'd turned onto the gravel road when his phone buzzed. Pressing it to his ear, he slowed to a crawl.

"Marcel."

The voice on the other end was his FBI contact, who informed him that he'd gathered what information he could find on Neville Morse and the Hopewell Clinic.

Nate passed Ellie's scorched house and pulled into his own driveway. He hopped out of his truck and entered through a side door that led directly to his small study. It took a few minutes to fire up his computer and download the waiting email.

In the meantime, he headed into the kitchen to make a pot of coffee. He hadn't gotten much sleep last night. And he had high hopes that tonight would be equally sleepless. He was going to need as much caffeine as he could pour into his body.

At last he was seated at his table with a stack of papers he'd just printed off and a hot mug of steaming coffee.

The top papers were devoted to the tedious forms that were required by state and federal agencies to apply for a grant. He quickly skimmed through them, his brows rising as he reached the official approval of the grant.

Almost a million dollars to build the clinic and to pay for a small staff.

Not bad.

He set aside the papers, and glanced through the rental

agreement between Neville Morse and the Hopewell Clinic. He was paid five thousand a month to have the place located on his land. More than generous, but not outrageous. Everyone tried to screw the government out of money.

The next page was the glowing résumé for Dr. Lewis Booker, who was listed as the senior consultant. Nate instantly recognized the name. The old doctor was still around, although Nate wasn't personally acquainted with him.

Perhaps he should take the time to seek out the doctor and find out his opinion on the sudden deaths of Daniel and Mandy, as well as Barb.

Shuffling to the next paper, he read through the legal mumbo jumbo that created a nonprofit corporation to run the clinic. There was a mission statement that hit all the usual promises. Serving the community. Elevating the futures of the clients. Blah. Blah. Blah.

Next was the creation of the board and their various duties. More boring legal mumbo jumbo. He was on the point of moving on to more interesting intel when he abruptly froze, his gaze locked on the list of board members:

Dr. Lewis Booker

Neville Morse

Walter Perry

Ruben Chambers

Colin Guthrie

Barb Adams, Secretary to the Board

The breath hissed between Nate's teeth. This was the connection. It had to be, right? Neville. Walter. Tia's father, Ruben Chambers. Barb.

And Ellie's father.

What the hell?

He dropped the papers on the table, his coffee forgotten

as he tried to logically sift through various possibilities. A futile task. He didn't have enough information to form any theories.

About to return his attention to the remaining papers, Nate was interrupted by the sound of a sharp knock on his front door. With a frown, he made his way through the house. He paused to glance out the window, his frown deepening at the sight of the sheriff's star painted on the side of the SUV.

Now what?

He took three steps to the side and pulled open the door, revealing the young deputy who was standing on his porch looking distinctly nervous.

"Hello, Clay," Nate said, his tone impatient.

The deputy cleared his throat. "Nate."

"Can I help you?"

There was more throat clearing. "Actually, I need you to come to town with me."

Nate stilled. There was something in the younger man's voice that warned this wasn't just a casual request.

"Why?"

"There's been some trouble at your building."

His mind leapt to the most obvious conclusion. Especially after what had happened to Ellie's house.

"A fire?"

The deputy shook his head. "No."

"Then what?"

Clay shuffled his feet, his discomfort etched on his face. "The sheriff just sent me to fetch you."

A deepening sense of unease spread through Nate. Why was the deputy being so cagey? Surely if it was a simple case of vandalism the younger man would simply tell him what had happened.

"Fine." Nate squashed his flare of annoyance. He could get back to his investigation of Hopewell Clinic as soon as he was done dealing with whatever had happened to his building. "I'll meet you there."

"I . . ." Clay coughed and flushed. "Okay. I'll follow you," he conceded.

Nate grabbed his keys and headed for his truck. It was obvious that Clay had been ordered to get him into town. It was equally obvious that he wasn't going to tell Nate why. There was no point in delaying the inevitable.

Ignoring the fact that he had an officer of the law on his tail, Nate drove at a speed that made his dashboard rattle and sent a plume of dust spewing behind him. He didn't like the knowledge that the sheriff had managed to manipulate him by using his hapless deputy. If the man had any spine, he would have come out and faced Nate in person.

His annoyance had reached a boiling point by the time he reached the town square, only to fizzle and die as he turned the corner. His eyes widened and his heart skidded to a halt.

There were enough flashing lights to make a Fourth of July parade proud. The sheriff's truck was parked front and center, an ambulance parked next to him, along with the fire truck and the coroner's vehicle. There were also two other deputies there, with their trucks turned to form a barrier to keep back the growing crowd of gawkers.

Nate swung his truck into the nearest parking spot. Switching off the engine, he jumped out of the truck and glanced toward Ellie's office on the east side of the square. He could see the outline of Doris at her desk through the large window and the ball of dread in his stomach eased. Good. The older woman wouldn't be sitting there so calmly if her boss was missing, would she?

Assured this had nothing to do with Ellie, he pivoted and sprinted to the front door of his building. The heels of his boots clicked loudly against the cement sidewalk, his adrenaline running high.

He might be relieved that Ellie was safe, but that didn't change his fear that something bad had happened.

Entering through the open door, Nate discovered the front store area was empty. He paused, momentarily confused. Then he heard the low murmur of voices coming from the back and he headed across the wooden floor to an empty storage room. Or at least it had been empty the last time he'd seen it.

Now it was filled with cops, EMTs and the coroner. It made the small space positively cramped as Nate squeezed in.

"What's going on here?" he demanded.

The men turned to regard him with varying degrees of suspicion.

"A question I was about to ask you, Marcel," the sheriff said, pushing his way to the front of the crowd.

Nate clenched his hands, glaring down at the man who barely came to his chin.

"I'm not in the mood," he growled. Then one of the men shifted to the side and Nate realized there was someone lying face-first on the ground. "Shit. What happened?"

The sheriff hitched up his pants, a hint of aggression in his jerky movement.

"What happened is that someone shot this man in the head."

Shot in the head? Nate stepped around the sheriff, crazily wondering if this was some god-awful joke. Nope. One glance was enough to assure him that this was no joke.

Careful not to disturb the body, he studied the small hole visible through the blood-matted hair. He would guess a small-caliber gun shot at close range. His gaze moved down the skinny body that didn't show any other obvious wounds, before returning to the head, where he could make out the man's profile.

Sharp features. A prominent nose and weak chin.

"That's Larry Harper," he breathed in surprise.

The sheriff moved until he was standing next to Nate, his eyes narrowed.

"He's a friend of yours?"

"No."

"But you recognize him."

It was an accusation, not a question. "Yes."

"How?"

Nate took two steps to the side, shutting out the low buzz of voices as he concentrated on the crime scene. He wasn't a medical examiner, but he'd been trained to notice important details.

Now he concentrated on the lividity of the body, as well as the pool of blood that was soaking into the wooden planks of the floor. He'd guess the man had been dead a couple of hours. No more. Maybe a little less. Next his gaze took in the flannel shirt and jeans that Larry was wearing. They were wrinkled, as if he'd slept in them, but they weren't bunched or rolled; that would have indicated that he'd been moved after death.

Last, he took an inventory of what was there. And more importantly, what *wasn't* there.

He could see the outline of a wallet in the back pocket of Larry's jeans, and a ring on his pinkie finger with a gaudy gold nugget. Which meant that he wasn't robbed. Unless whoever had been there had only been interested in drugs.

He turned his attention to what wasn't there.

A gun.

Which meant the killer had taken Larry's gun. Or that he'd been shot in cold blood.

Nate was betting on the cold-blood theory.

Busy sorting through the various possibilities of what had happened—including a drug deal gone wrong—Nate's thoughts were interrupted by the sheriff's sharp voice.

"I asked you a question."

He turned to impatiently meet the lawman's glare. "What?"

"How did you know Larry Harper?"

He resisted the urge to tell the man to shut up and let him concentrate. For once, Gary Clark was doing his job. Even if it meant he was being a pain in Nate's ass.

"I went to Tulsa to speak with him and his brother," he said.

Gary pulled a small notebook from his shirt pocket along with a pencil.

"When did this meeting happen?"

"Yesterday morning." The sheriff scribbled in his notebook. Was he trying to look official? Nate rolled his eyes. "Do you know how he got into my building?" he demanded. He hadn't noticed any broken windows.

Gary paused, as if debating whether he wanted to answer the question.

"There's a key in his front pocket. It fits the back door," he at last revealed.

Nate released a grunt of surprise. A key? That was the last thing he'd expected.

"You're sure?"

"Positive."

Nate's brow furrowed as he tried to imagine how the hell Larry had found a key.

"Did you give him the key during your meeting?" Gary asked.

"No, because I never had one to give him, or anyone else."

The sheriff looked skeptical. "You don't have a key to your own building?"

Nate shrugged. "Not one that opened the back door. I wasn't worried about it since I'm going to have the locks replaced."

More scribbling in the notebook, along with a glance filled with blatant disbelief. Gary Clark wasn't making any effort to hide his suspicion that Nate was lying.

"Why did you go see the Harpers?"

"I had a few questions."

"Questions about what?"

Nate made a sound of impatience. "Shouldn't you be concentrating on why he was here and who shot him?"

Gary puffed out his chest, looking like a chicken with his feathers ruffled.

"That's exactly what I'm doing."

Nate glanced toward the men who were watching the exchange in uncomfortable silence. Realizing that none of them were going to protest the ridiculous implication that Nate was involved, he returned his gaze to the sheriff.

"You can't think that I had anything to do with this?" he bluntly asked.

"I can think a lot of things," Gary said, his eyes narrowing as Nate snorted. "Do you think that your FBI badge protects you from the law?"

"I think my innocence protects me from the law," Nate growled.

"We'll see," Gary said.

A female voice sliced through the air with unmistakable authority. "Not without his lawyer present, you won't."

In one motion the group of men all turned to watch Ellie Guthrie, who halted at the entrance to the storage room. She was barely over five-foot-four inches, and with her hair pulled into a ponytail that made her look about ten years old, but there was an air of command about her that made all of them stand a bit straighter.

This was a woman on a mission.

And she'd knock down anyone standing in her way.

Nate felt a sizzle of heat race through him, even as he muttered an annoyed curse that she'd failed to keep her promise to him. So much for staying in her office until he returned.

Perhaps sensing he was about to lose control of the

situation, Gary Clark pocketed his notebook and pencil before he stepped forward.

"This is a crime scene," he snapped.

Ellie flicked a glance over the sheriff. It had the perfect amount of disdain.

"And you're questioning my client without allowing him proper representation," she warned in icy tones.

Gary's square face flushed. "He isn't under arrest."

She smiled. Or at least her lips curled. Nate shivered. He had a sudden image of a shark about to devour a hapless guppy.

"Then we can leave?"

Gary cleared his throat. He was smart enough to know he was out of his league.

"Let's take this to my office." He held up a hand as Ellie's lips parted to voice her protest. "Nothing official. Just a friendly chat."

Her gaze flicked toward him. "Nate?"

Nate paused. The last thing he wanted was to be stuck in a stuffy office while Gary played at being sheriff. Especially when Nate could be out investigating the murder with far more skill than the local cops. But without his usual contacts, the first thing he needed was information.

And right now, Gary Clark was the only person who could give him that.

"I want to know what happened here," he reluctantly conceded.

Ellie flattened her lips. He could almost see her debating the wisdom of cooperating with the authorities, against the fear he might say something incriminating. Then, as if sensing he was determined to get his questions answered, she gave an impatient wave of her hand.

In silence, the three of them left the building through the front door and crossed the street to the courthouse.

Once inside, they headed down the hallway and through an open doorway.

Escorting them past the reception area, Gary sent his secretary a stern glance.

"I don't want to be interrupted," he warned.

The secretary nodded, futilely trying to disguise her excitement. Nothing ever happened in Curry. Now every day had a new death or disaster. The secretary was clearly savoring the rare hubbub.

They entered the sheriff's dark, cavernous office and Gary crossed to sit behind his desk. A power move? Nate gave a mental shrug. It was doubtful the man had even a small portion of Nate's own training in interrogation. Either being the interrogator or the one being interrogated.

He wasn't worried about being lured into saying something he might later regret. He might no longer be an FBI agent, but he had the sort of friends who wouldn't be happy if some local yokel tried to railroad him into jail.

"Have a seat," the sheriff commanded.

Nate waited for Ellie to choose a wooden chair across from the desk before taking the one next to her.

"Who found the body?" he demanded, deliberately undermining Gary's attempt to establish his authority.

"I'm the one asking the questions," Gary bit out.

Nate settled in his chair and folded his arms over his chest. "This is a two-way conversation or I walk."

Gary's lips tightened. No doubt he wanted to say no, but he wasn't entirely stupid. He was way out of his depth and he needed Nate's help.

"I got a call an hour ago that someone heard gunshots in your building," he said.

"A call from who?"

"They didn't say."

"Did you trace the number?"

The sheriff's jaw clenched. Nate suspected the lawman hadn't even considered the idea of tracing the phone.

"Not yet," Gary muttered.

Nate felt a stab of irritation. When someone reported a dead body, it was surely common sense to try and find out who called. They were quite often involved in the murder.

Then he gave a shrug. Anyone who watched TV would know that a phone could be traced.

"I'll bet good money that it was a burner," he said, speaking more to himself than the sheriff.

Ellie leaned forward. "Why didn't you contact my client as soon as you received the call?"

Gary appeared confused by the question. "I was busy dealing with the dead body."

"A body that you found in a building you had no right to enter."

Gary's chair squeaked as he shifted uneasily. He'd never had to deal with murder before the past few days. He probably didn't have a clue if he could or couldn't enter the building.

Then, perhaps sensing that he was displaying his complete incompetence, he jutted his chin to a stubborn angle.

"Probable cause," he claimed.

"Doubtful a judge would agree. Which means your entire case will be tossed," Ellie drawled.

The sheriff hunched his shoulders. "I was told there was gunfire so I went in and found the Harper boy with a bullet in his head."

Nate hid a smile. As much fun as he was having watching Ellie demolish any case the sheriff might be trying to build against him, he had his own questions he wanted answered.

"Do you know the caliber of the gun?"

The sheriff jerked his head back toward Nate. "Why did you go to see the Harpers?" he demanded.

Nate swallowed a sigh as Ellie sent him the same annoyed glance the sheriff was using. Clearly, she wasn't happy that he'd already confessed he'd been to Tulsa to visit the brothers.

"After Daniel was found in the field, Walter asked me to look into his death," he said.

"Why?"

Nate gave a lift of one shoulder. "He wasn't satisfied with the suggestion his son died of an overdose."

An ugly expression crawled over the sheriff's beefy face before he was regaining command of his temper.

"And he asked you to interfere in my investigation?"

Nate held the man's gaze. "He was under the assumption that there wasn't going to be any investigation."

Gary clenched his hands on top of the desk, but he didn't try to deny Nate's accusation. They all knew that he'd dismissed Daniel's death as an accident. Along with the deaths of Mandy and Barb.

"What led you to the Harpers?" he instead asked.

Nate debated. He didn't make a habit of sharing the names of his informants, even if they hadn't asked for his confidentiality. But then again, he needed the sheriff to feel as if he was in control.

Otherwise he'd shut down the interview.

"The bartender at the Lodge let me look at the security tapes from the night that Daniel died. The Harpers were there with Daniel. I wanted to know why."

Gary suddenly leaned forward, resting his elbows on the desk.

"A convenient explanation."

Nate studied the man's suspicious expression. "Convenient? What's that supposed to mean?"

"There hasn't been a murder in Curry in a decade. Now suddenly people are dropping like flies."

"And?" Nate asked.

"And you seem to be personally involved in each death," Gary pointed out. "You're like some sort of black curse."

Nate felt a burst of anger. Not about the black curse thing. That was mild compared to what his brothers had called him.

But he'd be damned if the bumbling fool tried to pin the spate of killings on him.

"Me? Are you out of your fu—"

"Nate," Ellie interrupted, reaching out to touch his arm.

Gary pointed a thick finger in Nate's direction. "I know you think I'm a lazy yokel who can't do my job, but I'm not stupid," he said, almost as if he could read Nate's dark thoughts.

"Really?" Nate mocked.

Ellie dug her fingernails into his arm. "Nate." Her reprimand was more forceful this time.

Both men ignored her.

The sheriff lowered his hand, but his expression was accusing.

"You were seen talking to my deputy at the field where we found Daniel's body."

"We followed the ambulance," Nate retorted.

"Then you just admitted that you went to the Lodge and demanded to see the security tape."

"So? I told you, Walter asked for my help."

"Or maybe you wanted to make sure that you weren't caught on the video," Gary countered.

"I wasn't at the Lodge that night," Nate snapped.

Gary ignored his protest, clearly on a roll as he revealed his crazy theory.

"You might have been waiting outside. It would make sense that you'd want to check and see if the Lodge had any cameras that could reveal your presence."

Nate shook his head. Was the man serious?

"If I wanted to discover any outside cameras I wouldn't

need to ask to see the footage," he drawled. "I could find them myself."

Once again, the sheriff ignored him. Why bother with logic when he could toss around hypothetical allegations that didn't have to be based in reality?

"And perhaps you didn't know that the Harper brothers were there and they just happened to step out of the Lodge in time to see Daniel getting into a car with you," he continued.

"I don't have a car."

"Fine. A truck." Gary sent him an impatient glare. "Then they hear Daniel's dead and they call you to come to their apartment for a meeting."

Ellie's grip on his arm tightened, but Nate was unconcerned about the sheriff's attempt to paint him as a killer. It didn't matter that innocent people were arrested every day. Or that some were convicted. He had absolute confidence his lawyer could make sure he was protected from any bogus charges.

And he was hoping during the sheriff's wild accusations, he might reveal something that could help Nate figure out what the hell was going on.

"Why would they want to meet with me?"

Gary was prepared with his answer. "To demand you pay for keeping their lips shut about seeing you that night."

"They don't have the brains to figure out a blackmail scheme," Nate pointed out.

The sheriff slammed his hand on the desk. "You arrange a meeting promising to pay them and instead shoot one of them in the head."

Nate watched as Gary sat back in his chair, a smug expression on his face. The man obviously assumed that he'd just delivered the *coup de grâce*.

Nate tilted his head to the side, pretending to consider the accusation.

"Just one of them?" he at last demanded. "What good would that do me?"

Gary faltered. He hadn't considered the gaping hole in his theory.

"You were probably expecting both," he abruptly blustered. "Or you knew that killing one would keep the other one silent."

"I would never risk leaving a witness," Nate said with perfect honesty. Beside him Ellie muttered beneath her breath. Something about thick-skulled idiots. Nate pretended he didn't hear her, his gaze locked on Gary's square face. "And I certainly wouldn't do the deed in my own building. If I killed someone I would make certain the body was never, ever found."

The sheriff scowled in frustration. "If it wasn't you, then how did he get the key?"

Ellie dug her nails into his flesh hard enough to make him flinch. She wasn't fooling. She wanted him to shut up. He snapped his lips together.

"My client recently purchased the building and hasn't had the time to change the locks," she informed the sheriff.

Gary looked unimpressed. "So?"

"So we have no way of knowing how many keys the previous owner might have handed out to various employees or family members," Ellie said. "Plus, the real estate agent would have given them to prospective buyers as well as workers and cleaners." She gave a sweep of her hand, as if indicating a vast crowd of people. "Any one of them could have made duplicates. For all we know there are dozens of keys floating around town."

Gary's hooked nose flared. Ellie had scored a direct hit. Still, the lawman refused to concede defeat. He turned his attention back to Nate.

"Then there's the fact that you show up at Barb's house when she's dying," he growled, grasping at straws.

Ellie gave a click of her tongue. "I was there. She was already gone when Nate arrived."

Gary's gaze never shifted from Nate's face. "And, of course, you were seen enjoying a private conversation with Mandy only a few hours before she disappeared."

Nate sucked in a startled breath, for the first time seeing things from the sheriff's point of view. He'd assumed that Gary Clark was simply tossing out accusations in the hope he could find something to pin on Nate. The lawman had been daunted from day one at having an ex-FBI agent in Curry. It would no doubt give him great pleasure to shove Nate in a cell and throw away the key.

Now he had to admit that he would be on the top of anyone's suspect list.

Hell, he'd investigate himself.

Annoyed at being so slow to realize his danger, Nate did what he always did when he'd been stupid. He went on the offense.

"What do you know about the Hopewell Clinic?"

Gary's smug expression faded, replaced with genuine confusion.

"What are you talking about?"

"The rehab center that used to be in the same field where Daniel and Mandy were found," he clarified, not convinced by the man's seeming bewilderment.

He'd once fallen victim to the tears of a little old lady who claimed that she had no idea her grandson was selling drugs out of her house. Then she'd pulled out a gun and tried to shoot him in the heart. It was only because she didn't have on her glasses that she shot the fridge instead of him.

It'd been a memorable learning experience.

"Oh," Gary finally grunted. "I'd forgotten about that place. My mom worked there."

Nate jerked. He hadn't expected that answer. "Really?"

"She worked in the nursery a few months before it burnt

to the ground." Gary reached into his pocket to pull out a handkerchief. "I don't remember much. I was a baby at the time."

"Was there a daycare center for the workers?" he asked.

Gary shook his head. "No, for the clients. I think they specialized in helping female addicts who had young children. They came in from around the state."

Nate tapped a frustrated finger on the arm of his chair. It seemed that they kept collecting more and more puzzle pieces, with no clue how to put them together.

Hopewell Clinic had to be involved. It couldn't be mere coincidence that both Daniel and Mandy's bodies were found in the same place where it'd once stood. Not when both their fathers had been involved in the clinic.

"How did it catch on fire?" he asked.

Gary made a sound of impatience. "What does it matter? That was twenty-five years ago."

"There seems to be a lot of tragedy connected to a small plot of land," Nate pointed out. "The clinic catching on fire. And now two dead bodies."

Gary blinked, as if baffled by Nate's conclusion. "No one was hurt when the clinic burned down."

Nate continued to tap his finger, struck by a sudden hunch. What if there had been someone in the clinic when it'd burned to the ground? Maybe a client who died?

Still, why would the board members cover it up? Were they afraid they might be sued?

Or . . . had there been something suspicious about the fire? Maybe a deliberate arson to collect insurance money that had accidentally led to a death.

That would certainly be a secret that men in power would want to hide.

And keep hidden.

"You're sure no one was hurt?" he demanded.

Gary's brows snapped together. "That's what I just said."

Nate wasn't convinced. "There's never been any rumors about the fire? Maybe that it was suspicious?"

"You mean arson?" The sheriff started to shake his head, only to hesitate. "Wait. I think I overheard my mother whispering to a friend about something that'd happened at the clinic just before it burned."

Nate leaned forward. "What?"

Gary paused, hopefully searching his mind for the details of his memory. Finally, he heaved an annoyed sigh.

"I don't remember, and I don't care," he snapped. "We're discussing your connection to the string of tragedies in Curry."

Without warning, Ellie surged upright. "No. We're not."

Gary's mouth fell open as he gaped at the woman who was already walking toward the door.

"I'm not done."

Ellie turned, her expression hard. "Is my client under arrest?"

Gary opened and closed his mouth, like a catfish that'd been tossed on the bank. At last he conceded defeat.

"No."

"Then we're done." She glanced toward Nate. "Let's go."

"Yes, ma'am." Jumping out of his chair, Nate followed Ellie out of the office and down the maze of corridors to the front exit. He lowered his head to whisper in her ear as he reached around her to push open the door. "I like when you're a badass. It's sexy," he whispered.

She rolled her eyes, but he didn't miss her faint flush of pleasure before she was crisply stepping outside and heading down the cement steps.

Once confident they were out of earshot of anyone in the building, she halted so she could turn to face him. There was a glint in her eye that warned Nate she was about to give him a tongue-lashing about the stupidity of answering questions when he hadn't been officially arrested. But before she could launch into her tirade, she stiffened, her face draining of color.

Nate felt a prickle of unease as he turned his head to follow her gaze, realizing she was staring across the street at her office. Or more exactly, at the silver Rolls-Royce parked near her front door.

“Oh my God,” she breathed in horror.

Chapter Twenty

Ellie stared at the vehicle parked in front of her office as if it was a ticking bomb. Melodramatic, but that's exactly what it felt like.

She loved her parents. She truly did. But she needed plenty of forewarning, along with a generous amount of wine, to prepare for their rare visits.

To have them appear out of thin air was more than she could deal with when she already had on her plate a mysterious stalker, a burned house, and Nate almost daring the sheriff to arrest him.

"Ellie?" Nate reached out to grasp her hand. "Ellie, talk to me."

She gave a small shake of her head, hoping that might clear it. "That's my father's car."

"You're sure?" he demanded in surprise, only to grimace as he studied the expensive car. No one in Curry drove around in a Rolls. "Sorry. Stupid question."

She shivered. "Why would they be here?"

"I assume they miss their daughter and want to spend some time with you."

Ellie snorted. "You don't know my parents."

As if sensing her need for his warmth, Nate wrapped an arm around her shoulders.

"Why do you say that?"

She leaned closer, savoring his strength. Or maybe she was just savoring his rock-solid muscles. Whichever. She liked being pressed against him.

"My parents don't drop in unannounced," she informed him. "It takes weeks of pre-visit negotiations."

He looked predictably confused. "Negotiations?"

Her lips twitched. "The Guthrie clan consider themselves royalty, which means they have a detailed list of demands that must be met before they condescend to make the journey."

He remained confused. "What sort of demands?"

She ticked off the list on her fingers. "The specific brands of bottled water and coffee they prefer. New sheets on the bed. No household plants."

"What do they have against plants?"

Ellie's lips twitched. Her parents were difficult, overbearing, and treated her like a child. Oddly, however, she enjoyed their small quirks. It was what made them human.

"My mother dislikes the smell of nature," she said.

"I can't imagine that she enjoyed living in Curry," Nate retorted. "There's not much around here but nature."

"She never talks about her time here," she said, wrinkling her nose. "Actually, neither of my parents ever talked much about Curry, which I suppose is why I was curious to come here and discover more about the place where I was born."

"Understandable." He glanced toward her office. "I can't wait to meet them."

Ellie abruptly stepped away. It hadn't occurred to her to introduce Nate to her parents.

"You want to meet them?"

He studied her horrified expression, his jaw tightening with some inner emotion.

"Is there any reason you wouldn't want to introduce me?"

She licked her dry lips. It was difficult to pinpoint the precise reason. A part of her reluctance was the desire to keep her new life separate from her past. She moved to Curry for a fresh start. This place was her future. And Nate was very much a part of that future. Another part was the knowledge that her parents would never approve of Nate. Reasonable people might admire a man who'd served as an agent in the FBI and was now building his own business, but her parents were more interested in how much money a man had in his bank account.

"I just want to know why they're here," she hedged.

"Without me." His tone was flat, emotionless.

"For now." She sent him an apologetic glance. "Later."

There was a tense silence before he was turning his head toward his own building across the square.

"I have a few things to take care of."

Ellie was suddenly reminded of why they were standing in front of the courthouse.

She'd been at her desk when Doris had come in to say there was some trouble across the way. Ellie had strolled to the front reception area to check it out, more curious than alarmed. Only then did she realize that the emergency vehicles were parked in front of Nate's building.

Ignoring Doris's demand to know what was happening, Ellie had hurried out the door. Less than five minutes later she was shoving her way past the deputy to enter the storage area. She'd only been vaguely aware of the dead body on the ground. All her attention had been focused on Nate and making sure he didn't say something to incriminate himself.

Now, she reached out to lay a hand on his arm. "Nate."

He stiffened at her light touch, but he didn't pull away. "What?"

She ignored his sharp tone. She would find some way to soothe his ruffled feathers.

"Don't talk to the sheriff without me," she commanded.

His brows snapped together. "You don't think I'm guilty, do you?"

She sent him an annoyed frown. Did he truly think she would have spent the night in his bed if she thought for one second he could be a cold-blooded killer?

"Of course not. But Gary Clark doesn't like you, and he's lazy," she reminded him. "If he can pin the deaths on you, he'll do it."

He shrugged. "I don't have any intention of crossing paths with the sheriff."

She studied him with blatant suspicion. He'd agreed way too easily.

"You're not going to do anything dangerous, are you?"

Another shrug. "That's not on the agenda."

"Nate."

"Don't worry," he said. "I'm no longer that reckless boy who craves constant adventure."

"I wish I believed that," she breathed.

Perhaps sensing her genuine concern, Nate's features softened. Reaching out, he wrapped his arms around her waist and tugged her close.

"Believe it," he commanded, his voice husky as he lowered his head. "All I crave is you."

He brushed his mouth lightly over her lips. Ellie trembled, reaching up to place her hands against his chest.

"Just be careful," she pleaded.

"Call if you need me."

With one last, lingering kiss Nate dropped his arms and turned to walk away.

Ellie paused to admire his lean body, which moved with a lethal grace she could only envy. He might no longer be an FBI agent, but he moved like he was trained to kill.

Only when he turned the corner of the courthouse did Ellie square her shoulders and head toward her office.

She hadn't lied when she told Nate she was anxious to discover what had brought her parents to Curry. She didn't have a clue why they would be there. On the other hand, she found her feet dragging as she crossed the street and neared the door.

Her mind was already running through the list of complaints that would be waiting for her.

Her mother would criticize her casual attire and her hair that hadn't been trimmed or highlighted in over a year. Her father would belittle her small office and clientele who were basically petty thieves and drunken brawlers.

Grimacing, she stepped into the office and plastered a smile to her lips. She loved her parents, she silently reminded herself. And they loved her.

Her gaze landed on her father, who stood rigidly in the center of the office.

He was a large man, although he maintained his trim form, which was shown to advantage in a perfectly tailored charcoal-gray suit. His features were bold, with a straight nose and a square jaw. His eyes were as clear as emeralds, and had made criminals, attorneys, jurors, and his own daughter squirm in fear for years.

His dark hair was brushed with silver at the temples, and lay so perfectly against his head it was obvious he spent a small fortune to have it styled. Just as he spent a fortune on his smooth tan, his whitened teeth, and his Botox.

For Colin and Allison Guthrie, image was everything.

The sudden thought of her mother had Ellie's gaze roaming around the reception room. Behind the desk Doris was sitting in subdued silence, clearly overwhelmed by Judge Guthrie. It was a familiar reaction. But there was no sign of anyone else.

Moving forward, Ellie lifted her face. "Hello, Father," she murmured as he brushed her cheek with a light kiss. "Where's Mother?"

"She stayed in Oklahoma City," he said, stepping back to run a critical gaze over her. "She has her charity gala tomorrow night."

"Of course."

Her mother hosted an annual ball that raised money for a children's hospital. Ellie had never enjoyed the pompous gathering of the rich and powerful, but she admired her mother's ability to charm massive amounts of money out of her guests.

An awkward silence filled the office. Without warning, Doris scraped back her chair and jumped to her feet.

"I'll make some coffee," she muttered, heading down the hall to the small kitchenette at the back of the building.

Colin watched the woman's hurried exit with a lift of his brows.

"Is your secretary always so skittish?" he demanded.

Ellie nearly laughed. Doris was the least skittish person she'd ever met.

"Not at all. She's very efficient."

"Hmm."

"So." Ellie cleared her throat. "This is an unexpected pleasure."

Her father turned his head to stab her with his piercing gaze. "I don't know why it would be unexpected."

Ellie was confused. "Did I miss your call?"

"No, but you must have known I would be here to attend Barb's funeral."

"Oh." She made a sound of surprise. "It never occurred to me," she retorted with blunt honesty. "As far as I knew, you hadn't spoken with Barb since you left Curry."

"She was still an employee of mine for several years."

Ellie brushed aside her astonishment that her father would make such an effort to respect the memory of his old secretary. The Barb she'd known was a pathetic drunk, but

Colin would naturally remember her as an efficient, loyal woman who'd worked side by side with him.

"I'm not even sure when the funeral is," she admitted with a pang of guilt. There'd been so much going on, she hadn't had time to truly process the fact that the woman was dead.

"It's tomorrow afternoon," Colin said.

"So, you'll be spending the night?" Ellie was surprised. Her father could easily have driven up in the morning and then returned home after the funeral.

"I have a room arranged at the motel."

"I would invite you to stay with me, but I had a small fire at my house."

Colin reached up to smooth his burgundy silk tie, his features tightening with disapproval.

"So I heard, although not from my daughter."

He knew about the fire? "Who did you hear it from?" she demanded.

He waved aside her question. "That is not the pertinent point. Why didn't you let me know that someone has been pestering you?"

Ellie paused. For the first time, she realized she hadn't even considered calling her parents to tell them about her flat tires or the rats or the fire.

Instinctively she'd turned to Nate for comfort and support.

She should probably be worried about that, but right now, she had too much on her plate to give it more than a passing thought.

"There's been a spate of vandalism in Curry," she hedged.

His lips flattened. "I would say it's more than just vandalism."

"We both know that crime can happen anywhere, and I didn't want to worry you."

Her father didn't bother to disguise his dissatisfaction with her explanation.

"It's my duty as your father to worry."

She swallowed a sigh. Duty.

Sometimes it would be nice to be a daughter, not a duty.

"I'm fine," she said.

"For now."

She shrugged, trying to pretend she wasn't deeply worried. "I've taken precautions."

Oddly, her father's eyes darkened with anger. "There's no need for precautions. You'll return with me to Oklahoma City after the funeral."

Was he serious? Ellie studied her father's stern expression. There was an edge in his voice that warned he wasn't making a casual offer.

"I can't leave Curry," she slowly retorted. "I have clients who are depending on me. And my house has to be repaired."

Her father glanced around the reception room, his gaze lingering on the empty seats as if to emphasize the limits of her law practice.

"There's no need for you to worry. I will take care of sending someone to close down your office and collect your belongings from the house."

The words weren't an offer of assistance. They were a command.

A familiar sense of frustration churned through Ellie. Colin Guthrie was a man who expected obedience. Not only in his courtroom, but in his home as well.

Her mother was willing to bow to his authority. It was what a proper wife was expected to do. Ellie, however, wasn't nearly so accommodating.

She had the ability to think for herself.

She met her father's gaze squarely. "I appreciate your concern, Father, but I'm not leaving."

His nose flared with icy disapproval. "You've always been stubborn, Eloise, but while I was willing to allow you to assert your independence, the time has come for you to return home where you belong."

He'd *allowed* her to assert her independence? Yeah, right. She'd fought tooth and nail for it.

She tilted her chin. "This is my home now."

"Nonsense," Colin snapped. "I didn't invest hundreds of thousands of dollars in your education for you to throw it away in this backwater town with some rancher who will no doubt have you barefoot and pregnant in less than a year."

Ellie flinched. Not because her father just blatantly claimed he'd bought and paid for her future—she'd heard it all before—but because his words revealed that he was aware she'd been spending time with Nate. Perhaps even that she was staying with him.

The knowledge made her feel . . . raw. Exposed.

"If you feel cheated, I can pay you back," she informed him, her expression defiant. "It'll have to be an installment plan, but you'll get it all eventually."

He sliced his hand through the air. A motion she'd seen him practice in front of the mirror.

"It's not about the money."

"Then what is it about?"

His gaze once again swept over her small reception area. "You are destined for more than this."

Ellie refused to apologize for her highly successful law practice. She might not be sitting in a penthouse suite in Oklahoma City, or zooming her way to some political position, but she was happy. Which was more than her father could say.

"I think I should be allowed to choose my own destiny," she said with a quiet dignity.

"Not when your choices are foolish."

Ellie bit her tongue as Doris stepped back into the room. The older woman grimaced, clearly sensing the thick tension in the air as she hurried toward her desk.

"I think we should finish this conversation later," she told her father.

"As far as I'm concerned, it's finished," he said, lifting his arm to glance at the diamond-crusted wristwatch. Rolex, of course. "I need to check into my room, and then I have a meeting."

Ellie lifted her brows. A meeting? With who? She knew better than to ask.

"Fine."

Colin crossed the room, but as he reached the door he abruptly turned back to regard her with an unreadable expression.

"You were with Barb when she died," he said. It was a statement, not a question.

Ellie clenched her hands. Who the hell had been tattling to her father? The sheriff? One of his old friends?

Impossible to know.

"I was," she grudgingly conceded. "She called and wanted to see me."

"Why?"

Ellie shrugged. "I didn't get a chance to find out. When I arrived at her house I found her collapsed on the floor."

Expecting that to be the end of the conversation, Ellie was caught off guard when her father continued to study her with his piercing gaze.

"She didn't say anything?"

Ellie hesitated. She didn't know why, but she found herself reluctant to discuss what'd happened at Barb's house. Maybe because she didn't know who was feeding her father information, or why they had been spying on her.

"Why are you asking?"

"Last words can be important," he said in smooth tones.

Important for what? And to whom?

Ellie licked her dry lips. There'd been so many weird things happening that she couldn't be sure if she was overreacting to her father's strange behavior or not. All she knew was that she wasn't ready to discuss Barb's death.

"She mumbled something, but she was too far gone to make any sense," Ellie said, skirting the edge of truth. Hey, she was a lawyer. She was a master at telling not-quite-lies.

Colin pursed his lips. He wasn't satisfied, but he seemed to accept her answer.

"Did she give you anything?" he demanded.

"Like what?"

He shrugged. "If she wanted to meet with you I assume that she must have had a reason. Perhaps she had legal papers she wanted you to help her with. Or even assistance with her will."

Ellie frowned. "Why would she call me about her will?"

"You weren't her attorney?"

"You know I'm a defense attorney." She eyed him in confusion. "I don't do estate planning."

"Then she must have used Kenneth," he murmured, referring to the previous lawyer in town.

Okay, it was official. She wasn't overreacting. Her father was acting strange. Really, really strange.

"What's your interest in Barb?"

"As I said. She was an employee. I'd like to make sure that her affairs are all in order and her expenses covered."

"That's very thoughtful." She had to force the words past her stiff lips.

She must have done a poor job of hiding her disbelief. Her father sent her a sharp glare.

"I take my responsibilities for those I care about very seriously, Eloise. I hope you remember that."

With his chastisement delivered, Colin left the office and headed toward his car. Instantly the sizzling tension in the air began to dissipate. Like the passing of a thunderstorm.

Ellie sucked in a slow breath.

Had the entire world gone mad?

Chapter Twenty-One

Nate left Ellie in a foul mood.

He wasn't a complete barbarian. He accepted that not everything was about him. And it was perfectly reasonable that Ellie would want to meet her parents alone. Especially when she didn't know why they were there. The last thing she needed was him putting pressure on her.

Still, he couldn't deny a sense of disappointment that she hadn't turned to him for support. She no longer had to face her demons alone. Even if those demons were her family. Besides, he wanted to talk to the older man. Colin Guthrie had been gone so long from Curry it was hard to believe he had any connection to the current troubles, but he could answer questions about Hopewell Clinic.

His foul mood wasn't improved as he glanced toward his building to discover a large crowd standing in the street, gawking through the open door. Gossip spread like wildfire through Curry and by now everyone in town would know that a dead body had been found.

Nate clenched his teeth. There was no way to get to his truck without being seen. Which would mean a grilling by his friends and neighbors. Something he was anxious to avoid.

Squaring his shoulders, he took a step forward, only to come to a sharp halt. His gaze scanned the street. Directly in front of his building there were still a couple cop cars, along with a dark sedan that had official tags. CSI? FBI? It didn't matter. He was far more interested in finding the rusty yellow Camaro that belonged to the Harper brothers.

Where was it?

If Larry drove to Curry, it had to be nearby, right?

Heading to the west side of the square, he angled across the street to dart into the nearby alley. He walked down five blocks before turning back toward his building. It seemed impossible to believe that Larry would park his car this far from the building, but he wanted to make sure he didn't miss it.

He mapped out the area in a grid, searching each street until he reached the back of his building. The Camaro wasn't there.

So how had Larry gotten to Curry?

Had someone driven him there and dropped him off? His brother? Whoever had killed him?

Or had he driven the Camaro and his killer disposed of it? That seemed the most likely, but why go to the effort? It wasn't like they went to any effort to hide the body. In fact, they called the sheriff to make certain it was found.

He walked to the end of the alley, glancing toward Ellie's office. He desperately wanted to make sure she was okay, but he forced himself to resist temptation. She was an adult. If she needed his help she would call.

Instead he forced himself to concentrate on Larry Harper. Why had he come to Curry? Why had he been in Nate's building? How had he gotten there? Where was Bert? And most importantly, who'd killed him?

The questions churned through his mind as his feet instinctively carried him around the square to the large building on the corner.

The Lodge.

Hmm. Had his unconscious mind led him here? Perhaps a nudge from his FBI training?

It was early afternoon, but there were already several people sitting in the booths, and in the back of the long room, shooting pool.

Nate instantly felt the weight of a dozen gazes as he stepped through the door and headed for the bar. He ignored the waves to try and gain his attention, sliding onto one of the high stools so his back was to the other customers. It also ensured that he could speak with Paula without being overheard.

The bartender wiped her hands on the apron around her waist as she turned from the stack of lemons she was slicing. She looked surprised to see him before she was offering a practiced smile.

"What can I get you?"

"Whatever you have on draft."

With a brisk efficiency, Paula grabbed a glass and pulled one of the wooden taps to fill it with a golden brew. Then, with a flick of her hand, she had a paper coaster in front of him before setting down the glass.

"Here you go," she murmured, reaching beneath the bar to pull out a bowl of peanuts. "Bad day?"

Nate glanced over his shoulder at the customers who continued to stare at his back.

"I assume everyone knows I've had a bad day," he said, returning his attention to the bartender.

She offered a sympathetic smile. "Hard to keep a secret in Curry."

Nate snorted. "You'd be surprised," he said, thinking of the rash of recent murders.

At least one person in town was capable of hiding the truth of their evil nature.

She leaned forward. "Did they really find a dead body in your building?"

Nate picked up his beer and took a sip. It was cold and crisp with just a hint of wheat.

"It's true," he admitted, setting down his glass and using the tip of his finger to wipe away a bead of foam from the rim. He wanted her to think he was there to soothe his rattled nerves, not to pump her for information. "One of the brothers who was here with Daniel on the night he died, Larry Harper."

He lifted his gaze in time to see Paula jerk at his words. Surprise? Or a pretense of surprise?

Hard to say.

"No shit," she breathed. "Do they know how he died?"

Nate shrugged, not about to give out details that weren't yet public knowledge. He might consider Gary Clark a pathetic excuse for a lawman, but he wasn't going to deliberately undermine his investigation.

"I'm not sure."

She grimaced. "It's kind of creepy. First Daniel and now this Larry Harper. Makes you wonder if the two are connected."

It was the opening that Nate had wanted. "Did you see either of the Harper brothers after that night?"

"Nope." Paula gave a firm shake of her head. "And I would have noticed if they'd been here."

"Have there been any strangers hanging around?"

Her gaze flicked over his shoulder, taking in the crowd. "Just locals."

"What about a yellow Camaro?" he pressed. "Have you seen one parked around here?"

"I haven't really checked." Her gaze returned to study him with open curiosity. "Did you lose one?"

Reaching for his beer, Nate took a deep drink. He wasn't sure what he'd been expecting. Perhaps a description of a scary stalker lurking in a corner booth. Or a confession that Larry Harper had been in the tavern with whoever had eventually killed him.

It was clear, however, he was wasting his time.

"Thanks," he said as he reached into his pocket and pulled out his wallet. He tossed a few bills on the bar as he slid off the stool.

"Strange times in Curry," Paula murmured, reaching for the money.

It was the faint jangle of charms that drew Nate's attention to the silver bracelet around Paula's wrist. He abruptly froze.

"Wait," he rasped, reaching out to snap his fingers around her forearm.

"What the hell?" Paula tried to yank free of his grasp, but Nate ignored her struggles as he lifted her arm to study the cheap piece of jewelry.

The silver links with dainty charms looked ridiculous around her broad wrist. Paula was a tough, tattooed woman who looked like she would hate anything frilly. But it wasn't the fact that the bracelet seemed so out of place on her arm that captured his attention.

It was the fact that he'd seen one just like it.

In the same field where both Daniel and Mandy had been dumped.

"Where did you get that bracelet?" he demanded.

She glared at him in outrage. "Why?"

"It looks familiar," he hedged.

"So what?" She gave another jerk of her arm. "I'm sure there are thousands just like it. I don't make the kind of bank necessary to have custom jewelry made for me."

Nate wasn't convinced. What was the likelihood of two people in such a small town having the exact same bracelet?

"Where did you buy it?"

She scowled, her expression revealing that she was considering the pleasure of punching him in the face. A threat that Nate took seriously. He didn't doubt Paula could hold her own in a fight.

"None of your business is where," she snapped.

Nate met her scowl with one of his own. "It's important."

She faltered at his stern tone. It was his FBI voice. The one he used to intimidate hardened criminals. She muttered a curse before leaning across the bar, as if she was afraid someone might overhear her words.

"Look, I found it when I was cleaning one night," she confessed. "I put it in the lost and found box, but when no one claimed it, I decided I might as well get some use out of it."

Nate studied her petulant expression. Did he believe her? Not really. But he didn't have any evidence to call her a liar.

"Do you remember when you found it?" he asked.

"It was weeks ago." With an impressive burst of strength, Paula pressed her arm to the side, forcing him to release his grip or have his wrist broken. Once free, she sent him a warning glare. "I have work to do."

Nate studied her back as she marched away. No use in trying to force her to talk.

He recognized the rigid set of her shoulders and the stiffness of her spine.

She was done answering his questions. At least for now.

Leaving the tavern, Nate headed for his truck. He suspected that there were only two people who could tell him why Larry was in his building. One was the killer. The other was Larry's brother, Bert.

Time for a road trip.

I stand in the alley, careful to remain in the deepening shadows. It is late enough that most businesses are closed, but I prefer not to be noticed. I press my back against the brick building behind me and inch my way to the side. At last I reach the space between the dentist's office and the auto shop, where I can catch a glimpse of the local motel two streets away.

He's in room 112. I watched him carry in his suitcase, pleased to discover that he'd traveled to Curry without his wife. She might be fun to punish later, but for now I am only concerned with the men.

Neville Morse. Dr. Lewis Booker. Mayor Ruben Chambers. Sheriff Walter Perry. And at long last . . . Justice Colin Guthrie.

What a joke.

Justice.

I smile. Colin Guthrie might wear robes and carry a gavel, but he knows nothing about justice.

Or vengeance.

Those are my domain.

And I am about to inflict both of them on the men who once played judge, jury, and executioner.

Chapter Twenty-Two

Ellie was pacing her office when she heard the *tap, tap, tap* on the front door. Jolted out of her dark thoughts, she headed out of her office and into the reception room.

It was a surprise to find the room empty. She had a brief memory of Doris sticking her head into the office, no doubt to say she was leaving for the day, but Ellie had been too distracted to pay attention. Instead, she'd continued to brood on her father's sudden arrival in town and his adamant insistence that she return to Oklahoma City.

She grimaced. Thank God, her client meetings had been preliminary consultations. She clearly was incapable of concentrating on her work.

There was another tap, and she glanced toward the door. She smiled, a sizzling excitement flowing through her at the sight of the familiar male silhouette.

Nate.

She hurried forward, unlocking the door and pulling it open. A tiny part of her worried about her acute reaction to the man. It wasn't just lust. Or relief that she had a trained FBI agent to keep her safe.

This was soul-deep, gut-twisting awareness that was only

intensifying with each passing day. She swallowed a sigh, accepting that she'd already reached the point of no return.

Nate studied her with unmistakable concern, thankfully unable to read her mind.

"Ready?"

She glanced over his shoulder, noticing the darkness that shrouded the town square.

"What time is it?"

"Six thirty."

She hesitated, then gave a nod. "I can't get any work done today," she admitted.

Less than ten minutes later she had the office locked and was climbing into Nate's truck.Dropping her briefcase on the floorboard, Ellie settled back in her seat. She could sense Nate's lingering glances, but it wasn't until he pulled away from the curb that he spoke.

"I didn't see your father's car."

"He's spending the night at the motel."

"Oh." He sounded surprised. "Your mother isn't with him?"

She shook her head. "She had a charity event in Oklahoma City."

"It doesn't seem right to have him staying at a motel," he said. "He's welcome to stay at my ranch."

Ellie stiffened. Had Nate lost his mind? There was no way she was spending the evening listening to Colin Guthrie insulting Nate's decision to leave the FBI and become a simple rancher. Not to mention his opinion of her own intelligence in becoming involved with any man who didn't pull in a multimillion-dollar salary.

Yeah. That wasn't going to happen.

Not ever.

She intended to keep Nate and her father far, far apart.

"He's already made reservations," she said in a tone that revealed she was just fine with that.

He stopped at the corner, turning his head to study her in the glow from the streetlight.

"Are you having dinner with him?"

She shook her head. "Breakfast." Her lips twisted. "Unless he's too busy."

Nate's brows rose. A silent reminder of her own workaholic habits? She pointed a warning finger at his face.

"Don't say a word."

"I wouldn't dream of it." Turning the truck, he pulled off the square and wove his way through the nearby neighborhoods. "Do you want to eat at the diner or at home?"

"Home." The word slipped past her lips, sending a tiny burst of panic through her. Nate's ranch wasn't her home. Even if it already did feel like it.

He pressed his foot on the gas as they reached the edge of town. "Good choice."

Feeling oddly vulnerable, she cleared her throat. "How was your afternoon?"

A smile played around his lips. "I didn't get thrown in jail."

"A miracle," she said in dry tones.

"Not really. I spent most of the afternoon driving around Tulsa."

She sent him a startled glance. "Why?"

"I want to know why Larry was in Curry," he told her. "And more importantly, why he was in my building."

Ellie gave a slow nod. She'd been so focused on making sure Nate didn't get himself arrested for murder that she hadn't really considered the victim.

That was her job as a defense attorney.

"And you thought the answers would be in Tulsa?" she asked.

"I wanted to talk to his brother."

Ellie tried to remember what Nate had told her about

Bert and Larry Harper. She knew that they were drug dealers. And that they'd met with Daniel the night his body ended up in the field.

And now he was dead.

Was there a connection?

"What did he say?" she asked.

His hands tightened on the steering wheel, revealing his frustration.

"Nothing. I couldn't find him."

"He's disappeared?"

"He's not at his apartment. And it looked like he'd taken off in a hurry."

She turned in her seat, glaring at his profile. "You broke in?"

He shrugged. "I had a quick look around."

Ellie clenched her teeth. He'd trespassed in the apartment of a known drug dealer. Was the man deliberately trying to get himself in trouble?

"I've had clients who went to jail for less," she informed him.

He chuckled, as if she'd told a joke. "I have to get caught first."

She released a resigned sigh. Nate Marcel might be a rancher, and soon-to-be owner of a furniture store, but at heart he was still an FBI agent.

"So much for your pretense that you no longer crave danger."

He sent her a quick glance. "I behaved myself."

She snorted. "You illegally entered his apartment."

"Yeah, but I didn't track down any local druggies and threaten to have them castrated if they didn't tell me where I could find Bert Harper."

"That's behaving yourself?"

"I thought so."

She studied him with blatant suspicion. "So, you've given up on finding him?"

"I called a friend who might be able to trace him, but if he's gone to ground, I don't have a lot of hope that he's going to be found. At least not for a few days."

She released a small sigh. At least he wouldn't be charging around Tulsa threatening desperate criminals with slicing off their manly bits.

"Why would he just disappear?" she asked.

"That's the question, isn't it?"

She studied his profile. "Do you think he killed his brother?"

"I suppose it's possible. That would explain why I can't find his car."

"You don't sound convinced," she said.

"I'm not," he promptly admitted. "If the brothers got in a fight he would have shot him in their apartment. Or even on the street. Why drive to Curry? And how did he get a key to my building?"

She agreed. It did seem unlikely.

"So what's your theory?"

"I think he's running from whoever killed Larry."

Ellie settled back in her seat, staring at the headlights from Nate's truck, which sliced through the thick darkness.

"More questions without answers," she said.

A short time later they were parking in front of Nate's ranch house, and he was escorting her up the path to the front door. Entering the house, she headed for the spare bedroom, anxious to change into a casual pair of yoga pants and loose sweatshirt. She brushed her hair, allowing it to tumble over her shoulders, but she didn't bother glancing in the mirror as she headed out of the room.

The one thing she knew with absolute certainty was that Nate couldn't care less if she was plastered in makeup and draped in designer clothes. He wasn't interested in glamour, or money, or her father's power.

Which made him the complete opposite of every other man she'd dated.

Thank God.

Wandering through the house, she located Nate in the kitchen.

He held up a glass filled with a ruby-red liquid. "Wine?"

She reached to pluck it from his hand. "Do you have to ask?"

He chuckled, grabbing his own glass. "I defrosted a quiche my mother sent home with me after my last visit," he said, nodding toward the nearby oven. "It shouldn't take long to heat."

She sucked in a deep breath. The kitchen was already filling with the scent of bacon and warm pastry.

"It smells delicious."

Taking a sip of her wine, Ellie wandered toward the oak china cabinet set against the wall. She didn't have to ask to know that Nate had made it with his own hands. The wood was as smooth as glass, with delicate leaves carved along the edge. You didn't get workmanship like that from a factory.

She moved to the center of the room, halting at the table that matched the cabinet. Running her fingers over the smooth wood, she accidentally bumped against the stack of papers. About to straighten them, her gaze caught the name of Hopewell Clinic on the top sheet.

"What's this?"

She grabbed the papers just as he took a jerky step forward.

"Shit," he breathed. "I wasn't sure how to tell you about this."

Her mild interest turned to avid curiosity at his unexpected reaction.

"Hopewell Clinic is the place that burned down on Neville Morse's land, right?" she demanded.

"Yeah."

Her gaze skimmed down the page, easily processing the legal jargon that set up the clinic from federal grant money, and incorporated it as a nonprofit.

"Did you get this from your FBI contact?"

"No comment." He reached out his hand. "Ellie, let's wait until tomorrow."

She set her wineglass on the table and shuffled through the stack of papers.

"Why wait?"

"Because it's been a rotten day and I want to enjoy my dinner."

The words were smooth. Perfectly reasonable. But Ellie didn't believe him. There was something in the papers that he didn't want her to see.

So, of course, that made her all the more determined.

Taking a step back, she flipped to the next page. "I'm not a corporate lawyer, but this all looks in order," she said, confused why Nate was so tense.

Then she reached the portion that established the board of directors, and she gasped.

"Some familiar names," Nate said, easily realizing what had caused her shock.

"Colin Guthrie," she breathed, a ball of dread settling in the pit of her stomach. Why would her father be on the board of a rehab facility? And just how closely had he been involved in the clinic? She forced her gaze to continue down the list, her sense of unease deepening. "And Daniel's father and Mandy's father and Tia's."

"And Barb," he pointed out.

She lifted her head to study his stark expression. "This can't be a coincidence."

"No."

She dropped the papers on the table, her brain trying to process what she'd just discovered.

Hopewell Clinic had been formed thirty years ago from money that had been obtained through a grant acquired by Dr. Booker. It had been the doctor who'd presumably negotiated the contract to rent land from Neville Morse, to build the facility, and to invite her father, along with Walter Perry and Mayor Chambers, to be on the board. Five years later the place had burned to the ground and they'd made no attempt to rebuild.

On the surface, it seemed perfectly legit. Dr. Booker wanted to create a clinic to address the needs of addicts, and submitted a grant, which he received. He rented land that was far enough away from town to avoid any protests from the local citizens, and yet close enough to be easily accessable. And then he'd invited the most prominent citizens of Curry to sit on the board.

Even the fire could have been nothing more than a tragic accident.

But the recent incidents convinced her that there had to be some mystery connected to the Hopewell Clinic that was causing the horrifying events that were sweeping through Curry.

The deaths of Daniel and Mandy and Barb. Perhaps even Larry Harper. Plus, there was the petty harassment that was directed at her and Tia Chambers.

And now she knew that her father had been one of the board members . . .

"Oh." She began to pace across the kitchen, her thoughts whirling.

Nate stepped directly in front of her, grabbing her shoulders to bring her to a halt.

"What is it?"

She tilted back her head to meet her worried gaze. "My father."

"What about him?"

"Today in my office he was asking me about Barb."

Nate nodded, almost as if he'd expected her confession. No doubt he'd already accepted the fact that Colin Guthrie was somehow involved.

"Specific questions?"

She nodded. "He asked if she'd spoken to me before she died."

Now he was surprised. "He knew that you were with Barb when she died?"

"Yeah, there's someone in town who's been keeping tabs on me and passing the information to my parents." A fresh wave of anger raced through her at the knowledge she was being monitored like she was a child. "When I find out who it is, I intend to make them very sorry."

His lips twitched before his expression was once again set in somber lines.

"Why would he be interested in what Barb said before she died?"

"He gave some vague answer about the importance of last words and then he asked if she'd given anything to me."

"Given you what?"

She held up her hands in a gesture of confusion. "That was my question."

Nate took a few minutes to ponder what she'd told him, his brow furrowed with concentration. Ellie remained silent, listening to the tick of the old-fashioned clock on the wall. At last he lifted a hand to shove his fingers through his hair, as if he remained as baffled as she was.

"She could have some sort of information your father didn't want exposed," he suggested.

"Maybe. But why would she give it to me?" she asked.

During the long afternoon, she'd considered a dozen possible reasons for her father's strange questions, only to dismiss them. "Besides, when I got there she tried to warn me that people were in danger, not that she had something she wanted to give me."

Nate didn't remind her of her suspicion that someone might have been in the house when she arrived. Someone who might have been there to keep Barb from talking, or to find something that Barb had hidden in her house. She was already freaked out.

Instead he gave a casual shrug. "I think we should find out what your father thought Barb might have given you."

"How?"

"We search her house."

She paused, trying to decide if he was joking. When it became clear he was serious, she gave a shake of her head.

"We don't have any legal authority to go through her things."

"You were her lawyer."

"Not for her estate."

"Close enough."

"I doubt a judge would agree," she argued. "In fact, I'm pretty sure we'd be locked up for trespassing."

He smiled. "A good thing I can ensure that no one will ever know we were there."

She hesitated. She'd always been a boring, law-abiding citizen. She didn't seek danger, or take pleasure in bending the rules.

But now she had to admit that she desperately wanted to get into Barb's house, even if it did mean breaking the law. Maybe the older woman did have something that would reveal what was going on in Curry. Or how her father was involved with Hopewell Clinic.

If nothing else, they might discover if her death had

been a tragic result of her alcohol abuse, or something more sinister.

"How can you ensure we won't get caught?" she demanded.

He reached out to brush his fingers down the curve of her throat. "I'm good. Really good."

Heat spilled through her body. She shivered. How did he do that? He was barely touching her, but she was suddenly aching to strip off his clothes and get him naked.

She cleared her throat, hoping that her cheeks weren't as red as they felt.

"You're good at B and E?"

His fingers moved to lightly trace her lips. "At everything."

Another shiver snaked down her spine. She couldn't testify to Nate's every skill, but she did know that he was good at a few very specific things.

"Do you think Hopewell Clinic has some connection to Barb's death?" she managed to ask.

His eyes darkened as they swept over her face. "I think it's one possibility."

"We should go search Barb's house now," she said. "While it's dark."

"Tomorrow," he insisted.

She scowled with impatience. "I want to know tonight."

He cupped her chin in his hand. "You don't think it would be a little suspicious to have the lights blazing in the house of a dead woman?" he asked. "Or even worse, to have flashlights bobbing around, attracting the attention of the neighbors. Even our less than ambitious sheriff would have to come and check it out."

He was right, of course. There would be no way to search the house without some sort of light. And that would certainly alert the neighbors. Curry was too small not to have someone call 911.

She heaved a resigned sigh. "I hate this."

He stepped closer, the scent of his warm skin teasing at her nose.

"This?"

"The not knowing," she clarified. "I can face anything as long as I understand what I'm dealing with, but this stumbling through the dark is . . . terrifying."

"Put it out of your mind for tonight, Ellie," he said, lowering his head to skim a soft kiss over her mouth. "After a large slice of my mother's quiche, and a good night's sleep, you'll be back to your feisty self."

She felt herself melting as his lips brushed her cheek. "Feisty?"

He wrapped his arms around her waist. "I was trying to be nice."

"Hmm."

"Forget everything but me," he commanded in low tones. "Just for tonight."

Just for tonight.

Giving in to temptation, Ellie laid her head against his chest.

Chapter Twenty-Three

The cold shower did nothing to ease Nate's aching body. To be fair, he didn't think anything was going to help.

Having Ellie in his home, watching her eat the food he'd prepared and sip his favorite wine . . . well, it was custom-designed to stir his deepest desires.

Unfortunately, his heart had stepped in to overrule his body.

Ellie was shaken by the sudden appearance of her father, and the thought that he might somehow be involved with the Hopewell Clinic. She needed a good night's sleep before she had to face the man over breakfast.

Plus, he hoped to sneak out at the crack of dawn so he could search Barb Adams's house. Something that would be impossible if Ellie was in his bed.

Gritting his teeth, he stripped down to his boxers and switched off the overhead light. But even as he headed toward his bed, the door to his room was pushed open and Ellie stepped inside.

The breath was jerked from his lungs as the muted light from the bathroom fell over her slender form covered by a thin robe.

"Ellie, what are you doing?" he rasped.

He could see her smile as she moved to stand directly in front of him.

"Exactly what you assume I'm doing," she assured him.

He licked his dry lips, trying to remind himself of all the reasons he had urged her to get a good night's sleep.

"It's been a rough couple of days for both of us. You should rest."

She reached for the waistband of his boxers. "Later."

He grasped her hands. "You're upset about your father—"

"No," she sharply interrupted. "I don't want to talk about my father. Not now."

"Fair enough," he conceded. "But I want to make sure you're thinking clearly."

She gave a tug on his boxers, sending them plummeting to his ankles.

"I thought the whole point was to be feeling." She allowed her gaze to roam down his naked body. "Not thinking."

Desire blasted through him, his groin tightening. "I'm all in favor of feeling, as long as you don't regret this later."

She chuckled with wicked amusement as she pulled open her satin robe and let it slither down her body.

Nate groaned, his heart slamming against his ribs. She was stunning. The plush softness of her breasts, which were crested with rosy nipples. The slender curve of her waist and the swell of her hips. She might be tiny, but her feminine impact hit him with the force of a freight train.

"I want this." Placing her hands flat on his chest, she gave him a firm shove. Nate stumbled backward, hitting the edge of the bed and tumbling onto the mattress. "Do you?" she demanded.

Nate's body was hard with desire. A familiar sensation. But the squishy emotions that twisted and turned in the center of his heart were something he never expected to feel.

He held her gaze, which glowed in the dim light. "It might sound corny, but I don't have the words to express how much I want this."

A hint of vulnerability flickered over her face before Ellie was leaning over him. With exquisite tenderness, she pressed her lips to one of his numerous scars.

"This is the only sane thing in my world right now," she breathed against his heated skin.

Nate trembled, his hands lifting to grip her hips. This wild, reckless pleasure searing through him didn't feel sane. It was like an addictive madness. But he wasn't going to argue. If Ellie needed him to be her rock, that's exactly what he would offer her.

"Just hold on, Ellie. I've got you."

Her lips traced his collarbone as his hands slid up to cup her breasts.

"I'm pretty sure I don't deserve you," she muttered.

"Probably not," he teased, his thumbs stroking the tips of her puckered nipples. "But now you're stuck with me."

No surprise that she stiffened at his words. She avoided any mention of their future together.

That was okay.

He'd waited his whole life to find this woman. And now that he had her in his arms, he was determined to never let her go. Eventually she'd accept that their destiny was to be together.

Finally, she released a small sigh and crawled onto the mattress to lie beside him.

"Let's just make the most of this night."

Nate turned to frame Ellie's face in his hands. "I can do that," he assured her.

He leaned forward, fusing their lips together. Pleasure exploded through him, igniting a hunger that might have been unnerving if he hadn't already accepted that his need for this woman was as vast as it was eternal.

"Nate," she breathed, wrapping her arms around his neck.

He stroked a trail of kisses down the curve of her neck, thrusting aside his thoughts of forever.

Ellie was right.

They should make the most of this night.

The way things were going, who knew what tomorrow might bring.

Gathering her tightly in his arms, Nate rolled her onto her back, molding their bodies together.

"Don't forget to hold on tight," he warned.

Chapter Twenty-Four

Nate was fairly certain that he deserved sainthood as he slid out of bed and silently crept from the bedroom. What other man would leave the arms of a warm, naked woman before the crack of dawn?

It was only the pressing need to get in and out of Barb's house before Ellie woke that prompted him to hop in the shower, and pull on a pair of jeans and his favorite hoodie. It was still dark when he crept back through his bedroom and headed into the living room.

It was the scent of brewing coffee that alerted him to the fact that Ellie wasn't peacefully tucked in bed where he'd left her. Then the overhead light was snapped on to reveal Ellie standing next to the front door, dressed in the same stretchy pants and sweatshirt from the night before and holding a ceramic mug.

"Don't even think about it," she said, sipping her coffee.

He tried to look innocent. "Think about what?"

"Trying to sneak out of here without me."

"I'm not sneaking."

She snorted. "Bull. Crap."

"Is that a legal term?"

She wasn't amused. In fact, her eyes narrowed as she glared at him.

"You're going to Barb's house."

So much for his grand plan to sneak away and complete his search before Ellie was awake. Now he had to try and convince her that she should allow him to go without her. Like that was ever going to happen.

"I just want to have a quick look around," he said, knowing he was wasting his breath. "If I find something, I promise to bring it back here for you to look at."

She set the mug of coffee on a nearby table so she could slam her hands on her hips, her jaw jutted to a stubborn angle.

"Either we both take the risk, or neither of us take the risk."

"When did you get to be the boss?"

She flicked a brow upward, as if confused by the stupid question.

"I've always been the boss."

He heaved a resigned sigh. "My brothers are never going to let me live this down," he muttered, easily able to envision the Guthrie clan laughing with joy as he dutifully obeyed Ellie's commands.

"Are you ready?" She broke into his rueful thoughts. "I'll drive."

He studied her in exasperation. "Now you're pushing it."

She didn't look remotely apologetic as she moved to the couch to grab her purse.

"Your truck sounds like a battle tank and can be recognized by everyone in town."

"Like yours is any less recognizable?" he countered. The sleek BMW stuck out like a sore thumb in Curry.

She crossed back to stand next to him. "I can park it in front of my office and we can walk to Barb's. No one will notice it there."

He glanced at his wristwatch. "At six thirty on a Saturday morning?"

She shrugged. "It wouldn't be unusual."

He muttered a curse. She had a point. No one would pay attention to her car parked in front of her office.

"Let's go," he rasped, conceding complete and utter defeat.

They drove to town in silence, and he waited for her to park and turn the lights on in her office before they were hurrying through the shadows to Barb's house. Already the sun was creeping over the horizon, banishing the darkness and splashing a rosy glow over the neighborhood.

Taking the lead, Nate darted into the backyard, which was surrounded by a high fence. It would offer them a measure of privacy. Before he moved onto the porch, however, he turned to halt his companion near an overgrown lilac bush.

"Ellie."

"What?"

"I want you to really think about what we're going to do," he said in somber tones. "If we get caught they could take your ability to practice law."

She appeared undaunted by his warning. "You promised we wouldn't get caught."

He grimaced. His father had warned him that his boasting would come back to bite him in the ass.

"Nothing is one hundred percent."

"I trust you."

I trust you. The words whispered through him, tingling parts of him he didn't know could be tingled.

He swallowed a groan. This woman was truly going to be the death of him.

Turning back to the house, he headed for the electric box on the outside of the attached garage. He pulled open the metal door to inspect the wiring. It was all basic, and clearly marked. Which made it simple to be confident that Barb didn't have an alarm system installed. Still, he made a quick check around the house, peering through windows to look for any wireless alarms or cameras.

No surprise there was nothing. What thief would be interested in this place? From what he'd heard around town, Barb had hocked her valuables a long time ago.

Returning to the back door, he knelt down and pulled a leather case from his back pocket. In silence, he removed the slender tools and in less than a minute had them inside the house.

"Did you learn that at Quantico?" she whispered, pressing close to his back.

He glanced over his shoulder, taking note of her tense expression.

"I could tell you, but then . . ."

Her lips twitched at his teasing, a portion of her unease melting.

"Yeah, yeah. You'd have to kill me."

He turned to lead her into the kitchen, not about to admit that he'd learned how to pick locks when he was sixteen and his best friend's father kept a fridge in their basement, filled with beer. After catching them sneaking into his stash, his friend's father had started to lock the basement door. Within a week they'd bought the necessary tools and trained themselves to open the door as soon as his back was turned.

His nose wrinkled at the stench of rotting food and mold that had intensified over the past couple of days. Obviously, no one had been in to clean since Barb's death. No doubt the house would eventually be handed back to the bank to pay off Barb's loan, but for now it was being left to stew in its own filth.

Nasty.

He moved quickly into the living room, relieved to discover the curtains had been left open to allow the rosy dawn to spill through the front window. It would make the search a lot easier than fumbling through the dark.

His satisfaction, however, was short-lived.

Moving to stand at his side, Ellie grasped his arm. "Nate."

He grimaced at the sight of the cushions that'd been tossed onto the carpet and the coffee table that had been knocked over. Even the pictures had been jerked off the walls, as if someone had been looking for a hidden safe.

On instant alert, he pulled the gun he'd holstered beneath his hoodie, his gaze darting around for anyone lurking in the corners.

"Looks like someone had the same idea as we did," he growled, frustration churning through him as his searching gaze caught sight of the stain on the carpet. He bent down to brush his fingers over the damp puddle. Next to it was an empty glass that had been turned over. Recently. Which meant that they'd been beat by just a few hours.

"Who?" Her voice was a whisper.

"Impossible to know," he said, although they both knew who was the most likely suspect.

Colin Guthrie had arrived in town the previous day, asking questions about Barb. It seemed more than a little suspicious that her house would be searched just hours later.

Silently cursing himself for not having considered the possibility when Ellie had first revealed her father's interest in his old secretary, Nate headed toward the hallway.

"Stay behind me," he commanded, his stern tone warning he meant business.

She nodded, her face pale as they moved from room to room, searching for intruders. Once he was assured they were alone in the house, Nate returned to the spare bedroom, where he'd noticed a file cabinet. If Barb had anything of importance, that seemed a likely place to keep it.

As if reading his mind, Ellie headed straight across the room, pulling open the top drawer. Even at a distance, Nate could see that it was empty.

"We're too late," Ellie muttered, pulling open the other drawers to reveal they were as empty as the first. "If there was anything here, it's gone now."

Nate slid his weapon back into its holster. In his current mood, he was afraid he might start shooting something. Beginning with Colin Guthrie.

"Dammit," he rasped. "I'm constantly one step behind."

Ellie wrapped her arms around her waist, her expression troubled. Then, without warning, she abruptly darted out of the room and down the hallway.

"Follow me!"

Startled by her unexpected dash through the house, Nate jogged behind her.

"Where are you going?"

She continued through the kitchen to the narrow door beside the fridge. "When I helped Barb with her DUI, I asked to see the ticket she'd received from the highway patrol, along with the results from her Breathalyzer test."

"I don't think either of those things are going to help us."

She shot him a glance over her shoulder as she pushed open the door. "She had them stashed in a cooler in the garage."

Nate blinked. "A cooler?"

Ellie headed into the garage that was stuffed with as much crap as the house. There was a rusty car that was at least twenty years old. It was rare that Barb had a valid license, but everyone knew she would occasionally get drunk and climb behind the wheel. Around the vehicle were piles of trash bags and broken furniture that she'd tossed in the corners.

Ellie skirted past the mess to the four coolers that were stacked on the far wall.

"She said she kept losing things in her filing cabinets."

Nate wasn't a neat freak. He had a desk where he filed his important papers, but he didn't have them color coded and divided into some complex system. But how the hell could you find anything in a place that looked like a garbage dump?

He gave a shake of his head, following Ellie. "And she wouldn't lose them in a cooler?"

She grabbed the top cooler and pulled off the lid, revealing a stack of empty bottles.

"She kept her booze in here."

"Ah." Now it made perfect sense.

A drunk might not be able to find the toilet, but they would always have a primitive instinct that would lead them to their stash. Like bees to a hive.

He grabbed one of the coolers and popped off the lid. Inside were three full bottles of vodka. He grimaced. Poor Barb. It was a shame that she'd allowed her demons to destroy her life.

Tossing the cooler aside, he reached for the bottom one. Knocking off the lid, he peered inside, his heart leaping with hope at the sight of the brown grocery bag.

"I think I found something," he said, pulling out the bag and glancing inside. Despite the gloom in the garage, he could make out loose papers, stacks of envelopes held together by a ribbon, and a large manila envelope. "Bingo," he breathed.

Ellie leaned toward him. "What is it?"

On the point of pulling out the papers, Nate hesitated. They'd already pressed their luck far enough. He didn't want to risk being caught trespassing by some nosy neighbor. Or worse, having someone else arrive to search the place.

"Let's go back to your office and have a look," he murmured.

She nodded, clearly as anxious as he was to get away from the house that felt like it was shrouded in tragedy.

Quickly restacking the coolers to hide any trace that they'd been there, Nate moved straight to the door that led to the backyard. From there, he rounded the side of the house and paused to make sure no one was around. Moments later they were walking down the sidewalk like they were taking a casual morning stroll, the grocery bag of documents tucked at his side.

They maintained their pretense of nonchalance until they were back in Ellie's office. Wiping her hands on her jeans, as if her palms were sweating, she headed toward the kitchenette.

"I'll make some coffee," she said.

Nate grimaced. Ellie had many fine qualities, but her coffee tasted like black tar.

"No, I'll make it," he said in firm tones.

She rolled her eyes. "Coward."

With brisk efficiency, Nate had the state-of-the-art machine spitting out a steaming brew and they were headed into Ellie's office. They both chose to stand as Nate opened the grocery bag and started pulling out the contents to spread them over the desk.

Ellie reached for the stack of letters, untying the ribbon to glance through them.

"These were all addressed to my father's office in Oklahoma City," she said in surprise. "They were returned unopened." She lifted her head to meet Nate's steady gaze. "So much for my father's supposed concern for his secretary."

Nate wasn't so ready to condemn Colin Guthrie. Everyone in town knew that Barb had a bad habit of using her old friends to fund her drinking habit.

"He probably got tired of her begging for money," he pointed out.

"True," she muttered, sifting through the stack of

unpaid bills and the pawn tickets. "I'm not sure how she was surviving."

Nate grabbed the small account ledger that was nearly lost among the letters from debt collectors.

"She must have been on disability or Medicaid," he murmured. He flicked open the book, searching for any indication of monthly checks. There was nothing to reveal she was on government subsidies, but as he skimmed through the pages, he realized she hadn't always been living on the edge of disaster. "She had quarterly stock dividends." He flicked through more pages. "At least until the last seven years, when she started to tap into her original investment. She drained her account this past summer."

Ellie moved to stand next to him as Nate traced Barb's shaky entries into the ledger all the way back to the original sum.

"Fifty thousand dollars," he said in confusion. How the hell did a woman like Barb get that kind of money to invest?

Ellie pointed toward the date that was neatly listed next to the total.

"The same year that the Hopewell Clinic burned down." She sent him a worried glance. "A payoff?"

"That would be my guess." He paused. Crap. He didn't want to hurt Ellie. The past couple of days had been difficult enough. But they had to discover the truth. No matter what the cost. "I think we should have a closer look at those letters."

Ellie reached for the letters she'd tossed in the middle of the desk, opening the top envelope to pull out the single sheet of paper. Together they scanned the spidery handwriting that sloped at a sharp angle. Barb had clearly been sloshed when she'd been writing it.

As Nate had expected, the note was a plea for money. She started with a rambling demand for five thousand dollars, saying that she deserved the money after all she'd done for him. By the end, she grudgingly admitted that she would take any amount, no matter how small.

Ellie lifted her head to reveal her troubled expression. "After all I've done for you?" she said, quoting the letter. "That's pretty vague."

Nate snorted. "Yeah, it could mean anything from working late to having an affair to helping him cover up a crime."

She flinched at his bleak suggestions, but she didn't try to protest. They both understood that Colin Guthrie was involved in whatever was going on. The question now was just how deeply his connection ran. And what he was willing to do to keep his secrets hidden.

Ellie cleared her throat, her face pale but resolute. "The obvious solution is to ask my father."

Nate bit back his refusal. He couldn't order her not to speak with her own father. Even if the mere thought was enough to set off his inner alarms.

Instead, he tried for a distraction. Leaning forward, he grabbed the manila envelope and tore it open. He reached in to pull out a slender file.

As he'd hoped, Ellie was eyeing the file with a curious expression. "What is it?"

Nate flipped it open. His heart missed a beat as he caught sight of the bold letterhead at the top of the page.

"A patient file from Hopewell Clinic."

Ellie sucked in an audible breath. "What does it say?"

Nate read through the neatly typed intake form. "Jane Doe. Female. White. Twenty-five years old. Home listed as Omaha, Nebraska." He turned to the next page. "Addicted to alcohol. Crack. Tobacco. Three-year-old daughter. Admitted to the clinic May 12, 1995." He paused to calculate the time frame. "Six months before it burned."

She pressed against his side, glancing into the open file. "Is there anything else?"

Nate flipped through the forms. He didn't have any experience in medical jargon, but most of it was fairly straightforward. "The doctor and nurses have a few notes," he said. "A treatment plan. Several references to her oppositional defiant diagnosis." He paused as he reached the last page. It was a grid, with the days of the week listed at the top, and along the side were combinations of numbers and letters that made no sense to Nate. Many of the small squares had dots colored in. "And this," he added.

Ellie studied the form with the same confusion he felt. "What is it?"

"I don't have a clue."

"Maybe the clients were expected to do daily chores?" she suggested.

Nate shrugged. It made as much sense as anything. He replaced the paper and closed the folder.

"The more important question is why this particular file was in the cooler," he said.

"Without a name, it's going to be hard to discover who she is or what happened to her," Ellie pointed out.

Actually, it was going to be impossible, Nate silently conceded. Not even the power of the FBI could identify a mystery Jane Doe from Omaha with no fingerprints or social security number or even a picture.

For now, the file was a dead end. He tossed it back on the desk and glanced in the manila envelope.

"Is that all?" Ellie demanded.

On the point of tossing aside the envelope, Nate realized there was something stuck at the bottom.

"No." He shoved his hand into the envelope, snagging the object with the tips of his fingers and pulling it out. He felt a stab of surprise. "It's a newspaper clipping," he said.

He dropped the envelope on the desk. The clipping was fragile enough to disintegrate if he wasn't careful. Slowly he unfolded it, holding it toward the light that spilled through the window. The ink had faded, making it difficult to see.

He read the headline out loud. "'Mystery child found wandering near highway.'"

Ellie made a sound of surprise. "Mystery child?"

Nate allowed his gaze to move to the actual article. "'The unknown child was discovered by a couple from Indiana who were driving past late last evening. They reported that they searched the area, but were unable to find the parents. They took the child to the local authorities. Sheriff Perry asks anyone with any information to contact his office.'"

There was silence as Ellie clearly waited for him to continue.

"That's it?" she finally prompted.

Nate turned the article over. There was a coupon for toilet paper. Could that be the reason Barb had cut it out? No. She would never have put it in the envelope and hidden it in her special cooler.

"That's it," he said, his voice tight. "It doesn't give the age or gender or race of the child."

Her gaze was locked on the clipping in his hands, as if hoping for inspiration. At last she gave a shake of her head. "Do you know when it happened?"

"No. There's no date."

She wrinkled her nose. "We know it's the Curry paper if Sheriff Perry was in charge of the investigation. We might be able to search through the archives."

He crossed the office to xerox the clipping. He returned the original article to the envelope and folded the copy so he could tuck it into the front pocket of his jeans. It seemed unlikely that the mystery child had anything to do with the Hopewell Clinic or the crimes sweeping through Curry. It did, however, give him a perfect excuse to track down the former sheriff and question him.

"Actually, it would be a lot faster if I just ask Walter myself," he said.

Surprisingly, she nodded in quick agreement. "Fine. You tackle Walter and I'll go see my father."

Nate once again bit his tongue. She was going to eventually see Colin Guthrie. He would rather it be on her terms, and when Nate was in town. Carrying his handgun.

He brushed a light kiss over her lips. "Call me when you're done."

Chapter Twenty-Five

I watch as the men walk out of the motel room.

First out is the mayor. Of course. Ruben Chambers always shoves his way to the front. The man craves constant attention.

Next is Walter Perry. The onetime sheriff looks older than he did just a week ago. His back is stooped and his movements stiff. As if he is in pain.

Pleasure sweeps through me.

I want him to be in pain.

I want them *all* to be in pain.

Neville Morse is right behind the sheriff. Like Walter, he's aged. Not as dramatically. Perhaps he didn't really love his daughter. Or more likely, he's relieved it was Mandy and not himself who was sacrificed for his sins.

I chuckle.

Mandy was just a down payment.

The last man out the door is Dr. Booker. The thin, nervous man is swiveling his head side to side. Like a prairie dog in constant search of danger.

Can he sense my presence?

I hope so.

It would be another layer of fear.

And Lewis Booker has escaped my initial punishment. I'm going to have to do something very special to make sure that he suffers.

The door of the motel room slams shut, hiding Colin Guthrie from view.

No matter.

He's a delicious treat I intend to save for later. Along with the mayor.

For now, I move through the shadows, as silent as death. Ahead of me the doctor scurries down the street to his elegant Victorian home just a couple blocks away. His head continues to swivel. Side to side. Side to side.

Idiot. He has no idea that I'm on his trail.

He's so afraid of what is in front of him, he forgets to look behind.

Now it's too late.

Ellie took five minutes to make a fresh cup of coffee. Nate had many fine talents, but his coffee tasted like weak tea. She needed something with some actual punch to give her the courage to confront Colin Guthrie.

Not that she was afraid of her father. But he was an intimidating man who was used to having his own way. It made it difficult to stand up to him.

Draining her mug, she placed it in the sink and headed out the back of the office. It was still early enough that the nearby stores were closed, allowing an eerie silence to settle in the alley.

Ellie resisted the urge to glance over her shoulder as she hurried between the buildings. She wasn't going to start jumping at shadows. Or assuming that some unseen enemy was watching her every move.

Paranoia was as dangerous as sticking her head in the sand and pretending nothing was wrong.

She needed to take reasonable steps to keep herself safe, without locking herself in Nate's house and hoping it would all disappear. And just as importantly, she needed to focus her energy on solving the mystery surrounding the deaths of Daniel and Mandy and Barb.

Starting with a visit to her father.

She crossed the street, walking past the auto shop and through the parking lot of the motel where the silver Rolls-Royce stood out like a beacon.

With a small sigh, she headed toward the door next to the flashy car. There was nothing about Colin Guthrie that was ever low-key.

Sucking in a slow, deep breath, she lifted her hand and rapped on the peeling doorjamb. There was the sound of footsteps, then the curtains were twitched aside.

Ellie frowned as nothing happened. The sun had made its full appearance, spilling golden light over the parking lot. There was no way her father couldn't see that she was the one knocking.

At last the door was pulled open and Colin studied her with a frown.

"Ellie."

She determinedly stepped past him, entering the room and quickly glancing around.

There wasn't much to see. A bed with the worn quilt pulled up, as if her father hadn't even bothered to lie down. A packed suitcase on a faux leather chair. And a briefcase that was open on the narrow dresser.

"Good morning, Father," she said, her gaze moving to the man who'd raised her.

He wore a long robe and his face was damp, as if he'd just finished shaving. She'd clearly interrupted his morning routine, although his hair was perfectly groomed, and his Rolex was strapped around his wrist.

Colin glanced toward the parking lot, as if suspecting there might be someone out there. Then, closing the door, he turned to regard her with obvious irritation.

"Why are you here?" he demanded. "I told you I would call."

She resisted the urge to roll her eyes. So much for fatherly affection.

"We need to talk."

"We can talk when we return to Oklahoma City."

"This can't wait."

His annoyance deepened. He was a man who gave orders and had them instantly obeyed.

"Clearly living in Curry hasn't improved your manners," he chided.

She tilted her head, studying his familiar face.

Her father had always been a handsome man. And the years had treated him kindly. The few wrinkles that fanned from his eyes and the sprinkling of silver in his hair only emphasized his image of stately elegance. But for the first time she noticed the lines bracketing his mouth had deepened and there was a hardness to his jaw that she'd never noticed before.

"Aren't you interested in what I have to say?" she asked.

Her father glanced at his watch. There was nothing subtle about him.

"Not this morning. I'm busy."

"Busy?" Her attention turned toward the open briefcase. There was a stack of files inside. "I thought you were here for Barb's funeral."

"I am. I need to get ready." As if suddenly aware that the case was open, Colin briskly moved to push down the top. "I assume you plan to attend as well?"

She waited for him to turn back to face her. What was in the case? Work? Or something to do with his real reason for being in Curry?

"I haven't decided," she said.

"Perhaps it would be better if you didn't," he abruptly announced. "You should return to your house and start packing your belongings."

Ellie narrowed her gaze. The words were deliberately chosen to irritate her.

"You're not going to distract me," she warned.

"Ellie—"

"Tell me about Hopewell Clinic," she interrupted, going for shock value.

Her father stilled, obviously caught off guard by her question. Then, with a visible effort, he wiped his face of all expression.

"I don't know what you're talking about."

He was lying.

"It was an addiction treatment facility that was built on Neville Morse's land," she said. "I know you were a board member."

Having regained firm command of his composure, Colin offered a casual shrug.

"Was I? To be honest, I was one of the most prominent men in Curry when I lived here. I was on the board of the library, the church, and a dozen charities." The words weren't boasting. Just a statement of facts. "I can't remember them all."

"The clinic burned to the ground twenty-five years ago," she told him.

"If you say so."

"You truly don't remember?"

Perhaps realizing that Ellie didn't believe his pretense of ignorance, Colin changed tactics.

"What is your interest in the . . ." Her father allowed his words to trail away, as if he couldn't quite recall what she'd just said. "Hopewell Clinic?"

"I believe it's connected to the recent deaths in Curry."

His lips flattened. "What are you talking about? They died of an overdose. Sad, but unfortunately, an all too common occurrence these days."

There was no way to miss the absolute certainty in his voice.

"The cause of death has been determined?" she demanded.

Colin gave a firm nod of his head. "I spoke with Walter, who'd heard from the medical examiner. Both Daniel and Mandy were found with large amounts of heroin in their systems."

Ellie felt as if the ground was shifting beneath her feet. Was it true? Had they truly died from heroin?

It would be no surprise for Daniel. He'd been a hardcore addict for years. But Mandy . . .

The memories of the young woman flashed through Ellie's brain. Seeing her with little Charlie as they walked to school. And hearing them laugh when they were playing soccer on the sidewalk outside her office. Or Mandy's expression when she would sneak into the alley to smoke her one cigarette of the day. Ellie had caught her more than once, and the poor woman had looked as guilty as a child stealing a cookie. There was no way she would be so embarrassed if she was also shooting heroin into her arm.

"Mandy wasn't a user," she said with absolute certainty.

Her father made a sound of exacerbation. Had he expected her to simply accept that the deaths were an accident because the ME found heroin in their blood, and walk away?

She wouldn't be his daughter if she wasn't stubborn to the point of being downright pigheaded.

"This isn't a courtroom where you can try to sway a jury with pleas of innocence," he warned in stern tones. "The lab results don't lie."

She folded her arms around her waist. She didn't understand what had happened to Daniel and Mandy. Or how they'd ended up in Neville Morse's field, but she couldn't shake the suspicion that it had something to do with the past.

"Do you know how the Hopewell Clinic caught on fire?"

"If there was a fire, I assume it was an accident."

"Electrical? A lightning strike?" she suggested. "A patient leaving a candle burning?"

"I haven't the least notion. Nor do I care." A hint of color stained his cheeks, revealing his inner anger. It was something Ellie had never seen before. Her father was always so calm and in complete control of his emotions. She was clearly pressing on a tender nerve. "Return to your house and pack your bags, Eloise."

She stiffened her spine. "No."

"That wasn't a request."

"Thankfully I'm an adult," she reminded him. "I am perfectly capable of deciding if I want to stay in Curry."

He glared at her, but he didn't lose his temper. Instead, he went on the offense. It was what he did best.

"You know that your lover is suspected of murder."

Ellie didn't flinch. Instead, she silently shifted through the various people who could have told her father about Larry Harper's murder and the fact that Nate had been taken to the sheriff's office for questioning.

The sheriff was the most obvious choice, but Curry was too small not to have the gossip already sweeping through town. Anyone could have told her father.

Accepting she still didn't know who had been snitching on her, Ellie faced her father squarely.

"Nate is a man of honor."

Colin released a sharp laugh. "Do you know how many men of honor I've given the death penalty? Anyone can be lured into killing. They do it for greed. For revenge." His lips twisted. "For love."

An odd sensation clutched her stomach at his harsh tone. If she was foolish enough to listen to her gut, she might suspect that her father was speaking from personal experience. Thankfully, she was a woman who depended on her brain. Colin Guthrie was a highly respected judge who'd never had so much as a speeding ticket.

There was no reason to believe that he had ever broken the law.

The unnerving sensation, however, continued to nag at her.

Ellie cleared her throat. "Okay. If Nate killed someone, he's too intelligent to leave the body in his own building," she amended.

"He might have panicked."

Ellie snorted. It was obvious her father had never met Nate.

"He's a trained FBI agent. He doesn't panic," she dryly assured him.

"Unfortunately, I can't share your confidence in his innocence."

"You don't even know him."

Her father glanced away, trying to give the impression he was deciding whether or not to share some sort of unpleasant information.

"I have been doing my research since we last spoke," he said at last, glancing back at her. "I can assure you that Nate Marcel is not the man you believe him to be."

Ellie had never wavered in her trust in Nate. From the beginning, she'd sensed that he was a decent man, even when she was trying to keep him at a distance. And over the past year, her first impression had only been solidified.

Nate was the first to offer his help to his neighbors. He was kind and generous to everyone in Curry, not just those who could offer him something in return. He was charming. He was loyal. And he was strong enough to stand up for what was right, no matter what the cost to himself.

She gave a slow shake of her head, regarding her father with a small pang of regret.

"I'm beginning to fear that you're not the man I believed you to be."

Colin jerked, as if she'd physically struck him. "And what is that supposed to mean?"

She didn't answer. Because she didn't have one.

Not yet.

"Why did you leave Curry?" she abruptly asked.

"You know why. I was offered a judgeship by our state senator." He gave an impatient wave of his hand. "A man with ambition can't remain in a place like this."

She ignored his dig at Nate's decision to give up his career to move to Curry.

"When exactly did you leave?" she pressed. "In 1995?"

"What does it matter?"

"The clinic burned down in November 1995."

An emotion she couldn't decipher darkened his eyes before he was slicing his hand through the air.

"Enough," Colin snapped. "I need to get dressed and you need to pack."

He was starting to turn away and Ellie knew he was closing her out. Even if she stayed and yelled at the top of her lungs, he would ignore her as if she wasn't there. She'd learned that painful lesson when she was just a child.

She quickly formulated her next move. She had to force him to listen. Time to pull out the big guns.

"Barb happened to mention that you owed her money when she asked me to represent her," she said, fudging the truth.

She didn't want him to realize that she'd read Barb's letters. Not yet.

Her ploy worked. Even as she held her breath, her father curled his hands into tight fists. With a sharp motion, he pivoted back to face her.

"Barb had become a pathetic drunk," he said with a fierce insistence. As if trying to convince her that whatever Barb might have said couldn't be trusted. "A shame. She was once an efficient secretary."

"And loyal?"

He eyed her with suspicion. Did he suspect she was leading him into a trap? Probably. As a judge, Colin Guthrie had a reputation for detecting lies, no matter how small. And for ruthlessly punishing anyone who tried to deceive him. More than one convict was sitting in jail because they thought they could manipulate her father.

"I suppose," he agreed.

"She implied that it was her loyalty that had earned her a reward that you refused to pay," Ellie pressed.

"A reward?"

"Yes."

His jaw tightened. Ellie suspected that he was torn between the logical realization that he should deny any knowledge of Barb's demands for money, and the fear that the woman might have revealed something she shouldn't have.

"And that's all she said?"

"It's difficult to remember." Ellie offered a tight smile, tossing his own words back in his face. "That was several months ago."

"Eloise." Her father stepped forward, his face hard with

an expression she'd never seen before. At least not from him. "Don't play games with things you don't understand."

Ellie took an instinctive step back, her heart dropping to her toes.

"You don't give me any choice," she whispered.

He reached out, lightly touching her cheek. "Pack your bags and leave Curry."

She met his warning gaze. "And if I don't?"

He glanced toward the door of his motel room. "We'll both pay the price."

Chapter Twenty-Six

Nate knocked on Walter's door for the third time. The older man had to be there. Not because his shiny truck was parked in the driveway; Walter often walked around town. But because Nate could hear the TV blasting from the front room. Walter wouldn't go off and leave it running. People in Curry were raised to be frugal. No matter how much money they might have, they couldn't bring themselves to waste electricity.

When there was no response, he moved to the edge of the porch and jumped to the driveway. Then, ignoring the good manners his mother had instilled in him, he circled the house and opened the narrow gate in the fence. He entered the backyard and paused long enough to peer around the corner of the house.

He'd miscalculated the danger of a situation once before and nearly died. He wasn't going to bumble into another one.

A quick glance revealed a tidy lawn with a large square that was covered with straw at the back. Walter's vegetable garden. Closer to the house there was a raised patio with furniture that was still draped in tarps, and a metal railing that Walter was spraying with a power washer.

Nate cautiously moved forward, not wanting to startle the older man, but still keeping the element of surprise on his side.

He'd nearly reached the patio when Walter abruptly turned his head, his eyes widening.

"Nate," he growled, reaching over to flick a switch on the power washer, turning it off. "What are you doing here?"

Nate covertly studied Walter's faded flannel shirt that he'd tucked into jeans. He couldn't see any bulges that would indicate the man was armed, but that didn't mean he couldn't have a weapon lying around the backyard.

Leland the barber kept a gun in a drawer with his combs, and the owner of the local diner had a shotgun mounted over his cash register. The Wild West was still alive in this remote area of Oklahoma.

"We need to talk," he told the older man.

Walter dropped the nozzle of the power washer and folded his arms over his chest.

"If you're here about Daniel or Mandy, you can just turn around and walk away."

There was an undisguised aggression in the man's voice. Had someone threatened him? Or did he have something in his past that he was trying to hide?

Maybe it was both.

Nate lifted his hands in defeat. "Hey, if you're satisfied with leaving the investigation in the hands of the sheriff, I accept your decision."

Walter didn't look satisfied. No doubt because he realized Nate wasn't going to stop poking and prying into what had happened to his son.

"There is nothing to investigate," he snapped. "The coroner has officially listed their deaths as accidental overdoses."

Nate absorbed the information. He didn't believe for a

second that Mandy had overdosed on her own. Which meant someone had deliberately killed her with heroin.

Why?

An attempt to make her death look like an accident? A warning? A taunt?

He gave a sharp shake of his head. It was something he'd have to consider later. Right now, he wanted information from Walter.

"As I said. If you're satisfied . . ." Nate allowed his words to trail away with a shrug.

Walter muttered a curse. "Why are you here?"

"I have a few questions about an old business of yours."

"Business?" The older man lowered his brows. "I never had any business."

"The Hopewell Clinic," Nate clarified. "It was a drug rehab center that was located in the same field where they found both Daniel and Mandy. You were a board member."

Walter reached to grab the nearby railing. As if his knees had suddenly gone weak. His expression, however, remained hard with anger.

"Why the hell do you want to know about that place?"

Nate had decided on the way to Walter's house to confront him about the clinic. He wanted to compare notes with what Ellie discovered from her father, since he expected both men to lie. Between the two stories there might be a grain of truth.

"Barb mentioned the clinic before she died." He smoothly told his own lie.

Walter tried to wave aside Nate's words. "Barb was a drunk. She spent most of her days spouting nonsense."

"Not always," Nate corrected, taking a step forward. "Once upon a time she was a devoted secretary to Colin Guthrie. I believe he was also a board member of the Hopewell Clinic."

"So? I'm sure there were a lot of board members."

"No. Just five." Nate held up his hand to tick off the names on his fingers. "You. Colin. Neville Morse. Dr. Booker. And Mayor Chambers." He paused, as if he was trying to remember what someone had told him. "Oh, and Barb was the secretary."

Walter's hand tightened on the railing. Was he realizing that Nate wasn't going to be convinced that Barb was nothing more than a babbling idiot?

"What did the woman say?" he demanded.

"She implied there was something fishy the night the place burned down," Nate said, hoping to solidify his suspicion that the fire had been deliberately started. Or that it'd killed someone and they'd covered up the crime.

Instead, an emotion that might have been relief softened his expression.

"Places burn." Walter shrugged. "Nothing fishy about it."

"What happened?"

"Faulty wiring." Another shrug. "End of story."

"Was anyone hurt?"

"No."

Nate felt a stab of frustration. He'd really thought he was on to something with his assumption that the clinic had been deliberately torched. Or at least that someone had been injured during the fire. But Walter's casual reaction made him question his theory.

So, what was the connection between Hopewell and the events of today? And why did they threaten Ellie, who'd been just a young child when the place had burned to the ground?

"What happened to the clients?" he finally asked.

"I don't know." Walter's momentary relief disappeared as he scowled at Nate. "I suppose they were sent home. Or maybe they went to other facilities."

Nate was surprised by his sharp response. "You didn't keep records?"

"Why would I? If you have questions about the place, ask Dr. Booker. He was the one in charge."

Hmm. Walter hadn't been bothered by Nate's interest in the fire, but he didn't want to discuss the clients.

But why?

Had there been some sort of creative accounting going on? Back then there'd been an epidemic of insurance and Medicaid fraud. The five men might have been creating imaginary clients and charging the government for their housing and medical care. That would explain why Barb had kept the file. If Jane Doe from Omaha had never existed, the paperwork claiming she'd been a patient at the clinic would be a powerful source of blackmail.

"I intend to talk to the doctor," he told Walter, his words a warning. "But as the sheriff at the time, you should have known if there was something suspicious happening at the clinic."

"There was nothing going on. Like I said, if you have questions, then ask the doctor."

"Or one of my friends in the FBI," Nate said with a humorless smile. "I still have contacts."

Walter released his death grip on the railing and turned toward the house as if he didn't have a care in the world. Nate, however, had seen the fear that darkened his eyes.

"We're done," the older man announced, heading across the patio.

"I have one more question," Nate called out. Walter ignored him, pulling open the back door. Nate moved to the edge of the patio, raising his voice to ensure Walter couldn't pretend he didn't hear him. "What happened to the mystery child who was found near the highway?"

The older man released his breath with a loud hiss, jerking around to face Nate. Then, as if realizing he'd revealed more than he intended, he belatedly tried to act as if he was puzzled by the question.

"What child?"

Nate hid a smile. *Gotcha.*

"It was in the newspaper," he said.

"I don't know what you're talking about," the older man said.

He did. Nate was absolutely certain of that. Whether the child had anything to do with what was happening in Curry today, was another question.

"Maybe this will remind you." Nate dug into his pocket to pull out the copy of the clipping. He walked across the patio to shove it into Walter's hand.

With obvious reluctance, the man unfolded the paper to read the short article.

A muscle knotted in his jaw before he shoved the clipping back to Nate.

"That was a long time ago," he said.

Nate carefully folded it and slid it back into his pocket. "When exactly?"

"I don't know *exactly*," Walter snapped. "Twenty years or so."

"That's a little vague."

"That's all I got."

"Who was the child?" Nate demanded.

"I don't remember the name."

Nate displayed his disbelief with a dramatic roll of his eyes.

"A child is found roaming alone at night and you don't remember the name?"

The older man looked like he wanted to take a swing at Nate. He probably did. Not that long ago Walter Perry had been the law in Curry. He could tell people what to do and expect them to obey without question. It had to be hard for him to be in a position where he couldn't force Nate to go the hell away.

Or preferably, to shoot him.

"It happens more often than you think," Walter said between clenched teeth. "Kids have a habit of sneaking out of doors and windows or climbing over back fences. In this case I believe the grandparents were camping nearby and didn't even realize the child was missing until the next morning. They were scared out of their minds when they arrived at my office." He forced a smile. Nate shuddered. It looked weird. The older man's face looked like it had developed rigor mortis. "Thankfully for all of us, I still had the child there."

"Was it a boy or girl?"

"I think a boy," Walter said so quickly it was obvious he was just throwing out the words. "I reunited them, and they left the area."

It was a convenient story. A lost kid. Distraught grandparents. And then glorious reunion before they drove off into the sunset. It was also impossible to prove or disprove.

"Did you write up a report?" Nate asked, even though he already knew the answer. "That should have the names of the grandparents as well as the people who found the child."

"There's no report." Walter abruptly pointed toward the gate at the side of the house. "Now it's time for you to leave."

Nate held the older man's gaze. "You know I'm not going to stop until I have the truth."

He expected another attempt at innocence. Or even anger. Instead Walter backed toward the door, his breath rasping in and out like he was having trouble getting enough air.

"If you care about Eloise Guthrie, you'll let this go," he rasped.

Nate's hand instinctively moved to the gun he had holstered beneath his hoodie.

"Is that a threat?"

"It's a warning."

Clearly done with the conversation, Walter stomped into the house and slammed the screen door behind him.

Nate cursed, his feet frozen in place.

He could go inside and try to beat the truth out of Walter, which would probably land him in jail with no assurance that the older man actually knew who was responsible for killing his son. He couldn't risk leaving Ellie alone.

So what next?

With a grimace, he headed for the gate.

He'd been bluffing when he'd claimed he'd contact his FBI buddies for information on the clinic. He didn't want to take advantage of his old friends.

But there were still his brothers to tap.

It didn't matter if he was taking advantage of them.

They were family.

It's late morning before I can at last return home. Stepping into my shower I turn it on as hot as it will go, allowing the water to wash away the blood even as I savor the events of the day.

It'd all been so simple.

I'd followed Dr. Booker to his house and slipped in behind him, hitting him in his skinny ass with a cattle prod. Of course, I'd never used one before, so I had it set on maximum voltage. The good doctor had pissed his pants and careened across his room filled with frou-frou antiques. His flailing arms sent them crashing to the ground before he landed in a heap on the Persian carpet.

He wasn't out for long, but it offered me the chance to get him securely bound with duct tape I found in the garage. He wasn't much of a threat. Like all of my enemies, he was a pathetic coward at heart, but I didn't want any mistakes. Not when I was so close to my goal.

I adjusted the prod. I wanted pain, lots of pain, but I didn't want him passing out. Our time together, after all, was limited.

Waiting until he was able to form coherent words, I urged him to talk about the past. I wanted him to confess the truth. To reveal his sins.

He cried. He told me he'd been forced into making terrible choices. Boo-hoo.

Next, he'd moved on to the bargaining stage. He'd offered me money. And drugs. Finally, he promised to help me destroy the others.

There truly was no honor among thieves.

In fact, I've come to the conclusion over the years that there is no honor among the human race. Including myself.

We are all selfish. Greedy. And liars.

To ourselves and others.

Once I was sure that he accepted that death was in his future, I laid aside the prod and pulled out the knife that he'd helpfully had in his kitchen. It was big and sharp and it fit my hand as if it'd been made for me.

The drug overdoses had been fine for Daniel and Mandy, but the doctor's sins couldn't be washed away so easily.

He was special.

I didn't want a peaceful end. I wanted blood.

I'd moved toward the groveling weakling, and made my first slice. It was awkward and shallow, but the dark red liquid spilled down his face, dropping to the carpet.

Splat. Splat. Splat.

My heart swells with awe.

It's beautiful. Lovely, lovely death.

I slice again. And again.

At the time, I don't think of the tedious details. Like disposing of the body. Or returning home without anyone seeing the gory stains that cover me from head to foot.

All that matters is the knife as it arcs through the air, sending droplets of blood raining around us.

Only later will I concentrate on the next move in my intricate game.

I smile, the warm water of the shower pouring over me.

One stone. Two birds.

Chapter Twenty-Seven

Ellie and Nate stood near the treeline at the edge of the cemetery. A hundred feet away a large crowd huddled around a plain coffin as it was being lowered into the ground.

A shudder raced through Ellie. It had nothing to do with the brisk breeze that tugged at her black dress and tumbled her loose hair over her face. The afternoon sunlight was warm enough to chase away any chill. It was the pulse of dread that throbbed in the air. As if some dark premonition had settled over Curry, shrouding them in fear.

Or maybe it was just her.

She gave a small shake of her head, instinctively pressing closer to the man at her side.

"I think the whole town is here," she said, her gaze skimming over the horde of mourners.

A part of the reason she'd decided to attend the funeral was because she was afraid there wouldn't be anyone there. And of course, to keep an eye on her father and the other men connected to Hopewell Clinic.

She'd only had a couple minutes to discuss Nate's meeting with Walter Perry, as well as reveal her tense confrontation with her father, but neither she nor Nate had doubted that the men would be standing at Barb's graveside.

They held a secret that might very well have been the death of her father's onetime secretary. As well as Daniel and Mandy.

That secret would most certainly lure them to her graveside.

"Barb was born and raised in Curry," Nate pointed out in low tones, his arm circling her shoulders. "She probably knew everyone in town."

Ellie grimaced. When Barb had gone to jail for driving without a license, she didn't have one friend to call and bail her out.

"She might have been raised with these people, but none of them would talk to her when she was alive."

"Death erases a lot of sins," Nate said dryly. "And there are probably a lot of people here because they're scared."

She turned her head, studying Nate. He looked even more gorgeous than usual in his charcoal slacks and chunky ivory sweater, but she didn't miss the muscle twitching in his clenched jaw or the fact that she could actually feel the tension vibrating off him.

Over the past twenty-four hours he'd gone from full-alert to DEFCON 1.

"Scared of what?" she asked.

"What do you suppose Curry's death rate is?" Nate asked. "One a month? Maybe two. And the people who die are old or have been sick for a long time. Suddenly there've been four people dead in a matter of days." He turned his head, glancing toward the mound of dirt that now covered Daniel. "Three of them under the age of thirty. The town is searching for answers."

Another shiver raced through her body. Would she ever be warm again?

"Yeah, me too," she muttered.

His gaze returned to the group gathered around the open grave. "And then there's the inevitable sightseers."

"Nate," Ellie breathed in protest. Curry might have the usual nosy neighbors that filled every small town in America, but they didn't take pleasure in death. "That's just ghoulish."

"I'm not judging them, it's human nature," Nate insisted. "In fact, I had an aunt who attended at least three funerals a week."

Her eyes widened. Was he joking? Sometimes it was hard to tell with this man.

"Three a week?" she repeated.

"Yep." He kept his voice pitched low so it wouldn't carry. Not that anyone would hear him over the droning sermon from the pastor. The man hadn't known Barb, but that didn't stop him from offering a full-throated lecture on succumbing to temptation. Or had he moved on to the evils of the flesh? Hard to tell. "She'd get up in the morning and look through the obituaries in the paper. If there was a service nearby, she'd put on her favorite black dress and pearls and call my mother to drive her to the funeral parlor."

Ellie had never known any relatives beyond her parents, but she couldn't imagine having an aunt who went to random funerals. Her father would have locked her in the wine cellar.

"No one tried to stop her?" she asked, genuinely curious.

He looked confused by her question. "Why would we? It gave her a reason to get out of the house and socialize." He shrugged. "She met her third husband at a wake."

She swallowed an inappropriate laugh. "No way."

"She did." Nate lifted a hand in a solemn pledge of honesty. "Uncle Benny. You'll meet him at the annual Fourth of July picnic."

All thoughts of the morbid aunt and her new husband, Uncle Benny, were seared away by his casual words. He acted as if her presence at a family gathering was not only possible, but expected.

She waited for the panic to thunder through her. She had no interest in happily ever after. Not with any man. Right?

But the only emotion she could pinpoint was an unexpected tingle of anticipation.

Ridiculously, that was more unsettling than the more familiar reaction.

"I'm not really into picnics," she told him.

He smiled. Did he sense her inner conflict? Probably.

"You'll love this one, I promise," he said. "Fried chicken. Potato salad. Apple pie. Cold beer."

"And Uncle Benny?"

He nodded. "Plus a hundred other relatives."

It was disturbingly easy to imagine a holiday in the Marcel home. The comfortable ranch house in the suburbs of Chicago. The laughing children who would spill into the backyard to pester the men who would be gathered around the barbecue. And Nate's mother, supervising her kitchen as she glanced out the window to smile with pride at her sons.

A normal family who loved one another despite their differences.

"Can't we wait on the whole family meet-and-greet for a while?" she demanded.

He studied her wary expression, then without warning, his lips twitched. Did he suspect that her unease came more from her strange yearning than any fear of his family?

"How long?"

"I don't know." She cleared her throat. "Five or ten years."

"No way. As soon as they find out you're staying at the ranch they'll start descending on us," he warned, giving a swooping motion with his hand. "Like locusts."

Ellie's vision of a happy family-gathering transformed to one of buzzing insects chasing her around Nate's ranch.

"Then don't tell them," she urged.

"My mother's psychic. She probably already knows."

He wasn't helping. "Does she also know that I'll be returning to my own house once it's repaired?" she demanded.

His smile widened. "We'll see."

With a shake of her head, Ellie returned her attention to the crowd that was beginning to scatter. Like ants scurrying from a disturbed nest. They might have their own reasons for attending the funeral, but each of them was in a hurry to be away from the graveyard.

"I think it's over," she murmured, taking a step forward as she caught sight of her father making a beeline for the Rolls-Royce he'd left parked on the road in front of the cemetery.

Nate reached out to grab her arm. "Wait."

She sent him an impatient frown. "I want to speak with my father."

He leaned down to speak directly in her ear as the various citizens of Curry rushed past them.

"Let's see what happens."

"I don't understand."

"Trust me."

Frustration twisted her gut as her father turned his head, his gaze searching the crowd until he found her. His expression was unreadable as he crawled into his car and drove away.

He was up to something.

She was certain of that.

"Nate."

"I got this." Clasping her hand, he led her through the trees to his truck, which he'd left parked on a narrow dirt path.

Together they climbed in the vehicle and he fired the engine, turning onto a gravel road that led away from town. Ellie frowned, pulling on her seat belt as they bounced over the ruts.

"Where are we going?"

Nate kept his gaze on the road, his hands clenched tight on the steering wheel.

"I don't think your father is headed back to the motel."

Ellie parted her lips to demand exactly where he thought her father was going, only to snap them shut as they were almost bounced off the road as they hit a truly impressive pothole. Nate's precious vehicle was as smooth as a log wagon under the best circumstances. Now it felt like they were on a cheap carnival ride.

She wanted his concentration fully focused on keeping them out of the ditch.

They continued on the back roads that went from bad to worse. Ellie clung to the door handle, studying the empty prairie that gave no clue to where they were or where they were headed. Since moving to Curry, she hadn't spent much time beyond the outskirts of town. She went to work. She went home. And if she traveled, it was to Tulsa or Oklahoma City.

It wasn't until Nate was halting in the shadows of an old barn that she managed to get her bearings.

Nate switched off the engine and together they climbed out and crept around the side of the barn. Halting at the corner, they peered across the road at the field where Daniel and Mandy's bodies had been dumped.

Within a few minutes a truck and three cars were pulling to a halt at the side of the road.

"Neville. The Mayor. My father. The sheriff." Ellie named the men as they stepped out of their vehicles. As a group they moved through the open gate and into the field. It was too far to know exactly where they halted to huddle in a small circle, but Ellie suspected that it was near the crumbling foundation where the Hopewell Clinic had once stood. She frowned as she realized there was one missing. "Where's the doctor?"

"Good question," Nate said, sending her an approving glance. "He wasn't at the funeral."

"Could he be responsible for what's been happening?"

He tilted his head to the side, as if running the theory through his brain.

"He's familiar with Curry and has a connection to Hopewell Clinic."

"Along with the board members," she added.

"It's possible that he blames one or more of them for causing the fire that burned down his clinic."

"Or he burned it down and is warning the others not to talk."

They shared a grimace. The theories were lame.

They both knew it.

Nate turned his attention back to the group of men who looked like they were sharing an animated conversation.

"Damn. I hate this flat countryside. There's no way to get close enough to overhear them," he groused.

Ellie grabbed his arm. He was stubborn enough to try and find some way to sneak toward the group.

"It looks like they're arguing," she said, watching her father point his finger in the face of the sheriff. She recognized that finger-pointing. Colin Guthrie was chastising the man for having failed to fulfill his expectations. Something he'd done to her on a regular basis. "This has to have something to do with the clinic," she continued. "Otherwise there would be no reason to meet in this spot."

"It seems the most logical conclusion, but without proof we need to keep our options open," he warned.

"You sound like an FBI agent," she muttered, her hand tightening on his arm as Walter turned from the group and stomped toward his vehicle. "I think the meeting is over. Should we follow my father?"

Nate shook his head. "Let's go back to the ranch. I want to call my brother."

She hesitated before following him to the back of the barn and climbing into his truck. There wasn't any point in trying to confront her father again. Not until she had proof he was involved in something nefarious.

They waited in silence until the group across the road had driven away. Only then did Nate reach down to turn the key. A wise choice. The engine coughed and sputtered as if it was on its deathbed before it finally roared to deafening life.

Resisting the urge to tell him he needed to shoot the truck and put it out of its misery, Ellie instead concentrated on his decision to return to his ranch.

"Why do you want to call your brother?" she asked as they returned to the back roads to avoid the departing men.

"I want to see if he can discover any info on the mystery child who was found."

Ellie sent him a startled glance. Nate had made it clear that he didn't believe Walter's explanation, but it seemed an odd time to focus on the random newspaper clipping they'd found in Barb's envelope.

"Do you think it's connected to what's been happening?"

"I don't know."

There was an edge in his voice that warned he was on his last nerve. She sympathized. It felt like they were blindly floundering for the truth that remained just out of reach.

It was exasperating.

"Okay." She used her best lawyer voice. Whenever she was stuck on a case, she would clear her mind and start over from the beginning. "Let's try to piece together what we *do* know." She held up one finger. "First, Daniel either overdosed or was murdered and tossed in Neville's field."

Nate released a slow breath, visibly relaxing his clenched muscles. "Perhaps after he was hired to slash your tires," he added.

"Yes." Ellie wrinkled her nose. She'd almost forgotten

Nate's suspicion that Daniel had been paid to harass her. "So his death could be because he's the son of Walter Perry or because he could name who'd hired him."

"A few hours later someone calls the sheriff's office to report the body," Nate said.

Ellie nodded. They needed to know who made that call. It seemed hard to believe that someone stumbled across it in the remote field. But why would the killer call? Especially after they'd tried to make it look like an overdose?

Just another layer of confusion. She swallowed her frustration.

"We know that Tia was being followed," she continued. "And that Mandy was being pestered by vandals."

"It could have been the work of the killer or someone who was hired to continue the harassment."

She shivered. "Like the rats on my patio."

"Exactly." Nate slowed to a crawl, turning onto the main road that would lead to his ranch. "We also know that all of you are the children of the board members of the Hopewell Clinic. Daniel. Tia. Mandy. And you."

She didn't have to add that two of them were already dead. It hung in the air with a heavy sense of dread.

"Next, Barb contacts me," Ellie continued, resisting the sudden urge to glance over her shoulder. Whoever might be hunting her was a master at lurking in the shadows. He wouldn't be obliging enough to follow her in broad daylight. "But she dies before she can say more than that people are in danger."

Nate continued his leisurely pace as they neared his home. Ellie fully approved. She was still feeling bruised from their mad dash to Neville Morse's field.

"I wonder if an autopsy was performed," he mused.

Ellie felt a pang of annoyance. She should have put in a greater effort to discover if Barb had an heir, and if that person had demanded to know the cause of death. The local hospital had limited resources. Without family or law enforcement pressing for answers, they might have closed the file with the assumption it'd been a natural passing.

"I'll call the hospital when we get to the ranch. I did act as her lawyer. They might be willing to give me an answer."

Nate nodded. "We can't be sure what she meant by the warning, but it's possible that she was killed to prevent her from talking to you. We need to know how she died."

"And why the killer or someone else searched her house," she added. "We assumed it was for the file we found, but it could have been something they took before we arrived."

"In the meantime, Mandy was lured to the field and injected with enough heroin to kill her," Nate said, his thumbs tapping on the steering wheel.

Ellie felt a sharp pang of sadness. Not only at the thought of poor Mandy being killed and discarded like a piece of trash, but at the realization that little Charlie's life had been forever changed. Children never fully recovered from the death of their mother.

"The same field where the Hopewell Clinic used to be," she said.

"What does all that tell us?"

She heaved a sigh. She'd hoped that listing the events out loud would jog something in her brain. Instead, she felt as confused as ever.

"Absolutely nothing."

"I wouldn't . . ." Nate's words trailed away as he abruptly swerved the truck to the side of the road. "What the hell?"

"What's wrong?"

He unhooked his seat belt and shoved open his door. "I recognize that car."

Baffled by his twitchy reaction, Ellie glanced toward the yellow Camaro parked near the drainage ditch. She hadn't seen it around town. Nate, however, was climbing out of the truck and heading toward the vehicle.

Quickly scrambling to follow him, she reached his side just as he was leaning forward to peer through the front windshield.

"This belongs to the Harper brothers," he told her.

Ellie suddenly understood his tension. With Larry dead, and his brother missing, this car was a last tangible link to them.

"You're sure?" she demanded.

"Positive." He gave an impatient wave of his hand. "It's impossible that there's another car exactly like this one in the area. Look at those stupid dice."

Ellie wrinkled her nose. He had a point. The car had faded to a weird shade of jaundice and rust. Plus, the back window had been replaced with duct tape. And, of course, there was a pair of fuzzy dice hanging from the mirror.

It did seem like it was one-of-a-kind.

She glanced around. They were just a few feet from Nate's back pasture. To the east she could see the silhouette of his house, and if she turned toward the north, she could make out the roofline of her own home. But there was nothing else in sight.

She turned back to Nate. "How did it get here?"

He shook his head. "I don't know. It wasn't here when we left for the funeral."

Ellie thought back. They'd both been on the back porch to share a light lunch before they'd headed back to town. They would have easily seen the car from there.

"Which means that Larry wasn't driving it," she said, pointing out the obvious. "Do you think the killer left it here?"

"It was either the killer or Bert." Nate's face was tight with tension. He reached out as if he intended to open the door.

"No," she rasped. "Stay back."

Nate sent her a startled glance. "I just want to make sure there's no one inside."

"Don't touch it," she insisted. "It might be booby-trapped."

His brows arched. "Booby-trapped?"

Okay. That did sound stupid when he said it out loud. But that didn't ease the dread that was twisting her gut into a tight knot. Her feminine intuition was screaming that there was something wrong with the car.

Something terrible.

"You don't know." She clenched her hands, considering the best way to convince him to listen to her warning. "Besides, you don't want your fingerprints on there."

Nate abruptly pulled his hand back. "True."

She released a low breath of relief as Nate cautiously moved around the car, peering into the various windows. He was still closer than she wanted him to be, but at least he wasn't touching it.

"Is there anything inside?" she asked as he finished his circuit.

He straightened, giving a sharp shake of his head. "There's too much junk to know for certain. There could be a dozen bodies hidden beneath the trash."

Ellie flinched. "Don't even tease about it."

"Sorry."

She moved back to the truck to grab her handbag, pulling out her cell phone.

"We need to call the sheriff."

Nate started to reach into his pocket. "I'll do it."

"No. I will," she insisted. With crisp efficiency, she dialed the number to the office, leaving a message when she was told that the sheriff was in a meeting. Then, shoving the phone back in her purse, she moved until she was standing directly in front of Nate. "Look at me," she commanded.

He met her stern gaze with a hint of amusement. "What?"

"When the sheriff arrives, I'm not the woman who shares your bed, I'm your lawyer," she informed him. "Got it?"

He looked more curious than alarmed. "You think I need a lawyer?"

She resisted the urge to roll her eyes. She was used to dealing with people who were accustomed to run-ins with law enforcement. Which meant they understood the danger of saying anything that might aggravate the situation.

Nate, on the other hand, assumed his previous connection to the FBI ensured that he didn't have to play by the same rules as others.

It was an assumption that was going to get his ass thrown in jail if he wasn't careful.

"Yeah. I think you need a lawyer," she said, pointing a finger in his face. "Which means you keep your mouth shut and let me speak."

"I'm not very good at that," he drawled.

"Nate. I'm serious."

"Fine. Once the sheriff gets here, I'll keep my mouth shut," he promised, turning back to the car. He slowly shook his head. "I don't like this. It feels like a warning."

Ellie agreed. She stepped to stand at his side, that odd forewarning crawling over her skin.

"Or a setup," she said. She'd had one client framed for theft by his ex-girlfriend. It had been easy to do. She had a key to his house, so all she had to do was dump her jewelry in his underwear drawer late one night and then call the cops, claiming that he'd broken into her apartment and stolen her things. "The killer already left a body in your building and now the victim's car is left a hundred yards from your house."

Nate snorted, not looking nearly worried enough. "If he's trying to pin the murder on me, he's being a little too obvious."

She shook her head. "Not when you have a sheriff who has the investigative skills of a slug," she reminded him. "Besides, the killer's goal might not be to get you locked up for murder. He might be trying to keep both of us distracted."

Nate's breath hissed between his clenched teeth. "True. Which means we must be getting too close for comfort."

"Too close to what?"

"The Hopewell Clinic," he suggested. "The fire. The mystery child."

"Or none of those."

They shared a glance of smoldering annoyance. It was impossible to know why the car had been left in this particular spot. Or even for sure if it'd been the work of the killer.

Another question with no answer.

Ten minutes later the sheriff arrived in a cloud of dust. He pulled his SUV behind Nate's truck and climbed out with a sour expression on his square face. Behind him, Deputy Clay followed like an eager puppy.

"Remember," Ellie muttered as she felt Nate stiffen at her side.

Gary Clark was still a hundred feet away and already the air was bristling with male aggression.

Nate folded his arms over his chest. "Yeah, yeah. Keep my mouth closed."

The sheriff halted in the middle of the road, his gaze flicking over Nate before moving to study Ellie with blatant impatience.

"This had better be good, Ms. Guthrie. I don't have time to waste on wild-goose chases."

She ignored his chiding tone and pasted on her most professional expression.

"My client and I were driving to his ranch when we spotted this abandoned car," she said, nodding toward the Camaro.

Gary's face flushed and Deputy Clay took a hurried step backward. Was he afraid his boss might become violent?

"You called me out here because someone parked their car on the side of a public road?" he snapped. "Do you think this is some sort of joke?"

Ellie maintained her composure. "My client suspects that it might belong to Larry Harper or his brother."

Gary's bluster faltered. "Larry Harper," he repeated. "The dead man?"

"Yes."

The sheriff shot Nate a suspicious frown. "How did it get here?"

Ellie answered before Nate could be badgered into breaking his promise. "Obviously, we don't know."

"There's nothing obvious about it." The sheriff nervously hitched up his pants, his original impatience being replaced with anger. They all knew he was in over his head. Now he was once again being forced to display his lack of competence. And worse, it was in front of Nate, whom he clearly envied. "First a dead body is found in his building and now the man's car is at his house."

Ellie shrugged. "You just said it was parked on a public road."

Gary stabbed a finger toward Nate's house. "Might as well be in his driveway."

Ellie smiled. "But it's not."

Her refusal to react to his accusations only provoked the man's anger. Lifting his hand, he gave a snap of his fingers.

"Clay, start taking some pictures," he commanded. "I want the whole area photographed, including the road, in case these two didn't destroy all the tire tracks. Then, get the kit out of the trunk and start dusting the car for prints." Hitching up his pants, he headed toward the Camaro. "Did you touch it?" he demanded of Nate.

"He did not," Ellie quickly answered.

Gary glanced over his shoulder at Nate. "So if we find your prints, you don't have an easy explanation."

Nate reached his breaking point. He stepped forward, his jaw jutted to an aggressive angle.

"You won't find my prints."

The sheriff sniffed as he pulled a pair of rubber gloves from his pocket and snapped them on.

"We'll see."

Ellie elbowed Nate in the ribs. She understood his irritation. Gary Clark could test the patience of a saint. But the sheriff did have a reason to be suspicious. As he said, the body of Larry Harper had been found in Nate's building. With the key to the back door in his pocket. And now Larry's car was parked just behind his property.

Nate grimaced, clearly realizing that he'd allowed his temper to override his common sense. With a shrug, he snapped his lips shut as the sheriff pulled open the car door and started to rummage through the trash. The lawman looked under the seats and in the back, shuffling through piles of fast food wrappers and beer cans.

Finally satisfied there was nothing to be found in the junk, he opened the glove compartment. He pulled out the wad of papers, sorting through them with a frown before he tossed them onto the floor with the rest of the mess. Then he popped the trunk.

Circling the car, Gary kicked up tiny puffs of dust, impatiently waving away Clay, who had a camera and was enthusiastically snapping pictures of everything in sight. Then, grabbing the trunk lid, he shoved it up.

Instantly a gagging stench filled the air, sending the sheriff reeling backward to land on his ass in the middle of the road.

Ellie slapped a hand over her nose and mouth, frantically telling herself not to look. There was only one thing that could cause that particular smell.

Of course, she couldn't help herself.

She could no more stop her gaze from moving to the bloody corpse that was stuffed in the trunk than she could stop her heart from beating.

It was a compulsion.

"Oh my God," she choked out.

Even at a distance she could make out the horrific slashes that had been inflicted on the poor man. In places, they were deep enough to expose white bone. And the blood . . . She shuddered. It was everywhere. Soaked into his hair, his clothing, and the carpet of the trunk.

He looked like someone had taken an axe and tried to chop him into tiny bits.

Beside her Nate leaned forward, his muscles clenched as his breath rasped loudly in the awful silence.

"That's Dr. Booker," he at last said in grim tones. "I guess we know why he wasn't at Barb's funeral."

The sheriff managed to shove himself to his feet, his face white. But even as he visibly battled his urge to vomit, he was pulling out his handgun and pointing it at Nate.

"Don't move a muscle."

Chapter Twenty-Eight

Walter woke, dazed and confused.

It wasn't the first time. Or even the hundredth time.

Over the past twenty-five years, he'd spent the majority of his nights home alone, drinking his way to the bottom of a whiskey bottle.

It was a secret that he'd managed to hide from the world.

Not the entire world, a voice whispered in the back of his mind. His wife had tried to curb his nightly habit before she'd finally thrown in the towel and walked away. And in time, Daniel had grown old enough to realize that his father's slurred words and stumbles over his own feet weren't because he was tired.

A fact that Daniel had thrown in his face whenever Walter complained about his son's drug abuse.

"I don't take advice from a washed-up sheriff who is shit-faced by nine o'clock," the younger man would taunt.

Walter tried to move, grunting as a sharp pain shot through his head.

This morning was worse than usual. Probably because he'd started earlier than usual. As soon as he'd returned from that idiotic meeting in Neville's field.

It'd been Colin's idea to meet there. He said he wanted to

remind them all of what they had to lose. As if Barb's funeral hadn't been enough of a reminder. And then the arrogant ass had spent the next ten minutes chastising them. As if it was their fault that things were unraveling.

Walter muttered a curse. He'd not only lost his son to some madman, but he'd risked everything to break into Barb's house and search for the missing file that the drunken bitch had been trying to use to blackmail them.

And now Colin was insisting that he discover who was responsible before the mystery killer could hurt Ellie. How the hell was he supposed to do that? He was just an old man who'd retired a long time ago.

With a groan, he tried to sit up, only to discover he couldn't move.

What was happening? Fear blasted through him. Was it a stroke? The doctor had been warning him for years that his drinking was going to lead him to an early grave.

Just like Barb.

Then he managed to clench his hands, and he realized that his muscles weren't paralyzed. Plus, there was the rattle of metal when he tried to move. It wasn't a medical emergency. He couldn't move because he was cuffed to the bed.

His fear remained as he tried to process what was going on.

He was in his bed . . .

Wait. He blinked, trying to peer through the gloom. This wasn't his bed. He was in the basement. He could tell by the small window that was cut in the foundation near the drop ceiling and the faint smell of mold.

This was Daniel's room.

Or at least it had been before Walter had kicked him out.

How had he gotten here? Had he been pushed down the stairs? It felt like it. Not only did his head throb, but there was a deep ache in his body. He felt bruised from head to toe.

But how had he gotten in the bed? And who had stripped

him naked before cuffing his wrists and ankles to the bedposts so he was spread-eagled on the mattress?

His mouth went dry. His brain might be rattled and still fogged with alcohol, but he knew he wasn't going to like the answer.

Summoning the strength to try and struggle against the cuffs, Walter froze when he heard a rustle coming from the shadows on the far side of the room.

"Hello?" he called out, trying to tell himself that it must be one of Daniel's druggie friends. He'd always worried that one of them would come to the house to rob him. But why would they tie him up? That didn't make any sense. "Hello?" he called again. "I know someone's there."

"I began to wonder if you would ever wake up."

The voice was low and muffled, making it impossible for him to recognize. Hell, he didn't even know if they were male or female.

Walter frowned. The person had been hanging around, waiting for him to regain consciousness. Which meant this wasn't a simple robbery. It also made him suspect that it wasn't just his usual hangover that was making it difficult to think.

"You drugged me," he said, his voice hoarse.

"Just a few pills in your whiskey," the intruder drawled. "I didn't know you intended to drink the whole bottle."

Walter muttered an angry curse. No wonder he'd slept through his trip down the stairs. Not to mention being handcuffed to the bed.

"Who the hell are you?" he ground out. "Show yourself."

"Not yet. First we're going to have a little chat."

"I'm not in the mood to chat."

There was a creepy chuckle that made Walter's skin crawl. "I don't suppose you are."

Walter's burst of anger receded as his fear thundered back

with a vengeance. Was this the person responsible for killing Daniel and Mandy?

Was he next?

"Listen." He tried to make his voice cajoling. "Untie me from this bed and we'll talk like civilized people. I'll chat about anything you want."

"No," came the immediate response. "I like seeing you strapped down. Turnabout is fair play after all."

Fair play? Had he arrested this person in the past? That might explain why they wanted to hurt him. And even Daniel. But what about Mandy?

"I don't know what you're talking about," he said.

"Of course not," the stranger mocked. "You had nothing to do with Hopewell Clinic, did you?"

Walter jerked, as if he'd taken a punch to the gut. Oh God. It was exactly what they'd feared.

"What's your connection to the clinic?"

"We're talking about you."

Walter tried to think. Not an easy task when he was naked and chained to his dead son's bed. But he was a survivor. If he could just get his captor close enough he might be able to . . .

Okay. He didn't really know what he could do while he was chained. But as long as he had a breath in his body he was going to struggle to stay alive.

"I'm not saying a word until you show yourself," he blustered.

Without warning, there was a thin band of pressure around his neck. Walter gasped, belatedly realizing there was a wire noose around his throat.

"I don't like your attitude, Sheriff Perry," the person mocked.

"Stop," he rasped, tears trickling down his cheeks when the pressure slowly eased. It was one thing to contemplate death. It was another to stare it directly in the face. "Please. What do you want?"

"I told you. I want to chat."

He drew in a shaky breath. Deep down he knew that his tormentor hadn't gone to such efforts just to chat, but he clung to the futile hope that if he kept the person talking long enough, he might find a way to escape. Or someone might come looking for him.

Miracles happened.

"About Hopewell?" he asked.

"Yes."

"What do you want to know?"

There was another rustle. Was the intruder making himself comfortable? The thought was as disturbing as the noose around his neck.

It implied the person was supremely confident that there would be no interruptions.

"How did it start?" the intruder demanded.

Walter cleared the lump from his throat, forcing his thoughts back thirty years ago.

In those days he'd been the sheriff. A position that'd held a lot more respect than it did now. In the town of Curry his word had been law, and he'd enjoyed the power that had come with his shiny badge.

He'd also been married to his high school sweetheart, who was nagging at him to start a family, and in the middle of constructing a new house that was costing him a fortune.

"Dr. Booker received a grant," he said, offering the story that they'd all rehearsed for years. "I guess he thought he could make a difference with the patients who were sent to him."

"How very altruistic," the intruder said. "Now tell me the real story."

"That is the real story. The doctor built the clinic and asked me to be on the board. That's all I know."

There was a sound, like the clicking of a tongue. "You shouldn't lie to me."

"I'm not."

He caught a scent as if the person was leaning forward. Was it familiar? Maybe.

"The good doctor already told me that you were the one who came up with the plan to create the supposed clinic."

Walter flinched, rattling his cuffs. He'd wondered where Dr. Booker had been. They'd all expected him to attend Barb's funeral. Or at least make an appearance at the meeting that Colin had insisted on.

Was he dead?

Or had the bastard saved his neck by ratting out the rest of them? It wouldn't surprise Walter. The doctor had always been the weakest link. Unfortunately, he'd been necessary to their plans.

"That's bullshit," he growled. He wasn't going to be thrown under the bus. It was every man for himself now. "Booker was the chief of staff. Anything that happened there was his responsibility."

"He said you came to him," the stranger insisted. "That you'd heard the government was handing out money to keep junkies out of prison."

Damn that coward. "I might have heard about the grant—" Walter's words were choked off as the noose tightened.

"It was you who created that hell on earth," the intruder accused in his muffled voice.

"No."

"What did I say about lying?"

Walter gagged, his tongue hanging out as the noose squeezed his throat with enough pressure to cut off the air.

"You're killing me," he gasped.

"Not yet," the voice taunted. "Admit that you were responsible."

"I admit that I brought the grant application to the cabin," Walter rasped. Inwardly he swore that if he ever got ahold of Booker, he was going to kill him with his own hands.

The pressure eased. At least enough for Walter to draw in a gasping breath.

"The cabin?" the intruder demanded.

His memories once again wandered back in time. To the days when he'd been young and brash and certain that the world was his to conquer.

"It was a rundown shack on Neville's land where we used to get together on Thursday nights to play poker."

"Who?"

"Just a few guys," he hedged.

"Say the names."

"Me. Neville Morse. Dr. Booker." He was certain the intruder already knew they were involved.

"And?"

Walter hesitated. His life wasn't great. He'd lost his wife, his self-respect, and now his son. But that didn't mean things couldn't get worse if he revealed the entire truth.

The thought had barely flashed through his mind when there was the faintest tug of the noose.

Screw it. Right now, it was all about survival.

"Mayor Chambers. Colin Guthrie," he quickly confessed. "That's it."

The noose eased. "You convinced them to apply for the grant?"

"It wasn't like that."

"Then what was it like?"

Walter grimaced. The five of them had met at the Lodge, back when it actually was a Lodge and not a shady tavern.

They'd all been drawn together by their positions of respect in the community, as well as their unspoken ambition.

It'd been a natural progression to start getting together in private to share a few hands of cards, some fine whiskey, and a few hours of venting.

"We'd been complaining that we all worked in jobs that were meant to serve and protect the public. Even Neville was a volunteer fireman," he explained. "But we got crap pay for our sacrifices."

"Yeah. Such great sacrifices," the intruder mocked.

Walter bristled with a defensive anger. No one understood the pressures they'd had to endure. Especially him. How many nights had he worked late, breaking up a drunken fight between neighbors, or holding a woman's hand after her fine, upstanding husband had beat the crap out of her? It wasn't easy babysitting the citizens of Curry.

"We did our duty," he insisted. "We deserved more than the chicken feed we were paid."

They were words that he'd repeated to himself over and over. Sometimes he even believed them.

"And the grant offered you that opportunity?"

"It started as a joke." He tried to shrug, only to wince as the cold metal dug into his wrists. He'd never cared if he might be hurting someone when he slapped the cuffs on them. If he was arresting them, then they got what they deserved. "I brought the grant application and said we should get the money and run. A million dollars was a lot of money back then. But Neville said no, we should get the grant and put up a few pieces of plywood on his land and call it a clinic. That way we could keep the grant money, plus charge the government for monthly rent."

"But that wasn't enough for you?"

Walter shook his head. Looking back, it was easy to see how they'd goaded each other into behaving in a way none of them would have done on their own.

Group mentality. Or was it mob mentality?

It didn't matter. The results had been the same.

"It was the doctor who said the real profit was in the clients," he said.

"Profits." The word was spit out. "In human lives."

A chill inched down his spine. How much did the intruder know?

"He suggested that we have a few real patients who got treatment for addiction and then some fake patients who he could bill for services that he didn't have to provide," he hastily said. "That was the profit."

There was a long, tension-filled silence before his captor finally spoke.

"Fake patients."

"Yeah."

"Just so disappointing."

The words whispered through the air at the same time the noose was yanked tight. Walter screamed, his back bowing off the mattress. The pain was excruciating as the thin wire dug into his flesh.

Eventually the pressure eased and he managed to suck in enough air to speak.

"Okay," he squawked.

"The truth."

He hadn't been lying. After Hopewell Clinic opened, they'd filled a portion of the rooms with genuine patients. They'd even made certain that they were staffed with nurses, and a counselor who was in charge of the group therapy. Behind the scenes, however, the doctor was billing for twice the number of clients, while Neville had jacked up the cost of building the place, plus charging monthly rent.

It'd brought in a decent amount.

But money was as addictive as any drug.

No matter how much they made, they always wanted more. And more. And more.

"We started with the fake clients, then after a few months Colin said that he'd been approached by some powerful friends in Oklahoma City," he reluctantly admitted.

"Now we at last arrive at your most egregious sins," the stranger said.

Sins? The person sounded like a preacher. Or a judge.

Walter instinctively tried to deflect the guilt away from himself. "It wasn't me."

"Confess."

"It wasn't. I swear," he said in pleading tones. "Colin was the one to make the deal with those men."

"You mean the men who came to rape the poor women held prisoner in your clinic?"

Sweat dripped off Walter's naked body even as he shivered with fear.

He wanted to tell the intruder that if he could go back in time and change things, he would. That he would have stood up and said he wouldn't be a part of the sick scheme to allow Colin's powerful contacts around the state to use the women in the clinic for their own pleasure.

But the fear that the intruder would know he was lying made the words stick in his aching throat.

After all, Walter had been as eager as anyone when Colin first came to him with his plan. He'd sought out a few whores over the years and knew the dangers. No man wanted to troll the streets for a woman who might have a nasty disease.

They could charge a fortune to discreet customers who would enjoy the company of women who were regularly tested, bathed, and waxed, whether they wanted it or not, and who waited for them in comfortable rooms that were constantly monitored to make sure the women behaved themselves.

The truth was, they easily made five thousand dollars a night.

Pure profit.

"They weren't prisoners," he finally muttered.

"Bullshit."

"Colin brought in women to the clinic who wanted to trade off their jail time," he insisted. "It was their choice."

There was a scraping sound, as if a chair was being shoved aside. Or maybe the intruder had jumped to their feet.

"Did you warn them that the cost of avoiding jail was to service your rich and powerful buddies?"

"Most of the women were already prostitutes," he argued, falling back on the excuse they'd given to themselves.

"So you decided to become their pimps?"

Even though the voice remained muffled, it was easy to make out the person's anger. What was their connection to the place? One of the women who'd stayed at the clinic? If so, why would they wait so long to come back for revenge?

"They had a clean, decent place to live, plenty of food, medical services, drug rehabilitation, and free day care for their kids. Better than the streets."

A harsh laugh echoed through the basement. "As long as they didn't mind being raped several times a night, right?"

Walter's mouth was dry. He needed a drink. That was the only cure to block out the memories.

The women pleading for his help. The crying children. The smug smile on the men's faces as they strolled out of the private rooms in the back.

"We closed the place," he rasped, his hands clenching and unclenching. Abruptly he caught a familiar scent. Was that whiskey? Was his companion drinking?

Or was it a figment of his tortured brain?

"No, you didn't close it," the person countered. "It burned."

"I—" Walter bit back his words. The intruder didn't know the full truth. Thank God. "Yes, it burned."

"And now, old friend, *you* will burn."

"What?"

Walter was confused as he watched the heavily shrouded

form walk toward him. They couldn't actually mean that he was going to burn, could they? Then the figure held out an arm and Walter caught sight of the bottle. Whiskey. Just as he suspected. But the person wasn't offering it for Walter to take a drink. Instead the amber liquid was being doused over his naked body. Just like lighter fluid over charcoals.

Terror exploded through him as Walter frantically tugged at the cuffs, desperate to get free.

"No. What are you doing? I gave you what you wanted," he screamed, tears running down his face.

The intruder tossed aside the empty bottle, reaching beneath the heavy cloak. Seconds later there was a hissing sound and the scent of sulfur as the person lit a match. Walter watched in horror, realizing not even his worst nightmare could have prepared him for this end.

"No!"

Chapter Twenty-Nine

Ellie was tired. To-the-bone exhausted.

It wasn't just the fact that she'd spent the entire night at the courthouse while Nate was being interrogated by the sheriff. She'd spent a lot of long hours defending her clients from law enforcement without being near the edge of collapse. This weariness was a direct result of fear.

She knew Nate was innocent, but she couldn't deny there was enough evidence against him to give the sheriff ample reason to keep him locked up. She couldn't even argue when the lawman insisted on sending him to a holding cell.

Now she paced the hallway as the sun rose and the clock continued its relentless *tick tock, tick tock, tick tock*. Her feet were dragging, but her temperature was rising.

This was all so stupid. No matter how much evidence might be stacked against Nate, no one with a brain in their head would actually believe he was guilty. So why play this elaborate game?

Male ego?

She made a sound of disgust, whirling on her heel to head back into the office. Enough was enough.

As if on cue, Gary Clark stepped through the doorway. He was pulling on a black windbreaker with an official badge sewn on the sleeves and a matching baseball hat. He came to an abrupt halt when Ellie moved to stand directly in his path.

He didn't bother to hide his annoyance at the sight of her. "I told you to go home."

She planted her hands on her hips. "And I told you I'm not leaving until you release my client."

"I'm not done questioning him."

They both knew that he'd asked every question that could have some bearing on the death of Larry Harper and Dr. Booker. Plus a lot of questions that had no purpose but to annoy Nate.

"Then bring him back to the interrogation room so we can finish this farce," she commanded.

His jaw tightened. "I have every right to keep a dangerous criminal locked up."

"Not without charging him." Her voice rose an octave, echoing eerily through the empty hallway.

It reminded her that it was Sunday morning. Most people were no doubt still in bed. Where she would be if this stubborn fool wasn't so determined to prove who was boss.

"Don't push me, Ms. Guthrie," the sheriff growled, shoving past her to head for the nearby stairs.

He stormed away, not bothering to glance back. She expected him to flip her off. Before she could follow, his deputy, Clay, abruptly appeared. He was pulling on a jacket and had a determined expression on his face.

She hurried to stop him before he could disappear along with his boss. "Where are you going?"

The man hesitated, glancing down the hallway. Then, unable to resist the urge to share the latest gossip, he leaned toward her, speaking in a low voice.

"We just got word Walter's house burned down."

The ground seemed to lurch beneath her feet. "Walter Perry?"

"Yep."

"Was anyone hurt?"

He gave another look around, as if making sure the sheriff hadn't doubled back.

"The firemen just started the search, but just between the two of us, I heard on the scanner they found a body in the basement."

A body. The ground did that lurch thing again.

"The sheriff?"

He grimaced, his face draining of color. Had he just realized that the body would most likely belong to the man who owned the house?

"I guess it must be Walter, but we probably won't know for sure for a few days."

Ellie wrapped her arms around her waist, a cold horror spreading through her body. It was as if some malignant force was creeping through Curry, destroying anyone connected to Hopewell Clinic.

She gave a shake of her head. No. It wasn't a malignant force. It was a human with a pathological need to kill. And if they didn't discover whoever it was and stop them, the deaths would continue.

"This has to end," she told her companion in sharp tones.

Clay sent her a confused glance. "Beg pardon?"

"Release Nate." She reached out to grab his arm, willing to plead if necessary. "He's the only one with the skills to discover who is responsible for this madness."

He gently pulled out of her tight grasp, his expression wary. "That's not my call, Ms. Guthrie. The sheriff seems pretty determined to lock him up for some crime."

"You know he's innocent. Even Gary Clark knows he's innocent."

"The sheriff . . ." Clay allowed his words to trail away, lifting his hands in a gesture of defeat.

"What?"

"He's under a lot of pressure," Clay forced himself to explain. "Now's not the time to aggravate him."

Ellie snorted. She didn't believe it was pressure that made Gary Clark want to lock up Nate. It was plain jealousy. She also didn't doubt that the sheriff wasn't stupid enough to try and slap a murder charge on him.

Still, he had a lot of weapons to keep Nate in jail if he wanted.

"Meaning he'll keep Nate locked up on some petty charge just because he doesn't like him," she said in accusing tones.

Clay flushed. "I didn't say that."

"You didn't have to."

The deputy heaved a sigh. "Go home, Ms. Guthrie," he said, echoing the words of his boss. "It'll be a while before the sheriff returns."

Ellie clenched her hands into tight fists. This was no longer about an innocent man sitting in a holding cell just because a local lawman had his nose out of joint. There was someone out there hunting the citizens of Curry.

Someone had to stop them and she couldn't do it alone.

"We'll see about that," she warned, pivoting on her heel to head down the hallway.

"Ms. Guthrie," Clay called out.

Ellie ignored the deputy, picking up speed as she jogged down the staircase and out of the building. She blinked at the blinding sunlight that was a tangible reminder of just how many hours had been wasted trying to convince Gary Clark to come to his senses.

She was done being nice.

It was time to call in the big guns.

Angling across the patches of ground that would eventually be covered in grass, Ellie crossed to the corner where she'd left Nate's pickup.

After the sheriff had pulled his gun and cuffed Nate, they'd insisted on driving him to town in the official SUV. As if Nate was going to make a run for it. Ellie had jumped in the truck and followed just inches from the bumper. She wanted the sheriff to know that she was there, and that she wasn't going anywhere.

Once they were at the courthouse, she'd left the truck parked on the street. She'd completely forgotten that during Barb's funeral Nate had locked his cell phone and handgun in the glove compartment. Her focus had been on doing her job. That meant keeping her client from opening his mouth, and making sure he wasn't railroaded by the sheriff or his deputies.

Only when she'd been faced with the absolute certainty that unless she got Nate out of jail, someone else was going to die had she been struck by inspiration.

Or was it desperation?

She shrugged. It didn't matter.

She dug the keys out of her purse as she reached the truck. Pulling open the passenger door, she glanced around to ensure there was no one lurking around. The square was empty. She didn't know if the citizens were all at church, or if they were gathered around Walter's burning house, but right now her only interest was making her call without anyone interrupting her.

Unlocking the glove compartment, she pulled out the handgun and carefully laid it on the front seat. She briefly thought about shoving it into the waistband of her skirt. She didn't like guns, but she wasn't stupid. The very air hummed with a sense of danger. It couldn't hurt to be armed.

Of course, she didn't know a damned thing about pistols. Including whether it was loaded, or if there was a safety that she had to release. It was just as likely she'd end up shooting her own foot rather than the bad guy.

Ignoring the weapon, Ellie reached back into the glove compartment. She located his phone that had slipped between the folds of the tattered owner's manual. Turning it on, she was relieved to discover he hadn't put in a passcode.

She hesitated, knowing that Nate might be angry with

her decision. Then, squaring her shoulders, she scrolled through his contacts. She found his mother's name and pressed the screen to call her.

The older woman answered on the second ring, her voice bright and cheerful.

"Ms. Marcel, this is Ellie Guthrie," she said in a breathless voice, feeling awkward talking to the woman who might someday decide she wasn't good enough for her son. She quashed the ridiculous thought and concentrated on why she'd contacted the older woman. "I'm a friend of Nate's and I need your help."

Five minutes later she ended the call, satisfied that Ms. Marcel understood what she needed. In fact, if Gary Clark wasn't such an ass, she would almost feel sorry for him. Trying to decide whether to return to the courthouse or wait in her office, she was distracted by the shiny Rolls-Royce that drove slowly past her.

Her father. Had he been searching for her in the hopes that he could force her to return to Oklahoma City with him? Or did he have a more nefarious reason for cruising the streets of Curry?

The car turned the corner near Nate's building, pulling to the curb. Ellie grimaced. He'd clearly caught sight of her and was waiting for her to come and speak with him.

It was the last thing she wanted to do. She was tired, scared, and in dire need of a shower. Not at all in the right frame of mind to argue with Judge Guthrie.

Unfortunately, she knew her father too well. He wasn't going to leave until he'd said whatever it was he had to say. End of story. Plus, she had a few questions she wanted to ask him.

Stiffening her spine, Ellie tossed the phone on the seat with the gun and slammed shut the door. She'd return as soon as she was done talking to her father to lock everything up. For now, she could keep an eye on the truck from across the street.

She headed toward the car at a brisk pace, rounding the corner and halting next to the passenger door as the window was buzzed down. Leaning forward, she prepared to warn her father she was staying in Curry.

The words never left her parted lips.

She hadn't even managed to glance through the open window when pain exploded in her brain. It started at the back, as if someone had used a baseball bat to smash in her skull and swiftly radiated through her head and down her spine. Her teeth clenched, weird lights dancing in front of her eyes before they were rolling back. At the same time her legs suddenly felt like soggy noodles, refusing to hold up her weight.

A setup. It had to be.

Someone had been waiting for her with every intention of knocking her unconscious.

She tried to scream for help as she collapsed onto the sidewalk, but nothing emerged but a low grunt. She tried again, but her throbbing head smacked against the concrete and everything went blessedly dark.

Nate had been in trouble before. When he was young it was natural that he would rebel against his father. And the best way to do that was to break the law that the older man was sworn to uphold.

It'd never been serious. A party where there was underage drinking. Sneaking out after curfew. A rock thrown through the bedroom window of the jerk who'd given him a black eye at school.

And on one memorable occasion he'd taken his father's motorcycle for a joyride. The older man had been angry enough to have his young son tossed into a cell at the county jail for a few hours. He'd intended to teach Nate a lesson.

He'd succeeded. The time had dragged like molasses for Nate and he'd sworn to himself that he would never, ever end up in a cell again.

He'd managed to keep that promise until last night.

This time, however, he wasn't angry at having his freedom stolen. Or even the fact that he was being punished for a crime he didn't commit. He was furious that he was separated from Ellie. How the hell was he supposed to protect her when he was locked in a cramped room that was designated as the holding cell?

If something happened to her, he was going to hold Sheriff Clark personally responsible. And the man would suffer.

They would all suffer.

His dark thoughts were finally interrupted when the door was abruptly pulled open. He stormed forward, surprised to find it was the sheriff. He'd expected a deputy to take him back to the interrogation room. He glanced over the man's shoulder, his gut twisting when he didn't see Ellie.

"Where's Ms. Guthrie?" he demanded.

"She isn't here." The sheriff's words were clipped, his face screwed up like he'd just swallowed a lemon. "Follow me."

Nate allowed the man to lead him through the jumbled maze of rooms that had served as the county jail until the new facility had been built.

"You can't question me without my lawyer."

Gary climbed the steps that led them out of the basement to the first floor. He turned to enter the official sheriff's office and moved to the reception desk that was currently empty.

"I'm releasing you." The man turned to shove a small box in Nate's hand.

Nate stiffened. This was the last thing he expected. Was it some trick? Some idiotic attempt to play good cop and lure him into saying something he shouldn't when his lawyer wasn't around to stop him?

He wouldn't put it past the man.

"Why?" he demanded.

"You wanna stay in jail?"

"Did you discover who killed Dr. Booker?" Nate pressed. It still felt like a trap.

Gary sent him a jaundiced glare. "I think it was you."

"Then why aren't you charging me with murder?"

The sheriff pointed toward the old-fashioned phone on the desk.

"In the past twenty minutes I've received five phone calls that included threats from the FBI, the Justice Department, and the Chicago Police Department." His lips twisted with a bitter humor. "It must be nice to have friends in high places."

Ah. Now that made sense. Obviously Ellie had decided to contact one of his brothers. Or maybe his parents. It was something he would have done if worse had come to worst, but he hated the thought they would now be worried about him.

Still, he couldn't deny a flare of pleasure that Ellie had reached out to the Marcels. She clearly knew that they could be depended on to solve their problems.

"Actually it's nice to have a family who loves me," he said, pulling the top off the box to retrieve his belongings.

"Whatever," Gary muttered, watching with obvious impatience as Nate bent down to pull on his shoes and then threaded his belt around his waist. It wasn't until Nate had tucked his wallet in his back pocket that the sheriff continued. "If I decide to charge you with murder, not even the president will be able to stop me."

Nate resisted the urge to roll his eyes. Instead he glanced toward the hallway, where he heard the sounds of footsteps passing by. He only caught a quick glance at the two men, but it was enough to determine that they were strangers.

And that they were both wearing jackets with official titles embroidered on the back.

He turned back to the sheriff. "Fire investigation?"

Gary hunched a shoulder, his face suddenly revealing the strain the past few days had taken on him.

"Walter Perry's house caught fire this morning."

Nate hissed in shock. When he'd been hustled down to the holding cell he'd assumed that it was a ploy to try and rattle him. As if an FBI agent didn't know all the tricks of interrogating a suspect. Now he realized that the sheriff had yet another disaster on his plate.

"How bad?"

"Burned to the ground." The words were clipped, trying to give nothing away.

"Was Walter inside?"

"That's classified information."

Meaning he was inside. No reason to hide the fact if the onetime sheriff had survived.

Silently he ticked off the names. Daniel. Barb. Mandy. Larry. Dr. Booker. And now Walter.

Someone was picking them off one by one. So who was next? Neville Morse? The mayor? Colin Guthrie?

His mouth went dry, a sudden urgency pounding through his body.

"There's no message from Ellie?" he asked, his voice harsh. "She wouldn't have left without telling someone where she was going."

The sheriff scowled. "This isn't your secretarial service. You want to know where she is, then call her."

Nate instinctively reached into the pocket of his slacks before remembering that he'd left his cell phone in the truck during the funeral. Had Ellie driven it to town? Yes, he'd glanced out of the back of the SUV to see her following them. She'd been close enough for him to see her grim expression.

Without bothering to ask the sheriff if he could go, Nate

headed out of the office and down the stairs. Distantly he could hear the chatter of the visiting fire inspectors, but he didn't need them to know the cause of the fire was arson.

And that Walter had been murdered.

Once outside, he walked around the courthouse, spotting his truck parked at the back. He paused, sucking in a deep breath at the sight of it. Surely it meant that Ellie was nearby? Probably at her office.

Deciding to grab his phone before going in search of her, Nate jogged forward, pulling open the door of the truck. It was only then he remembered that Ellie had the key. Damn. He couldn't get into his glove compartment.

The thought had barely formed when his gaze landed on the phone that had been left on the seat. Along with his gun.

The fear he'd momentarily eased blasted through him. Ellie might have left his phone lying in plain sight. Curry wasn't usually a hotbed of crime. But she would never have been so careless with his gun. Not when a child might have come along and gotten their hands on it.

Which meant . . . what?

He didn't know.

Nate grabbed the cell phone and scrolled to her number. He hit the screen, and held it to his ear. He impatiently tapped his foot as he heard her phone ringing before it switched to her automated message telling him to leave his name and number.

Cursing beneath his breath, Nate shoved the phone in his pocket before reaching for his handgun. With a quick efficiency, he ensured that it was still loaded and the safety was on. Then he tucked it in the waistband of his slacks and pulled his sweater over it.

He slammed shut the door and rounded the back of his truck. The square was eerily silent as he jogged down the street. There was no traffic, no pedestrians, and all the businesses were locked up tight. It only increased Nate's unease.

Picking up speed, he jumped the curb and aimed directly for the door to Ellie's office. He grabbed the handle, not surprised to find it locked. A glance through the glass door revealed the reception area was shrouded in darkness. That didn't mean she wasn't in the back.

Not bothering to knock, Nate retraced his steps to the end of the sidewalk, turning the corner so he could approach through the alley. Instinctively, his hand reached beneath his sweater to grasp the butt of his gun. This was a perfect spot for an ambush.

He climbed over the hedges that surrounded Ellie's back patio and moved to peer into her window. His heart sank to his toes. Empty.

Where the hell was she?

Nate pressed his back against the building and forced himself to quash the rising panic. Right now he had to think like an FBI agent, not a man whose lover was missing. He closed his eyes, trying to imagine Ellie waiting for him at the courthouse. She'd been there for hours, sitting at his side as he was interrogated. Then the sheriff had hauled him to the holding cell.

From there she'd gone to his truck to use his phone, where something must have startled her. Or . . .

No. He wasn't going to allow himself to think the worst. Not yet.

He formed the picture of Ellie standing next to his truck, the silence of the square around her. Then abruptly his eyes snapped open. The town was quiet now, but it hadn't been a few hours ago. There must have been sirens blaring and people scurrying toward Walter Perry's burning house. The only reason he hadn't heard was because he was locked in that damned basement.

Pushing away from the building, Nate crossed the patio and bounded over the hedge before running down the alley at top speed.

At the street, he turned to head away from the square, weaving his way through backyards and the crowded church parking lot before he at last turned the corner to see Walter's house.

He grimaced. The brick home hadn't burned to the ground, but it was close. The roof was gone, along with the windows and the front door, leaving behind an empty shell. The bricks were charred to an ugly black and soot was drifting over the front yard like gruesome flecks of snow. An acrid stench clung to the air, coating Nate's tongue and seeping into his skin. It was overpowering enough to make him gag.

He shuddered, turning his back on the house. There was nothing he could do for Walter. It was too late for the retired sheriff. Instead he studied the crowd gathered behind the police tape.

There were fewer than a dozen onlookers. No doubt the majority had dispersed along with the fire trucks and ambulance. It wasn't like there was anything to see beyond the destroyed house. Which meant that it was easy to determine that Ellie wasn't there.

Pretending he didn't see the waves from several in the crowd, Nate spun on his heel and retraced his steps. The last place he knew Ellie had been was the courthouse. Which meant that was where he needed to start his search.

He was jogging past the barbershop when he caught sight of Leland arranging a display in the front window. On impulse, he doubled back and pushed open the door. The older man glanced at him in surprise.

"Hey, Nate. I'm not open today," he said, glancing down at his dark slacks and white shirt that had been carefully pressed. His Sunday best. "But if you need a shave, I'm happy to do it."

Nate gave a quick shake of his head. "Thanks, but I was just wondering how long you've been here."

"Oh." He considered for a second. "Twenty or thirty minutes, I suppose. I meant to come straight after church, but I stopped by Walter's house." The barber heaved a dramatic sigh. "Did you hear there was a fire?"

"Yes. A damned shame."

Nate tried to sound sympathetic without encouraging the older man to become distracted with the latest gossip.

A wasted effort.

Leland leaned toward Nate. Almost as if he was afraid he might be overheard by some phantom customer.

"No one will say anything, but I saw the ambulance parked right in front of the house, which means Walter must have been home when the fire happened, right?" he questioned. "You don't have that unless there is a body found. Or bodies." He shuddered. "Who's to say? There's a new death in Curry every day. Or at least that's what it feels like."

The older man wasn't wrong. There was a new death every day. The thought made Nate's stomach clench.

"Did you happen to notice Ms. Guthrie?"

Leland studied him with a curious expression at the unexpected question.

"You mean at the fire?"

Nate tried to disguise his throbbing fear. "Or walking past your shop."

Leland once again paused, considering the question. "Hmm. There was quite a crowd at Walter's," he finally answered. "You know how people are. They have to stand around gawking at a tragedy."

There was no trace of irony in Leland's voice, despite the fact that was exactly what he'd been doing.

"Did you see her?" Nate prompted.

"No. I don't think so." Leland paused before he gave a low grunt, as if he'd been hit by a sudden thought.

"What?"

"That father of hers was there," Leland said.

"Judge Guthrie?" Nate blinked in surprise. Why was Ellie's dad still in town? And was it possible that Ellie was with him now?

Nate gave a small shake of his head. If Ellie had decided to visit her father, she would have left a message for him. Or at least picked up the phone when he called.

"I suppose that's his fancy title now." Leland shrugged. "When he lived in Curry he was just plain Mr. Guthrie."

Momentarily distracted, Nate studied the man's lined face. The barber wasn't precisely subtle.

"You didn't like him." The words were a statement, not a question.

Leland grimaced, probably remembering a time when Colin Guthrie had the sort of power and influence in town to make life miserable for someone who spoke badly about him. Then, the barber shrugged.

"He always acted like he was too good for this small town. He got even worse when he married that snooty wife of his. No one was sad to see him move away."

"I haven't had the pleasure of meeting him yet," Nate said, trying not to think about the looming encounter. Ellie didn't have to tell him that her father was going to be less than impressed with a small-time rancher who didn't have an extra dime to his name.

"Good luck with that," Leland muttered, before he grimaced. "Sorry, Nate. Ellie is a lovely woman. We're all very happy she's moved back to Curry."

"She is," he agreed, dismissing his vague dislike for a man he'd never met. "Did you speak with him this morning?"

"Nope. He was standing off by himself. To be honest,

he looked white as snow. Like he was really upset at Walter's death."

"I heard they were friends, so I suppose it's natural he would grieve his loss," Nate said even as he inwardly wondered if it'd been sorrow or terror that'd turned the judge's face white.

He was betting on terror.

Almost as if able to read his mind, Leland glanced toward the window at the sheriff vehicles parked across the street.

"I think they were close for a while," he said, turning his gaze back to Nate. "Walter Perry liked rubbing elbows with the bigwigs. I know he belonged to the Lodge back in the day, and a few of them liked to get together and play cards out at Neville Morse's place, but from what I've seen, Walter and Guthrie had a big falling out."

Nate leashed his impatience. As desperate as he was to find Ellie, anything he could discover about the men involved with Hopewell Clinic was important.

"Do you know what it was about?"

"Nope, I'd gotten lunch at the diner and since it was a nice day, I decided to eat it on one of the benches near the courthouse." His eyes grew distant, as if he was lost in his memories. "While I was sitting there the two men came around the side of the building. It looked like Guthrie was telling Walter something he didn't like and I could see the sheriff reaching down to grab his gun. As if he was thinking about shooting Guthrie." Leland shook his head. "I was afraid it might get out of hand, so I hurried toward them to try and break up the fight, but by the time I could reach them, Guthrie was strolling away, as cool as a cucumber. A week later the Guthrie family were packed up and moving to Oklahoma City."

Nate was instantly reminded of watching the men standing in Neville's field just twenty-four hours ago. Colin

Guthrie had been shaking his finger in Walter's face, clearly chastising him for something.

Was it the same thing that'd caused their argument years ago? And did it have something to do with the reason Colin Guthrie had moved his family away from Curry?

He resisted the urge to press for more details. If Leland had overheard the conversation he would have told Nate. The barber had a pathological urge to share whatever he knew with the world.

"So you haven't seen Ellie all day?" he demanded for the last time.

"Can't say I have." Leland studied him, at last catching the tension in Nate's voice. "Is something wrong?"

"I need to speak with her. It's urgent."

"If you want me to help look for her, I can," Leland readily offered, waving a hand toward the plastic shelves he'd placed on the ledge beneath the window when Nate had first walked in. "I'll finish straightening out these trinkets later."

Nate cast an indifferent glance toward the gold and silver necklaces arranged on the top shelf. It wasn't until he caught sight of the bracelets that were in a small pile on the bottom shelf that he froze in shock.

He took a jerky step forward, reaching to grab the top bracelet. It was made of cheap gold, but it was almost an exact replica of the silver one that he'd found in Neville's field. As well as the one he'd glimpsed wrapped around Paula's arm.

"Where did you get those?"

Leland frowned, obviously confused by Nate's sharp tone. "My wife makes them," he said, eyeing Nate warily. "At least she attaches the different charms onto the chain that she buys by the yard. In a moment of weakness last year I agreed to let her sell them in the shop." He shrugged. "After a few months I moved them to the back. You know how the men are in this town. They were making fun of me for trying to turn the shop into a frou-frou hairdressing place. They kept asking if I was going to start painting their nails and toes. Unfortunately, my wife doesn't care what my customers think. She wants her wares in the window where people just passing by can see them. She's convinced they'll sell better."

Nate had a fuzzy memory of seeing the display case when he'd been in the shop, but he'd never paid attention to it. Not until now.

He held up the bracelet. "How many of these have you sold?"

"I don't know." The old man gave a vague wave of his hand. "A few."

"Please, Leland. It could be important."

Leland snapped to attention. He'd spent time in the army. It might have been forty years ago, but he recognized an order when he heard one.

"I write down the sales," he told Nate. "My wife wants to know how much I owe her."

"Can I see your list?"

"Should be in the back. Wait here and I'll get it." Leland turned to make his way to the rear of the shop. He disappeared through a curtain that blocked off the storage room and what Nate assumed must be an office. There was the sound of a drawer being pulled open and a rustle of paper. A few moments later, Leland was returning with a small notebook in his hand. "Here it is," he called out, hurrying to stand next to Nate. He flicked through the pages, his lips moving as he silently counted the sales he'd written down. "Looks like I sold ten bracelets in the past year." He lifted his head to meet Nate's steady gaze. "Do you want to know about the necklaces?"

Nate shook his head, the terror he'd tried to deny blazing through his body even as he'd tried to call Ellie over and over. In the back of his mind he'd tried to convince himself that she was getting coffee. Or a muffin. It was the only way to keep the panic at bay. But he'd known deep inside that she was in trouble.

She'd gone to his truck, made the call to his mother, and then disappeared. Which meant the killer had snatched her off the street in broad daylight.

"No. Just the silver charm bracelet."

Leland didn't hesitate this time. He already understood that there was something terribly wrong.

"Silver." He flipped through the pages. "Most people bought the gold. There were only two silver ones that I sold."

"To who?"

"Paula Raye."

Nate jerked. "Paula. You're sure?"

"Yeah. I remember," Leland assured him. "She said she was buying one for herself and one for a friend. I gave her a discount." The older man looked up and gave a small grunt as he hurriedly reached out to grasp Nate's upper arm. "Are you okay? You look sick."

Nate felt sick.

How could he have been so stupid? He'd seen the bracelet on Paula's arm. He'd known that it matched the one in the field. But he'd let himself be distracted.

His stupidity had left Ellie vulnerable. If anything happened to her . . . Nate slammed the door on his grim thoughts. Later he'd wallow in self-reproach. For now, he had to concentrate on what he'd discovered.

Just because Paula had bought the bracelets didn't necessarily mean she was involved, but it was the only tangible clue that he had.

"Did she say who she gave the bracelet to?" he asked his companion.

Leland shook his head. "Nope. Just said a friend."

Of course she hadn't told him who it was for. That would

have been too easy. He was going to have to track down Paula. Now.

Turning away, Nate was on the point of charging out of the door when he abruptly remembered it was Sunday. The Lodge would be closed and he had no idea where the bartender lived.

He glanced back at Leland. "Do you know where Paula's house is?"

The barber's voracious love of gossip once again came in handy. "When she first came to town I think she was living out of her car. I noticed it parked behind the Lodge even after hours. But a few months ago, I heard that she rented out the old Hollister place." He shrugged. "Kind of a surprise to all of us."

Nate sent him an impatient frown. "Why would it be a surprise?"

"Well, for one thing, it's even more isolated than most places are around here," Leland explained. "It's almost thirty miles away from town, and nothing but prairie grass for neighbors. Plus, it's a huge, rambling place that hadn't been lived in for years. It had to have been filled with cobwebs and rats when she moved in."

It sounded like a lot of places in the area. Remote. Isolated. But Leland was right. It was a long way from where she worked. Especially since she had to drive home late at night. And why would she need a huge home? Why not choose a small place on the edge of town?

There were probably a dozen explanations, but for now Nate was concentrating on the fact that Paula had chosen a place that would be perfect for a psychotic killer. No neighbors to see her coming or going. And seemingly lots of space to hide Daniel and Mandy before she murdered them and dumped them into Neville's field.

"Where exactly is it?" he demanded.

Leland waved his hand toward the back of the shop.

"Take the road past the farmers' co-op. It comes to a dead end north of town. You can't miss it."

"Thanks." Nate raced to the door, yanking it open with enough force to send the bell attached above it sailing through the air.

"What's going on?" Leland called from behind him. "Nate?"

Chapter Thirty

Ellie struggled through the darkness that clouded her brain. She didn't have to open her eyes to know that she wasn't in Nate's bed. Not only was she missing the warmth of his arms wrapped tightly around her, but she was sitting upright in a chair.

The last time she'd fallen asleep like that she'd just celebrated her twenty-first birthday with cherry fizzes and every time she tried to lie down the world would spin in a sickening motion.

Her head had also throbbed like someone had used a jackhammer on it.

She felt exactly the same as she lifted her heavy lids, only this time she was fairly certain that cherry fizzes weren't the cause of the relentless agony.

It took a few minutes for her eyes to focus. How long had she been asleep? An hour? A day? The fact that she didn't know made her heart skitter against her ribs. As did the memory of what'd happened just before she'd blacked out.

She'd been leaning down to glance into the Rolls-Royce. Then someone had hit her on the back of the head and she'd been knocked unconscious. So what had happened to her father? Or had he even been in the car? Had someone stolen it to lure her to that precise spot?

Blinking until she could at last make out her surroundings, she cautiously glanced downward.

She'd been right. She was sitting in a chair. Not a hard, wooden chair. Or an office chair. This was a cushioned recliner that might be found in someone's family room. Her hands were cuffed together, but otherwise she wasn't bound in any way.

Warily she raised her gaze to scan the room. It was dimly lit with open rafters above her and one bare bulb that hung from its own electrical cord. Beneath her feet was a cracked cement floor that looked like it hadn't been scrubbed in the past fifty years. The air was thick with mold. And something else . . .

Fear? Did that have a smell?

Her mouth went dry at the strange thought and she glanced toward the blankets that had been draped from the rafters in the center of the long room. Like when kids performed a play in their grandparents' basement. Creepy.

What was hidden behind there?

The washer and dryer? Storage containers? Dead bodies?

She had a horrible suspicion she didn't want to know.

Trying to lift her heavy head so she could look behind her, Ellie groaned. The cherry fizz hangover had nothing on the agony that was currently drilling through her brain.

"Awake already?" a voice drawled. "You must have a thick head."

Ellie forgot how to breathe. She'd been scared when she'd awakened in this weird-ass basement. Even with her brain pounding she'd realized she'd been kidnapped by whoever was responsible for the killing spree in Curry. But the terror that burst through her at realizing she wasn't alone defied description.

Her mind went blank, her heart lodged in her throat. Which

would explain why she couldn't breathe. The knowledge that she had to think clearly if she was going to survive was the only thing that kept the panic from overwhelming her.

"So I've been told," she finally managed to croak. "What's going on?"

"A little show-and-tell," the voice answered.

There was a squeak of springs, as if someone was lifting out of a chair, or maybe climbing out of bed, followed by the shuffle of footsteps. Icy dread spread through her veins as Ellie forced herself to turn her head and discover who was responsible for the murders.

The shadowed figure stepped close enough to be bathed in the harsh glare coming from the bulb and Ellie's mouth fell open. She'd expected it to be one of the men involved with the Hopewell Clinic. Or one of their friends. Who else would have a reason to kidnap her?

But it wasn't one of the men. It wasn't even a man.

It was Paula Raye. The bartender at the Lodge.

"Paula?" she breathed.

The woman moved to stand directly in front of her. She was wearing an old flannel shirt and jeans that had suspicious splotches on them. Mud or blood? Ellie shuddered.

"Surprised?" the woman demanded.

"I'm confused," Ellie admitted with complete honesty. "Did you knock me out?"

The woman hesitated before giving a small shrug. "It was necessary to get you here."

She was hiding something, but what? Right now, it was the least of her worries.

"Where are we?"

"My temporary home." Paula glanced around, her face twisting with distaste. It emphasized just how unattractive a woman she was. "It's not much, but it's better than my last lodgings."

"Your last lodgings?" Ellie parroted. It was such an odd choice of words.

"Oklahoma State Penitentiary."

"You were a prisoner?" Ellie asked before she could stop the stupid question. You didn't have lodgings at the Oklahoma State Penitentiary unless you were a prisoner.

"Yep. For almost twenty-five years."

Well, that explained the bad tattoos. And the haircut. She swallowed a hysterical urge to laugh.

There was nothing funny about the crazy ex-con.

"What did you do?"

Ugly hatred darkened her eyes. "The charge was trafficking drugs, but it was bogus. I was jailed to keep my lips shut."

"Keep your lips shut about what?"

"The Hopewell Clinic, of course."

Ellie's initial shock faded to stark acceptance. And then self-disgust. She'd known the trouble in Curry had something to do with the clinic, and she'd let that suspicion allow her to commit the cardinal sin when exploring evidence.

She'd assumed.

She'd assumed that it must be someone who'd lived in Curry all those years ago. And that it was a man. And that the villain's motives had something to do with money and greed.

"You were there?" she asked.

A muscle next to the woman's mouth twitched. There was some strong emotion she was trying to keep hidden.

"Unfortunately."

Ellie carefully leaned forward, using the motion to inch toward the edge of the cushion. The squishy material was as effective in keeping her trapped as if she'd been tied to the chair. It was like moving through molasses.

"Why unfortunately?" she asked, trying to keep the woman distracted. "I thought it was a rehab facility that was created to help people."

Paula released a short, angry laugh. "That's what was listed on the brochure."

"But it wasn't?"

"So innocent," Paula mocked, reaching down without warning to grab Ellie's chin in a brutal grip. "Did you like my gifts?"

Ellie swallowed her cry of pain. She wouldn't give the woman the satisfaction of knowing she was hurting her.

"Gifts?" It took an effort to speak. The woman was strong. It felt like she might crush her jaw. "You sliced my tires and dumped the rats behind my office?"

She slowly released her punishing grip and straightened. A mysterious smile tugged at her lips.

"Daniel took care of the tires. I personally delivered the rats." Her smile widened. "And set fire to your house."

"Daniel worked for you?"

Paula shrugged. "Until it was time for him to pay for the sins of his father."

Nausea rolled through Ellie's stomach. This woman had obviously taken pleasure in tormenting her. And worse, she'd lured other people into helping with her nasty pranks. Until she'd decided their use-by date had arrived.

"You killed him."

Ellie expected the woman to laugh. Or gloat. Instead, she turned away. As if hiding her expression.

"The drugs were a nice touch, don't you think? A moral symmetry."

"Nice? You murdered a man who did nothing to you."

Paula jerked her head back to glare at Ellie. "I told you. The sins of the father."

Father. Ellie shuddered. "Is that why you killed Mandy?"

"A necessary sacrifice."

"Just because Neville Morse was on the board of Hopewell Clinic?"

"God says an eye for an eye."

Ellie studied the woman's face that had flushed with a dull color. It wasn't guilt. Or remorse.

It was anger.

"Was Barb an eye for an eye as well?"

Paula scowled, almost as if she was offended by Ellie's accusation.

"That wasn't intentional," she said. "I never meant to kill her."

Ellie gave a small shake of her head, instantly regretting the unconscious gesture. It sent sharp darts shooting through her brain.

She clenched her teeth, focusing on the woman's strange behavior. The older woman had seemed smugly proud when Ellie had mentioned the deaths of Daniel and Mandy, but she was on the defense when it came to Barb? Why?

"You accidentally murdered her?"

The dull color deepened at Ellie's disbelief. "She came into the Lodge a few nights ago. Nothing new in that. The woman was a pathetic drunk whose only friend was a bottle of vodka."

"What happened?"

Paula hunched her shoulders. "I'm not sure. Maybe she had a weird flashback. Or maybe the fog in her brain simply cleared long enough for her to see what was standing in front of her."

"She recognized you," she said, puzzled why it would matter. Surely there'd been lots of clients who had been in and out of the clinic.

"Yeah. She tried to confront me that night, but I managed to shake her off."

Ellie was still confused. "That's when she tried to contact me," she said, recalling Nate telling her that Barb had been to the Lodge just hours before her frantic calls had started.

Paula spat out a foul curse. "I knew the stupid bitch would try to warn her precious boss." Her gaze flicked dismissively over Ellie. "Barb worshipped the ground your father walked on. I could tell that whenever I saw them at the clinic together. I imagine that's why she turned to drinking. Because she couldn't have the man she wanted."

Ellie dismissed Paula's mockery of Barb's unrequited love. She'd already sensed that the poor woman remained desperately infatuated with Colin Guthrie, despite the fact he'd moved away with his family years before.

Instead she concentrated on the fact that Paula had been worried that Barb might reveal her presence in Curry.

"What did you do to her?"

"I snuck through the window," Paula admitted. "I only meant to convince her to keep her mouth shut."

Once again she was struck by Paula's odd response to Barb. Why just scare her? She'd been a part of the board.

"I heard you when I was at the house," Ellie said, easing another inch forward on the cushion.

Paula didn't notice. She'd turned to pace from one side of the narrow room to the other. She didn't seem nervous. It was more anticipation. As if she was waiting for something.

"I found Barb in the living room. Before I could say a word she was screaming at the top of her lungs. And then she clutched her chest and fell on the floor." Paula gave a dismissive wave of her hand. "I assumed she was having a heart attack. That's when I heard the door open and I knew I had to bail. I could only hope that she was too sick to rat me out."

Ellie didn't miss the indifference in her tone. Paula didn't care that Barb was dead, but she hadn't wanted to dirty her hands doing it.

"She must have died of natural causes," Ellie said, more to herself than her captor.

"If that's what you call drinking yourself into an early grave," Paula drawled.

Paula had a point. Barb had been racing toward death for twenty years or more. Of course, having someone break into your house didn't help an already weak heart.

The thought of breaking into a house sparked a thought in Ellie's fuzzy brain. "Why did you go back to Barb's place and search it if all you wanted was for her to keep her mouth shut about you?"

Paula halted, turning to face Ellie. Her blunt features held an expression of puzzlement.

"I didn't."

Ellie grimaced. She believed her. Which meant that someone else had snuck into Barb's house. Not that she intended to waste time thinking about who it might have been. Not now. She had enough troubles, thank you very much.

"Why did you kill Larry Harper?" she instead demanded. "He didn't have anything to do with Hopewell Clinic, did he?"

Paula glanced toward the back of the room. Had she heard a noise? Or was she considering her answer?

"After the Harpers discovered that Daniel might have been murdered, they decided they would add blackmail to their list of crimes," she at last said, glancing back at Ellie. "They didn't have any more talent for that than they did for dealing drugs. I could have run circles around them if I'd still been in the business."

Ellie flattened her lips together, resisting the urge to point out that Paula had just admitted to being a drug dealer when she'd earlier claimed she was framed for her crime.

She wanted to keep her talking. Once she stopped . . . Well, Ellie assumed that bad things were going to happen.

Besides, she couldn't deny a morbid curiosity. She'd spent days churning the various possibilities through her brain. She wanted to know what had happened. So far she'd discovered that Daniel had been responsible for the vandalism before he'd been killed. And that his death was related to Mandy's. She'd also learned that Barb had probably died of a heart attack, and that Larry had been stupid enough to try and squeeze money from a murderer.

"And your answer to his blackmail was to kill him?" she asked.

"He deserved to die." Her tone indicated that Paula thought a bullet to the head was a perfectly reasonable response.

"What about his brother?"

"He's on the run." Paula made a sound of disgust. "He's too much a coward to ever show his face around Curry."

Ellie didn't know Bert Harper, but she suspected that Paula was right. From Nate's description of the two brothers, it sounded like they were typical bullies. All bluff and bluster until someone stood up to them. Then they bolted like spineless cravens.

"Why shoot Larry in Nate's building?"

A strange glint flared through her eyes at the question. "It was convenient. When I first arrived in Curry I'd considered opening a small coffee shop. I've always wanted my own business. I looked at a number of empty buildings around town, but in the end I realized I didn't have enough money. I had to go to work at the Lodge."

Ellie tried to imagine Paula standing behind a counter serving dainty coffee cups with muffins and fresh cookies. It boggled the mind.

Ellie cleared her throat, at the same time scooting a fraction forward.

"You stole an extra key from the Realtor?" She asked the question loud enough that it hid the rattle of her handcuffs.

Paula shrugged, not seeming to notice that Ellie was almost at the edge of the cushion. Or maybe she just didn't care. It wasn't like Ellie had much of a chance to escape. She didn't have a clue where they were, or how many people might be waiting upstairs.

"An old habit," Paula readily confessed. "One that came in handy. Not only did I have a private place to get rid of Larry, but it would pin the blame on Nate." She lifted her arm to lightly touch something that was wrapped around her wrist. "He was becoming a pain."

Ellie frowned. Was the woman wearing a bracelet? Hard to see from her angle. Then she dismissed the thought. She was more concerned with the reason Paula had tried to frame Nate. And what she intended to do to him in the future.

For the first time in her professional career, Ellie was relieved her client was currently locked in a holding cell.

"I suppose that's also the reason you left Larry's car with Dr. Booker in the trunk parked behind his house?" she demanded, unable to halt the edge in her voice.

Paula smiled, clearly pleased that Ellie was angered by her games.

"Yes. That dipwad sheriff was anxious to blame someone for the trouble in Curry and it was obvious he resented a good-looking FBI agent in town. It was easy to make sure that he had a reason to toss your boyfriend in jail. Once he was out of the way I could bring you here without worrying about being interrupted."

Regret formed a heavy knot in the pit of Ellie's stomach. She'd feared that she was putting Nate in danger. Her father's connection to Hopewell Clinic made her an obvious target. Plus, his choice to investigate what was happening was directly because of his need to protect her.

But only now did she realize it was entirely her fault that he'd been arrested for murder.

"Why me?"

Paula's face lit up. Like a child who'd just been offered a treat.

"I thought you would never ask." The woman moved toward the blankets that divided the room. Glancing back at Ellie, she reached for the rope that held them up and gave a sharp tug. On cue, the blankets dropped to the cement floor. Paula chuckled with glee. "Ta-da."

Ellie jerked, wondering for a crazed moment if she was hallucinating. It wasn't an old washer and dryer behind the blankets. Or storage containers. Instead it was her father and Mayor Chambers, tied to crosses made from rough wood and attached to the back wall.

For a horrifying second, Ellie thought they were dead. That the crazy-ass Paula had actually crucified the men. Then, sucking in a deep breath, she forced herself to take a closer look.

The mayor was disheveled, with rips in his slacks and shirt and dirt embedded in his skin. His hair was standing up straight in some places and matted in others, and his eyes were swollen shut. He slumped against the thick ropes that held him to the cross, clearly unconscious. There was a gag shoved between his bloody lips. He looked like he'd been tied to the back of a truck and dragged through the back roads.

And maybe he had.

Still, she caught the small up and down movement of his chest. He was alive. For now.

Her attention turned to her father. He was battered and bruised, but he looked considerably better than the mayor. As the blanket fell, he lifted his head to glare at Paula with an expression of extreme contempt. He would no doubt have blistered her with a furious tirade if he hadn't been gagged.

Colin Guthrie would remain defiant to the end.

At last he turned his head to take in the sight of his daughter, who was cuffed and seated a few feet away. His jaw tightened. Whether with anger or fear, it was impossible to know.

"Oh my God," Ellie breathed. "What have you done?"

Paula waved a hand toward the men. "Justice."

"Justice for what?"

Paula strolled to stand next to Ellie's father, a smug expression on her face.

"Do you want to tell her, or do you want me to?"

Colin turned his head away. Paula laughed. As if it was a great joke.

"Fine. Then I'll do it," she said, swiveling to face Ellie. "Your self-righteous prick of a father used to be my pimp."

Ellie studied the woman with a blank sense of disbelief. Was it some sort of sick joke? Or just her way of trying to embarrass Ellie's father? Colin Guthrie was a man whose entire existence was grimly dedicated to upholding the law. There wouldn't be anything more horrifying to him than being accused of involvement in the sex trade.

When Paula simply met her stare with a mocking smile, Ellie gave a shake of her head.

"That's a lie," she rasped, flinching as pain shot down her spine.

"Oh no. It's the god-honest truth," Paula assured her, reaching out to pat Colin's shoulder. "Isn't it?"

The judge kept his head turned away, but there was a tightening to his jaw that sent a strange chill snaking down Ellie's spine.

"I don't believe you," she forced herself to say.

Paula's fingers tightened on Colin's shoulder until her knuckles turned white. "The Hopewell Clinic that passed itself off as a rehab facility was no more than a whorehouse for the rich and powerful in Oklahoma."

Ellie watched her father's reaction. Even though he was no doubt in shock at being held a prisoner in this basement, there should have been outrage at the accusation. Or revulsion. Instead, he tilted his chin to a stubborn angle. Like he did when he knew he was in the wrong, but he was going to dig in his heels.

Her stomach cramped, her aching brain trying to wrap around the vile allegation. Could it be true? She'd suspected there was something strange going on at the clinic. Perhaps even criminal. But prostitution?

Her mouth felt as if it was stuffed with cotton wool as she tried to control the emotions that swirled through her.

"My father was only a board member," she ridiculously blurted out. "Even if what you said is true, I'm sure he didn't know—"

"He knew." Paula cut through her words, her features hardening with an ugly emotion. "He was the one who negotiated with my lawyer and the prosecutor to offer me the opportunity to avoid a seriously long jail sentence by going to rehab. Of course I chose to go to the clinic. What woman wouldn't?"

There was such conviction in her voice. She truly believed that Colin Guthrie had deliberately lured her to the clinic to sell her body.

Oh God. Ellie heard the sound of her cuffs rattling and realized she was trembling.

"That doesn't mean he knew what was happening," she insisted.

"He personally delivered his friends to the clinic," Paula spat out. "For all I know he watched as they raped me."

Ellie shook her head. "No."

Paula glared at Ellie's obstinate expression, then without warning, she reached to grab the gag tied around her father's mouth. With a violent wrench, she jerked it out of his mouth.

"It's the truth, isn't it?" she rasped. "Tell her."

Her father spit the blood out of his mouth before he turned his head to send Paula a glare filled with pure loathing.

"Bitch."

Paula ignored the insult as she reached down to grab a long, thin object that was leaning against the bottom of the cross. At first, Ellie assumed it was a steel pipe, but as Paula lifted it, she could see the handle and small prongs on the tip.

"I bought this cattle prod at the farm store." She held it in front of Colin's face. "It's surprisingly handy. Let's see if it will encourage you to talk."

Ellie barely kept herself from leaping from the chair. She didn't want to startle the woman. Not when she was holding the prod less than an inch from her father's face.

"Stop," she pleaded.

Paula didn't even glance in her direction. "Confession is good for the soul, isn't that right, Judge?"

Colin sniffed in scorn, his nose flaring. It was exactly the wrong thing to do. Paula released a hissing breath as she jabbed the prod against his neck.

Colin's body bowed and jerked as the electrical jolt blasted through him. At the same time his eyes rolled back and flecks of foam formed at the edge of his mouth. Ellie cried out as Paula pulled back and her father abruptly slumped, the rope tightly bound around his wrists and ankles the only thing keeping him upright.

Paula sent Ellie a warning glance, the prod held close to Colin's neck as Ellie started to rise.

"Sit."

Ellie obeyed. What else could she do? Another jolt from that damned prod might kill her father.

They waited for Colin to recover, his breath a harsh wheeze in the silence. At last he managed to lift his head, his face as white as snow and his eyes dazed.

"Answer the question, Judge Guthrie," Paula commanded.

The older man opened his lips, but it took several tries before he could finally form the words.

"Yes," he hissed. "I knew what was happening at the clinic."

His gaze was locked on Paula, so he didn't see Ellie sway, feeling as if she was going to pass out.

He knew. Her father knew the clinic was being used for prostitution. And worse, he'd been responsible for bringing Paula to the place with the promise it would keep her out of jail.

She'd been sick with fear before. Now she felt sick with horror.

She'd known this man forever. She would have sworn on her life that he was the most tight-laced, respectable man in the entire state of Oklahoma. He was devoted to his family, he went to work each day, he paid his taxes, and gave generously to charities.

Surely this all had to be some hideous misunderstanding.

"It was your idea." Paula continued to press for a confession. "Admit it."

Colin's head dropped back against the wooden cross. Ellie inanely wondered if Paula had installed them herself, or if they'd been a fixture from the previous owners.

"I might have suggested we could make extra money, but I wasn't alone in the decision," Colin protested.

"Decision." Paula's humorless laugh scraped over Ellie's raw nerves. "You make it sound like you were deciding what pizza to order, not forcing women into the sex trade."

"You were already a prostitute."

Paula held the prod less than an inch from the judge's heart, naked hatred in her eyes.

"And you were an immoral bastard."

"Why?" Ellie sharply interrupted.

In the back of her mind an angry voice whispered that

she was being an idiot. She should use Paula's distraction with her father to try and escape. But she couldn't make her heavy muscles move.

She needed her father to explain. There had to be a reason why he would do such an awful thing.

Turning his head in her direction, Colin grimaced. He looked at least a decade older than when he'd arrived in Curry.

"For everyone else it was the money," he said, his words faintly slurred as if his tongue was swelling. "For me it was an opportunity to get out of this town before I was buried alive."

Ellie studied him in frustration. Her father had rarely discussed his past. She assumed it was embarrassment that he'd come from such humble beginnings. After all, most of the social elite in Oklahoma City didn't have parents who were poor farm workers. But it was disgusting to use his childhood poverty as some sort of excuse.

"You weren't held here against your will. You could have left any time you wanted," she said.

He shook his head, then immediately winced. Ellie sympathized. Her own brain continued to throb with a ruthless pain.

"Just like my parents left," he muttered.

Ellie frowned. "What are you talking about?"

"My mother ended up pregnant when she was just fifteen. As soon as the rumors began circulating through town, she and my father were driven out of Curry. The good citizens weren't so forgiving back then," he explained in derisive tones. "Three years later they came crawling back with a young son they couldn't afford to feed and another on the way. My grandfather allowed them to move in with him, but he treated them like dirt. My mother died in childbirth a few months later, and my father died working the fields before he ever reached his fortieth birthday." His expression hardened, revealing the steel that had always lurked beneath his polished façade. "That wasn't going to happen to me."

Ellie felt a pang of regret for the grandparents she'd never had the opportunity to meet. Their lives had clearly been ones of brutal survival, but her father had managed to graduate from high school and had gone on to become a lawyer.

"It wasn't the same," she argued. "You weren't dependent on your family to earn a living. You had a career."

His bloody lip jutted out. It was a familiar gesture, but for the first time, Ellie realized how childish her father could be when he wasn't getting his way.

He'd always been so cold and authoritative, but beneath his aloof composure was a petulant toddler. Was it because he'd lost his mother at such a young age? Or because his father had been a broken man? Whatever the cause, it had obviously allowed him to remain dangerously egocentric.

"I had a law degree, but to have a career I needed contacts. The sort that could help me get out of the prosecutor's office and into a position as a judge." His petulance became more pronounced. "Most men had families with the right contacts. I had to make my own networks."

Ellie lifted her hands, ignoring the rattle of the cuffs. It felt like someone had reached into her chest and was squeezing her heart. She'd wanted her father to reassure her; instead he'd only made everything worse.

"I can't believe it," she croaked.

Colin looked offended by Ellie's blatant horror. Had he expected her to offer him forgiveness?

"I did it for your mother," he said in an attempt to deflect his guilt. "And for you. How do you think you were able to live in a big house and attend the best schools?"

Ellie held his gaze. "I never asked for any of that."

His lips parted, only to snap shut. They both knew that

she'd hated moving from one house to another. And the fancy clothes that had itched her skin. And stupid dance lessons her mother insisted on when all she wanted to do was play softball.

"I can assure you that your mother did," he muttered.

She didn't doubt his claim. Her mother had been addicted to the finer things in life. But she wasn't the one who'd sold her soul to acquire them.

"You can't blame her," she snapped.

The color returned to her father's face, an ugly flush at her refusal to accept that he was above reproach.

"There was no blame," he rasped. "It was a business decision. Pure and simple."

As if tired of being forgotten in the drama between father and daughter, Paula gave a sudden wave of the cattle prod.

"There was nothing pure about it," she snarled. "You sold women to have a big house and wear those fancy robes."

"I did what I thought necessary for my family. I wasn't going to follow in the footsteps of my father," Colin insisted.

Was he trying to convince them that he'd been forced into becoming a part of Hopewell Clinic? Or himself?

"Such a sob story," Paula mocked. "Tell me, Judge, do you want to hear about my past? How my daddy would sneak into my bed late at night? Or how my mother gave me my first hit of meth when I was just twelve? I ran away at sixteen to go to Omaha for a fresh start, but there's never a fresh start. Not for women like me." She managed to reveal the stark brutality of her past with a few words. "There're always creeps like you, whether they're wearing T-shirts and boxers or expensive suits, waiting to take advantage of young girls."

Ellie had tried not to listen to the woman's story. It truly was heartbreaking, but that didn't excuse what she'd done. And what she might be intending to do in the near future. Still, her attention was captured by one word.

"Omaha?" The fact that this woman had come from Omaha and the file folder that had been hidden in Barb's cooler had listed the hometown of the patient as Omaha couldn't be a coincidence. "You're Jane Doe," she burst out.

The older woman sent her an annoyed glance. "What?"

"Your patient file was in Barb's cooler."

Paula shook her head. "I don't know what you're talking about."

Ellie felt another flare of disgust. Of course Paula didn't know about the file. But someone else did. Someone who'd searched Barb's house trying to find it.

She turned her attention toward her father. "It was you. You knew about the file and you went looking for it."

Colin didn't try to pretend he didn't know what she was talking about.

"Barb had attempted to use the file years ago to try and force more money out of me. I knew she would never go to the authorities, so I ignored her threats," he said, and Ellie wondered how he'd been so sure Barb wouldn't rat him out. Had he known his onetime secretary had been desperately in love with him? Probably. "When she died I knew we had to destroy it," Colin continued. "We broke into her house, but obviously we were unsuccessful."

Ellie released a choked laugh. So much for her father's claim that he'd rushed to Curry to attend his loyal employee's funeral. He'd come because he wanted to ransack Barb's house in case someone discovered he wasn't the upright citizen he pretended to be.

Abruptly, Ellie jerked her gaze back to Paula. She couldn't bear to look at her father.

"Why didn't you leave the clinic?" she demanded.

Paula's face darkened, an ancient fury smoldering in her eyes.

"They were smart enough to fill the place with women

who had young kids," she said. "I either did what they wanted or they threatened to take away my daughter."

A daughter. She had a daughter and they'd used that innocent child to force her to . . .

Ellie lowered her head, her hands clenching and unclenching in her lap. There had to be something mentally wrong with her father and the other men who'd been a part of Hopewell. What other explanation could there be?

"I can't listen to anymore," she whispered.

Clearly angered by Ellie's reluctance to continue with the dark reminiscences from the past, Paula stormed forward to grab her chin. Digging her fingers into Ellie's skin, she yanked her face up.

"But I was too smart for them," she assured Ellie, her eyes glittering with a hectic excitement. "When I realized I'd been scammed I didn't cry and whine like the other women. No, I convinced one of my johns to bring me a camera. I told him I wanted pictures of us together. The dumbass believed me," she boasted. "I used it to document what was happening at Hopewell."

"You have proof?" Ellie demanded in surprise. Why hadn't she revealed what she had?

As if able to read her mind, Paula released Ellie's chin and straightened.

"Yeah, I had proof." She spat out the words. "But, I couldn't go to the authorities. Not when they were the ones in charge." Paula glanced toward the judge and the still unconscious mayor. "Instead I called a reporter who I was friendly with."

Ellie frowned. "One of your customers?"

"No," the woman snapped. "It was a female reporter who'd done a story on prostitutes in Omaha. She interviewed me for hours. She told me that she wanted to shine a light on what was happening to women who were forced into the sex trade. Once I watched it I realized that it really was just a way to make the housewives in the suburbs feel better about having crappy husbands and boring lives. They at least weren't having to sell their bodies." Paula shook her head in disgust. "I thought it was all a bunch of hooey, but I kept the woman's business card. I thought I might have some other stories she might be interested in. Only the next time, I was going to get paid."

Ellie ignored Paula's rambling explanation. She was far more interested in why no one had tried to bring an end to the clinic.

There had to be someone who was willing to step up and protect those poor women.

"You sent the picture to the reporter?" she asked.

Paula gave an impatient shake of her head. "No. I asked her to meet me near the clinic. I wanted to personally hand over the pictures," she explained. "I couldn't risk having them stolen or destroyed."

Understandable. Ellie would have done the same thing. And, of course, Paula was no doubt hoping she'd get a few bucks for handing the woman a blockbuster scoop on the most powerful men in Oklahoma.

"What happened?"

Paula hunched her shoulders, her expression oddly vulnerable before she was giving a sharp shake of her head and her lips curved into a bitter smile.

"I don't know if the woman decided not to come or if she was late, but while I was waiting for her, your father and his buddies showed up. I was hauled to the courthouse and thrown in jail."

Ellie leaned forward. At the moment, she'd forgotten that she was in a damp, musty basement with a crazed killer. She was lost in the nightmare of the past.

"What about your daughter?"

Paula released a grating laugh, turning her head toward the judge. "Ask your father."

She didn't want to. Any love or respect that she'd ever felt for Colin Guthrie was being stripped away. But she had to know the truth.

"Father?"

He didn't answer, the stubborn expression returning to his face. Paula angled the prod until it was just an inch from his neck.

"She'd violated her parole, plus she was found with drugs on her," Colin snapped, sweat dripping down his face.

"Drugs you planted," Paula accused.

"It was your word against mine," Colin protested.

"And we both know you're a lying sack of shit." Paula turned to glance back at Ellie. "It was my third strike. They sent me to prison and threw away the key."

Ellie's attention remained locked on her father. "What about the child?"

"We put her in the back of Dr. Booker's car," he said. "In the confusion she managed to wander away."

The truth hit Ellie with the force of a freight train. Now she understood why Barb had hidden the newspaper clipping in the same envelope as the patient file.

"The mystery child," she breathed. "She was found near the highway."

Paula made a sound of pure fury. "Not that they cared. She could have been hit by a car. Or kidnapped."

Colin glanced down at the prod less than an inch from his throat. "She was found and taken to the sheriff," he reminded the woman in a hoarse voice.

Ellie swallowed a curse. Nate had confronted Walter, and the ex-sheriff had lied right to his face. Of course, that was the least of his sins.

"What did you do?" Ellie asked her father.

Her father hesitated and Paula leaned toward him. "Tell her," she hissed.

More sweat poured down Colin's face. "We put her in a place where we knew she would be safe and well cared for."

"You put her in a place where you knew you could keep me from using the pictures to expose your sordid business," Paula shot back. Her gaze flicked toward Ellie. "You see, I was quick enough to hide the camera before they could get their greedy hands on it."

Ellie no longer cared about the pictures. She didn't need proof of the evil done by her father and his partners.

"Where is your daughter?" she demanded.

Chapter Thirty-One

"Here."

The word came from the darkness behind her. Ellie craned her head around, ignoring the sharp pang behind her right eye. At first she couldn't see who was speaking. There was just a vague shadow.

Then the form moved closer and the overhead light revealed the last person Ellie had expected to see.

"Tia?" she gasped, her gaze moving over the woman's sturdy body stuffed into a red sweater and too-tight stretchy pants. She had a purse hanging from her shoulder like she was going to the store, not entering a basement where there were three people being held captive.

"Hello, Ellie," she drawled, circling the chair to stand directly in front of her. There was a smug smile pasted to her lips.

Ellie knew her mouth was hanging open. She couldn't help it. Her battered brain was struggling to process yet another shock.

Her gaze moved between the two women, taking in their large, stocky figures and the blunt features. They weren't identical, but there was no doubt a resemblance.

"You're Paula's daughter," Ellie said, as if it wasn't perfectly obvious.

Tia continued to smile. "I am."

"But I thought . . ." The words dried on her lips as she glanced toward the mayor, who hung loosely from the cross.

Who'd beaten him? Paula or Tia? Both? Not that it mattered.

Tia didn't bother to glance toward the mayor. Instead her gaze flicked over Ellie, a hint of disdain in her expression.

"So did I. At least until I was sixteen and I overheard the ladies in the church gossiping about the mystery of my arrival in the Chambers' household when I was just a babe. No one seemed to know where I'd come from, or why the mayor would want a child at his age." A muscle next to her eye twitched, as if there was some dark emotion churning just below the surface. "I confronted my parents and they told me that I was a foster kid they decided to adopt. At first I was angry, but eventually I realized that it answered a few questions for me."

She studied Ellie, clearly waiting for her to respond.

"What questions?" she forced herself to ask.

Tia looked pleased. "Like why I had nothing in common with my supposed parents. And why they didn't love me."

Ellie felt an odd twinge in the region of her heart. Tia's words echoed what she'd endured her entire life. The knowledge that she was an outsider in her own family. That her parents had never expressed their love.

Still, the dysfunction of her childhood had driven her to become a defense lawyer, not a homicidal maniac. And no matter what the public might think, the two were very different things.

Ellie cleared the lump from her throat. "How did you discover the truth?"

"My father." Without warning Tia spun around and smashed her fist into the face of the unconscious mayor.

The sound of her knuckles hitting the man's fleshy cheek made Ellie wince. Suddenly she knew exactly who'd beaten the man. Tia turned back, her expression remarkably bland. As if she'd handed her father coffee, not a punch to the face. "He accused me of being a talentless slug. But I proved him wrong," Tia continued. "It turns out that I have a talent for detective work. I started searching through his office when he was gone. I knew there had to be paperwork if I was adopted. Do you know what I found?"

Ellie gave a wary shake of her head. "No."

"My birth certificate."

It took Ellie a second to realize why the birth certificate would matter.

"You found the name of your mother."

"I did." Tia glanced toward the silent Paula. "And I'll admit that after some research I was deeply disappointed when I discovered she was in jail." She heaved a dramatic sigh, clearly relishing the fact that she was the center of attention. Strange. Ever since Ellie had known the woman, Tia had always tried to fade into the background. "It meant that my parents had been right. My real mother was a loser who chose her drugs over her own daughter."

Ellie grimaced. "They said that?"

"That was one of the nicer things they said about her." She paused, drawing in a deep breath. The muscle beside her eye continued to tick. "It wasn't until a year ago I finally decided that I had to meet her. After all, she'd been in jail for years. She had to be clean and sober by now."

"I couldn't believe when the guards told me that my daughter was there to see me." Paula broke into the conversation, beaming like any proud mother. It made Ellie's stomach curl with revulsion. "It was the best day of my life."

"And mine," Tia agreed, waving a silencing hand in her mother's direction. This was her moment of glory. "She told me everything. About the clinic and how she'd tried to rescue us. And how those bastards had thrown her in jail to hide their disgusting"—her lips curled as she sought the appropriate word—"business."

Ellie shuddered. She couldn't imagine the earthquake that had shaken Tia when she learned the truth. Not only had she been kidnapped when she was barely more than a baby, but the people who'd pretended to be her parents had forced her real mother into prostitution and then sent her to jail to keep her mouth shut.

That would be enough to screw with anyone's head.

Perhaps it wasn't surprising that she'd gone batshit crazy.

The realization sent a violent surge of adrenaline through Ellie's body. Tia was going to kill them all. She could read it in her cold, demented eyes. And she intended to inflict as much pain as humanly possible.

Ellie had to escape. But how? She was trapped in the basement with no hope that a rescue was on the way.

What she needed was a weapon.

"But you didn't tell anyone what you discovered?" she asked, in the hope of keeping Tia distracted as she covertly glanced toward Paula.

The older woman was gazing in blatant rapture at her daughter, the prod held loosely in her hand. She was too far away for Ellie to risk making a grab for it. She had to hope the woman would step closer.

Tia shook her head, unaware of Ellie's distraction. "I had a better idea."

It took a second for Ellie to realize what Tia meant. "Bringing your mother to Curry?"

"Yes," Tia eagerly agreed. "She wanted justice."

"What did you want?"

Tia arched a brow, as if wondering whether Ellie was being deliberately stupid.

"I wanted revenge."

Ellie stiffened. She'd assumed when she'd been talking to Paula that the older woman had been responsible for the murders. Hadn't she confessed to them? Ellie thought back. There had been some hedging when it came to discussing the deaths. Had she been trying to cover her daughter's involvement in the crimes?

"You helped her kill all those people?"

"Help?" Tia laughed. The sound echoed eerily through the room, just like something out of a horror show. "I was the one to kill them. Except for Barb. I suppose you could say my mother scared the life out of her." There was another insane burst of laughter.

Ellie stared at Tia. It was easy to accept that Paula Raye was responsible for the deaths. She was a stranger who'd mysteriously appeared in town. None of them could have suspected the truth about her, or her past.

But Tia . . .

She'd been in Curry for her entire life. She'd gone to school with Daniel and Mandy. She'd attended church. She'd been a member of the community. How could no one have sensed her violent instability?

"It was you," she muttered, not sure what else to say.

Tia preened, proud of her accomplishments. "Odd, isn't it? My mother is the convicted felon, but she couldn't bring herself to actually do the deed. But I could. In fact, I relished it. Killing is another of my hidden talents." She abruptly reached into the large handbag she had slung over her shoulder, bringing out a knife. "See?"

The air was squeezed from Ellie's lungs. Tia held up the weapon to reveal the six-inch blade coated in a wet, sticky substance.

Blood.

Fresh blood.

Ellie flinched at the sickening memory of seeing the dead body stuffed in the back of Larry Harper's car. It'd been slashed with a viciousness that made it look like a wild animal had attacked him.

"Dr. Booker," she muttered.

Tia gave a slow nod. "I made him cry. And then beg. And then I sliced him into tiny bits."

She slashed the knife through the air, mimicking how she'd murdered the doctor.

Ellie grimaced. "God."

Clearly pleased by Ellie's horror, Tia gave one last slash with the knife.

"I just finished with Neville Morse."

It was Paula who responded to the chilling announcement. "He's dead?"

"As a doornail," Tia assured her mother before she wrinkled her nose. "Whatever that means."

Ellie abruptly slumped to one side, allowing her hands to dangle over the arm of the chair. It wasn't just anguish that made her go limp, although she felt like she'd endured one horrifying shock after another. But Paula had taken an unconscious step forward. She was close enough that a desperate lunge might allow Ellie to grab the cattle prod.

Knowing that she had to keep Tia distracted until she'd summoned the courage to make her move, Ellie glanced sideways, meeting Tia's fevered gaze.

"Why did you kill Daniel and Mandy?"

"That's obvious," she said. "Their parents needed to suffer as my mother suffered. They took me away from her, so I took away their children. They didn't suffer." She shrugged, indifferent to their deaths. "I meant for you to die after Mandy, but since your father was ultimately responsible for Hopewell Clinic, as well as sending my mother to jail, I wanted something special. What better revenge than forcing him to watch as the life drains out of you?" She used the knife to point at the wooden crosses. "When Mother moved into this place and I found these on the wall, I realized that it would be the perfect setting for my ultimate sacrifice. Everything is perfect."

"Tia—" Ellie started to plead for her life. She wasn't too proud to beg.

"Shut up," Tia snapped, a volatile anger darkening her face. "I don't like to be interrupted. My parents were always doing that. As if what I had to say wasn't important. That won't happen again. Never, ever again."

With a jerky motion, she turned to glare at Ellie's father. The older man had remained silent since Tia had entered the basement. Had he suspected that she was the one responsible for the killing spree? Or was he just a coward who was hoping that the younger woman wouldn't notice he was strapped to the cross?

Now he paled as Tia moved to press the knife against his neck. "I have one question, old man. Why did you burn the place down?"

Colin tilted back his head, futilely trying to escape the sharp edge that was slicing deep enough to cause tiny beads of blood to drip down his throat. There was no doubting that Tia meant business.

"The reporter showed up," he stammered. His early arrogance had been shattered, leaving behind a pathetic shell of a man. "She demanded to know where Paula was. We explained that she'd been sent back to jail, but it was obvious she was suspicious of the place and what was happening there. I couldn't have her poking around, so I made the executive decision to burn the place and walk away."

Tia made a sound of disgust. "Just like the coward you are."

Ellie could see Tia's muscles tighten as she prepared to

slice Colin's throat. Before she could halt the impulse, she was crying out.

"No."

Tia froze, caught between her bloodlust and the need to complete her demented plans.

"You're right," Tia at last muttered, lowering the knife to turn and glare at Ellie. "First my dear father. And then you. And last, the monster responsible for destroying all our lives."

Great. She'd saved her father, but she was second on the list of people to die.

She leaned farther to the side. Time was running out. She was going to do something. Soon.

"And then what?" she pressed.

"Mother and I leave this godforsaken place and start over." Tia waved the knife, sending droplets of blood spraying through the air. "Together."

Tia appeared to be on edge, as if resisting the urge to slice Colin Guthrie's throat was causing her extreme distress. Ellie sensed that she was about to snap. The question was, did she push the crazy woman over the edge, or try to soothe her?

Ellie decided on the push.

She didn't want either woman thinking clearly when she attempted her escape.

"They'll know you were responsible," Ellie warned. "You'll be fugitives for the rest of your lives. Or more likely, you'll be captured and face the death penalty."

Tia's eyes darkened, but she managed to curl her lips into a confident smile.

"Do you think I'm stupid? I've already thought about that." She stretched out her arm to show a deep gash just above her wrist. "I trashed my room and left behind smears of my blood. That idiotic sheriff will assume that I was taken by the same person who killed everyone else."

Ellie hid her grimace. Tia wasn't wrong. Gary Clark would eagerly leap to the wrong conclusion. Clearly, however, she hadn't realized that Nate wasn't so easily fooled.

Not that Ellie was about to point out the danger. If Tia and Paula managed to kill her and escape, she didn't want them going after Nate.

Instead, she glanced toward the silent Paula. "And your mother?"

"She already has a new identity ready to go." Tia glanced toward Paula with a wry expression. "The bonus of spending your life behind bars means she knows lots of people who are capable of making her disappear." She turned back to Ellie, who remained slumped, pretending to be defeated. "Plus, I intend to release the photos as soon as we're out of here. The scandal will keep people too occupied to worry about me or my mother."

A groan of panic was wrenched from Colin's lips. Almost as if the fear of being exposed was worse than the fear of death.

And for a man with his bloated ego, it probably was. What could be more devastating than the thought of being smeared as a disgusting pervert who sold sex like a common pimp? His career would be gone. His reputation. And probably his membership to the country club.

Everything that mattered to him.

"You have the camera? After all these years?" Ellie demanded.

Paula stepped toward her daughter, unaware that she'd just moved closer to Ellie.

"I grabbed a small backpack before leaving the clinic so I could stuff in a few clothes for my daughter," she said. Did she need to remind everyone that she'd been the one who'd actually had the guts to try and destroy Hopewell Clinic? Or was it just a subtle reminder to her daughter that she had her uses? After all, Tia was a ruthless killer. Who knew when she might decide Paula should be punished like the others?

"I also put the camera in there, and when I realized that I'd been followed to the spot where I was supposed to meet the reporter, I dropped the backpack in a dried-up well."

Tia touched her handbag. "I retrieved it after my mother told me where she'd hidden it. Then tonight, I decided to dump Neville's body in the same well. It seemed like poetic justice."

Ellie couldn't think about Tia dragging a mutilated Neville to the well and tossing him in. That would be a nightmare she would add to the others. Assuming she got out of there.

"It will never work, Tia." She focused on taunting Tia. "You aren't nearly as clever as you think you are. One of Paula's criminal friends will turn you in. Or you'll be caught on video and they'll realize you aren't dead. The authorities will figure it out and you'll be strapped in an electric chair alongside your mother."

Ellie had a talent for swaying juries. She could pluck the perfect words and phrases to tug at people's hearts when she was in a courtroom. Right now, she was babbling like an imbecile. Not that she was going to be too hard on herself. It was nothing less than a miracle that she could speak at all.

She was scared out of her mind.

Thankfully, it didn't take skill to aggravate Tia. The mere implication she wasn't some criminal genius had her eyes widening as she lifted the knife over her head.

"I told you to shut up," she hissed.

Ellie tensed her muscles. *Crap.* She'd wanted to annoy the woman, but she hadn't intended to provoke her into attacking her. Not yet.

But even as Tia started to move forward, she abruptly pivoted on her heel and lurched toward Ruben Chambers.

"You shouldn't make her angry," Paula muttered, her gaze riveted to the gruesome sight of her daughter lifting the knife and stabbing it directly into the center of Ruben's heart.

Ellie sharply turned her head, trying to block out the sound of the knife being pulled out of the man's chest and then shoved back in.

There was nothing she could do for the mayor. He'd sealed his fate when he'd stolen Paula's baby and raised her to become a cold-blooded killer.

But she could save herself. And potentially her father.

Clenching her teeth, she gathered every ounce of her strength and lunged out of the chair.

Her movements were stiff and awkward, and the handcuffs kept her from spreading her arms. But she had surprise on her side. Plus the added distraction of Tia slicing Ruben to death like a crazed maniac.

Paula didn't stand a chance as Ellie snatched the prod from her loose grip. A second later she had it pressed against the older woman's lower back. There was a faint buzzing sound, then Paula parted her lips and screamed before she tumbled to the ground, her eyes rolled back in her head and her body twitching.

Nate had arrived at the house not long after Tia had arrived. Leashing his surprise at the sight of the younger woman, he'd cautiously followed her into the house.

Unfortunately, there'd been no way to enter the basement without revealing his presence before he could get down there. And without knowing if Tia was armed, he'd been forced to retreat long enough to make a call to the sheriff's office, along with his friend in the FBI, and demand they get there ASAP. He wasn't going to risk getting Ellie killed because he wanted to play hero.

Then he'd gone back into the house and crouched at the top of the stairs with his gun in his hand. If things started heading south he wasn't going to have a choice. He would have to go down there.

He'd listened to Tia boasting about her kills, and he realized that Paula was actually her mother, but he didn't try to process what he was hearing. He'd been with the FBI long enough to know that when he was in the middle of a mission it was dangerous to let himself be distracted by emotions. Later he would sort out why they'd started killing the citizens of Curry. Right now, he was single-mindedly focused on keeping Ellie alive.

He was still squatting at the top of the staircase when he heard the scream.

His primitive brain didn't try to process if the sound came from Ellie, or one of the other women. It just urged him into action.

Holding the gun over his head, he leaped down the stairs, taking them four at a time. He hit the cement floor and scurried toward a broken armchair that had been shoved in the corner. It wasn't exactly bulletproof, but it was the best he could do. And thankfully, no one seemed to notice his impulsive entrance into the basement.

Forcing himself to take in slow, deep breaths, he glanced around the chair. Adrenaline was the enemy when he needed to shoot with accuracy. But even as he tried to remain calm, his heart stopped at the sight of Tia racing toward Ellie with a huge knife in her hand.

Rising to his feet, he prepared to squeeze the trigger. He hesitated. Dammit. He couldn't get a clear shot. Not from this angle.

Tia was screaming a stream of curses, swinging the knife at Ellie at the same time the smaller woman was fending her off with a thin pole. Nate circled around the stairs, trying to move as silently as possible.

It wasn't silent enough.

Either he made some noise, or Tia simply had a premonition that there was someone else in the basement. With astonishing speed she was darting toward Colin Guthrie, who was hanging on a wooden cross. She pressed the knife to his neck as she scanned the darkness for some sign of the intruder.

"Stay back or I'll kill him."

Nate ignored the woman, stepping forward to hold out his hand.

"Ellie."

Making a strangled sound, Ellie limped toward him, her hands cuffed together and what he realized was a cattle prod held tightly in her fingers. There were tears openly streaming down her cheeks, but she kept her head held high.

Her courage made his heart swell with pride.

"I mean it," Tia screeched, clearly realizing that she'd lost the upper hand. "I'll slice his throat."

Ellie stepped into Nate's waiting arms, leaning her head against his chest.

"Then do it," she told Tia. "I don't care what happens to him."

Tia blinked in shock. Clearly she'd never considered the idea of failure. Now she floundered at how to force Ellie to continue playing her sick game.

"You don't mean that," she desperately rasped. "He's your father."

Ellie gave a pained shake of her head. "No, he's a stranger. The man I thought was my father never existed," she rasped. "Do whatever you want."

"No, this time I win." Unable to accept defeat, Tia released a harsh cry. Then, clearly out of her mind, she leaped over her unconscious mother and charged toward them. "I win."

"Stop or I'll shoot," Nate commanded, pushing Ellie behind him. Tia continued forward, her face twisted into an expression of pure hatred. "Stop or I'll shoot," he repeated in a loud voice.

The maniac was beyond hearing him.

Continuing to race forward, Tia lifted the knife, her gaze locked on Ellie. Nate didn't hesitate. Raising his hand, he aimed the gun and with one smooth movement, he pulled the trigger.

Epilogue

The nineteen fifties ranch house in the suburbs of Chicago was exactly how Ellie imagined it would be. Set on a small lot with a fenced-in backyard, it had white vinyl siding and a new roof. The garage was attached, and looked like it had recently been extended so there was only enough room in the driveway for one car.

Inside it was shabby and cozy, with a living room that opened directly to the L-shaped kitchen and a narrow hallway that led to the bedrooms.

The entire structure would have fit in her parents' dining room, but there had never been the same warm, welcoming atmosphere that seemed to ooze from this house.

Of course, her parents would quite likely have to downsize drastically. In the four months since Nate had helped Ellie limp out of the basement, her father had retired from the bench, retreated from society, and separated from his wife. Ellie hadn't seen him, but Nate had kept her up-to-date on the investigation into Hopewell Clinic. It was hard to say if any charges would be pressed. Not only because of the statute of limitations, but because the men who'd been the clients of the clinic had the sort of power to put an end to any criminal proceedings.

Whether or not he went to jail no longer mattered to Ellie. There was no punishment that could adequately compensate the victims. He would wither and die alone. Probably sooner rather than later.

Paula and Tia, however, were another story.

Paula had been hauled straight to jail by the sheriff when he'd finally arrived at the ranch, and Tia had been taken to the hospital, where the doctors had removed Nate's bullet from her shoulder.

They were awaiting trial. According to Nate, both were trying to negotiate their way out of the death penalty by blaming the other for the crimes.

So much for the mother/daughter reunion.

Ellie had more or less recovered from her ordeal. She still had nightmares, but she was back at work and she'd finished the repairs on her house.

Not that she'd moved back home. She kept finding reasons to remain with Nate.

Which was how she'd been caught in a moment of weakness and convinced to travel to Chicago to spend the Fourth of July with his parents.

Standing next to Nate on the back porch, her eyes widened. When they'd first arrived in Chicago, only the immediate family had been gathered in the living room. Ellie had been so nervous she could barely speak, but everyone had been so kind and gracious, she'd soon lost her reserve.

She hadn't realized until Nate had escorted her through the French doors that the backyard was overflowing with guests. Circles of men gathered around the barbecues. Women laughed and chased young children. A huge group of teenagers jumped on a trampoline.

Her nerves returned and she instinctively reached out to grab Nate's hand.

"Good Lord. When you said a family gathering, I was expecting a dozen people," she complained. "Not a horde."

He chuckled, giving her fingers a reassuring squeeze. "The Marcels don't do anything small." He sent her a charming smile. "You have to admit that they are all on their best behavior."

They had been. And while she'd been impressed with their manners, not to mention their drop-dead good looks, she hadn't missed the hint of devilment that lurked in their eyes.

"How did you get your brothers to agree?" she demanded, skimming her gaze over the crowd to see the Marcel men tossing around a football and tackling each other with enough force to make her wince.

"I threatened to tell my mother that it wasn't a baseball that broke the front window when I was ten," Nate said.

"What did break it?"

"They double-dog dared me to ram my head through it."

Her eyes widened. "You didn't."

He looked offended. "Of course I did. It was a double-dog dare. I had to."

Ellie shook her head, all too easily capable of seeing a young Nate running across the living room to smash his head into the window.

"That explains so much."

He reached up to brush a finger over her cheek. "Any of it good?"

Warmth cascaded through her. If it hadn't been for this man, she didn't know if she would have recovered from Tia and Paula's crazed attempts to kill her, and the discovery her father was an immoral bastard.

It was Nate who'd held her when the nightmares made her cry out in the middle of the night. And Nate who'd stood at her side when she'd forced herself to return to work. And Nate who'd protected her from any backlash.

Thankfully most of the people in Curry had been anxious to put the past behind them. They were all related to at least one of the men involved. And while there were a few who would never trust her because of her father, the vast majority had returned to treating her as just another citizen who owned a business and paid her taxes.

"Maybe a little," she murmured, lost in his eyes that were more blue than gray today.

"Don't worry." His thumb traced her lower lip. "I'm sure our kids will take after you. Or at least I hope so."

Ellie stiffened at his offhand words. "Kids?"

He arched his brows. "Oops. Did I say that out loud?"

She rolled her eyes. This man was like the old Chinese water torture. A steady drip, drip, drip that could wear away the most resilient resolution.

"Aren't you getting ahead of yourself?" she chastised. "I agreed to meet your family. Nothing else."

He smiled, completely unrepentant. "A man can dream."

Her heart lurched and skidded, slamming against her ribs. Instinctively she turned from his probing gaze. She couldn't think clearly when she was looking in his eyes.

Unfortunately, she immediately caught sight of June Marcel. The small woman with a halo of dark curls and dimpled face barely looked old enough to be married, let alone have a litter of grown sons. And she was without a doubt the heart of the Marcel family.

Not one of them would allow anything or anyone to hurt this woman.

"Nate," Ellie breathed.

Easily sensing her sudden distress, he wrapped a protective arm around her shoulders.

"What's wrong?"

She licked her dry lips. "Do they know?"

"Know what?"

"About my father."

She felt his muscles ease at her question. As if he was relieved that's what was troubling her.

"They do, and they don't give a shit," he bluntly told her.

She snorted. Easy for him to say. "I find that hard to believe."

He waved his free hand toward the milling crowd. "Look at the size of this clan."

She grimaced. It was still overwhelming. "I already did."

"Do you think that we don't have a few rotten apples in the bunch?" he demanded. "At least three cousins are currently in jail and my great uncle was connected to the mob. Nothing fazes us."

"They can't be as bad as my father."

Without warning, Nate grabbed her by the shoulders to turn her to face him. His expression was oddly somber.

"No one here is concerned with Colin Guthrie or what he did in the past," he assured her in fierce tones. "All they care about is how happy you make me."

Her heart did more of that lurching and skidding. This man . . .

Somehow he'd become everything to her.

"Do I make you happy?"

"Words can't describe how I feel when you're near," he said without hesitation.

Ellie reached up to touch his beautiful face. She could remember opening her door and finding him standing on her porch. She'd known in that moment she was lost.

It just took some time for her to admit the truth.

"I'm glad you're so stubborn, Nate Marcel," she breathed.

He laughed. "I'll remind you of that when you want to hit me with your shoe."

"Actually, I've discovered a real fondness for a cattle prod," she warned him.

"Yikes. I'll keep that in mind." Releasing her shoulders, he took a step back and held out his hand. "Are you ready to join the family?"

They both knew he was asking for more than just a few hours at a picnic. Ellie tentatively reached out to lay her fingers in his palm.

"I'm ready."

And she was.

HEADLINE
ETERNAL